The Blood Stained Canvas concept was created and
written by Daniel J. Barnes.

All characters in this publication were created
by Daniel J. Barnes and all the characters in this publication
are fictitious, any resemblance to real persons, living or dead,
is purely coincidental.

Blood Stained Canvas was edited by Sarah Barnes.

For Dave, Gone to soon.

<u>Dedication</u>

To my wrestling hero, Bret 'Hitman' Hart, still my biggest
influence in professional wrestling.
If I had not seen you perform, I would never have even
believed I could do it.

Thank you Bret, I owe it all to you.

Acknowledgements

I would like to thank every artist that breathed life into the
characters in some way or another,
Danny Kelly, Russ Walton, Phil Buckenham, Lewis Tillett
& Jussi Dahlman.

I apologise that this was the avenue I have taken the project,
but with how I have envisioned it, this is the only way
I would be completely happy with its outcome.

DJB

BLOOD STAINED CANVAS

STUDD CITY

ALASKA

SANCTUARY CITY

SKELTER PRISON

CANADA

GULF OF ALASKA

NORTH POINT

GRENOBLE

BLACKFOOT

MAPLE FALLS

ROYALE

MONTREAL

CRIMSON

VELVET BEACH

ALEXANDREA

PEPPERVILLE

ROMA

CHINATOWN

BUTTERWORTH

VENTURA

THE BOROUGH

JONES

FORGE CITY

ST. PATRICKS

OAKLAND

ST. GERMAIN

UNITED STATES

BARNVILLE

CALHOUN

PACIFIC OCEAN

SOUTH POINT

THE ISLE OF DIKAKU

djb

From the Diary of Randall Rogan

Friday, April 19th.
The Duggan Inn, Forge City.

Where should I start? I've been involved in the wrestling business for 36... No, 38 years now. I was 16 when I started running for Max Crawford, you know collecting the wrestlers ring jackets and gimmicks when they'd made their entrances, then I'd bring the items back to the locker room. I'd just about do anything to be around the business, selling programs and popcorn, sweeping the ring canvas, picking up the debris that hit the ring after a Captain Propaganda match, believe me there was a lot! The guy had heat! But he did portray a Nazi sympathizer, so it's easy to see why.

I'd even run errands for the wrestlers themselves, carrying their bags to and from their cars. Even passing messages back and forth between the rats that came to see them each week, some of those notes contained information that almost blinded this 16 year old, but I still read them.

This was back in Long Island, where I grew up, where I still live with my family. I say live, I'm never home.
Max Crawford... what a card he was... haven't thought of him in... I can't actually remember the last time I thought about him. He was the promoter and booker in Long Island, ran

shows every Friday & Saturday night out of the old coliseum for near on fifty years!

And that is some feat, let me tell you! Sold out most weekends too... It's a Franken Burger restaurant now.

Well, It turned out 'Crooked' Crawford (That's what the boys called him) was a complete snake! He was sweet as cherry pie to me when I was a kid, but when I grew up and I was making some serious money, well let's just say this business breeds conmen and he was one of the biggest I have ever met. But I can't speak ill of the dead he gave me my start so I guess I owe him a lot, Hell, I owe him everything! Or I could put it another way and say its all his fault I'm still stuck in it, the rat bastard!

Now here I sit in some grubby motel room in... where are we again... Forge City... yeah, sat here 36 years later on the verge of throwing the towel in. Now don't worry this isn't going to be a long drawn-out memoir, where I go back to the beginning and tell you everything from each pair of trunks I wore or each time I scratched my ass. No, I can't stand those, most of the time it's a fabricated life that's portrayed in those type of books anyway. No, you don't need to know all that and to be perfectly honest I don't want to tell you everything! That's my life and my business, what does a man have left if he tells you everything? Now, granted there may be a few little excursions up and down memory lane but no, this isn't a memoir.

I'm broken, the list of injuries and niggles I'm carrying is endless. Some of them I've been dealing with for near on ten years now. But the truth of it all is I miss my family. Hell, I've already missed most of my son's childhood... Jimmy... I miss him so much and Martha, what a woman she is, a real rock if ever there was one.

No, this is no life for a family man.

The thing is I'm "The American Man" Randy Rogan. Wrestling legend and icon (to some) and the current Heavyweight Wrestling Champion of the World and... I'm, well... I'm done.

CHAPTER 1

Delaware, 1986.

Randy Rogan's young naive eyes widened like saucers at what he was witnessing. The single strip light that hung above in the neglected claustrophobic locker room flickered annoyingly, repeatedly flashing on something metallic that caused it to violate his fresh green eyes.

But still through the barrage of attacks to his eyes he did not squint, or even blink. He remained entranced by what was taking place before him, almost hypnotised by it.

"It's a tool that you'll have to learn to live with, Kid." A gravelly voice said.

He heard the words and could feel his head nodding, his mouth gaping in awe, but still he remained focussed on what was occurring.

"It isn't difficult to do. Even a greenhorn like you could do it." Chuckled the voice.

Rogan laughed under his breath, still focussed and a little bemused.

He'd been wrestling for around two years, about the amount of time that all rookies think they know the business inside and out, which could not be further from the truth. The truth being that you are always learning, every single night you step through those ropes you are learning something new. In most cases until their final match they are still learning, the lightbulb doesn't go off for everyone. Some don't shut up and just listen to those that have already walked a thousand miles on the same journey, they don't soak up the knowledge that falls from the branches of the learning tree, some just step over the leaves and ignore them, or crumple them underfoot, these are the ones who don't get it.

In 1986 Rogan was one of these very rookies, he'd been around the business since he was 16, but obviously didn't know all the in's and outs. Now he'd been smartened up and was living life on the road as a professional wrestler. He'd been doing it for a few years, so he too thought he knew how it all worked.

He was wrong.

But this one moment changed how his mind worked, It was like a hidden door had been opened up for him that nobody else could see, he walked through it and never looked back.

"Yep, just one of the tools of the trade!" Came the growling voice again, before coughing and spluttering.

'Uncle' Sam Reagan was what you'd call an old timer, but he'd been to the top of the mountain, where he had stayed for a long time. He was one of the most successful World Heavyweight Champions of all time, capturing the prize on three occasions. He had been at the top so long that he probably had the view from that mountain top memorised.

"Sorry, kid." He coughed and yakked, spitting up a mass of thick tarry saliva onto the stained linoleum flooring "Too many cigars, got my lungs in a bear hug." He chuckled at this and shook his head before focussing back on his task.

He'd already made one of his 'tools of the trade' which had captivated young Rogan and he'd sat down opposite to watch as all the other youngsters had gone off to chase rats.

"Is this for real?" Rogan asked with all the innocence of youth.

Reagan's old eyes came up to meet his, he looked angry at first and then sighed, the anger leaving his body with the exhaling of breath that smelt of stale cigars.

"I mean it's not a rib or something?" He asked.

He stared at Rogan, and with all sincerity in his voice said, "This is as real as this shit gets, kid!" before his eyes dropped again to the matter in hand.

Reagan leaned forward on the bench, his spinal cord performing the famous ballad that all veteran wrestlers sing. He dived into his frayed and worn-out gym bag, that looked as though it has seen as much action as its owner. He rummaged inside it and pulled out the small rectangle packet that Rogan had seen him throw back in earlier.

"I'll show you again from scratch." Reagan spluttered "You can keep the left overs and make more." He continued nodding at the pile of metallic fragments sitting on the bench next to him "But you've got to know how to make your own, you dig?"

Rogan nodded.

He opened the box and let the contents softly fall into his wrinkling cupped hand. A razor blade slid out and fell into his palm. He held it up to the flickering light in his rough fingertips, turning it slowly.

"Isn't she beautiful?" He asked but wasn't looking for an answer "Remember to give her the respect she deserves, she can fuck you up if you're not careful."

Rogan nodded again leaning forward on his bench, catching his reflection in the blade as it twirled around in Reagan's fingertips like a prima ballerina.

"Yeah, Don't you go getting attached to her, she'll be gone by the end of the night."

He lowered the blade and it hung in his loose grip between his bare legs that were wrinkled, tanned and free of hair.

"Think of her as one of those rats. I'm sure you've had experience with those haven't you?"

Rogan blushed slightly and nodded with a wry smirk slithering across his face.

"Yeah, I bet you have you lucky fucking dog!" He laughed "Ah, to be a youngster again. The rats left this sinking ship along time ago." He shook his head and gazed off somewhere, maybe into a nostalgic muse of a special night spent with a particular rat. Whatever it was, it left enough impression for him to remember it, but he returned quickly and looked at Rogan again.

"Treat her like you would a rat. She'll be here for you tonight, but as soon as you've gotten the use out of her, throw her away."

Rogan sniggered, understanding the metaphor perfectly.

"Trouble is with the real rats they keep coming back, whether you want them too or not! Am I right?" Reagan laughed and slapped Rogan on the pad that fit snuggly around his kneecap, decorated with bright fluorescent shapes.

He held the razor blade in both hands between the thumb and index fingers and aggressively snapped it in half, then he placed one half of it down on the pile of debris.

"That's what you want, that clean snap. No jagged edges." He held it aloft showing half of the blade to him "Now you want to use some scissors with this next part, you don't want to go snapping away at it, that may create craggy parts that will slice you up. You don't want that happening, no sir."

He leaned forward again, the ballad of Sam Reagan's spine serenading Rogan once more. He sat back up with a small pair of scissors in his hand, and then tested them as if to demonstrate to this rookie how scissors worked.

"Snip, snip!" He smiled, showing his surprising pearly white teeth which sat in an old face that had the texture of leather about it, 'The teeth of a champion' he had once said. Being a champion for a few years pays for some top of the line dentures.

With his tongue protruding out of the corner of his mouth, the way some do when concentrating, he held the blade out in front of him and then snipped a small corner of it off. It fell to the linoleum and there it sat between the torn up and scuffed toes of his white leather boots.

He discarded the scissors and the bigger half and picked up the piece he had cut off. He held it up again and stared at it shaking his head.

"Funny how something so small can have such an effect isn't it?"

He placed the shard on his bare thigh as he dived into his gym bag once again, his spine treating Rogan's ears to an encore. He came back up with a small square packet, Rogan's face flickered with confusion for a moment as he thought it was a rubber but then breathed a sigh of relief when he realised it was actually an antiseptic wipe. He opened the packet and discarded the rubbish on the floor, not that one would be able to tell in such a flea-bitten pit.

"Gotta make sure she's clean." He said as he wiped the small shard all over with the wipe "Don't want to go catching anything now do ya?" He then broke out in hysterics "Exactly just like rats!"

Rogan laughed too and after a minute or so and Reagan went back to wiping his blade. He discarded the wipe and placed the blade back down on his thigh once more and again it was into the bag he went.

Rogan looked at the tiny triangle the size of a fingernail, to him it looked just like what it appeared to be, a useless piece of broken razor blade, which would have been most peoples reaction to such a sight too.

"Fucking bastard!" Reagan shouted at the top of his voice as he sat back up with an almost empty roll of athletic tape in his hand.

Rogan flinched in his seat as Reagan's bawling startled him.

"That fucking Samoan bastard!" He said holding out the roll of white wrist tape and shaking it in front of Rogan's face "You let people borrow your wrist tape and they take the piss they do! Fucking liberties! Sina! That fat piece of Samoan shit!"

He grumbled several more racial obscenities towards fellow veteran wrestler 'The Samoan Warrior' Sina, before going quiet again and pulling the tape away from the roll, a sound that Rogan had already heard thousands of times, a sound he will forever hear throughout his career.

Another snip of the scissors and he'd cut a small piece of tape off and then picked up the shard.

"Now you've got to wrap her up nice." He wrapped the tape tightly around one end of it leaving just one point protruding from one end.

"And there's your gig." He said and again gave it the ballerina in a music box treatment as Rogan watched on.

"Here, take it." Reagan said handing it to Rogan.

"You're giving it to me?" He asked in awe.

"Yeah, why not!" He said pulling up his faded blue kneepads into place.

"Thanks!"

"Well, we don't have time to make anymore, we're on in ten minutes."

Rogan looked around for a clock or any indication that they were soon going out to the ring.

"But, how do you know?"

"I can sense it."

Rogan looked at him puzzled.

"When you've been doing this dance as long as I have you get a sixth sense. It's the sound of the crowd. Can you hear them?"

Rogan listened and listened hard, he heard nothing.

"I can't hear anything."

"Exactly!" Reagan smiled "They're dead. Sina and Giant Nagata have done their job, they've brought them down, ready for the main event. So they'll be ready to come back up again for us. It's important not to burn them out."

Rogan sat nodding like some bobblehead toy, his head on a spring, moving forward and back in awe, as leaves from the learning tree fell all around him and he knew enough now to pick them up.

"I like you, kid. Don't be such a mark though, okay?" He said laughing and slapped him on his large muscular tanned thigh.

"I'll try." Rogan said looking at the blade in his hands.

"You know what you've gotta do with her, yeah?"

"I think so." He muttered.

"Whoa! There's no think so's when it comes to juicing, kid. You gotta know so!"

Reagan takes the blade from his grip and demonstrates by placing the blade next to the areas on his head. "You can go on the eyebrow if you want to get the subtle flow where maybe you've taken a stiff right hand." He clenched his fist up and mimicked thumping himself in the temple. "Or the hairline is good if you want to make more of an impact, say after a chair shot. Go in and then twist the blade slightly, don't hack and slash at it or else you can end up in all sorts of trouble." He hands the blade back to him and stands up, his tired joints singing again. Rogan follows suit, something he'll be doing for the next couple of years.

"Avoid the forehead it'll scar up and look awful, you don't want to mess up that babyface of yours, that's your money maker right there, Pal!" and with that gave him a playful slap on his smooth shaven cheek.

"Yeah, you're best going along the hairline tonight as you'll be taking a chair shot, it'll hide the scar when it's healed. And be ready because Colt will swing that fucker. You need to be ready for it, okay?"

"Yeah."

Rogan had just realised that this was real, as real as it gets and had spent the last several years thinking that blood packets were used like in the movies when wrestlers bled in their matches.

He realised he had a lot to learn.

Reagan handed him an aspirin "Take it."

"What's this for?"

"It'll help to thin your blood."

Rogan watched as Reagan swallowed one down, and again followed suit.

"When it's time for you to get colour, hold your breath for a little bit, the blood will rush to your head and you'll get that flow, that crimson mask."

Reagan smiled at him, a look that was almost fatherly. Maybe he saw a bit of himself in Rogan and that's why he offered up his knowledge to him.

"You'll do fine, Kid. Just keep your ears open out there and you'll do fine."

"Sure, thanks."

"Now, we've got to hide the sharp little señorita haven't we?" He said and picked up his gig that he had made earlier.

"Some guys hide their's in their boots, or trunks, I've even heard of guys concealing it in their mouths!"

Rogan's eyes grew wide again.

"But, that's just crazy if you ask me, extremely dangerous. Some even tape theirs to the tips of the fingers, but I think that can be dangerous too. Accidents happen you know?"

Reagan smiled again as Rogan looked at him petrified.

"You do it that way too if you've gotta break in a new guy that doesn't know how to juice and you've gotta do it for him."

Rogan's eyes are even wider and stared at his tag team partner for the evening in terror.

"But, we're not going to do that tonight. I trust you enough that you can do it yourself, I recommend the inside of the wrist." He grabbed Rogan's arm and balanced the blade in place on the inside of his already taped wrist and then tore off another piece of tape and covered it. It was now unnoticeable.

"Then when it's time you simply tear off that strip and do the deed. Make sure you're facing the canvas so it's not obvious, don't want to give the magic away now do we?" He said with a wink.

"What do I do with it afterwards?"

"Don't worry the ref will deal with it."

Rogan still looked terrified, but Reagan laughed and slapped him on the back, the sound of his hand striking on his muscular back echoed in the empty locker room.

Reagan slipped on his star spangled tailed jacket and he plonked a top hat that was patriotically emblazoned with the red, white and blue of the American flag on a nest of greying hair. He hoisted up his slack blue trunks, pulling them around his overhanging gut and pushed his chest out to its maximum.

"How do I look, kid?" he asked with a cheesy grin flashing across his ageing face.

"Like the man!" Rogan said with all sincerity.

Reagan smiled at the youngster who was looking back at him in anxious awe and told him something that he later said his trainer The Wizard once told him.

"Welcome to a bizarre strange place, Where things may not make sense to you, the outsiders. Witness a sport. A circus. A way of life! Come with me as we delve into a world of lies, deceit and politics. A world of smoke and mirrors. A place for many lost souls, all searching for a purpose in and yearning for acceptance in a make believe world. For the majority it is a short stay, For others it's a slow agonising death! But it all happens on a Blood Stained Canvas!"

CHAPTER 2

Sanctuary City, Present Day

A bland grey Volkswagen Jetta rolled into the lonely carpark of the Sanctuary Arena. Slowly the tyres groaned as the vehicle sniffed out the perfect parking space.

As close as you can get to that backdoor. Don't want to be mobbed by marks on the way out.

It moved slowly and methodically toward the large futuristic building, that doomed in an amalgamation of glass and metal as steel girders protruded out of its roof and seemed to claw the dome as if protecting it from something. The afternoon sunshine emerged through the greying clouds and glistened on its windows.

Almost reluctantly the car came to a full stop in between two others.

"Looks like Seb and Jim had the same idea." Rogan said glancing at the two cars that had become the bread to his filling.

The engine clicked off and a Randy Rogan sat in silence, almost holding his breath as the sound of the tired engine ticked over.

He sighed a heavy sigh and rubbed his hand over his full beard softly as he sat deep in thought.

I guess most of them will already be there by now. The young hungry kids have probably been here for hours, getting some ring time in to try new shit out. I remember when I used to be that eager.

A smile wriggled through his beard and then disappeared, it was almost as if he had remembered some fond memory and then it had left a bitter taste in his mouth. But to be honest, that is exactly how he felt about the wrestling business now.

In one hand it held amazing fond memories and experiences for him and in the other hand it was like holding a fresh steaming pile of horse shit. The yin and the yang, the good and the bad memories as well as the shit. For him personally, the scales had started to lean in favour of the shit.

He stepped out of the car and slammed the door behind him. He stretched out his back and it sang that same song that his mentor 'Uncle' Sam Reagan used to sing all those years ago.

"Oooh!" Rogan groaned "The Ballad of Uncle Sam!" He chuckled.

He looked around and noticed how empty the carpark was, there were only a few of them scattered around the dark concrete, sprouting up like weeds almost.

I remember a time when the carparks would have been half full from workers rentals before the fans even showed up. Hardly anyone drives these days.

He popped the trunk and hoisted out his suitcase, dumping it down on the concrete, the worn wheels made an unpleasant scraping sound and no doubt lost another few fragments of plastic. It had seen some action but it was still pretty modern for an old timer like Rogan. But he did appreciate these new wheeled suitcases, they were a Godsend really in his profession, held more than his old gym bag anyway and a lot easier to move around. Yes, this was one thing that had changed for the better he thought. He pulled out the handle and started to move toward the building, making sure the rental was locked up before he did. *Yeah, I remember all piling into a car and driving three, four, five hundred miles without even giving it a second thought. Taking in a few road beers, enjoying each others company and telling war stories. Those were the days. Oh, there I go. I've said it. You're officially a dinosaur.*

He moved towards the door of the building.

"Mr Rogan, Mr Rogan!" Came an excited squawk that actually caused the unbeknownst Randy Rogan to jump.

"Jesus!" He blasted, almost falling over as he saw a small round man, who must have been in his thirties, staring back at him with the wide eyes of awe through thick lensed glasses.

"It's me! I made it!" He snorted scratching frantically at a red rash on his neck.

"Oh, yeah, it's you..." Rogan replied, knowing the face (because he'd seen it a lot).

"It's Mark!" He answered a little annoyed that Rogan didn't remember his name.

"Yes, you are." Rogan smiled.

"Mark Schroeder? From Illinois?"

"Of course I remember you!" he smiled again looking down at the magazine that he was gripping in his chubby sweaty fingers. "Would you like me to sign that?"

"Oh, Yes, please, Mr Rogan!" He answered excitedly, handing him the magazine that had an old picture of him on the cover.

"Didn't think I'd see you again so soon." Said Rogan, while he leant awkwardly on his knee to sign it with a marker (one that he also had with him, stuffed in his pocket for such occasions).

"Oh, I'm your biggest fan! I get to every big show I can!" He answered, sweat trickling down from his receding hairline over a face caked with bulging puss filled acne.

"Awesome!" Rogan said and handed him back his magazine.

"Thanks so much!" Mark snorted "See you in New York!"

Rogan smiled and walked towards the door to the building, looking back over his shoulder a few times to see Mark just standing in the same spot grinning at him.

I must have signed a thousand autographs for that guy. He always tells me he's my biggest fan. I should be grateful, and I am! Don't get me wrong, it's my fans that have put me where I am today. But, some of them can be a little bit over familiar and teeter on the verge of... well, creepy.

He walked inside and was faced with a long narrow corridor, everything looked so clean and fresh, the tiled floor, the walls and the ceiling all looked white to him. He felt like he was dying and that this was a tunnel of light leading him to heaven. The smell of cleaning fluid attacked his nostrils and made him focus again as an old man waddled past with a mop bucket on wheels.

The old man smiled at him and seemed very pleased to see him.

"Mr Rogan! It's great to see you again! It really is."

"You too..." Rogan had no idea who the old fellow was but knew the drill and acted like he remembered him too "... Larry!" looking down and reading his name badge.

"How have you been?" Rogan asked sincerely, granted he couldn't remember the guy but he was still kind and polite.

"So, so. Ready for the scrapyard I think. My hips aren't what they used to be!" he scoffed.

"You're preaching to the choir my man." Laughed Rogan and patted him gently on the shoulder. "The usual changing rooms?"

"Yeah, they've got you guys in the visitors side."

"Gotcha. Thanks, Larry. You take care now, you hear?"

"Will do, champ!" Chuckled Larry and slowly moved along in the other direction with his mop bucket.

Look, I can't remember everyone. It's been about two years since we last ran this venue and I meet so many people every night. I do feel bad sometimes but I try and stay respectful and polite. There is no way I can remember them all.

He walked slowly down the corridor, his heavy duty workman style boots clunking as his moved along, the wheels of his case chattering nonsense behind him.

I know some guys who would've just ignored that guy, and there is no need for that, always stay respectful. That's something Old Sam taught me. He realised how important we were to fans, how much happiness we brought into their lives. Even if I haven't met people before, they talk to you like they know you. I've been on their television screens for the past thirty years and they've been through everything with me, they were there when I tagged with Uncle Sam to take the tag straps from the dastardly Tokyo Giants in '88. They were there when I won my first World title from 'The Reflection' Rex Regal in '94. To them they do know me, I'm like their extended family. Always remain respectful and courteous, that's what I was told and that's what I do.

As he walked he started to make out figures in the horizon of this sickly bright hallway. His eyesight had been starting to dwindle and from this distance he could only see the silhouettes of people, he couldn't tell you who they were. He wore glasses for reading and watching television, but maybe he needed to start wearing them all the time. He sighed again with the thought of that, he really was getting old now.

Here we are again. Venue to venue, hotel to hotel, city to city, state to state it all just becomes one hazing blur. It's been three weeks since I slept in my own bed! Or played with my son or even fucked my wife! It can really take its toll on you.

He could now make out the figure of a man leaning up against a Koko Pop soda vending machine and swigging on a cherry flavoured can of soda. His thick black moustache contorted as he smiled and waved at the approaching Rogan. He had a slender but athletic build, and had a neatly tied ponytail sprouting from the rear of his head.

"Randy!" Came the voice, that had an upbeat Spanish twang to it.

"Hey, Pedro! How's it going?"

"It goes well. You took your time. The champion likes to be fashionably late, no?" Laughed Pedro.

"Perks of the job!" Rogan laughed back, extending his hand, Pedro shook it.

"Have you seen the card yet?" Rogan asked.

"Yeah!" He rolled his eyes and had another swig from his can, hundreds of tiny pink bubbles appeared on his moustache and then burst immediately.

"Not good?"

"It's so, so." He said, his head swaying from side to side, his hair flicking out from either side of his head.

"Oh!" Rogan sighed.

"No, you're okay, Randy. You've got Kami."

"Oh!" Rogan answered pleasantly surprised "Then why is it so, so?"

"I've got Glen." He rolled his eyes again and shook his head. "I feel my back will be aching after tonight, no?" He laughed.

"Yeah, good luck with that! Just keep it simple." Rogan chuckled. And walked on.

"Simple is the word!" He heard Pedro call from behind and Rogan shook his head and laughed.

Ring crew members whizzed past him carrying all manner of tools. He smiled and said hello to each one as they hurried on past.

Gotta feel for Pedro if he's gotta lead Glen around tonight, he isn't the greatest worker. But then again, he isn't the worst, you've just got to know what to do with him. 'Play to the strengths and hide the weaknesses' That's what Sam used to say, 'If you're good, you could have a match with a broomstick! And get the damn thing over!' And he was right. You do have to lead some guys, but that's the nature of the beast, some still don't get how it all works and others are just not good. But then it's up to you to get something out of them. No, Glen isn't the best but he isn't the worst. The worst? Well, from my personal experience, it's Shaun Strikes. That match was a black smudge on a relatively solid career of decent matches.

"Randy! There you are!" Came a voice that halted Randy and he turned to see a small, fragile looking Wally Dominguez, (personal assistant to the promoter, Louis Raggu) frantically scuttling down the hallway towards him. He was smartly dressed and had a bright red bowtie on, peeping out over the top of a clipboard that was grasped tightly to his chest.

"I wondered where you were, Randy!" he announced, sweat trickling from his hairline "We were starting to get worried about you!" he continued looking up at the 6 feet 5 inches of veteran champion, pushing his thick bottle lens glasses back up the bridge of his long slender beak.

"I'm here, Wally. Don't get your panties in a twist." Rogan replied with a roll of his eyes.

"You know that Mister Raggu, likes you here..." Wally Dominguez droned on tilting his wrist to check the time.

"Look!" Rogan interrupted "I'm here, I've had a long drive, I wanna just say hello to everyone and then relax before it's showtime, okay?"

"Yes, of course that is acceptable. I just need to go

through your match with you at some point."

"Well, can I get in the building first?"

"Yes, sir!"

"Besides, there isn't anything you need to tell me about my match, other than who is going over. Kami and I will do the rest." Rogan said walking away towards the locker rooms marked visitors on the door.

"Yes, but..." Wally tried but he sighed knowing that he wasn't going to get anywhere.

"Oh, that's the wrong dressing room, by the way."
Rogan stopped just as his hand pressed against the door to push it open.

"But I thought..."

"You've been moved to the home side as the facilities are better over that side of the building."
Rogan sighed and walked away towards the main hall of the arena.

So much for my quick getaway tonight, there's no rear exit on that side of the building I know that much, so we are going to have to wait until all the fans have gone home tonight before we can come back this way to get out.

"Logic!" he sighed as he stepped into the main hall.

CHAPTER 3

The ring was set up and crew members scuttled around carrying things, putting out chairs, adjusting the steel barricades into their correction positions. Rogan nodded at them all and smiled, pleasant greetings and handshakes to the people he knew well.

In the ring, a few wrestlers were going over their match that would happen later tonight and Rogan smiled at the sight of this "Ah, the eagerness of youth."

He looked around the vast main hall, taking it all in, this was something he'd always done. He didn't feel nerves at all when he was in a building that he had performed in before, he had wrestled here many times and it felt comfortable to him. The ceiling seemed to rise forever curving at its highest point he always felt as though he was trapped in a snow globe. He carried on towards the ring, the screeching howl from the wheels of his case echoed in the main hall and descended up to touch the dome.

The ring consisted of two brutish looking fellows, a tag team known as The Rhino Bros. Stomp was the taller of the two, towering over even the impressive stature of Randy Rogan, and an impressive bright green mohawk exploded out of his large head. He was doing all the talking as his partner, Tusk, watched on nodding along in agreement with what his partner was saying. He was much smaller, not tall at all but rotund and built, ginger hair sprouted over everywhere on his pale flesh, but most recognisably on his chin in a long pointed beard. Ironically there was not one hair on his shaven head.

"...That's what we gotta do." Stomp said, his gruff intimidating voice bellowing around the hall.

The two guys that stood opposite them, looked on casually, taking in what Stomp was saying. The young looking duo were an exciting tandem known as The Firecrackers. Both of them looked very similar, both were tall and athletic, which may have been the reason they were put together in the first place. The most differentiating feature was their hair. Although they had both grown it out, Lenny's hair was bleached blonde and Duke's hair was a nice shade of hazelnut.

"I get what you're saying." Said Duke "But we gotta get some offence in there!"

"Of course, you will!" Tusk said.

"We know you can fly and flip flop around the ring, we get that!" Said Stomp "But it has to be done at the right time." They all nodded in agreement.

"We gotta get our shit in you know?" Lenny laughed, they all followed suit.

"You will!" Stomp chuckled slapping him on the shoulder.

"Shall we go through the finish again?" Tusk asked.

There was a babble of agreement and they all attempted to take their places around the ring for a dress rehearsal.

"So Duke, you're shit-canned out by Tusk and we set up

like we're gonna finish Lenny with the spike pilderiver..."

"Sorry, to interrupt fellas!" Rogan called from outside the ring, staring through the red, white and blue ropes at the hungry talented youngsters in the ring.

"Randy!" Comes the chorus of enthusiasm from the ring full of wrestlers that probably grew up watching Rogan, idolising him and wanting to follow in his footsteps. There was nothing but respect shown as they all waited their turn to reach through the ropes and shake his hand.

"You boys play nice." Rogan said before heading for the East side of the building where a black curtain had been erected, this would act as the evenings entrance and the way to the correct locker rooms.

"I'd love to work with him one day." Duke pined as they all watched him waddle away, a noticeable limp to the left side of his body due to bad knees and a dodgy hip. Injuries that always seemed to disappear when it was go time and the adrenaline was flowing.

"I did!" Stomp announced arrogantly.

"No shit!" Came the Firecrackers reply.

"Nothing major, small town show. Worked the main with him in Hope Springs, back in '03."

"Damn!" The Firecrackers said shaking their heads.

"Do you know something? I learn't more in that one match than I had in a hundred leading up to it."

Rogan appeared on the other side of the curtain and again was met by the chaotic rushing of crew members trying to get everything in place and ready. He wheeled his case along towards a bunch of wrestlers that were standing around staring at a piece of paper that was tacked to the wall. Jungle Jim stood shirtless with his incredible rippled physique on display, his brown dreadlocked hair cascading down his golden tanned trapezius. His hands were casually tucked in the pockets of his jeans as he looked on seemingly pleased with the match he had been given. Nemesis stood beside him, a man of decent size in an orange and purple flashing of colours streaked across his singlet, which had the name NEMESIS graffitied across it in a shocking ice blue colour. He nodded his head agreeing with something that was said to him his brown mullet fluttered around behind him.

"Yeah, we'll just keep it nice and simple, only a ten minute match. No point pulling out all the stops for that one." Announced the gargantuan man that stood beside him, Nemesis agreed again nodding at him. The large man was known as 'The Slammer' or 'The American Hero' to some. At 6 feet 10 inches tall and built as though he had been chiselled out of granite, he looked like a real specimen. His long spandex tights clung to his bulging tree trunk type thighs and topping his outfit was a blue mask that covered his entire head and laced up at the back. Eyes, nose and mouth holes were cut out of it and trimmed in white and red, the theme and design that was emblazoned on his ensemble was a stars and stripes motif, much like Randy Rogan's persona.

There he is. The big man, The Slammer. The man that will take my place. The next hero to don the patriotic gimmick. Now don't get me wrong, I'm not bitter, not at all. I know how this business works, I know that we are cogs in a machine. A machine that will continue to turn forever. I realise I am just one of those cogs and when that cog is no longer able to turn the works at the desired speed, then they're replaced. He has been groomed to take my place for the last few years now, and I'm fine with that, it's time that somebody else took the helm and I'd rather it be someone that I like and someone I have invested so much of my time and effort in helping get to where he needs to be. He's the blueprint for what every promoter wants a wrestler to be like, he's a beast, a promoter's wet dream. He's over like fucking rover and most importantly of all he'll make money. And that's what it's all about! My only worry and concern is if he has the temperament for it. Carrying the whole business on your shoulders is a huge undertaking, you have to be in the right frame of mind or else you're fucked! And you'll end up just another flash in the pan.

"I see all the waifs and strays are loitering as usual?" Rogan said announcing his arrival.

They all turned and greeted him with warming smiles, it was a nice feeling for him to get such genuine pleasantries from his peers, in some ways that meant more than anything else. He just wished that all his peers shared that same sentiment towards him, some were jealous, cruel or just deceitful and would go to any lengths to cause trouble for their own amusement. Some of his peer's egos were such that they despised his success and flicked their fork tongues in poisonous whispers to any naive ears that would listen. Politics, a tradition that was seemingly as old as the business itself. But over the last year or so Rogan had ignored such blather, vowing that he would soon be done with it all, and really wanted to try and enjoy his time with the people he liked instead of focussing on the people that didn't like him, they no longer mattered.

They greeted him with handshakes and friendly pats on the back. The Slammer didn't shake his hand, instead he moved on in and gave him a hug.

"Good to see ya, Champ!" Slammer said with a toothy smile peeking out from underneath his mask.

"Easy, you big gorilla! You'll crush my old bones!"

"Ha!" The Slammer laughed "Nobody's won with a Bear Hug for twenty years!"

They all laughed.

"So what we got?" Rogan said turning his attentions to the evenings card that was unceremoniously tacked up on the white pristine wall on the back of a flyer.

"You've got Kami, in the main. 25 minutes." Nemesis said pointing it out with his index finger that was wrapped in an unnecessary amount of athletic tape.

"Easy night for you then, Champ!" Jim said smiling at him.

"Yeah! 25 minutes is doable. Just about!" Rogan chuckled.

"Yeah, the days of one hour Broadways with Rex Regal, are long gone, huh?" The Slammer playfully mocked with his gigantic arm draped across Rogan's shoulders.

"Damn straight!" Rogan laughed.

SANCTUARY CITY ARENA

OPENER
~~JUNGLE JIM~~ v PEDRO PASSION (8 MINS)
SUNSET GLEN

RHINO BROS. v FIRECRACKERS (20 MINS)

UNITED STATES CHAMPIONSHIP
~~MR CANADA~~ v YELLOW FEATHER (C) (15 MINS)

NEMESIS v ~~THE SLAMMER~~ (10 MINS)

INTERVAL

TAG TEAM CHAMPIONSHIP
~~DEVASTATION~~ v BRONX & ACE (15 MINS)

JUNGLE JIM v SEBASTIAN CHURCHILL
(DOUBLE COUNT OUT) (12 MINS)

~~JOHNNY MIDNIGHT~~ v EL FLAMINGERO (8 MINS)

~~MEGAN POWERS~~ v MISTRESS EVIL (6 MINS)

MAIN
WORLD HEAVYWEIGHT CHAMPIONSHIP
~~RANDY ROGAN(C)~~ v KAMI KAJEU (25 MINS

CHAPTER 4

Rogan moved on towards the dressing room door that sat at the end of another long corridor. The door had the word 'VISITORS' emblazoned on it in sharp black font. The door next to it had a scrap piece of paper stuck to it, the word 'WOMEN'S' scribbled on it.

Rogan opened the door and walked into the male locker room, he was immediately hit by a room filled with humid steam bellowing out from the shower block and the sight of naked bodies waltzing around in various stages of getting dressed. His nostrils were immediately invaded by the peculiar but routine aromas. The stale sweat absorbed spandex that seemed to fill the air every time someone opened up their case, paired with the warming and overpowering smell of muscle rub.

He stood in the doorway and his face contorted as the ghastly sight of Kami Kajeu's naked buttocks gawked back at him.

"Jesus!" Rogan groaned as Kajeu bent over to rummage in his case that was strewn on the clammy tiled flooring. His flabby cheeks wiggled with the movement, parting like the curtains on a stage to reveal his hairy scrotum, a dangling pendulum swaying from side to side like the clapper of a bell.

"Shut the fucking door! There's a breeze going straight up my asshole!" Kajeu shouted in his broken American accent.

"Okay, keep your balls on!" Rogan shouted back.

On hearing Rogan's voice, Kajeu peered around to see him. His silky dark hair was long and draped over his chubby face but a smile could be seen appearing through the veil of hair.

"Randy! You funny bastard!" He chuckled and stood up. Rogan entered and let the door close behind him as he approached the large bulging specimen that was Kami Kajeu.

"You good?" Rogan said as they shook hands.

"You know me, Randy. I'm always good."

"Have you lost some weight?" Rogan mocked, looking down at the large sagging stomach that hung over his tiny penis and massive balls.

"I'm down 3 pounds!" Kajeu laughed and slapped his stomach, the sound like a gunshot going off and it echoed through the locker room.

"Good, you'll be a bit lighter for me tonight then when you sandbag me."

They laughed.

"We'll have some fun." Rogan laughed and nodded.

"Easy night!" Kajeu said and bent back over to rummage in his case.

Rogan cringed again at the sight of his large wrinkled ass bent over in front of him. It reminded him of something you may see on the African plains, the rear end of a bull elephant or rhinoceros perhaps.

He walked towards an empty space in the corner, he passed several wrestlers going about their business and smiled, greeted them, and shook their hands.

Ace Armstrong was a blonde haired good looking guy, he was

what was known as a utility man, could fit in anywhere on the card and have a decent match and delivering whatever you needed from him, but was never going to be a main event player. Unfortunately for him, he lacked that mysterious 'It Factor'. He was clad in eye-catching lime green spandex tights and frantically stuffed something in a locker, quickly slamming the door concealing what every mysterious treasures lay within. He smiled at Rogan, it was a nervous smile.

God knows what he's got hidden in there. That kid is such an oddball.

The Native American, Yellow Feather, stood pruning his beautiful flamboyant headdress, removing any stray feathers.

Characters, that's what pro wrestling needs again. More characters like Yellow Feather. There has always been a large following in the Indian community, always good to have someone who represents that history on the roster.

"Hey, Willie!" Rogan said walking past.

"Hi, Randy!" Yellow Feather nodded back.

Willie's Uncles both donned the headdress and proudly displayed their heritage before him, as The High Chief and Flying Eagle. It will be a sad day when the promoters call an end to the gimmick. Some call it stereotyping, but that's his heritage and he's proud of it, he should be able to express that. The gimmicks are slowly fizzling out and being replaced with more 'real' characters, with bland names and vanilla personalities. I'm a true believer that people watch professional wrestling for the larger than life characters and to escape their normal lives and lose themselves in a world of fantasy. What happens when the fantasy world becomes the same as their reality? Then there is nowhere to escape to.

A large muscular black man warms up with a resistance band, stretching the rubber to its full capacity, as veins pop out all over his rock hard biceps.

"How's it going Champ?" Says Billy Bronx who greets him with a fist bump and friendly smile.

"All good, Billy!" Replies Rogan as he walks on by.

A youngish guy, wrapped in a towel casually lolls on a bench, his wet dark hair slicked back, his attention fully on the screen of his cell phone. He glances up at Rogan as he passes and ignores him, turning his attentions back to his screen.

Rogan finally parks up his case next to a bench in the corner and removes his leather jacket, hanging it up on a peg that protrudes from the wall behind him. He turns to look at the guy on his cell phone again and shakes his head.

'Magnificent' Johnny Midnight! The future of this business! I know that he saw me, I could see him glance at me but then to not have the respect to even acknowledge me makes my blood boil...well it used to, nowadays I'm not too bothered about that because I know what he's like. He's everything about this business that I despise, and he is the future of it! Now don't get me wrong, the guy is one hell of a talent, and he knows what he's doing in there, very technically sound, knows how to tell a story. His persona is one that is arrogant and thinks he's better than everyone, but it's no gimmick, that's exactly what he is like out of the ring too. I guess that's why he garners so much heat from the fans. He does think he's better than everyone and has

shown a lack of respect to several of us veterans that have paved the way for him to even be here.

Rogan sighs and shakes his head.

"Hi, Johnny!" he calls down the bench.

Johnny looks up from his phone and forces a smile that was so obviously artificial "Oh, Hi, Randy. Didn't see you there."

The two stared at each other for a moment before Midnight's gaze dropped back to his cell phone, leaving Rogan shaking his head again.

He'd screw over any one of us in this dressing room to get what he wants.

Before Rogan could dwell on such negative vibes, he heard the loud yell from the entrance to the showers "Randall!" He looked up to see the plump physique of Sebastian Churchill, wrapped in a towel.

"Oh, here he is!" Rogan laughed "The pig in a blanket."

"Fuck off mate!" He growled in his strong British accent as he approached Rogan who had stood up to meet him "That hurts my feelings that does!" he continued before they both burst out laughing and embraced.

"Missed you last night mate." Churchill said with a warm smile "Tagged with Ben Gali against those young Firecrackers."

"Shit, I haven't seen Ben in an age, how is he?"

"He's good, put on a few pounds now though. But haven't we all!" He laughed "But yeah he's good. Those Firecracker kids are good though."

"Yeah, I've heard good things."

"Just needed to slow them down a little, you know? Little fuckers wanted to do everything and do it yesterday!"

They laughed.

"Where were you last night anyway? Were you in Blackfoot?" Churchill asked, whipping his towel from around his waist and rubbing his platinum hair up with it. Rogan ignored the huge penis that hung between his legs, he'd seen it before, it was legendary to some.

"No, I was over in Forge City. Doing a show for Bobcat!"

"Good old Bobcat! Salt of the Earth that lad. He promoting outside Ontario now then?"

"He's merged with Arnie Gareljich. They're co-promoting." Said Rogan "I worked against Bobcat's son, Bret. Very good, going to be something I'd say."

Churchill smiled and nodded.

"Got that old school mentality and respect for the business." Rogan continued "That seems to be disappearing these days!" and with that glanced at Midnight.

Churchill looked in the same direction too and nodded "I know exactly what you mean, mate. 'Mean' Micky MacGyver would have slapped the shit out of him!" He laughed and with that he left to where he was sitting to prepare.

He manoeuvred his case onto the bench, unzipped it and then sat down next to it, his old joints creaking like a flight of old stairs.

It all comes down to respect I guess.

He opened up his case and on top of all his paraphernalia sat the World Heavyweight Title belt. He stared at it as the strip lights gleamed onto its golden plates, his face bathed in its reflective glow.

But, I know my old friend, my mistress, she respects me and I her. She's been part of my life for so many years. Just seeing her made him smile. To think I first cradled her in my arms at aged seventeen. She belonged to Captain Yankee back then and he let me carry her to his car. Even then she called to me.

He ran his finger tips over the centre plate, feeling the intricate design of the American eagle's wings that were painstaking engraved over fifty years ago.

I have witnessed this beauty around the waists of legends such as Dan Dynamo, The Marauder, Magnus Meadowlark, Abullah 'The Screaming Sheik' and even my hero and mentor 'Uncle' Sam Reagan.

He could feel the allure just from touching her cold golden plates that lay on a thick black leather strap.

And still she calls to me telling me to stay, promising that she will be mine forever if I do.

His smile disappears and he closes his case.

But I can't.

CHAPTER 5

The word 'Office' was scribbled on a piece of paper and tacked to the door of this particular dimly lit room in the Sanctuary Arena. The room itself didn't resemble an office at all, but a storeroom, complete with a large section of shelving homing all manner of items from stationary, spare arena uniforms and cleaning equipment. A table had been brought in from one of the VIP lounges and looked obviously out of place next to a vacuum cleaner, a step ladder and a floor buffer.

A small balding fat man sat on one of two folding chairs that had been arranged either side of the table. A chunky cigar stuck out the corner of his mouth and smoke puffed out filling the dim room in a thick grey haze. The hair that he had on his head was greasy and seemed to cling to his clammy skin. He chuckled to himself about something as he chewed on the butt end of his cigar. Suddenly there was a knock at the door, Louis Raggu looked up at it but said nothing and looked back down at the table which homed a pile of magazines and a notepad with a sharp pencil on top of it. The eraser that once sat proudly on the end was worn down to nothing. A cell phone also sat in front of him and a pile of dollar bills lay discarded on the table, next to a black money tin. He began to scrape up all the bills that depicted various presidents throughout American history, gripping them with his podgy greasy looking fingers, they looked as though he had eaten fried chicken and not bothered to clean his hands. Several gold rings gripped his fingers tightly, so much so that his fingers looked a different shade to his hands as though the circulation were being cut off.

The door knocked again.

"Give me a second!" Raggu snapped in annoyance.

He put the last of the money into the tin, it was so full that it was hard to close the lid and even when it was shut, some still sprouted out from underneath the confines of the lid.

"Come in!" He bellowed, the cigar shaking in the corner of his mouth. As the door opened up he picked up his cell phone and pretended to be on a call.

"Can I talk to you, Mr Raggu?" Came the meek voice of a man, clad in mustard coloured trunks, and black ankle boots, his white sports socks underneath pulled up so they could be seen over the top.

Raggu signalled for him to come in with a wave of his hand and a nod of his head as he serenaded the cell phone with several 'Huh, huh's'.

The man walked in and closed the door behind him.

He stood uncomfortably there for a minute looking around at the makeshift office. He scratched at his shaven head and sniffed, he remembered having a full head of hair, so long and wavy he could tie it back in a pony tail, it had gone now. Three months ago he lost a hair versus hair match with Sebastian Churchill. Raggu had said a new look may be what he needed to get over with the crowd. So he lost his hair and grew a neat looking goatee beard.

The crowd unfortunately still didn't care.

Raggu pointed to the chair and the man sat down on it, the cold steel caused his buttocks to contract being taken by surprise by the shocking change of temperature.

Raggu hung up the cell and placed it down on the table smiling at the man that sat adjacent.

"Sorry, Glen! It was a very important phone call, you understand?"

"Oh yeah, of course, Mr Raggu!" he nodded frantically.

"Now what can I do for you?" He sneered, his chunky digits interlocking together and coming to rest on the table in front of him.

"Well, I was wondering about maybe the possibility of an increase in wages?" He reluctantly asked, his face cowering as he said the words, a sentence that he'd been practising in the hallway for the last half an hour or so.

Raggu looked at him and then at the money tin, that was spewing out dollar bills.

"I mean, price of living life on the road has gone up for me." Glen pleaded "There's food, hotels, car rental, gas! Everything seems to be on the rise."

"Why don't you ride with someone else? Share the rental and gas costs?" Raggu said leaning back in his chair and sucking on his cigar.

"Nobody ever wants to ride with me." He said lowering his head in embarrassment.

"Nonsense!" Raggu said nonchalantly "I'm sure somebody will. Ask again!"

Glen looked up at him and just sat there.

"Something else you wish to say, Glen?"

"Well, yeah. I mean I think I should be paid what some of the other guys are getting."

"How'd you know what the others are getting?"

"I..." he stuttered.

"You've been sticking your nose in others private affairs?"

"Well, I just happened to see..."

"Is it any wonder nobody wants to ride with you, Glen?" Raggu spat, saliva spraying out over the table.

"I mean not to be disrespectful, but even some of the girls are getting paid more than me now." Glen moaned. Raggu shook his head and made a tutting sound with his bulbous lips.

"Sorry, I know that probably sounded really sexist, but..."

Raggu Interrupted him "Glen, Glen ,Glen!" he sighed again leaning back to enjoy his cigar.

Glen thought that the cigar looked expensive, as did the rings on his fingers, and the gold watch stretched around his fat wrist as did the chunky medallion that hung around his neck.

"You ask me the impossible, Glen." Raggu sighed.

"Why?"

"Times are very hard, Glen!" he said blowing smoke out into the air.

Glen's eyebrows rose up to meet the wrinkles that crimped across his forehead in shock after such a statement. Glen was a simple soul and not too bright but he knew bullshit when he smelt it.

"Do you know how much it costs to put on theses shows?" Raggu asked.

"No."

"A fucking lot! That's how much!" He spat again. Glen felt some of his spittle drop onto the exposed flesh of his thighs and grimaced.

"The girls get paid more than you because they are talented, they draw and not to mention they're hot!" He smiled and licked his lips.

The sight of this sickened Glen.

Raggu sieved through the magazines until he came to a copy of Heyboy. He opened it up and unveiled the centrefold which happened to be the female French Canadian wrestler, René. The spread featured her lying on a chaise lounge. Her back arched pushing out her perfectly shaped breasts, while a long flowing pearl necklace dripped down her cleavage and then disappeared between her legs.

"Take René for instance. Now if you looked like that Glen, I'd fucking pay you a lot more!" He laughed and slammed the magazine back down on the table, not before having another quick glance.

"But to be honest, I'd probably be fucking your ass right now if you looked like her!" He laughed, thumping the table, bursting into a coughing fit, spluttering a spitting everywhere.

Glen grimaced again at not just the thought, but of the sight of this disgusting looking individual that was able to abuse his power.

"So what can I do?" Glen finally asked after Raggu had finished his coughing fit.

"You have to remember your place in this business, Glen. Some are eagles and meant to soar through the sky, others are chickens that peck around at the scraps."

"I'm a chicken?" Glen asks in a defeated manner.

"You're a chicken!" nodded Raggu. "See! So you do get it after all!"

Glen stared at him and sighed again.

"You're a jobber. That's what your role is here, your job is to put other people over."

"Oh!"

"It's an important fucking job! You must embrace your role. If I'm to have eagles soaring in the skies I need plump chickens to feed them. Do you understand?"

"Yeah!" He sighed.

"Don't be disheartened, Glen. You see the truth of it is, that a chain is only as strong as the weakest link, and you are that weakest link."

Glen's heart sank, he felt his bottom lip quiver underneath his thick goatee, his eyeballs started to glaze with moisture, he felt at that moment he could actually cry.

What the hell am I supposed to do? I've done everything you've ever asked of me, you crooked bastard! I had new trunks made when you said my gear was bland. I shaved my head for you

and changed my looked for you. I spent $2000 of my dads
money on a new sequinned entrance robe and then you told me
I couldn't wear it because Churchill already wears one like that.
I mean what have I got to fucking do here!

He wished he had the balls to say what he was thinking, but he
didn't. He just bit his quivering lip and controlled the urge.

"Look, by all means go somewhere else and try your
luck, I won't hold it against you."

"I don't want to go anywhere else." Glen sniffed, still
fighting back those emotions.

"Good, I want you to stay. You do what you do very
well."

"What? I lose well?" Glen chuckled shaking his head in
disbelief.

"Yes!"

Glen was taken aback, he still didn't fully understand the
business even though he had been wrestling for around 11 years
now. He didn't get it and thought that winning was all that
mattered. He thought that Randy Rogan was the top dog
because he won all the time, he didn't see that he needed the
other guys to lie down for him to help him make it to the top.

"The marks come to see the underdog win, Glen. You're
that underdog! But you have to find some way of connecting
with the crowd, I've tried everything, it's really up to you now."
Glen didn't know what to say or to do. What could he do to stand
out, to connect with the fans?

"I could paint my face?" He said out of the blue.

"The Devastation boys do it though. Can't have everyone doing that gimmick can I? It'll dilute it and it won't be special any longer?"

"How about being in a tag team?"

"With who?"

"I...I don't know." He sighed seeing no more straws to clutch.

There was silence between the two and smoke bellowed out of Raggu's mouth like he was a steam locomotive, that was usually a good sign though, it meant he was thinking. Usually cooking up a scheme that would be proposed to help someone out but in the grand scheme of things only help himself.

"Listen, Glen. You're never going to be a headliner until you're a draw. Until you are the one putting the asses in the seats! Or at the very least selling some merchandise! We all want to make money, but it's down to you!"

Glen sat and his cogs started to turn over, granted a little slower than most peoples, but turning nonetheless.

"Will, I ever win a match? Maybe that would help get me over with the fans, if I won a match?"

"Glen!" Sighed Raggu, rubbing at his greasy forehead with his equally tacky fingers "You're still not getting it are you? It's not about winning or losing it's about..."

"Entertaining a crowd and sending them home happy?" Glen blurted out with enthusiasm, like a lightbulb had just gone off. Raggu rolled his eyes and then a huge fake smile formed, his gold nugget sunken into one of his teeth twinkled as he grinned.

"Yeah, that's exactly what it's about! You do that every night and you'll soon have them on your side."

"Right!" Glen said jumping out of his seat with optimism "That's what I'll do. I'll give them my best every night, they've got to start appreciating me then haven't they?"

"Yes, Glen!"

"Thanks, Mr Raggu." Glen said and left.

Raggu sighed a huge sigh of relief. He knew deep down that however unmarketable 'Sunset Glen' was he knew that he needed someone like him in his roster, if he wants to build killer heels they have to have some lambs to slaughter. He knew that Glen would never get over, but at least Glen had something to focus on and keep him quiet for the next few months.

"Entertaining a crowd and sending them home happy?" He scoffed as he opened up his money tin again and watched as the mass of bills spewed out over the table.

"Yeah that's exactly what it's all about!" he laughed.

CHAPTER 6

There is a rumble of excitement working its way around a now jam-packed Sanctuary City Arena. Music bellows out of the buildings sound system and the spotlights dance around the enthusiastic fans, who scream and jump up and down. Gigantic foam hands wriggle in the air and handmade signs can be seen cut into a mass of writhing bodies.

The spotlights spiral around the room, flashing past the 20 by 20 structure in the centre of the hall, an artists canvas unconventionally made up of steel, wood and rope, wait patiently for the brush and paints.

The ring is surrounded by rows upon rows of metal guardrails, these serve a duel purpose. Not only to keep the fans safe if the action spills out of the ring, but it is also there to keep the wrestlers safe. There have been many times when some members of the audience have gotten carried away and rowdy and either took a swipe at the wrestler or in some severe cases, attacked them with weapons! Days before the guardrails and security, various wrestlers suffered stab wounds or found themselves caught up in a riot.

One famous story involved a gigantic man by the name of The Marauder! He stood almost 7 feet tall, his face and bald head painted with a red hand print. He scared the living daylights out of many a crowd. One night during his reign as the World

Heavyweight Champion in the 60's, he made his way to the ring clad from head to foot in fur skins, a helmet homing one horn breaking out of one side of it's rusted metal shell and his trademark long auburn beard that had red food colouring spewed down it for effect.

He was that hated that he'd whipped a Philadelphian crowd into such a frenzy by taking a swing at them with a massive femur bone that he carried everywhere, that when he finally got into the ring and spewed 'blood' all over his opponent (Which happened to be local babyface hero, Jon Michaels on this occasion), the crowd exploded and rushed the ring, The Marauder had to be escorted back to the dressing room area, literally fighting his way through punches, kicks and even thrown chairs! He managed to take a few out with his flailing femur, but in the melee he was stabbed in the side by what police later said was a homemade shiv. It was found on the floor, the blade smothered with The Marauder's blood. The Marauder didn't sell the stabbing at all and waltzed into the dressing room like nothing at happened hollering at the top of his voice "Now that's how you get heat!"

Riots are no longer commonplace as the attitude of the fans has changed. Knowing now exactly what they're watching, after the curtain had been pulled back a few years ago it changed the scene for good. A safer environment granted, but business has suffered financially, struggling to get back to the heights it once had, when people still believed.

The lights stopped swirling around and it all went dark. Screams and whistles echoed through the arena and one light came on and shone on the ring illuminating a man with a microphone, much to the pleasure of the crowd who shouted, chanted and laughed in anticipation.

"Are you ready!" The announcer said through the microphone, his voice boomed around the arena and was matched for volume by the hungry crowd. As the announcer talked about safety information, the close circuit television cameras turned their attention to a small table at ringside. Two men sat at the table, one a small man with large square glasses, dressed smartly in a tuxedo and next to him a fat man in a hideous looking Hawaiian shirt, with palm trees and pineapples emblazoned on a turquoise background. The fat man even had a toupee that seem to slide to one side every time he moved. They made their final adjustments to bow ties and hair pieces as they went live in TV land.

"Welcome everyone to another thrilling night of professional wrestling brought to you LIVE from The Sanctuary Arena in Sanctuary City!" The little man said enthusiastically in a tone that a gameshow host might use "I'm Milton McQueen and with me as always is Bunk 'The Hunk'!"

"That's right folks!" He said in a Southern drawl "Once again the love muscle has come to flex just for you!"
He flexed a thick bicep at the camera and winked, his toupee slipped out of place and he nudge it back to where it should be.

"Well, I hope you'll only be flexing your vocal cords tonight, Bunk!"

"Let's hope there's something for me to sink my teeth into then, McQueen!"

"Oh boy! Do we ever! Tonight we're bringing you not one, not two, but THREE! Championship matches!"

Bunk looks at him gobsmacked.

"Holy cow!" He drawls.

"That's right, Bunk! Devastation will defend their World Tag Team Championship against the new and exciting tandem of Ace Armstrong and Billy Bronx!"

"That is a formidable team, but I don't like their chances against a seasoned duo like devastation." Bunk grimaces and shakes his head.

"Well, how about this! The United States Champion, Yellow Feather, puts his title on the line against the undefeated Mr Canada!"

"It's about time that all these peons gave Mr Canada some respect! All this animosity towards Canada has to stop and it will stop tonight when Mr Canada takes that United States Title!"

"And what about the big one? 'The American Man' Randy Rogan defends The World Heavyweight Championship, against his arch nemesis, 'The Korean Kraken' Kami Kajeu!"

"Rogan's American dream is about to become a nightmare! Kajeu's beaten Rogan before, he can beat him again!" The bell sounds, its high pitch sing seems to last forever and a hush falls over the crowd as they turn their attentions to the dark curtain at the corner of the hall.

"Ladies and Gentlemen!" Growls the announcer "This match is scheduled for one fall!"

The crowd repeat the words 'one fall' and it trails off to touch the roof of the dome somewhere in the darkness above.

"About to make his way to the ring..." The ring announcer growls again and pauses to allow the start of the wrestlers entrance music to kick in. A spotlight splashes light on the curtain and the subtle sound of saxophones leave the speakers, like the sensual soundtrack of some late 70's pornographic film.

There is a groan of boos from the people in the crowd who realise just who it is.

The commentary team let the viewers at home know what's happening.

"Oh here we go!" Bunk announces "Those sexy saxophones can only mean one thing!"

"It's Pedro Passion!" Elaborates Milton McQueen.

Pedro Passion gently pushes aside the curtains and arrogantly struts down the aisle towards the ring. A sour serenade of boo's rain down on him from the crowd, intwined with a berating of several obscenities from very passionate fans that don't appreciate Pedro's flamboyant persona.

Cooly gliding past the mass of downturned thumbs, as if his glittery pink sequinned trousers (held up by braces) and a matching bow tie wrapped tightly around his neck wasn't enough to stir the pot, he began blowing kisses at them all.

"Yes, yes! I know that you want a piece of this!" He grinned obnoxiously, stopping just as he reached ringside to do a turn on the spot so that everyone could take in his ripped and tanned physique.

"You like that don't you?" He asks, nodding in agreement with his own ego.

The crowd groaned and let him have it again.

He skipped up the steps to the ring and effortlessly slunk in between the ropes before twirling around in the middle of the ring, the spotlight catching each shimmering cerise sequin and making him sparkly under the warming light.

"Hailing from Paradise City, Las Vegas, Nevada!" Announced the ring announcer, who still stood in the ring but had sunk back into a shady nook near the one corner, allowing Pedro the room to manoeuvre on centre stage. Waylon 'The Voice' Voight was a ten year veteran of this business and knew that the crowd had not come to see the ring announcer and just got on with the job in hand.   "Weighing in at 240 pounds... PEDRO PASSION!"

The crowd erupted again with a chorus of boos and Pedro grabbed the microphone and yanked it out of Waylon's hand.

He held it ever so limply in his hand, and stood loose and casual, almost feminine. As he waited for the music to fade he wiped his finger tips across his thick black moustache.

"I know what you want!" He said, his voice resounding around the dome "I know what you need!" he hissed seductively as he paused. This was routine and he knew when to stop and when to go and when to milk it, this was one of those times. "You came here to..." He waited for the boo's to die down so his catchphrase had maximum impact.

"WATCH ME DANCE!" He shouted and dropped the microphone to the canvas, aggressively whipping off his trousers and launching them out of the ring as he began to wriggle his body, gyrating his hips, while the spotlight glistened off his baby oil soaked jagged abdominal area.

"Oh that is disgusting!" McQueen groaned to the people watching at home, as they were treated to an extreme closeup of his thrusting crotch area on their monitors that sat on the table in front of them.

"You just don't appreciate what a great dancer Pedro is, McQueen!" Bunk chortled.

"Would you please stop dancing, Bunk!" McQueen sighed.

The music cut out and Pedro stopped dancing. He waltzed to a neutral corner removing his bow tie as Waylon picked up the microphone, shaking his head and glaring at Pedro who winked back at him.

"And his opponent!" Roared Waylon.

The crowd roared, whoever it was about to come through that curtain was surely already a made man. Pedro had riled them up and they were looking to a hero to come and save the day and make everything right. A generic eighties rock ballad had kicked in and as the electric guitar wailed, the wrestler arrived right on cue.

"C'MON PEOPLE!" Shrieked Sunset Glen as he burst through the curtain as though he were actually on fire.

The crowd immediately deflated in a lackadaisical murmur of disinterest.

Sunset Glen waited for the response, there wasn't one and then made his way to the ring looking to slap hands and kiss babies.

There were no hands to slap and no babies to kiss, Glen had received the worst thing a wrestler can get, nothing. Granted if you are a babyface and come out to a chorus of boos then at least that can be worked into the program, maybe even the match if the worker is good enough and knows enough that the crowd isn't with them. The worker could then work an aggressive heel style in the ring. Same with a heel making his entrance and being showered with love and affection, somewhere down the line you can turn these wrestlers to what the crowd want. But to walk out here and not receive cheers or jeers that is a death sentence. Glen was doomed.

"For fuck sake!" murmured Pedro, his reaction unheard by the crowd because of the yowl of the eighties rock band Razor Snake.

"Good luck trying to get the crowd back." Waylon said to Pedro under his breath.

"Tell me about it!" He sighed with annoyance, as he tried hard not to break character and let his disappointment show in his body language. He knew he would have to work extra hard to even get anything from the crowd now. As the heel of the match they would normally heckle his antics but now he is wrestling someone that they don't care about then the match is probably doomed from the start.

"The crowd are really getting behind Sunset Glen here in Sanctuary." McQueen lied through his teeth, hoping that they could edit some cheers in there when the show airs.

"Yeah..." Bunk started but then trailed off into suppressed laughter, hysterical and unable to talk.

"I think we have lost Bunk 'The Hunk' for a second due to a technical difficulty with his headset." McQueen carried on the true professional that he was.

Sunset Glen steps through the ropes as 'The Voice' finishes his introduction.

"From Salem, Oregon, and weighing in at 228 pounds, SUNSET GLEN!"

Nothing.

Glen raised his hand in the air to no reaction and then some wiseass in the crowd growled, "You suck, Glen!"

It snowballed and the whole crowd erupted in unison with "YOU SUCK! YOU SUCK! YOU SUCK!"

Glen was frozen like a deer stuck in the headlights of an oncoming truck. He could feel the warm spotlight cooking him in his own embarrassment, his bottom lip began wobbling and tears filled his eyes. To make matters worse for him he couldn't see anyone in the crowd, the light shown on him and everything in the background looked dark, all these unpleasantries aimed at him came out of that darkness and it made him feel so small.

The veteran referee, Bernie Barnes, waddled over towards him looking like he was checking his wrist tape "Forget everything you had planned for the match. He's hitting you with the finish straight away." He murmured and then backed away into the middle of the ring.

Glen stood there lost.

The bell rang and Pedro went straight for the dazed Glen and span him around by his shoulders so that he was facing him and whispered "We're going home!" and gave him a swift kick to the gut, the toe of his white leather boot just making enough contact for Glen to react and he instinctively doubled over in front of Pedro. He then hooked both of Glens arms behind his back and interlocked his fingers tightly in a butchers grip, before throwing himself backwards with velocity driving Glen headfirst to the mat. Glen's head didn't touch the mat, Pedro supported his upper body but to the audience the manoeuvre appeared to drive poor Glen's face into the canvas.

The crowd actually cheered.

"THE PASSION KILLER!" McQueen screeched "Straight away and this one is over!"

Pedro let go of the lock that he had tightly sunk in and rolled Glen's lifeless body over and lay across his chest.

"You really fucked us both here, man!" Pedro murmured as Bernie quickly slid down on the canvas and slapped his hand three times.

Glen said nothing.

The bell rang again, this time to indicate the match had ended, the saxophones hit and Pedro Started to dance again, this time to cheers.

"For fuck sake!" Pedro said to himself as Waylon announced he was the winner, again to resounding cheers. Pedro didn't want to be a face, and he hoped that this was just a blip and that they can turn it around.

Years ago something like this wouldn't have been a problem, it would only have been seen by those in attendance. Nowadays there are eyes everywhere and news will spread immediately on the internet and social media, there's no escape from it.

Everything becomes common knowledge. Wrestlers could hone their skills and work the same opponent every night in a different town, almost practicing that big payoff match that would appear on pay per view, making sure the match was perfect.

This would also help when the chemistry is not there and opponents don't gel well together, the wrestlers could use those matches to iron out the creases. They don't have that luxury now, by tomorrow every wrestling fan will know the results, no longer having to rely on weekly or monthly magazines for their dose of wrestling news. Some think that the internet has ruined the wrestling business, it has helped to tear down that veil of mystique that hung in front of it for so many years. In a way it as humanised the characters and made them approachable, making them real and no longer those larger than life individuals that you could only see if you paid money and purchased a ticket. For all the positives, there are negatives and vice versa. Sunset Glen rolled out of the ring and sadly walked to the backstage area with tears in his eyes.

CHAPTER 7

Rogan's worn white leather boots hit the damp tiled flooring of the locker room. The toe ends were scuffed and peeling, reminiscent of his mentors all those years ago. Long white ice hockey socks were pulled up under blue knee pads emblazoned by a bright white star that was trimmed in shimmering gold, and were then slotted into the boots. This was a pleasant place for his feet, as familiar as ones own pillow, comfortable and cosy. His feet seemed to spread out and relax, as they found that comfortable position. It could be seen as comparable to that of a dog or cat that circles its favourite spot in front of the fire before settling.

He started to thread the off white stained laces through the metallic eyelets that glittered in the strip lights. As he pulled the boot in tight and into place, his ankle cracked and he whined, but his toes danced with excitement and anticipation.

Bob Dylan once sang '...For the times they are a-changin'. And boy was he right. This business has changed, it's time this old bull was put out to pasture. I'm not being bitter nor cynical of the direction the business has gone, I get it, it's exactly that, 'a business'. They'll do what they think will draw them money. But a lot of these new promotions popping up are just full of spot matches. That's all very well, who doesn't like a nice high spot?

But when there are seven, eight, nine all in one match and then the next match has gotta top that, well, where does it all end?

Kami Kajeu waddles over, his massive bulk stuffed into knee length spandex tights that are half black and half smothered with a North Korean flag design. White athletic tape peeps out as it is wrapped heavily around his knees, serving as some kind of moral support to keep his heavy mass upright. His black shiny hair had been painstakingly tied tightly into a knot on his head and a North Korean motif sat in the middle of his forehead on a red cotton bandana.

"So what d'you wanna do tonight, champ?" Kami asked sitting down next to Rogan on the bench.

"I'm easy. Got anything in mind?"

"Well, I was thinking..." Kami trailed off a list of old spots and sequences that were already programmed into Rogan's brain, he knew them all by heart and could easily perform them in his sleep. He drifted off to his thoughts again as Kami continued.

There is always a place for the high spots and the 'flipping and flopping' I'm not against any of it, but it needs to be woven into a story that makes sense instead of just being done for the sake of doing it. If you give the fans a little bit more each match, it keeps them coming back for more, plus you've always got something special in your reserves. If you're gonna go and shoot your load in a 10-15 minute slot, then sooner or later they're gonna get bored of you and move on. And who can blame them? They've seen everything you've got to give.

"...On the double down I was thinking, maybe we both hit a flying crossbody! It'll be like a fucking train wreck! We can milk the shit out of that!" Kami announces excitedly.

Rogan finishes lacing up one of his boots and nods in agreement. *And it keeps coming back to characters and stories, that's what these guys don't understand that's what keeps the people coming back each time. It's Hollywood! It's circus! It's soap opera! It's theatre! That's what it is, physical theatre. They want to connect and latch on to characters and stories the way they do when they visit the cinema or watch their favourite series on TV. Emotional attachment is what has kept me at the top for so long. I'll take emotional attachments over Phoenix Splashes every time.*

"...Then it'll be time for your fire. The usual? Axe Handle, Clothesline, Bodyslam?"

"No! I think I'll mix it up tonight."

"Okay!" Kami nods.

"Clothesline, Clothesline, whip reversal, up and over and I'll hit a Back Suplex on your fat ass!"

"Sounds good to me," smiled Kami.

But with pro wrestling everything moves in cycles and it'll all come back to characters and storytelling, you mark my words. Look, these guys today... amazing athletes! Better athletes than us and the generations that have gone before them, fitter and healthier? Damn straight! They have a better understanding of nutrition and know the pitfalls of drugs and alcohol. They are better wrestlers than any of us that have come before them, better than me, better than Kami, better than Sina, 'Uncle' Sam

Reagan and Captain Yankee! All of them! But we're better workers, storytellers and sellers. These are the ones that make the money at the end of the day, check the record books and see who made the most moolah.

"...The finish? Randy?"

"Huh?"

"You spaced out on me there, Champ. You feeling okay?"

"Yeah, was just thinking. What did you say?"

"For the finish, I was thinking you go up top, I cut you off and then launch you off the top, then..."

"You go for the Bomb's Away splash." Rogan interrupts "I move and as you sell that and turn over slowly I'll go up and hit..." Rogan stopped himself mid-sentence and looked around the locker room that was almost empty now, only Sebastian Churchill and Jungle Jim stood huddled together going over their match.

"Jim!" Rogan shouted.

"Yeah?" Jim said turning around.

"Are you going over tonight?" Rogan asked.

"No, double count out."

"Can I borrow the Top Rope Elbow tonight?"

"He means can he steal it!" Chuckles Sebastian slapping Jungle Jim on his wide tanned back.

"Yeah, sure! I'm not using it tonight." Smiled Jim.

"Thanks, Brother!" Rogan said turning his sights back to Kami "Top Rope Elbow drop then!"

"You sure you got what it takes old man?" Kami laughed.

"I'm willing, but don't know about being able." Rogan said joining him in a playful chuckle.

"Have you ever done it before?" Kami asked, a look of concentration furrowed underneath his bandana, obviously thinking back to past matches together and wondering whether he can ever remember him doing the move before.

"No!" laughed Rogan.

"Oh! Well, this should be fun." Kami burst into hysterics.

Like I said never give them everything! Pulling one out for a special occasion. Biggest pop of the night I guarantee.

CHAPTER 8

Several wrestlers congregate around the curtain, discussing things that they're going to do in their matches. Wally Dominguez frantically flits around like a chicken that's had its head cut off, flicking through the pages on his clipboard as sweat cascades down his temples. For him every night on the road is a headache having the unenviable job of rounding up all these egos and getting them into the right place at the right time. The guys and girls call him 'Mother Hen' and he hates that, they don't show him any respect and don't see what he does as being important, but it is, without him to usher them to where they need to be some of them would miss their cues entirely. Wally likes to think of himself as a shepherd in charge of a flock of unruly sheep.

As the action continues on the other side of the curtain, the noise from the crowd thumps around the dome, and becomes muted in the backstage area. To the wrestler's it sounds as though they're under water and they can hear the cheers and jeers somewhere off in the distance.

Mr Canada adjusts the eye and nose area of his red mask that is stamped with a white maple leaf on his forehead, and intricately trimmed with white and black around the eyes, nose and mouth area.

"Fucking stupid thing!" he moans. He was once known as 'The Canadian Kid'. But since coming to the United States he had been given a new persona and a new look, he was still not used to the mask yet. He is smaller and lean, but still athletic looking, but from a wrestling standpoint looks beatable, which is exactly what the intent was with the character. A sneaky heel that cheats and manipulates the rules to come away with victories. Clad head to foot in Canadian patriotism, from his red singlet and long tights combination, mimicking the design of his mask throughout, as well as a huge Canadian flag attached to a pole that is lent comfortably on his shoulder.

"You got it all, kid?" asked Yellow Feather.

"Can we go over the finish one more time?" Mr Canada asked hesitantly.

A paternal smile stretches across the tan leathered skin of the older and wiser Yellow Feather.

"You nervous, kid?"

"Yeah!" Mr Canada nods.

"It's okay to be nervous. If you're not getting those butterflies in the pit of your stomach and that excitement building inside you, then it isn't worth doing!"

Mr Canada nods in agreement.

"The time when those butterflies stop flying is the time to hang up your boots, kid."

"Yeah, well, their fucking fluttering now I can tell ya!" Mr Canada chuckles.

"Good!" Laughs Yellow Feather loudly slapping him on the shoulder.

Yellow Feather looks majestic in his gigantic traditional headdress, large feathers of yellow trimmed with red, burst from his head like flames. His tights of yellow and red are trimmed with black in all manner of traditional Native American symbols, the reason for the symbols and their meaning would be lost on the ignorant, but to him displaying his culture and heritage in such a way means the world to him. His boots are an expensive pair of real buffalo skin, in a tasseled moccasin style. To top off his exceptional attire is the 10 pounds of gold wrapped around his waist, The United States Championship. The main plate of the title is forged into the obscure shape of the United States of America with the flag visible in the centre, glistening in pristine gold on a red leather strap. The importance of the title is obviously not as illustrious as The World Heavyweight Championship, but still meant something. It had a long history, it had been baptised by people in the business as 'The Workhorse Belt' and was usually given to technically sound workers who could have great matches on demand.

Yellow Feather was one of these very workhorses and was already a two time United States Champion. His current reign had seen him hold the title for 250 days, this reign was to come to an end tonight.

"So, you try to waffle me with the belt..." Yellow Feather says.

"Yeah!" nods Mr Canada "A swing and a miss...I drop the belt..." He then looks a little lost and fidgets with his the eyeholes of his mask again.

"I pick it up!" Yellow Feather says, staring wide-eyed at Mr Canada trying to get the cogs turning again.

"The ref takes it off you?" Mr Canada asks a little unsure of his answer, but Yellow Feather meets him with a nod "Then while your back is turned I roll you up and grab a handful of tights"

"You got it!" Yellow Feather smiles.

"Cool!" Mr Canada sighs a nervous sigh as somewhere in the distance a bell rings and the muffled sound of boos shudder around the dome.

"You'll be fine, kid." Yellow Feather says gripping his shoulder firmly and giving it a little squeeze of encouragement "It's all in there trust me, if you get stuck I'll be there, don't worry."

"Okay." Smiled Mr Canada, the mask concealing the gesture.

"Just keep talking out there, we got this."
The tag team of The Firecrackers burst through the curtain, caked in a glowing layer of sweat, their flame designed tights soaked through, as if the flames were being extinguished. Duke cups his Jaw in his hand and struggles to move it.

"Man, those guys are fucking stiff!" he groans through his fingers.
Lenny stands shaking his head, a look of annoyance blushes his face.

"Was it that clothesline?" Lenny asks.

"Fuck yeah! The clumsy bastard nearly took my head off with it!" Duke whines.

Lenny's face contorts again and a smile slithers across it "It looked good though." He scoffs, slapping him on the back.

Duke looks at him and laughs "That's all that matters then!"

The Rhino Brothers plough through the curtain, the curtain sticking to the their large tacky frames, before falling back into place as they stepped on through.

"Bro!" Tusk whined in an apologetic tone, his round face wearing a mask of sweat clad guilt "I'm so sorry about that line!" They approached and both placed their large mitts on Dukes shoulders in earnest concern.

"It's okay, I'll be fine. Don't worry about it!" Duke said smiling and wincing at the same time.

"Oh man, that doesn't look good!" Stomp said leaning over and having a closer look. Duke glared at him wide-eyed and terrified as the others looked at each other in shoulder shrugging confusion.

"What's wrong?" Duke gulped.

Stomp draped a caring arm around him and with all sincerity sighed "Well! How are you gonna suck dick now?"

They all burst out laughing and Stomp slapped him playfully on his backside.

"Great match though boys!" Stomp announced swiping back his wet green mohawk that was no longer standing to attention, but had deflated and now lay sticking against his clammy skin.

They all hugged and smiled and then began to walk down the corridor towards the locker room.

"They've gotta put the titles on one of us soon!" Lenny said.

"Tell me about it!" Tusk agreed "We're having fucking five star matches out there!"

"We're the fucking future man, can't they see it?" Duke added.

"Now, don't get me wrong..." Stomp announced and then looked around before lowering his tone "...I like Devastation, they're nice guys, but, they're getting too long in the tooth now. Especially Famine!" He shakes his head "I was in there with him the other night and he..." Their conversation trailed off as they passed a door that stood ajar, an aluminium plate was screwed on it depicting the universal signage for a disabled toilet.

The light in the bathroom flickered rapidly like the wings of a humming bird. The door was closed abruptly and then locked. The Slammer stood looking at himself in the mirror that hung over the washbasin. He sighed, and turned to look at his mask, which was hung on a peg situated on the back of the door.

The mask stared back at him with black hole eyes.

"Fuck off!" he growled at it, saliva spraying from his mouth.

Under the mask, Joseph Fox, Jr had the look of a neanderthal, with a bulbous brow and sharp edged cheeks and jawline, he'd thought many times this was why they put the mask on him in the first place, because he wasn't a pretty boy. He was covered in a couple of days worth of stubble, which was one of the benefits of wearing a mask, he didn't have to stay clean cut all the time, plus he could move around in public without anyone knowing who he was. This allowed him to skip past a lot of the meetings with fans that the others had to endure. Not that it was awful meeting them, but it was 24/7 when they knew what you looked like, you always had to be switched on. The Slammer didn't really like meeting them though, so the freedom of coming and going when he pleased suited him down to the ground.

He had a messy mass of hazel hair that sat plonked on his head, again he needn't run a comb through it as the mask would conceal it and it would soon be matted in sweat anyway.

"I said fuck off!" He snarled at his mask again, his heavy bagged eyes almost mirroring those deep black sockets of distain that looked back at him.

He turned away and ran the tap, looking into the mirror again. His eyeballs were almost red as veins bulged from them, looking like they were about to burst from their sockets.

He splashed his face and turned off the tap. He leant on the basin, amazingly the sink didn't break away from the wall and fall to the tiled floor under his massive bulk. Whatever could be said about his looks could not be said about his physique, he was colossal. Every single muscle on his huge 6 foot 10 inch frame was primed and ready, bulging in places some people don't even have places. He was a freak of nature, but sometimes even Mother Nature needs a helping hand.

He grabbed his spandex tights by the waist band and pulled them down so they hung just above his knees. He scratched frantically at his testicles and his large girthed penis swung two and fro between his massive hairy thighs. The boys called this his 'Mong Dong'.

He opened up his travel wash bag that was placed on the downed toilet lid behind him. All the usual accoutrements could be found in it, the traditional tag team for teeth, Paste and Brush. Aftershave, Shampoo, Shower gel, etc. There was also some stowaways not found in everyone's luggage, a bottle of prescription pills, as well as syringes and all manner of other strange items wrapped up in packets, like something that maybe found in a hospital. On top was a small bottle of liquid, the word Testosterone printed across it.

He bent over the toilet, if anyone was to burst in now they'd be met with his big hairy rear end looking back at them.

Luckily for them he'd locked the door.

He rummaged around in his bag and started to open the packaging for the syringe, an alcohol swab, an injection needle and finally the blunt fill needle. He left these all ready on the toilet lid protruding from its protective packaging. This was a routine that he had become accustomed to every couple of weeks.

He tore at the packet that concealed the alcohol swab and rubbed it over a patch of area on his right buttock, he then threw the used swab onto the floor.

He took the blunt fill needle out of the packaging, he had learnt lots about injecting steroids over the last couple of years he'd been using them, he knew the importance of drawing the liquid out of the bottle (which happened to be thick like an oil) with a blunt fill 18G needle. He struggled to remove the bottles lid, a dainty piece that looked ever so tiny in his bulging ape hands. The yellowing liquid swished around before calming when the lid was removed.

The needle entered, it sat there for a small amount before the liquid was drawn up into the syringe itself. He quickly swapped the needles from the fill needle to a 25G needle and the safety cap of the business end of the syringe was disposed off unceremoniously.

He grasped the syringe in the correct position in his giant hands and slowly the needle was forced into the thick gluteus muscle, he looked strange and off kilter like some modern art statue that had been constructed into a peculiar stance.

He craned his neck to make sure there was no blood seeping back into the syringe and then pushed down slowly on the plunger.

The testosterone left the confines of the syringe and entered his body. He slowly removed the needle and collecting up all the debris, he disposed of it in a feminine sanitary bin that was sitting next to the toilet. He yanked up his tights and manoeuvred his bulging girth into a comfortable position and again returned to face the mirror. The mask whispered to him again and he turned to face it, the look of distain on his face was unpleasant. When he looked at the mask he saw his stepfather (that he had had a rocky relationship with all his life) staring back at him, judging him, condemning him and his choices. Sometimes he heard it hiss at him, but it was for his ears only.

"Shut up!" He growled.

The mask just hung there.

"This is what I want to do with my life, okay?"

The mask mocked him with those dark sockets.

"It's not stupid!" He shouted "And I ain't no faggot!"

The Slammer sighed and then his face winced, pain shot through his head as though a hot poker had been slid through his ear, skewered his brain and began to turn it like a kebab over a flaming hot grill.

He dropped to his knees and grabbed at his head.

"FUCK!" He shrieked.

He fell to the floor into a foetal position, as if this favoured posture would shelter him from the pain.

It did not.

His brain throbbed and he crawled across the floor in agony towards the travel bag, he clawed at it and knocked it onto the floor, all the paraphernalia from inside fell out and splayed off in all directions. He grabbed at the bottle of pills and again struggled with the lid, finally he popped it off and swigged at the bottle the way a drunk would with a beer. He swallowed some pills, how many he didn't know, and he lay motionless on the cold tiles of the bathroom. He couldn't tell you how long he'd lay there because he didn't know, it was all a dark blur.

His head started to throb less and he relaxed, his body had become tight and all his veins were now snaking up over his muscles, especially those wrapping around his head from his temples. He looked up at the flickering light and then at the mask again.

"No, you're not right at all!" He panted "I'm not a loony, I'm not a freak!"

A tear started to roll down from his eye as he could hear the laughter from his stepfather cackling somewhere in his head.

As he pulled his massive bulk up off the ground he knew that he did have some kind of mental disorder, the doctor had called it IED (Intermittent Explosive Disorder). He had gotten checked out after a few severe concussions, but he didn't really know what it all meant, he just knew that he got angry and pissed off a lot and his head really hurt when that happened, the constant steroid abuse probably wasn't helping matters either.

With an increased level of testosterone some can suffer from psychotic episodes known as 'Roid Rage'. All of this together was not a pleasant combination.

The Slammer stood over the basin again, his skin glowing beetroot red, veins continuing to throb and he cried into the mirror, ashamed of the reflection he saw staring back at him. He turned on the tap again and there was a gush of cold water exploding from the tap, he cupped the running water in his hands and splashed his face again. It was cold and soothing. It was almost over.

He made the mistake of looking over at the mask again, emblazoned in the stars and stripes of the American flag, a positive message of hope to some, but to The Slammer all he could see were those judging black holes.

"GODDAMNIT!" He howled before curling up a gigantic fist and driving it into the mirror. The mirror shattered under the velocity of the thrust and glass exploded around his mitt, shards lacerated his knuckles and blood seeped across his hand and was left to drip and fall with the cascading glass into the bowl and onto the floor. He sighed and lent on the basin as his tears washed away with the tiny blood stained broken remains of the mirror.

CHAPTER 9

The moist palm of referee Kenny Campbell slapped the canvas hard and the word three left his mouth and seemed to carry through the air of a startled crowd, a crowd that had been stunned into silence by Mr Canada pinning Yellow Feather.

"Wait a minute!" Gasped Milton McQueen, in a tone that suggested that a mistake must have been made.

"We've got a new champeen!" Yodelled Bunk 'The Hunk' over excitedly.

"He had a handful of tights!" Growled McQueen in a gravelly annoyed tone.

"What?" Bunk gasped "I didn't see that from my vantage point, McQueen. Maybe your monitor is faulty."
Mr Canada is handed the title belt by the referee and he knelt in the middle of the ring cradling the United States Championship like it was a newborn baby.

"Well done, Kid!" Yellow Feather murmurs as he gets to his feet, arms out to either side and mouthing nothingness at the referee "Hell of a match, you deserve it." He added before grabbing the rear waistband of his tights and frantically tugging at them, informing the referee of what dastardly shenanigans had just taken place.

"Thanks!" Mr Canada managed, physically trying to fight back real tears as the blinding spotlight that hung above the ring shimmered on the golden plate, picking out the word 'Champion'. He rubbed a thumb over the letters, it felt good, a fulfilment like no other. Yellow Feather's 250 day reign as United States Champion had come to an end, why? Because wrestling promoter and booker, Louis Raggu had said so. Mr Canada did not really beat Yellow Feather for anything, he'd been the next wrestler chosen to hold the title. So why would Mr Canada become so emotional by such a predetermined set of circumstances? Passion and love, love for the business and a passion to be the best you can be. Yes, the champions are chosen but it is still a lot of hard work and dedication to get to the level where a promoter chooses you as their champion. It means that they have faith in you and your ability, plus they believe that with you at the helm they will draw more people which inevitably means more money.

The reason behind this particular title switch is simple, The United States Championship is seen as a part of America itself. It holds a special place in fans hearts who are patriotic to their country. The tale to be told here is as old as the hills, putting the title on a foreigner works, it's money! Because the patriotic fan with red, white and blue running through their veins will feel that an injustice has taken place and a foreigner is walking around with their title, the people's title if you will. And they will pay handsomely to see this usurper dethroned and the championship back where it belongs, around the waist of one of their own.

When the realisation had sunk in to the stunned crowd, the dome was a buzz with boos, whipping angrily and violently through the atmosphere like a swarm of irritated hornets.

Yellow Feather rolled out the ring shaking his head, hands clasped on his hips, shock and confusion carved into his face, playing the part of someone who'd been duped. The crowd sympathised with pats on the back as he shuffled slowly and unhappily up the aisle towards the curtain. Was he unhappy? Of course not. His part was played well and for anyone keeping score will know that although Yellow Feather had just lost the title and the match, he was still kept strong as a character, he wasn't beaten clean.

As the replay was played in slow motion for the people at home, the announcers got to watch it for a second time.

"He clearly gained an illegal advantage by holding onto the tights for extra leverage!" came the voice of Milton McQueen.

The video showed the referee snatch the title belt from Yellow Feather's hands, who was wearing a bemused look on his face, and as his focus was elsewhere, Mr Canada crept up behind him and hooked one of his legs pulling him down to the ground backwards like antics in a schoolyard. The referee was quick to join them on the mat and to check the shoulders were down. As he counted Mr Canada grabbed the waistband of Yellow Feather's tights and yanked them up, exposing his backside and then applying all his bodyweight on top of Yellow Feather's torso making it impossible for him to escape before the three count.

"If the referee didn't see it, it didn't happen!" Bunk chuckles.

"Well, I for one do not condone the underhanded tactics that we've just witnessed! Unfortunately folks, it looks like this one is going to stand and controversially we have a new United States Champion in Mr Canada!"

Mr Canada stands in the middle of the ring holding aloft his new United States title for all to see, as he is bombarded with rolled up pieces of paper and half filled cups of soda that ricochet off him.

The purpose was served and with Yellow Feather not beaten cleanly, his reputation is not dented in the slightest, still keeping him as a threat for whatever comes next. A rematch could be on the cards after a few months of playing cat and mouse. Mr Canada ducking and diving Yellow Feather before the two ultimately collide for the title again, in what could see Yellow Feather claim a third run with the title. This was just one of many stories that could be told here.

When the story is built up correctly, it writes itself.

CHAPTER 10

The Slammer lumbered down the corridor towards the area situated behind the curtain. He slid his mask on and tied the laces at the rear to secure it into place, to lose the mask in the middle of the match would ruin his gimmick, there would be no place to hide out there, especially with all the cell phone cameras poised and ready. His rugged face would be on the internet within minutes, then all years it had taken to build the character up into such an excellent position would be ruined.

He passes a bunch of wrestlers gathered round in the corridor, either discussing their matches to come or the matches they've already had. One of them informs him that Wally was looking for him, he doesn't know who said this, nor does he care, he doesn't care about many people in all honesty. Already his position in the industry is going to his head. He ignores them all, apart from Sebastian Churchill who appears in front of him in a flamboyant red and silver sequinned entrance robe.

"Hey Joe! Have you seen Crystal anywhere?" Churchill asks looking a little flustered.

"Sorry, Seb!" Shrugs The Slammer "I haven't."

"Cheers!" he sighs in his sharp English accent "Where the bloody hell is she?" He moaned to himself as he walked away.

The Slammer realises he is late and will no doubt receive a verbal tongue lashing from Raggu for this, he likes all the ships in his armada to sail on time.

He thought that he may get lucky and Raggu might not be there and all he'll have to contend with is his gopher, Wally, and he is easily dealt with, nobody takes him seriously.

As he gets closer he can hear his opponent's music erupt from the sound system, nothing like a popular eighties rock ballad to get the people going. They do not disappoint and there is a decent reaction from the crowd, his opponent for the evening is the veteran, Nemesis.

"Shit!" He curses under his breath, as he notices Raggu and Wally waiting for him. Wally is sweating as always, and worry has drove him to perform a jittering dance on the spot moving as if he were in urgent need of the bathroom.

"He's here." The Slammer murmurs to himself. Of course he is there, he always turns out to see his main guys, the guys that can make him the money. He has a lot of money tied up in my gimmick.

But that's something else that The Slammer doesn't realise, but he has no legal ownership of the name or likeness of his character. If he doesn't play ball Raggu can replace him and find someone else that looks like him to keep the character going. Granted almost seven feet tall adonis' don't grow on trees, but it could happen. The Slammer has been treading on thin ice for sometime now and the realisation has never hit home that if he walked or was fired, he'd have to start from scratch. The whole persona that he has built up and made into one of the most popular wrestlers in the world doesn't belong to him, and who would want to come and see the dreary, ugly Joe Fox without all the bells and whistles?

Raggu looks at him through a furrowed brow of annoyance, shaking his head and tapping at his watch.

"Where the hell have you been?" Raggu seethes.

"I'm here now aren't I!" The Slammer fires back as he walks straight up to them.

Wally cowers as they are caught in his intimating shadow, but Raggu just stares up at him unfazed, nonchalantly puffing on his cigar.

"Nemesis is already out there! We've had people looking all over for you…"

"Look! I'm here! The bell hasn't rung has it? So what's the big deal!"

Raggu took a drag and exhaled, the thick smog danced around them and concealed them in their own private cloud. Raggu squinted as he looked through the mask and at Joe.

"You look like shit, Joe!" He whispered "What crap are you on?"

"I ain't taking anything!" He snarled.

"Well, whatever it is, it's fucking you up!"

The Slammer didn't reply he just stared at him with those bulging pinkish eyes of his, veins rippling across them as if they were daggers looking to pierce his pupils.

"I'm not an idiot you know. I know all you guys have some kind of vice."

"I'm not fucking taking anything!" The Slammer growls defensively.

The steroids are not a factor here, the majority of the roster are on some kind of testosterone increasing supplements legal or otherwise, but it's the use of real dangerous recreational drugs that is being implied by Raggu. He has seen way too many greats fall from such habits. But in this particular case The Slammer is telling the truth, but he daren't let on about his mental health issues. If that ever came out it could spell his demise and he doesn't want to jeopardise his place in the grand scheme of things, especially now, now that he is being groomed to be the top guy in the company.

"I don't believe you, Joe." He whispers again and the two generate towards each other.

The Slammer's veins start to pulsate and his skin glows with a tint of warmth, he clenches his teeth hard, and they unpleasantly grind down on each other, all signs that the rage is coming.

"Don't fuck this up!" Raggu says.

The Slammer manages to take control and calm himself, he has done this a few times, but sometimes it's too far gone and then the red shroud descends and the rest as they say is history.

"I won't!" He says and stomps past them heading for the ring. An enhanced version of 'Star Spangled Banner' explodes and he charges out of the curtain, he is greeted by what can only be described as a delirious scream of excitement.

"Wow! What a pop!" Wally said open mouthed in awe. His gaping was mirrored by all that stood around and heard the eruption "That's the loudest pop I've ever heard!"

Raggu just carried on sucking on his cigar seemingly unfazed by it, but approaches the curtain anyway, Wally scurries behind him.

The Slammer bounds down to the ring and Raggu peers through the gap in the curtain and scans the audience, everyone is on their feet, arms raised with fists pumping the air. There isn't one face in the crowd without that enthusiastic wide eyed, wide mouthed expression on it. The flailing waves of arms is almost hypnotic, and their reaction to him is so loud that it almost drowns out his entrance music.

"They really like him, Sir." Wally announces.

"I had noticed, Wally!" Raggu says rolling his eyes.

Wally looks away a little embarrassed for pointing out something so blatantly obvious.

"I haven't heard a pop like that since Rogan made the step up in '93." Raggu announced.

"Is he the next guy then?"

"Oh, yes, Wally he most definitely is!" Raggu said smiling and chewing on the end of the cigar, that was now sodden and thick with saliva.

"He's still a bit green though." Wally added.

"I don't know about that. A little Clumsy maybe? Besides..." Raggu says laughing "...Green is my favourite colour."

CHAPTER 11

The delicately manicured fingers of Miss Crystal gripped the top of the toilet cubicle in the ladies bathroom. Her large shapely backside collided with the flimsy wall that separated the ablutions, with each thudding of her backside on the dividing wall she groaned with ecstasy. Inside the cubicle, 'Magnificent' Johnny Midnight stood cradling her bottom-half in his hands. His cerise glittery spandex trunks pulled way down around his black leather boots, as he thrust his pelvis frantically forward to meet hers in a loud moist slapping of flesh.

"Oh Johnny! Give it to me!" She groaned, through a mass of platinum hair that had drooped over part of her face. This only spurred him on and the thrusts became harder as his exposed buttocks clenched with each lunge.

"Don't...you...worry!" He panted "I'll give it to...you!" His mop of black hair flicking back with each passionate advance.

Her long red sequinned evening gown didn't hinder their animalistic love making. The gown hauled up to her waist, exposing her thong which had been pulled away to one side to make way for Johnny's manhood. She groaned again, her one stockinged leg wrapped around his waist had lost its red patent stiletto and had fallen to the tiles below. The other stiletto held on for dear life as it clung between her foot and the rim of the toilet bowl. It was almost as if the two had done this before.

He slowed down for a moment and pulled his penis out, it pulsed and panted like a thirsty dog, but it wasn't done, not yet.

"No! Don't stop!" she moaned.

"I just need a minute." He said as he nuzzled into her neck and kissed her, before plunging face first into her bulging bosom that rose out from the provocative low cut neckline of the dress.

His fingers caressed the shape of her pubic bone and slipped in between her sodden labia's, then two of them disappeared into her vagina. She smiled and bit her bottom lip, the thick Ruby Red brand lipstick stained her teeth pink as he discovered the Gräfenberg spot just a couple of inches in on her inner wall. She groaned again with ecstasy.

Sebastian can never find my G spot! She thought and then put the thought out of her head before the enviable guilt had a chance to creep in and ruin the moment. His thumb and fingers worked in tandem as his thumb caressed her clitoris and his fingers worked their magic out of sight.

That sensation of needing to pee suddenly took hold and she knew that she was near to climaxing.

"Fuck me, fuck me!" She groaned.

He removed his fingers and drove his penis inside again, vigorously he penetrated her and her body arched, as she came loud and proud, her screams echoed around the bathroom. Luckily for them they had found a bathroom over the other side of the building that wasn't being used.

It didn't take Johnny Midnight long after hearing her wailing of elation to unleash all he'd been harbouring, and with a growl of rapture, he ejaculated inside her.

He slowed down and then the two fell into each other, breathing heavily and smiling.

"How was that?" He asked.

"Magnificent!" She giggled and the pair kissed each other and then burst into laughter.

CHAPTER 12

Megan Powers waits anxiously behind the curtain, she stretches her legs into a splits position, sinking slowly down onto the concrete floor. The sensation is cold but not unpleasant as her exposed buttocks and thighs come into contact with it. She peers through a gap in the curtain and can see the action taking place as 'Magnificent' Johnny Midnight tangles with the flamboyantly masked, El Flamingero. The crowd moves in flurries and she can feel their emotions change on the wind of those flurries.

The sound of their cheering and jeering relentlessly attack her ear drums, as she closes her eyes for a second to be alone with her thoughts.

It's been a long time coming. But, finally after years and years of slaving away it would appear that we are to be put into the prominent parts of the show. For as long as I can remember women have never been taken seriously in this sport, or entertainment, or whatever the hell they're calling it these days. To me it's pro wrestling and it will always be pro wrestling. But, yeah, people have started to sit up and take notice that we can do what the boys can do. That we are as good as, if not better than the boys and now that the voice of the fans can clearly be heard, we are now being seen on the same level as the men, equals and no longer treated like second class citizens.

She smiled to herself, her plump lipstick smothered lips making her appear smug, and she had every right to be. Megan Powers is what the internet have been calling a... Pioneer.

Well, I don't know about a pioneer! It's all very flattering. But, I've been doing this shit for about fifteen years now and though some would like to believe I'm in the twilight of my career, I'm actually only 34 and I'm just getting started! I got bit by the bug young that's all. I dropped out of college when I was 19, because this was what I wanted to do. I was studying law at the time... My Father wasn't happy. He's come to terms with it now though.

She laughs to herself and shakes her head.

And now suddenly he's taking a huge interest. It's amusing to me that there are some people that were never there for me when I needed their help and support, when I was sleeping in my car, or eating cold beans straight out the tin. Or when my electric and gas had been cut off and I had nothing. They didn't care then, because I was a nobody, a daydreamer. No, there was nobody there when I was crawling through all the shit to get to the top. Yes, it's very amusing to me that those people are now the ones waving the Megan Powers flags in the air and shouting from the rooftops 'I knew she could do it' and 'I've always been there to show my support' when in reality they never have been. My relationship with my Father is like this. We didn't speak for the longest time when I dropped out of college, he said I was throwing my life away... but it's my life to live. My experiences to have. What is life if it's not yours to live?

We are in a better place now though and he shows his support, but I wish he'd have given it to me back then. I guess that's what spurred me on, what made me into a strong independent woman. It gave me the urge to make him eat his words and that has made me the woman I am today. That attitude has made me mentally strong, so really I should thank him.

She works her way back to her feet, the rubber souls of her red boots squeaking like injured mice with each movement. She starts to rotate her neck all the way around, stretching it and working out the kinks. Her mass of brown lacquered hair swaying with each rotation, but never coming out of place. She looks behind her and sees her opponent for the evening, Mistress Evil, clad from head to foot in black leather, her skin as pale as snow and her bright red hair slicked back. She looked like a cross between a vampire and a dominatrix mistress, which was exactly the look she was going for.

Mistress Evil was in fact going through exactly the same motions for her pre match warm up ritual that Megan was, and their eyes met and then they nodded and smiled at each other.

But, I can't stand here on my soap box tooting my own horn. No, there has been generation after generation of females that have tried so very hard to break down the wall of male chauvinism and scepticism that has stopped us from showing the world what women are capable of. But, their efforts were not in vain, each pioneer of their generation has chipped away a chunk of that wall and made it easier for the likes of me to break through. The likes of Queen Georgina, The Squaw, Mildred Mae and Golden Velvet, the list goes on and on. We are not just eye candy or tits and ass any longer. We're no longer put on as a pre show dark match to warm up the crowd, nor are we half time entertainment or even 'popcorn matches'. We are important! I can stand here proud as a woman and as a wrestler! I couldn't have done this without the likes of Emily Kincaid, The Grass Snake, Mistress Evil and Big Bella-Marie. It needed us all working together and not against each other to bring that wall down, and that's just what we've done.

She quickly snaps her neck back from side to side and shakes her arms as she jogs up and down on the spot, her athletic slender physique hugged tightly by a red spandex swimsuit style unitard, trimmed with vibrant yellow, and a lightening bolt design throughout the material.

It's great to know that women are finally being taken seriously in this industry.

If Megan Powers could hear what was going in the ring at that moment she may think that feminism had moved back a few paces. 'Magnificent' Johnny Midnight crouched behind the seated masked individual called El Flamingero, his forearm clasped loosely under the chin as the two take a breather and discuss where they're going next.

El Flamingero's character was over the top and flamboyant, his pink Mexican style mask saw an unusual and large protruding beak sprouting from the front of it and black feathers exploding from the top and rear of his head. His full bodysuit was matching electric pink in colour and trimmed with lavish black feathers.

At this moment in time his facial features that could be seen by the jeering crowd display pain and anguish as Johnny appears to have him trapped in an unescapable headlock.

"El Flamingero seems to be fading here. The fans are trying to get behind him, but it's maybe too late!" Milton McQueen's words help tell the story to those watching on in TV land, helping to add that element of drama as it looks like there is no escape for their hero.

"Rat alert at twelve o'clock!" Johnny murmurs, his mouth hidden behind the mass of feathers sprouting from El Flamingero's mask. He smiles at a pretty young woman that he had found while scouring the crowd. She smiles back at him pushing out her large bosom that was doing a grand job of trying to explode out from the Randy Rogan t-shirt that concealed them. He winks at her and she coyly flutters her heavily made up eyelids at him. El Flamingero stops grimacing for a moment to open up his squinting eyes to see what Johnny is talking about.

"Damn! What a rack!" He says before going back to selling the effects of the brutal headlock he was in.
Johnny blows her a kiss, the crowd erupt with a chorus of boos aimed towards him, but he isn't listening to them at this point. She winks back and Johnny smiles.

"Looks like I'm on for tonight."

"Aren't you still screwing, Crystal?" El Flamingero asks through the gritted teeth of torment he is portraying.

"You know it!" murmurs Johnny, his fingers clapped tightly in a butcher's hook that seem to constrict and tighten the hold.

"Man, you're a lucky son of a bitch, you know that?"

"I nailed her before I came out here." He laughs.

"No way!" El Flamingero gasps.

"Yeah! That's my warm up."

The pair laugh and Charlie the referee joins them on one knee in front of El Flamingero asking him whether he gives up.

"You guys ready to start going home?" Charlie asks.

"Yeah, yeah! Give us another few seconds. There is something I want Mr Flamingo to do for me before we go home."

"What's that?" El Flamingero asks.

"Smell my fingers!" And with that he stuffs his fingers right under the nose of the unsuspecting opponent.

"Jesus!" He cries.

Charlie the referee covers his mouth and stops himself from laughing out loud, but his shoulders rise up and down vigorously and uncontrollably.

"For fuck sake, Johnny!" laughs El Flamingero.

"If that doesn't spur you on for a comeback, nothing will." Charlie sniggers.

El Flamingero starts to reach to the crowd who cheer louder for him, he starts to slowly get to his feet and they get louder still.

"These sucker's think that they're the reason for your surge of power." Johnny says in a gravelly tone, mimicking that of movie trailer voice over "But! We all know that there's only one thing that can inspire, El Flamingero!"

"Pussy!" Roars El Flamingero as he climbs to his feet, the words of his fiery comeback lost in the cheering crowd. The three men in the ring do their upmost not to burst into fits of laughter as El Flamingero breaks the headlock with three sharp elbow thrusts to Johnny's torso.

"Pussy!" He screams again and unleashes several strikes at Johnny, who reacts to each blow.

He looks out to the crowd and points to the ropes wobbling two and fro in front of him and asks them 'Shall I?' at the top of his lungs, the crowd reply back positively. He nods back at them and then sets off running towards the ropes. He uses the middle rope as a springboard, he strides onto it and then spins around in the air, seemingly defying the laws of gravity, before body blocking Johnny. The two of them hitting the mat with El flamingero on top of him for the cover, Charlie is quickly down and counts.

"Only a two count there!" Milton McQueen says for the folks at home "Midnight just came out the backdoor in the nick of time."

El Flamingero stands and looks out at the people, all of them cheering at him, he nods in response and points to the top turnbuckle in one corner.

"We going home, Johnny?" He asks under his breath.

"Yeah!" Murmurs the grounded Johnny who is slowly pulling himself off the mat. He looks over at the woman in the crowd again who has been joined by a friend, another attractive woman in a figure hugging dress, showing off her petite physique. Johnny smiles at them and the two wink at him with their arms wrapped around each other, they begin to kiss and the petite girl paws at her friends ample breast, before the two of them start laughing.

"Yeah! We're definitely going home now!" Johnny said rising a little quicker now.

The crowd clap in unison as El Flamingero effortlessly climbs to the top rope, the way some would find ease in skipping or riding a bicycle. He stands with his hands out either side of him like a messiah on a cross, and the crowd are electric. Johnny turns to face him and he launches himself of the top rope feet first to deliver what would be a devastating missile dropkick, but Johnny manages to grab his legs as he approaches and the intervention causes El Flamingero to take the impact on his back.

"Wait a minute! Midnight had that one well scouted!" Screams Milton McQueen.

"Johnny Midnight is not just a pretty face, McQueen!" Adds Bunk 'The Hunk'.

Johnny Midnight seizes his moment and holding both ankles of the prone El Flamingero, he steps into him, entwines his legs around his own and then quickly turns him over onto his front, before sitting down on the small of his back in what has been known as a Scorpion Lock. This variation was known as The...

"Midnight Feast!" Screams Milton McQueen.

El Flamingero looks in terrible pain and screams "I give!", while slapping the mat in a frenzy. The bell rings, Johnny Midnight lets go of the hold and struts to the centre of the ring where Charlie grabs his arm and holds it aloft for all to see, the crowd unleash a melody of boos, jeers and insults.

The announcer's silky tones explode from the sound system and echo around the dome, informing everyone that, 'Magnificent' Johnny Midnight was indeed the winner of the match.

Johnny eyes the two girls in the crowd again as they lick their lips at him while touching each other.

"Damn right I'm the winner!" He yells smugly.

CHAPTER 13

Randy Rogan lay on the uncomfortable looking bed in only his underwear, the phone receiver held to his ear and a bag of ice on his hip, dulling the after effects of the top rope Elbow Drop.

"Yeah, I'm fine." He lies as he checks in with his wife, something that he has done every night on the road since forever.

"Yes, I'm sure!" he sighs manoeuvring the bag of ice around the now numb hip. He knows she can read him like a book, she always has been able too. He often joked that she had a built in bullshit detector.

It's a good job that I'm not one of these guys that likes to sleep around. Because she'd know.

"Okay, nothing major just a bit bruised up. I'll be fine." He couldn't lie to her, not that he wanted to, but he didn't want to worry her either.

"Is Jimmy okay?" He asks and a proud smile beams across his bearded face when he is told how well he is doing at school.

"That's great!" he yawns "Yeah, I guess I am a little." He rubs at his eyes, heavy bags already hanging low, his freezing cold hand that's been holding the ice pack on, was enough to wake him up momentarily.

"Okay, okay I will. Yeah! What's that? Yeah, Astoria, Oregon tomorrow, then back home."

He tries to manoeuvre himself into a more comfortable position, he's been lying on his left side so long that his other hip is now just as numb as the iced one.

"Flying! I know, but it will be quicker. I miss you guys and want to get back sooner. Yeah, okay, I love you too. Sweet dreams."

He reaches over and hangs up the phone, each movement causing him to wince. Finally the receiver is cradled back into place and he glances at the digital clock next to his bed. The digits all reading zero, like four red eyes glaring back at him. It startled him a little and a shiver produced gooseflesh all over his body. The significance of this he put down to it being midnight and it would be Johnny Midnight that would no doubt be taking the title from him.

"Weird." He said to himself.

Looking around him he is reminded where he is, yet another hotel room, like every one he's ever stayed in. He ponders for a moment and asks himself if he's actually stayed here before, maybe he has, maybe he hasn't. The room was as generic as they come. There is nothing of any interest in the room and that doesn't matter to him, all he is looking for is a place to get his head down for the night and sleep. Or try and sleep.

The aftermath of an adrenaline rush can really mess with ones sleeping pattern, making it sometimes impossible to sleep no matter how tired you are.

He tries to lie down and his head is submerged into an irregular looking pillow, he beats at it and manipulates it into some strange shape, but still it's not right. He lay there for a few minutes staring at those red digits, willing them to change. Finally it did and 00:01, looked back at him and somehow that didn't freak him out as much.

He closed his eyes. Inside his head visions of the evenings match raced through his head at 100 mph, over and over again. The paranoia from mistakes that he may have made haunt him repeatedly, like wailing banshees with laughing faces swooping in front of him. But he knew how to deal with that, years of this business had taught him...

It doesn't matter that you missed that spot, Randy. So there's no need to beat yourself up over that one. You gotta ask yourself did the crowd know? No, they didn't. They didn't know what you and Kami had planned, so it doesn't matter does it? No, it doesn't.

His eyes open again and he sighs "I can't sleep."

He pulls himself back up into some kind of seated position, still favouring his right hip. He lifts the now melting ice from his hip, already there was some discolouring rearing its ugly head.

"Yep, that was a stupid fucking move to do wasn't it, old man." He shook his head at his own stupidity. It wasn't that he did the move wrong, as he sat there and replayed it over in his head, he hit it perfectly. In fact that was what probably did it, it was too perfect and his right hip took all the impact.

He placed the ice back and actually smiled.

Got the biggest pop of the night though. Those fuckers didn't know this old fella could fly.

He notices his bag is still on the bed and he opens it up and removes his diary, something he'd been adding to over the past few months, something that he wanted to do for his last year in the business.

From the Diary of Randall Rogan

Saturday, April 20th.
I guess it's Sunday now... Sunday, April 21st.
Windham Lodge, Sanctuary City, Alaska.

Note to self: You're too old to be doing top rope Elbow Drops now. Leave the highflying to the kids.

Another easy night, obviously the bruised hip is a blip, but it isn't serious and I'll just patch it up and move on to the next one. Always a pleasure to work with Kami, what a class act he is. Been in the game nearly as long as me and for a man of his size, can still move around that ring like a cruiserweight. He'll go down as being my greatest nemesis, our feud spanning twenty years, so was nice to have that final dance with him. Not that he knows it was our last outing, nor anyone else for that matter.

I called Martha... She's just the greatest, she's such a rock. Nobody else could put up with the shit that leaks out of this world into the real world. Most people wouldn't get it or care, she gets it and she cares, well about me. I think she worries that I'm alone out here in the trenches. I guess I am. Friendship can be hard to find in this world. Everyone has an ego and wants to be the best, wants to be the one to hold the strap, be on the magazine covers and TV interviews. Everyone just wants that opportunity and I get that, I appreciate that and that's why I'm not bitter towards the eight guys lining up behind me chomping at the bit for my spot. But it's that competition that makes getting close to people difficult, yes I have friends within this bubble, but when I leave this bubble will they still be there? I doubt it. Again I get it! It's nobodies fault, it's just out of sight out of mind. They'll be carrying on with what they do and I won't be part of that anymore. So in a way I guess they become acquaintances or colleagues, work colleagues really. For example, if you work in an office and you work with these people everyday, talk to them, eat lunch with them, gossip at the water cooler with them, but you wouldn't necessarily call them friends would you? You wouldn't socialise with them, go on vacation with them or invite them round for dinner would you?

But real friends? People who are there for you when the chips are down? There's only a few. Seb is one of the few, he was one of only five people within the industry that I heard from when Martha had a cancer scare a couple of years ago. It turned out to be nothing thank God! But it hits home when out of a thirty year career in this business only five people contacted me to show their genuine love and support. It kind of puts things into perspective. Not that I don't like most people in the business it's just, well, people are all different and live their own lives that's all. We have all been brought together through our love of wrestling and the same dream to become one, doesn't mean we all share so many similarities outside of this world. You can't get on with everyone that's just the way of the world, it would be a boring fucking place if we were all the same now wouldn't it.

I guess time will tell, when I'm out of it, who will still be there. He puts down his pen and rubs his tired eyes, finally he may be ready to go to sleep.

CHAPTER 14

The sharp vanilla spotlight light cuts through the darkness and onto the ring. Randy Rogan's body lies prone on the sweat stained canvas, his breaths are slow and heavy, the sound of the crowd seems so far away and muted to him. He peels himself from the mat, his body clad in a layer of moisture that weeps to the canvas below and soaks into it, merging with the sweat of a dozen others that have already lay on it before him that evening.

Rogan's limbs shake as he manages to pull himself up onto his hands and knees. He gasps for air, only managing to suck in the rife thick stench of body odour, it burns the back of his throat causing him to cough and splutter. The thick rubber soul of a motorcycle style boot connects with the side of his head, causing his head to be violently whipped back and forth, sweat leaving his long brown hair like sailors fleeing a sinking ship.

He collapses to the mat again, the smell of the stale bodily fluids from that warm canvas violates his nostrils and for a moment he feels nauseous, but he does not vomit, he has no time to vomit as a huge hand grabs a handful of his sodden hair and yanks him up. He moves with it and staggers to his feet, he looks around a look of dazed bewilderment on his weary face. The crowd are just moving shapes in the darkness, occasionally being illuminated by the spotlights. There is an abundant of camera flashes and an array of cell phone lights that flicker and dance in that darkness, like the frolicking of fireflies on a summer evening.

"Ready to go home?" Comes a voice and he turns to look at the gigantic man that holds a clump of his hair in his hand.

"You okay?" Comes the lowered voice of Stomp, as he stands over him, lights splashing off his bulging physique, and catching the piercings that protrude from his ears and nostril, causing them to glitter like the grandiose contents of a treasure chest. He looks a little concerned when Rogan doesn't answer, a look that appears out of place on his craggy features and savage persona that happens to be capped off with a green mohawk that stands to attention like the fin of a shark.

"Yeah!" Rogan winks, still looking though he had been run over by a bulldozer "Just selling."

"Damn, you're good!" Stomp answers shaking his head. Stomp pulls back one of his large arms balling a fist for all to see and brings it down rapidly to connect with Rogan's forehead, but Rogan blocks it with a flailing forearm and slaps Stomp in the chin hard with a right hand. This was expertly done for all the naysayers who mock the art as being fake. They could not deny that Rogan just punched Stomp in the jaw. Stomp's head snapped back and leant forward for another one of the same and another and another, and that was the art. The fist was balled to look like a punch, but in reality the hand was cupped, with nothing in it to cause Stomp any pain. He just moved with it and the rest is history, or art, however you look at it. Stomp cuts off Rogan's flurry with a well placed knee to his midsection, his body contorting around his massive thigh like all the wind has been knocked out of him.

Stomp grabs Rogan's hair again and screams in his face, the words seem incoherent and are lost in the hum of the frenzied crowd. Then mouths to Rogan "Are you ready?"

Rogan looks over Stomp's bolder like shoulders to share a glance with his partner for the evening which happens to be, Jungle Jim. He stands waiting in their corner, bare feet gripping the apron, clad in fur trunks and nothing much else apart from a crocodile tooth necklace.

"Yeah!" Randy murmurs giving Jim the look and he nods back knowing that they are now about to go into the finish of the match.

Stomp grabs Rogan by his arm and yanks him toward the ropes, but Rogan reverses the whip attempt and instead sends him hurtling towards the ropes. Stomp's gargantuan mass collides with the taught ropes, they swell but thankfully are strong enough to take the force and propel him back towards Rogan who waits in the centre of the ring. Rogan drops his head, bending over as Stomp nears quickly, when the two meet Rogan jolts back up and flips Stomp over his shoulder into a Back-Drop which vaults Stomp into the air. He turns his body in mid air and safely lands on his back.

The crowd erupted in unison for Rogan, but he collapses to a knee, reeling from fatigue and the effects of vaulting such a mammoth of a man. The crowd chant his name in unison, willing him on to get back to his feet and make the tag. He staggers over towards Jungle Jim, whose hand is out stretched and willing him forward as much as the crowd. His corner looks so far away and he collapses to a knee again, if it was possible the crowd grew louder, forcing him to muster all he had to get back to his feet. He manages to and his journey begins again, closer and closer he shuffles towards his partner, his saviour as sweat shimmers off his moist muscular physique. His face looks weary and troubled as he fights on, his bones creak and his bruised hip throbs, those pains are real, but amazingly he doesn't sell those pains. He can see the whites of Jungle Jim's bulging eyes and reaches out to make that all important tag, their fingertips almost brushing as Rogan swipes at his hand and misses.

"Where's Tusk?" Rogan calls through gritted teeth.

"He's coming!" Jim calls back as he dances on the apron stretching his arm over the rope in desperation for the tag.

Suddenly Tusk hurtles past him like a freight train and ploughs into the unsuspecting Jungle Jim who is thrown from the apron and to the floor. The crowd show their displeasure and the wailing of boos cascade down on the despicable Rhino Brothers. Tusk clasped his hands together as if holding an axe and brings them down hard on Rogan's back. He collapses onto the canvas again and each time he attempts to get to his feet, Tusk brings those heavy blows down again as if he were some deranged lumberjack chopping wood.

Stomp re-enters the ring and both of them unleash a flurry of clubbing blows down on 'The American Hero'.

The referee shouts at them like he was telling off two petulant children, they ignore the tongue lashing and Stomp grabs the beaten carcass of Randy Rogan by the scruff of his neck like he were some prize from a hunting excursion.

Tusk and Stomp, slide their thumbs across their throats calling for the end of Rogan and then playfully head butt each other.

The crowd hiss and spit venom towards the two bullies. Jungle Jim slowly gets to his feet on the outside of the ring as Stomp pushes Rogan's head down between his massive thighs. He grabs a handful of his waistband to keep him there as Tusk positions himself into a seated position on the top rope. They signal to each other as the referee unleashes the rulebook five count indicating how long they're allowed to be in the ring for together. It would be just enough time to unleash their dreaded Tag Team finishing manoeuvre, a spike piledriver (or what they liked to call 'Endangered Species')

Tusk stands on the middle rope as Stomp interlocks his fingers around the waist of Rogan and hoists him upside down, Rogan's head trapped between Stomp's thighs, blood rushing to his head. Tusk means to grab his ankles and jump down from the ropes adding an extra 300 pounds of pressure to drive his head into the canvas.

Jungle Jim pulls himself back up onto the apron as The Rhino Brothers look like they've got this one won. Rogan starts to kick his legs and the movement unbalances Stomp and he lets go of Rogan who lands back on his feet. He grabs at Stomp's legs and trips him backwards before hooking them under his arms and falling back. His momentum causing a seesaw action and forcing Stomp up off the ground and being slingshotted into his partner. Tusk falls from his seated position on the top rope and tumbles to the outside of the ring as Stomp sways to and fro, groggy from the impact.

The crowd roar as Rogan staggers over to the corner. The slap of palm on palm indicates to all that the tag has been made.

Jungle Jim immediately climbs to the top rope as Stomp staggers out of the corner like a zombie in some bad B-movie horror. When in position, Jungle Jim launches himself off the top rope and soars through the air. It was a sight to behold and camera flashes spit in the darkness with a rapid succession of bursting bulbs, everyone hoping to catch the moment for themselves.

Rogan looked on as his partner spreads his arms like a bird of prey. For a moment he appeared to fly and everything moved in the slowest of motions. For a split second Rogan stood in awe and asked himself why he couldn't do something like that, the answer came quickly, because he'd never had too.

Jungle Jim came crashing down on Stomp who fell to the canvas, the referee counted three and the roof of the Astoria Municipal Auditorium almost came detached.

CHAPTER 15

From the Diary of Randall Rogan

Sunday, April 21st.
The Blassie Motel, Astoria, Oregon.

Hip still hurts like a bitch. The boys looked after me in there though, was a nice little match. Those Rhino Brothers may appear that they work like two bulls in a china shop, but they're as tender as kittens when it comes to working. For me anyway, I guess I can't talk for anyone else. Speak as you find.

And Jim, well we go way back. He's a good guy and a true professional. He actually may be just what this generation is looking for in a babyface champion. Maybe I'll put in a good word for him when I finally get to sit down with Raggu and tell him I'm done. He was preoccupied with Nemesis tonight, I don't actually know first hand what happened in his match with Joe, but he looked pissed. Seb said something about Slammer taking some liberties in the ring with Nemesis, maybe some potatoes were thrown in there, Joe can be a little reckless. We've always got on well and I like Joe, but I don't think he's playing with a full deck sometimes. He can be riled up very easily and doesn't think of the consequences of his actions sometimes. Seb also said he pinned him with one foot which would make Nemesis look like shit out there. What's known in the business as being squashed! Now, again I reiterate I'm hearing this second hand so I can't pass judgement, but if that is the case it's a shitty thing to do. Granted, The Slammer is the new rising star and probably the next guy to wear my... the world title, but you have to be respectful of the guys you're working on the way up, because they may be the guys that you'll be working on the way down.

Wrestling... never without the drama.

The rest of the guys, well the majority of them, went to a local bar, One Eyed Willie's in Astoria, which happened to be a regular haunt for wrestlers. They asked me to tag along for a drink or two. I declined. It's been years since I've been out drinking and to be truthful I never actually enjoyed going. It's nice to reminisce and talk about old times with the guys. But, most of the workers these days are a lot younger, from another generation and they probably see me as an old grumpy dinosaur. The generation gap is rapidly increasing.

No doubt it will all end in a ruckus with egos colliding between the boys or with some drunken locals thinking they can take on the phoney wrestlers.
Considering we're 'phoneys' it never seems to end well for the people that try us. I remember 'The Samoan Warrior' Sina, bite off a man's ear one time. Believe me, you don't forget something

like that. The hilarious thing was that that act actually started a mass barroom brawl with wrestlers and locals, and while the earless man was rolling around the floor in agony, and violence erupted all-around him, Sina just sat back on the barstool and continued with his drink.

Yeah, I'll just get some shut eye here in another cheap motel, hey, gotta save those pennies, they're for my boy's college fund. I could tell you just what they're all doing now...

CHAPTER 16

The bar is reasonably quiet and mostly filled with wrestlers unwinding from the evenings events. It's a dark and dingy bar decorated with wall to wall wood panels, making it appear darker. Some neon lights bathe various parts of the establishment in pinkish, purple tints and the atmosphere is calmed by the vocals of Cyndi Lauper's classic 'True Colors' seeping from the old jukebox. The busty barmaid leans up against the bar, chewing gum and wiping glasses.

On a quick tour of the bar, The Rhino Brothers, Pedro Passion, Big Bella Marie and Billy Bronx are congregating, chuckling and cackling.

The booths that are fitted into the rear wall sit under a collection of mounted pirate gimmickry and several objects that look as though they were fished out of the Pacific and placed there to give One Eyed Willie's authenticity.

Booth one homes 'Magnificent' Johnny Midnight, celebrating another victory (this time over Billy Bronx) by sipping champagne while being sandwiched by two local females, that sprawl all over him.

Ace Armstrong, who is considered as bit of a loner, sits at the next booth, swishing the remains of a Bobby's Light around in the bottom of his bottle while his cell phone is pressed up against his ear. He looks around shadily and talks very quiet to whoever is on the other end of the call, not wanting anyone to overhear his conversation for some reason, "I'll be in New York tomorrow." He whispers "That sounds fantastic! Just make sure you bring your toys!" He smiles almost sadistically.

Booth three is empty, possibly because the table hasn't been cleared or cleaned. The stickiness of spilt beer can be seen glistening under those neon bar signs, making it not very inviting.

Booth four homes Sunset Glen, sitting on his own with half a cola in his glass, looking around and hoping someone will come and sit with him, or even acknowledge his existence.

Various smaller tables sit in the centre of the bar, randomly scattered here and there, and this is where the remaining wrestlers are sitting. Jungle Jim sits discussing property with Yellow Feather. They'd both recently purchased new homes.

On the last occupied table sits Megan Powers and Emily Kincaid, best friends and travelling companions. Wrestling had brought them together and they'd bonded while on several loops.

In a quiet corner of the bar, in a booth on its own, Louis Raggu and his assistant Wally convene. Louis grips a small glass doubled with Hackenschmidt brand whiskey, his eyes fluttering around the room, keeping an eye on the wrestlers, but mostly straying to the females. Wally's head is buried in a notepad busily writing something down as his orange juice stands untouched on the table.

"So that's it? Nemesis is fired?" Wally asks, nervously twiddling his pencil in his fingers.

"Yep!" Raggu answers nonchalantly.

"But…" Wally attempts to try to change his mind, knowing how few wrestlers are actually on their roster right now.

"But, nothing, Wally!" Raggu snaps and turns his attentions away from glaring down Emily Kincaid's low-cut blouse for a moment. "He disrespected me in front of everyone and he had to be made an example of. These fuckers have got to know who is actually in charge around here and that's me, Wally! I'm in charge!"

"I know, Sir."

"Yeah, well, some of these pencil neck geeks seem to forget that sometimes and need a reminder."

"What will Nemesis do now?" Wally asks, more to himself than anyone else "He's got a wife and three kids."

"Oh, boo fucking hoo! Play me a tune on your violin, Wally! He brought it on himself! He's only got himself to blame. Besides, he's a good hand. I'm sure he can get a gig with Bobcat and Gareljich or maybe with Roussimoff down south. It's really none of my concern anymore." Says Raggu taking another swig of whiskey "And it shouldn't be yours either, Wally. This is business!"

"I know, sir. I just can't help but think of his family."
Raggu cuts him a look and Wally blushes. Try as he might, he'll never be the voice of reason to Louis Raggu, the stubborn mule never changes his mind.

"But, what Slammer did to him was a little disrespectful." Wally persists again.

"Will you just leave it, Wally! I've spoken to Slammer and told him if he dicks with me he'll be out of the door too! But,

I have invested too much into this Slammer character to pull the plug on it now. That big son of a bitch is going to make me a rich man. He may even draw better than Rogan!"

"You've tried to replace Rogan before and every time it's failed."

Wally gulps as he is met by those cutting eyes again.

"Sorry Sir, I meant no disrespect. It's just all those guys who you tried to build just didn't connect with the audience. Axel Jackson, El Corazón De Plata, Hiro Shinzaki. They all failed. The people just want Rogan."

Raggu looks at him and sips his whiskey.

"Drink your OJ, Wally." Raggu said calmly.

Wally puts down his pencil and gulps down some of his orange juice.

"You're right!" Raggu continues "They did fail. Rogan is an anomaly. There will never be another like him, No Sir! He has such a connection with the people, because he's one of their own. They feel like he's one of them, a man of the people. That's why they will always love him. Do you know I toyed with turning him heel back in '01"

Wally gulps and nearly sprays his orange juice everywhere, but manages to swallow it and save him the embarrassment.

"No, sir!"

"Yep, well, when the internet got word of it they soon put the kibosh on it. Nobody wanted it. So I never ran with the angle, and I'm damn glad I didn't. That could have ruined me. At the end of the day it's who is good for business. I've never heard a reaction like the one that the Slammer gets when he steps out there. He's the total package, the next American hero! I mean what a specimen he is and with the mystique of the mask element it just works. I'm almost ready to pull the trigger on him, and tonight it came down to me making an example of either him or Nemesis and I chose Nemesis. He's never going to be the guy and for that reason he was the one I had to let go."

Wally looks down into his orange juice watching the little pieces of pith circle like carps in a pond.

"I'll send him a cheque for two weeks wages." Raggu sighs and is immediately met by a shocked looking Wally.

"What? I'm not a complete cunt, Wally! Now write that down before I change my mind."

"Yes, Sir!" he smiles and scribbles it down on his notepad.

"Do you have a replacement in mind for Nemesis? The roster is looking a little thin on the ground at the moment."

"I've already made arrangements, Wally. We have The Masked Mandrill, Krong and El Corazón De Plata coming in for New York. Plus I'm going to give René another tryout."

"Another one? Isn't that three now?"

"Yeah!" Raggu smiles and appears to drool, almost salivating over something. "She still needs some work."

"It looks like we'll have just enough for the annual Battle Royal."

"Yep! Heck, if we're short, we can throw some Tag Teams in there, or some of them will have to do double duty."

"This event always seems to draw well." Wally says as he scribbles on the pad, again adding the new names to his list.

"Yep, stuff the ring full of wrestlers and it'll always go over well. Those schmucks think they're getting more bang for their buck."

Wally delves back into his notepad and starts scribbling something down and circling it.

Raggu looks around the bar and settles on the booth where the party seems to have already started for one man. 'Magnificent' Johnny Midnight pours champagne from a huge bottle into the flutes of two beautiful looking women, whose names have already escaped him. They giggle at everything he says, even if it isn't funny and as they begin to kiss his neck and their roaming hands disappear under the table, he fills his glass to the brim letting it overflow and down the exposed cleavage of the one girl. He stuffs the bottle back into the ice filled bucket that sits on the table, Raggu could have sworn that he heard him say, "I'm such a klutz, let me help you with that!" and his face submerges itself in her ample bosom slurping up the spilt champagne from her flesh.

"Would you look at that lucky bastard!" Raggu says shaking his head.

Wally looks over and looks almost embarrassed and what is taking place in front of his eyes.

"Disgusting! I'm just glad you're not thinking about putting all your eggs in his basket."

"Oh, but I am, Wally!"

"But what about your proposal for The Slammer?" Says Wally, again with that bewildered look of worry moving across his forehead.

"All in good time, Wally. We need a good heel to take that title from Rogan first. The money is in the chase and with the amount of heat Midnight can muster, he's the perfect candidate."

"Really?" Wally asks unconvinced.

"Yes, really! He's one talented son of a bitch!"

"He's a self-centred asshole!"

"Maybe that's why I like him." Raggu laughs "He has all the tools that we need a heel champion to have. He'll duck and dive and stay away from The Slammer for a few months until the inevitable happens and he has no way out and then we crown The Slammer."

Raggu turns his attentions back to Johnny's booth and he can see his hand slip between the open legs of one of the ladies, he stares at them and can't help but feel that tremble in his own loins. He then notices that Johnny's eyes are fixated on the busty barmaid who is also giving him the eye, casually chewing on her gum like a gurning cow. She leaves the bar and walks towards the ladies room, all the while her eyes fixated on Johnny. As she disappears into the bathroom, Johnny rises from the booth informing the girls that nature is calling and follows the barmaid.

"The lucky son of a bitch!" Raggu murmurs under his breath shaking his head in disbelief at the fortune of some people. He looks over at the two ladies now enjoying their own company and entertains the wild thought that he could actually go over and keep them company for a while, he even licks the palm of his hand and wipes it across the greasy receding strands that sit on his flaking scalp.

"I've got it!" Wally pipes up with excitement and makes Raggu jump, spilling a little whiskey over himself.

"Fucking hell, Wally! What are you talking about now?"

"I've got an idea for The Slammer."

"Oh shit!" Whines Raggu rolling his eyes "Your ideas usually costs me money."

"We get a bus!"

"A bus?"

"A bus!"

"Why do we need a bus?"

"Slammer can do a tour of every major state in it and do meet and greets! Getting him out there to talk to the people. That should help build him up."

Wally looks on in anticipation, thinking he's onto a winner with this idea.

"What a shit idea, Wally! That would never work."

Wally looks dejected.

"You'll be asking me to book a show on an aircraft carrier next and want him flown in on a fucking helicopter!"

There is a moment of silence as Wally sits pouting like a puppy dog who has just felt the brunt of its masters boot, then realises that he does indeed have another query.

"What ideas do you have for Glen?"

"Lost cause that one."

"Yeah, I still don't think he gets it."

"Do we still have the Dr X mask?" Raggu asks before sipping his whiskey and becoming mesmerised by Emily Kincaid's breasts again, the soft neon caresses her pale virginal flesh as they jiggle when she laughs.

"Raggu's looking at your tits again" Megan informs Emily.

"Oh, I'm used to it now. The fucking pervert!" She makes eye contact with him, which causes him to squirm in his seat as he tries to look anywhere but at her chest.

"That guy's such a sleaze ball! You know he once asked me to give him a hand job for a spot in a main event?" Seethes Megan while shaking her head. "What a jerk off!" She adds before taking a big swig from her bottle of Bobby's Light.

"Did you do it?" Emily looks at her with her naive country girl eyes.

Megan almost spits the beer over the table but ends up swallowing it all and then is hit by a coughing fit.

"Fucking hell, Em! What do you take me for?"

"I don't know... I mean..."

"No, I did not give that slimy little slug a tug job! Jesus!" Megan says wiping beer from her mouth.

"Sorry!" Emily apologises in a shroud of blush and daintily sips her wine.

"You're so naive to the world, Em."

"I know." Emily sighs, bowing her head a little in embarrassment.

Megan is a strong female, and has made it her mission to look out for Emily since she joined the fraternity. A country girl who was plucked out of obscurity to join this circus, who hasn't seen what a terrible place the world can be outside of her family's farm in Nashville.

Megan drapes an arm around Emily's delicate frame. "I'm sorry if I went off on a tangent there, Em. I just don't want to see you fucked over."

"I know. Sometimes I just don't know what people are talking about. They treat me like I'm stupid or something y'know?"

"You're not stupid, Em. You've just got to be on your toes with some of these guys, they'll try and take advantage of ya."   Emily nods and smiles at her friend, she feels safe when she's around her, content in the knowledge that she is there to look out for her and keep her safe.

"Yeah, well, I wish he'd take advantage of me." She giggles and stares at Johnny Midnight who is strutting across the bar zipping up his jeans.

"Emily Kincaid! You dirty little slut!" Megan laughs.

"I got needs, Meg!" she giggles back.

Her eyes fixated on Johnny as he slinks back into his groupie sandwich.

"But seriously Em, you don't want to get involved with a guy like that."

"Don't I?" She says meekly as if she's in a daydream and all that she can see is Johnny, no doubt surrounded by clouds and a halo.

"Hell no! Just look at him with those two! Goddamn rats! They've got no shame!"

"Yeah!" Emily sits up straight and announces "Fucking bitches!"

Megan looks on shocked "Emily!"

"What?"

"I don't think I've ever heard you curse before!"

"Oh, sorry!" Emily again flushes with embarrassment "I don't know what came over me. I guess I'm just jealous."

"But, seriously, he's not a nice guy, Em. Did you know he's been screwing around with Crystal?" Megan says matter-of-factly taking a big swig of her beer.

"Yeah!" Again she finds herself staring at him like a teenager with a crush, her pretty freckled face cupped in her hand as she leans on the table "She said his dick was enormous." She added, sighing in a musing state.

Megan's beer bursts from her mouth and sprays into the air.

The congregation gathered at the bar see this and let out a resounding cheer.

"Always knew you were a spitter!" Calls Pedro Passion, laughter is unleashed by everyone.

The unfazed Megan smiles and brandishes a middle finger salute in his direction. The laughter dies down and they all tune back in to Stomp and his tale he was in the middle of telling.

"So, as I was saying we're all in there for this rumble in... erm... oh fuck where was it again!"

"Detroit!" Billy Bronx adds smiling like a Cheshire cat.

"Yeah! Detroit! Oh, yeah, Billy! You were there weren't ya?" Stomp smiles and Billy nods. A meeting of knowing smiles indicates to the others that Billy already knows the punchline.

"Well, this happened to be Glen's first appearance." He sniggered and lowered his voice, they all look over at Glen, who is still alone sipping at his cola.

"Well, Raggu had him travelling with Bunk and Dirty Martin."

"Oh God!" Chuckles Big Bella Marie "Those two are the last guys you'd wanna be learning the ropes from!"

"I know, right!" Stomp laughs "So…"

"Wait, was this when they were tagging?" Asked Tusk for confirmation.

"Yeah! Near the end of their in-ring careers though." Stomp nods.

"Space Cadets?" Pedro asked.

"Space Mountaineers!" answered Tusk.

"That's it!" Pedro nods.

"So, he's been riding with those fuckers to Detroit, from… wherever it was…"

"Kentucky!" Billy added.

"Right, Kentucky. So that's like a good six hour drive. They've got six fucking hours to get over the inner workings of a rumble match to him."

"Damn, imagine six hours on the road with those douchebags! I don't think I could last six minutes!" Bella scoffs.

"Six hours they have to tell him how this type of match works, right?" Stomp starts laughing a little to himself and then downs some of his beer to wet his whistle "You know, Raggu is trusting them to help this kid. Now, I don't know what the fuck was actually said in that car, but we're at the arena and we're all gathered around the curtain ready to go out. You know it's Battle Royale rules so we're just waiting for our names to be announced. Well, I turns to Bunk and I asks 'Does this Mark know what he's doing?'" Stomp's eyes actually start to well up with tears as he fights back the laughter.

"Now!" Stomp sniggers before starting again "Glen is standing there twiddling his thumbs, in his little red budgie smugglers, shaking like a squatting cat! He looked terrified. Then Bunk grabs him by the shoulder and shakes him and asks 'You know what you've gotta do don't ya kid?' Well, Glen grins at me and sticks his thumb at me. Martin and Bunk smile too and stick their thumbs as well. Now I'm thinking okay, he get's it, he's ready, he's just nervous." Stomp stops for a breath and wipes away at his eyes, the others are leaning in know and wanting to know where this is going.

"So our names are called and we go out to the ring. Now Glen is the furthest thing from my mind as we're in the ring and we're doing the usual shit. You know holding people in the corners and telling dirty jokes, and see who you can get corpsing in there. Well, all of a sudden I hear someone shout 'YOU MOTHER FUCKER!' I think nothing of it, maybe someone just took a potato or something, right?"

Billy is looking at him now and shaking with laughter and Stomp starts to do the same.

"Then I hear it again, but it was someone else shouting it. Then I hear an 'Asshole!' then a 'Faggot!', then a 'What the fuck!'. Now, I've got my back to the other guys and I'm holding Yellow Feather over the rope, so I don't know what's happening behind me." Stomp puts his bottle down on the bar and he's mimicking holding an imaginary Yellow Feather over the ropes.

"Yellow Feather says to me 'What's going on, Brother?' And just as I go to tell him that I ain't got a clue, I feel something jam itself up my asshole! And I answer by going 'OOOOOH!'" His face goes long and his eyes saucer, as he rises up on his tiptoes showing everyone just what happened.

They all laugh at him, Billy has tears streaming down his face, and Bella Marie crosses her legs in an attempt to stop her from peeing herself.

"So, I turn around and see Glen standing there with his thumb up in the air and smiling!" Stomp bursts out laughing and then struggles to tell the rest of the story "And, and Bunk and Martin... are standing there laughing their asses off with their thumbs in the air too!"

"Oh my God! That is hilarious!" Laughs Tusk.

"So, they'd told Glen to go around and stick his thumb up everyone's ass? And he didn't know it was a rib?" Pedro asks.

"Yeah!" Laughs Stomp.

"What a fucking Mark!" Pedro laughs shaking his head.

"Oh, that's too much!" cries Bella Marie, bouncing up and down, now much in need of the bathroom.

"That's not all though!" Billy chimes in "Tell them what happened to Glen."

"What happened?" Tusk asks shocked that there could be possibly more to this tale.

"Oh, shit no! I don't think my bladder will take anymore!" Bella Marie chuckles, in desperate need now, but must hear the rest of the story.

"Well, he got his damn nose broke. That's what happened!" Stomp says and the others stop laughing for a moment, as they seemed to sense that the story had taken a serious turn.

"What Happened?" Pedro asked.

"Stuck his thumb up the wrong person's keister. That's what happened!" He said giggling. "He only went and jammed it up old Giant Nagata's hole!"

"Damn!" They all said in unison.

"Nagata turned around slowly and said..." Stomp now did the best mixture of neanderthal and Japanese accent that he could muster "...Wus tha yo fumb?"

Laughter boils on the surface again as their shoulders start to shake rapidly.

But, Stomp is still not finished.

"So Glen, sticks his thumb up to him and smiles that goofy ass smile again." Stomp continues tears streaming down his cheeks with laughter. "He just nods at big old Nagata, who recoils and potatoes him straight in the face! Floored the fucker, broke his damn nose!" Stomp collapses onto the bar as the others writhe in laughter.

"The poor bastard!" laughs Perdo.

"You mean stupid bastard!" Tusk intervenes.

"Oh, shit I'm gonna have to go!" Bella Marie laughs, twirling on the spot like some obese ballerina.

"Wait!" Stomp announces standing upright and wiping his eyes "Watch this!" he adds and turns his attention to Glen who is still finishing off his cola, hoping that someone will talk to him.

"Hey, Glen!" Stomp shouts. The group all turn to look at Glen, who is now looking up and smiling.

"Yeah, Stomp?" Glen calls back in excitement. Maybe they want to call him over and let him in on their conversation he thinks.

Stomp sticks his thumb up to him, the others chuckle, as Pedro takes a swig of beer at definitely the wrong time as Glen gestures back with a thumb and a smile of his own.

"Wus tha yo fumb?" Stomp shouts and Glen's face drops and so does the thumb as they burst out in a fit of hysterical laughter, doubling over and falling up against the bar. Bella Marie finally made the dash to the ladies room, a lady her size should not be able to move that fast, but she really needed too. Its still unknown whether she actually made it in time.

Pedro's ill-timed swig came back out of his mouth in a drizzling mist covering everyone.

"And I thought you swallowed, Pedro!" Megan taunted from her table.

Pedro doubles over coughing and spluttering but manages to gesture back towards her with his middle finger.

CHAPTER 17

The laughter from the bar could still be heard out on the dark damp street outside of One Eyed Willie's. The gargantuan frame of The Slammer strolls down the sidewalk, being careful not to step in the abundance of rain puddles that are spread out before him, the streetlights helping to guide his way around them. The cold sea air blows across his path and he shivers, stuffing his hands into the pockets of his jacket.

"Fucking damp and depressing fucking place!" He moans, as the gust swipes across his face pushing back his thick brown hair and showing off that rugged appearance of his that is hidden by a mask most of the time.

As he approaches the bar he sees the silhouette of a man leant on the wall of the alley next to it. He is always wary, growing up on the streets of Forge City had taught him to be. He stares at the dark figure, he's big, not as big as him (but who is), but still he's cautious.

"Fucker!" Comes the word from the mysterious man, the world spluttered in drunken slur, but spat with venom.

The Slammer stops, his feet sliding into a puddle and causing it to ripple around his heavy duty workman style boots.

"You say something, ya bum?" He growls at the mysterious man.

The man laughs, it's the deranged laughter of a drunk.

"You fucking bum! Get a fucking job!" The Slammer says before moving along.

"Where you going, Joe?" The words spill out, stopping him in his tracks again.

"Do I know you, guy?"

"You fucking should! You piece of shit!" He spits, and stumbles forward out of the darkness of the shadow and into the glare of the streetlights "I'm the guy you just fucked over!" His long dark hair covered his face and he staggered out in front of The Slammer, it was Nemesis.

"Oh, it's you!" The Slammer dismisses and attempts to walk on into the bar.

"Don't you walk away from me! You retarded piece of shit!" He spits, swaying too and fro on the spot, an almost empty bottle of Volkoff vodka being swung around loosely in his hand. He dragged himself through the puddles as he tried to stay upright.

"What do you want from me?" The Slammer growls turning around to face him, his hands leaving his pockets, his arms stretching out either side of his body, opening himself up to him.

"What do I want from you?" He drools "What do I want from fucking you?" He cackled "An apology would be nice for starters!"

"Sorry!" The Slammer shrugs.

"Is that it?" Nemesis fires back, stumbling forward closer towards him.

"Yeah, sorry you fucking take this bullshit personally!" The Slammer scoffs.

"Personally? Your damn right I've taken it personally! I lost my fucking job because of you!" He points the bottle at him and the remains of the vodka spills into the rain puddles under his feet "You went into business for yourself and now, I've got nothing!"

"Hey, it's your own fault, brother! You kicked up a stink about it to Raggu. Shoulda just let it go and moved on."

"Oh, Fuck!" Nemesis cried bursting into laughter and staggering into the road, falling up against a parked car. He leant up against the car looking at his haggard reflection and started to cry.

"I've got a wife at home, with three kids! A mortgage to pay!" he sniffs.

"That isn't my problem." The Slammer shrugs and turns to walk away.

Nemesis' face contorts as if suddenly possessed by some demon not of this earthly plane and he growls with pure hate in his eyes "You heartless bastard!"

Nemesis lunges at The Slammer and swings the bottle with all his might, shattering it over the back of his head. Blood and glass cascades around him as he teeters and falls up against a parked car. Amazingly he doesn't fall to the floor. He turns around to see the seething Nemesis, broken bottle neck gripped in his hand breathing heavily and drooling.

"Are you fucking crazy!" The Slammer yells at him and then that pain shoots through his brain, and the red misted blur of violence takes over. Before either of them knows it, The Slammer has hoisted Nemesis up into the air by his throat and brought him down with reckless abandonment onto the hood of a parked car. It dents from the impact in a Nemesis shape and immediately the car's alarm is echoing through the damp streets of Astoria. The Slammer doesn't hear the constant call of the car for help nor the breaking of bone in Nemesis' skull, as he relentlessly rains down with fists into his face. Finally The Slammer is dragged off the prone body of Nemesis, that is lying on the hood of the car, his face pulverised to a pulp, as drool, vomit and blood seeps from his orifices.

"Joe! Joe! What the fuck are you doing?" He hears somewhere far away as he staggers back and then sees his handiwork. He stares wide-eyed, blood matted together in his hair and glass glistening in it and has no recollection of what has just happened.

"Joe!" He hears again and turns to see Jungle Jim and Yellow Feather holding him, shaking him out of this trance.

"What?" Was all he could muster.

"What the hell are you doing?" Jim yells at him as Yellow Feather hurries to check on Nemesis.

"We need to get him to the hospital!" Yellow Feather cries.

"What the hell happened, Joe?" Jim yells again but The Slammer goes to walk away.

"Joe!" Jim growls pulling back.

The Slammer glares at him and for a moment the mist threatens to return, but instead The Slammer grabs at his head and falls to his knees screaming like a banshee.

Jungle Jim and Yellow Feather look on dumbfounded as he claws at his head and shrieks. The shrieking stops and The Slammer looks down into the rain puddle below him, his breathing heavy, causing a ripple in the water, distorting his reflection. For a split second he could have sworn he was wearing the mask.

"Are you okay, Joe?" Jim asks.

"I'm fucking fine!" The Slammer snaps and climbs back to his feet.

"What the hell is going on here?" Jim asks in a calmer nature hoping it will get an answer. The Slammer looks at him and then looks at Nemesis who is being cradled in Yellow Feather's arms on top of the car's hood. His bloodied face spluttering up all manner of bile. For a second he looked in Jim's eyes and saw hope, he saw that there was someone here who wanted to help him.

I need help.

But, the thought never made it to his lips as Johnny Midnight staggered out of the bar, the two beauties cradled in his arms.

"Whoa!" He snickered "What the fuck happened here?" With that the moment to ask for help was over.

"Now is not the time, Johnny." Jim pleads.

"Okay, it's cool! I got better things to do with my night than watching this freak show anyway!"

"What d'you call me?" The Slammer growls at Johnny, who looks startled, but not about to lose face in front of his ladies fires back with a provoking retort.

"Oh nothing, Sasquatch!" He smiles.

The Slammer reaches out and grabs Johnny by the throat. The girls scream at the sight of Johnny's face turning an unhealthy shade of beetroot and look on terrified at this monster they see before them. It's those petrified gazes that brings him back again and he relinquishes his grip on Johnny who then collapses into the arms of the ladies.

"I need a drink!" groans The Slammer and he disappears into the bar.

CHAPTER 18

High above a bed of ever-changing white cloud, there soars the massive frame of a Boeing 747 from Liberty 3 Airlines. Running currently at around 490 knots, through a tranquil cornflower sky, as it makes its way to New York City.

Rogan fidgets in his seat, even without a sore hip, air travel for a man of 6 feet 5 inches tall and weighing around 275 pounds, was never comfortable. No room to stretch out his legs, seats built for the 'average' man or woman gave him little in the way of stretching out anywhere else either. Plus having somebody in front of you constantly reclining and inclining their seat as if they were a patient in a dentist's dental engine, made watching the inflight movie near impossible too. But it was only the latest Bret Lennox offering, 'Love, Sex & Laughter' which critics had been quick to slap flop on it as soon as it hit the theatres.

He sighed and looked around, unfortunately he didn't have the window seat so getting lost in the Earth's natural beauty was a no go, instead he had the aisle seat and every time the stewards were serving something (which seemed to be every fifteen minutes) they had to ask him to tuck his bulging arm in so they could pass with the trolley, this also meant that he couldn't get a decent sleep. He turned and looked at the old lady situated in the middle seat of the three, she was reading some romance novel, on its worn cover, there was a cavorting young couple intwined in a sensual embrace. It was written by the infamous romance author, Sybil Stasiak.

She caught him eyeing up the cover and she stared at him over the thick frames of her glasses, her eyebrows raising in a mass of wrinkles under a pink rinse that looked like spun sugar.

He smiled at her "Any good?" He asked.

"Too rich for your blood, sonny!" she smiled before turning her attentions back to the bisque tinged pages, most of them turned in at the corners.

Rogan smiled and looked away thinking that the book looked like it had seen some action, worn down by time and ragged around the edges. It reminded him of himself.

He decided now was as good a time as any to carry on with his journal, being back at home tonight he may not have the chance, or want to if he was honest. He dove into his carry on that was tucked neatly under the seat in front. He sifted past his wrestling boots, knee pads and a pair of trunks, the smell of stale sweat greeted him as they were disturbed. Out the corner of his eye he could see the old lady's nostril twitch and that made him chuckle to himself, 'Too rich for your blood, lady?' He thought.

Carrying his wrestling gear in his carry on had become second nature to him when travelling by plane. The airlines have always had an annoying habit of loosing luggage and when that's your uniform getting lost it can be huge ball ache. Back during the boom in the late eighties, early nineties Rogan flew everywhere, yes it was quicker and at that time it was being paid for, so he made the most of it. Losing his trunks became a fortnightly occurrence and borrowing a moist red pair from 'The Mad Scotsman' Raging Red, was not ideal.

The last time the airline lost an item of his, it happened to be his brand new cowboy style boots he'd had custom made. He had only worn them three times and they cost him a good few Benjamin Franklin's. He never saw them again.

Three years ago they popped up on EarlBay, selling for a whopping $25,000! Where they had been for thirty years, who knew. But during this frustration he was on a flight back from Cuba when he was given a piece of advice from a masked wrestler called Starburner. He had been a sensation on the independent scene before making it big so he knew all the in's and out's of air travel.

"Always use your carry on for gear, man!" he'd said in his laid back Spanish drone.

And Starburner was right.

The novelty for flying soon wore off when the industry started to struggle financially, when its popularity wained and workers were informed that if they wanted to fly then it would have to come out of their own pocket. The majority went back to riding the freeways together again.

So, to this day whenever Rogan flies, his gear comes with him.

He knew he still had about an hour to go so, he took out his journal and unhitched the clasps that held his small table in place in the seat in front of him, he guided it down and pulled it into position. He opened up his journal and grasped his pen tightly in his tripod grip preparing to write.

"Can I get you anything to drink, Sir?" Came the programmed voice of the steward.

He looked up to see a false smile staring back at him as a beanpole of a young man stood hovering over his trolley.

"Yeah, can I get a can of Koko Pop?"

"Sure, what flavour would you like, Sir?"

"Erm... I'll have a Carmen Miranda!"

"Sorry, Sir?" Asked the steward with a confused look on his face.

"Right, you're a bit young to remember her, aren't ya. A mixed fruits, please."

"There you go, Sir." The steward said as he handed him his can. "Any snacks?" He added.

"No thanks!" he answered, while rummaging through his bag he'd spied a Red Alert protein bar, so he was good if he got a little peckish.

He heard the steward ask the old lady and the man at the window seat if they wanted anything, they declined.

He pulled back the ring pull and a fresh fruity spray escaped into the air and satisfied his nostrils, he looked at the can and remembered a time when the ring pulls had to be removed.

That thought made him feel very old.

From the Diary of Randall Rogan

Monday, April 22nd.
Flight L3 1012, From Oregon to New York.

Nearly home. Be good to get home and give my two favourite people a big hug and a kiss. God, I've missed them. I love what I do (sometimes) but going out drinking or to the clubs isn't my scene and it just makes me want to be home with them. But then sitting in an empty hotel room also makes me miss them. It's a catch 22, I can't win.

I heard there was a ruckus at the bar last night. I called it!
I can't believe that Paul is in hospital and has been let go! That's too fucking bad it really is, I get that he wasn't going to let Joe go because of having so much invested in him and with him being so over an all, but it's pretty shitty for Paul. He was a good worker, solid and dependable.
I fear that Raggu may have shot himself in the foot with Joe, who is at the opposite end of that spectrum, he's unpredictable and heavy-handed. God knows what is going on in Joe's head. But, it's Raggu's money I guess, so it's totally up to him. We all make mistakes in life and in business. Heck, I've made my fair few, never malicious nor intended, but mistakes are made and usually upset someone down the line. Leaving them with your mistake as their lasting image of you, defining you unfairly by that one mistake. It's a shame that people dwell on the negative, it's such a waste of time and effort. We are only human after all

and will fall off the horse many times before we learn to ride it. In my reckoning it's best to just forget about it and move on.

Will this be a mistake that Raggu will come to regret?

CHAPTER 19

Thousands of feet below flight L3 1012 from Portland International to La Guardia in New York, Backyard Brawl XVI is just about to kick off in Morgantown, West Virginia.

The usually immaculately kept garden of The Norris family was now a cluster of random items, from industrial equipment to home furniture. Ten year old Davey Norris had been busy on that first morning of Spring Break. He had been rushing around since sun up, clearing out his Father's shed. With a layer of perspiration glistening on his round ebony face he dragged out the old wooden stepladder. It was infested with woodworm and encrusted with dry flicks of paint from decades of decorating jobs that had taken place throughout the house. The ladder was a palette of history, every colour his Mother had ever had on the walls of the lounge was there, and with Juanita Norris that was a lot of colours. She was never satisfied and got fed up pretty quickly, some years Davey's Father had to paint it multiple times to meet her high expectations.

Davey set the ladder up on the patch of fresh green grass that had started to already yellow with the lack of rain that they hadn't been having lately. The ladder stood around 5 feet tall, but to Davey it looked 7 feet at least! He'd paused and looked up at it daydreaming of jumping off the top rung, cameras flashing all around him, swan diving like he'd seen his favourite Tag Team, The Firecrackers do a hundred times on his TV screen.

Next came out his Father's wooden workbench, his Grandpops had made it, apparently he was one talented carpenter, but that was way before Davey's time. He dragged it level with the stepladder.

A black plastic trash can was next to be heaved out of the cobweb ridden shed, it was a struggle as it was filled with all manner of 'Junk!', well that was what Davey called it, but it happened to be his Father's fishing equipment. He dumped the 'junk' on the floor at the entrance of the shed and dragged it towards the stepladder and workbench that were already in place. He turned it over and situated it opposite the workbench. He beat it like a drum for a moment and listened to the sound reverberate inside. He threw himself at the bin and head butted the top of it, that droning sound reverberated again as he fell onto the grass in a heap laughing.

"That'll do nicely!" he said to himself grinning ear to ear, before scrambling back to his feet and heading towards the backdoor to his house.

"What's all that racket going on out there now, Davey!" His Mother blurted out from her stationary position at the kitchen sink, her hands submerged in a mass of hot bubbles "It's enough to wake the dead!" She added as he stood in the doorway.

"Nothing, Momma!" He answered.

"See as it isn't!" she snapped.

"Is Paul awake yet?" He asked.

"Hell No!" She moaned "It's only just gone eight!"

He nodded and stood staring at her, looking as though he wanted to ask her a question but not sure if she was in a good enough mood to even dare.

"What y'all gawping at me like that for? Y'all be wanting something no doubt!" She said aggressively.

He nodded.

"Well, c'mon, boy! Spit it out! I ain't got time to be gabbin' to you! I got jobs to do! Now what d'you want?"

"Can I take the spare chair, please, Momma?" He whispers, almost cringing as he awaited a response.

"Why the hell d'you want that old thing for?"

"I need another corner for my ring."

"Goddamn, kids!" She groans before sighing "Take it!"

"Thanks!" He smiled grabbing the back of the old kitchen chair that sat in the cupboards that nobody every sat on, apart from their pet cat Pepé now and again, hence why it was known as the spare chair. It usually only ever made a special appearance when there were visitors for dinner or at Christmas time.

Davey dragged the chair outside, the legs screeching and scraping unpleasantly on the floor as he made his way to his construction. He heard his Mother yell at the top of her voice to keep the noise down, ironically her yelling was louder than any noise coming from Davey's travelling spare chair.

"There!" He said proudly, hands gripping his hips, surveying his work.

Off he ran again, this time around the rear of the shed where the garden fence cordoned off The Norris family's land to a dirt road and then woodland. That particular road had become ripe with fly tippers, dumping all manner of rubbish there and leaving it to fester for months before the powers that be finally get round to clearing it up.

It also happened to be on Davey's route to and from school, and just yesterday he and his best friend Deeks had spied some interesting new paraphernalia that had been recently disposed of.

He jumped the small chainlink fence and landed in the knee high debris of other peoples unwanted trash and began to dig around in it.

"Got it!" He said excitedly and flung the trash bags, newspapers and leftover scraps of peeled vegetables out of the way, some of the potato and carrot peel settling in the curls of his short afro, but he didn't care.

He grabbed hold of a hefty piece of rolled up carpet, that was tied tightly with a piece of string, this made it easier to manoeuvre and he pulled it out and leaned it up against the chainlink. He stood to catch his breath for a moment, the carpet was cumbersome and was a weight for a scrawny kid. He swept away the peel that was caught in his hair and then noticed something else in the trash. The carpet had been lying on top of a mattress.

"Oh, Jackpot!" He squealed with excitement and again started digging out the mattress like a dog would to retrieve a bone it had buried.

Five minutes later the single bed mattress that was infested with all manner of bugs and stamped with several suspicious stains stood upright against the fence next to the roll of carpet. Davey breathed heavily already tired from his morning's adventures when he heard a voice.

"What'cha doin', Davey?"

"Shit!" Davey cried, grasping a now rapid beating heart "Paul! You scared the crap outta me!"

His younger brother Paul (who was eight years old) had his little round face pressed up against the chainlink, his dark eyes staring inquisitively at him.

"Why are y'all in the trash?" He asked.

"I found some great things we can use for the BYB. Here now, give me a hand!"

Davey picked up the bottom end of the rolled up carpet and pushed it up onto the top of the fence where it teetered for a second or two before Paul could grab the end and guide it down to the other side. They did the same with the mattress, Paul's face contorted like he was about to vomit. "This thing stinks!" He said letting go of it and letting it fall to the grass "Am I gonna catch cooties off that?" He grimaced rubbing his grubby hands down his t-shirt that had a faded picture of Randy Rogan printed on it.

Davey jumped over the fence and smiled at Paul "Yeah! Big gigantic cooties!" He said grabbing him in a Headlock.

"Hey, Watch it!" Paul moaned.

"They crawl in your hair and your fro will fall off! Right on the floor it will! Happened to a friend of mine. Had to go and see a special hair doctor to sew it back on."

"No, Davey, no! Please tell me y'all be messing?" Came Paul's muffled cries from underneath Davey's sweaty armpit.

"Of course you ain't gonna get no cooties!" Davey sighed letting go off him and giving him a friendly shove.

"Momma said I can catch cooties messin' around in the trash!"

"Jeez Louise!" Groaned Davey, rolling his eyes "D'you believe everythin' your Momma tells ya?"

"Yeah!" nodded Paul.

Davey laughed.

"C'mon and help me move this stuff."

It didn't take the two of them long to manoeuvre the mattress in the middle of his square that had been formed earlier and then the carpet was draped over it.

Paul smiled, it had finally clicked what all the fuss was about and why his brother was so excited about an old mattress and a dirty carpet.

"Now we can thump on it!" Davey said rubbing his hands together like a shifty car salesman.

"Thump?" Paul enquired looking up at his brother.

"Yeah, Thump! That's what wrestlers learn to do. Y'all need to learn to thump if you're gonna be a wrestler, Paul!" Davey said so matter-of-factly as if he himself was the voice of experience.

"Oh, Okay!" Paul said nodding along.

"Like this. Watch!" Davey said and with that he threw himself backwards, wriggling in the air like a trout caught on a fishing line, before landing on the carpet/mattress combo with a thump, a cloud of dank dust rising up around him and disappearing into the air.

"Wow!" Paul whispered, thinking that his brother was indeed the coolest person on the planet.

"Now all we need is some rope. Think there's some in the shed hanging up. Y'all wanna go get it Paul?"

"Okay!" Paul said before racing off towards the shed.

"Oh, the guys are gonna love this!" Davey beamed.

"They're not coming you worm!" hissed a voice from behind him.

"Yeah! Worm!" Came the voice of a toddler, with just as much gumption as the voice she was mimicking.

"What d'you want, Jenny?" he sighed, turning around to see his teenage sister, Jenny and his baby sister Sharmell staring at him, arms crossed and judging him through matching pouted lips and high brows.

"Y'all trippin' if you think those piss ants be coming here!" Jenny spat with all the venom of an older sister.

"Piss ants!" Mimicked the three year old, Sharmell.

"Sharmell!" Davey said in shock "Y'all can't be saying words like that! Pop will tan your hide!"
Sharmell stuck out her tongue and then began dancing on the spot singing "Tan your hide, tan your hide!"

"Y'all ain't listenin' to me, Davey! AJ called and him and his brother got the pox." Jenny said smugly "So y'all got nobody to do your fag ass wrasslin with!"

"Shit!" Davey whined.

"Momma!" Jenny called at the top of her voice "Davey's cursin'!"

"Bitch!" He growled.

"Jenny! Leave those boys alone and get your ass back in here!" Came the bellowing cry of Momma Norris, that made Jenny jump out of her skin.

"Comin' Momma!" She called before giving her brother the evil eye "C'mon, Sharmell, we got serious shit to do!" And with that she strutted off towards the house.

"See wee us shit!" Sharmell said pointing at Davey before tottering after her sister.

"Damn it!" Davey cursed and kicked the workbench, it collapsed slowly into the thick grass.

"What's wrong, Davey?" Paul said as he came trundling along, struggling with a mass of rolled up blue rope that was covered in cobwebs.

"AJ and Danny can't come. They've got the pox!" he moaned.
They both looked sad for a moment until they heard a voice call over the chainlink.

"Don't worry, y'all still got me!"

"Deeks!" Came the cry from the Norris brothers in unison.

"At your service!" he smiled as he jumped over the fence and approached them. His attention was immediately directed to the monstrosity that Davey had constructed in his backyard.

"I like what you've done here!" he nodded, his bottom lip sticking out, his long fair hair falling over an eye before brushing it behind his ear.

"Just putting the rope on now!" Paul said, holding out the reel of rope in his hands.

"Lets do it!" Deeks said, and they all helped untangle it. They tied the rope around the stepladder, then stretched it out to the workbench and tied it around before weaving it through the spindles of the spare chair and coming a little stumped by the upside down plastic trashcan, with nowhere visible to tie it to. They pondered this for a few minutes when Deeks had the bright idea of just winding it around the whole thing. Which they did before stretching the remaining length of rope out and tying it to the other side of the stepladder.

They stood back in awe, proud of their accomplishment. No longer would the members of The Backyard Brawl have to wrestle on the haystacks over on Farmer McGuirk's field. No Sir, now they had their very own wrestling utopia (well until Davey's Mother or Father told him to take it down)

"You know something?" Deeks said draping an arm around the shoulders of Davey.

"What's that, Deeks?" Davey asked.

"I betcha my weight in Pizza Wolf Pizza, that nobody's ever done this before."

"You think?" Davey asked.

"Yeah! We must be the only kids in the world to think this up."

They stood in awe for another few minutes taking it all in. Maybe they were the only people ever to make a wrestling ring in their backyard and live out their dreams. The likelihood of that being true is improbable but to them that's how it felt.

"Dibs on The Slammer!" Davey calls .

"Oh!" Groaned Paul and Deeks in unison "You're always The Slammer!" Deeks moaned.

"That's because I'm the best!" Davey grins.

"Yeah Right!" Scoffs Deeks.

"Besides, I've got the mask!" And with that revelation he pulled out a homemade wrestling mask from the rear pocket of his dirty jeans. He had made it from one of his Mother's old stockings that happened to be red and white striped.

"I'll be Johnny Midnight, then. He's gonna be World Champion one day!" Deeks announced.

"No way!" Davey fires back shaking his head "The Slammer for sure!"

"Can I be Rogan?" Paul asks.

"Sure you can." Smiled Deeks and gives him a high five.

They all race to get into the ring, Davey jumping over the rope in one big stride and then jumping into the air again, doing his best flailing fish impression before crashing down on the mattress. Deeks follows suits and he flips forwards and gambols onto it. Paul lags behind going underneath the rope and connecting with his best bellyflop attempt, dust bellowed up and caked his face, everybody laughed as Paul wiped the dust out of his eyes.

"Oh! There's one thing I forgot!" Davey pipes up and then runs off towards the shed again.

"What's he got?" Deeks asks but is met by a shrugging of shoulders by Paul.

Deeks looks down at Paul and smiles, he'd always wanted a brother, but with his Mother and Father now divorced it didn't look like he ever would. He liked Paul and he knew that when he came round that Paul kind of got pushed aside by his brother sometimes.

"Paul?" Deeks asked.

"Yeah, Deeks?"

"Do yo wanna have the first match with Davey?"

"Can I?" Paul gasped, his dark little eyes shining with happiness.

"Sure thing!" Deeks smiled.

Davey burst from the shed roaring and bellowing, with the stocking over his head and holding aloft an old beaten and battered steel chair.

"Whoa! That's awesome!" Deeks yelled as Davey jogged over swinging the chair around recklessly.

"Now we can have some hardcore matches!" Davey said enthusiastically.

"I don't think I wanna be in any of those types of matches, Davey. Momma wouldn't like that." Paul whined.

"There's nothing to it, Paul!" Davey said, "Watch!"

Davey lifted up the steel chair over his head, the sun glistened on the bent metal frame as it hovered above Paul's head. Then Davey did what he'd seen hundreds of times on the television, he brought the chair down with all his might on the top of Paul's head.

Deeks and Davey froze as Paul lay on the grass, his body twitching like a blue bottle that had just felt the business end of a rolled up newspaper. His eyes looked glazed and drool seeped out of the corner of his mouth.

"Paul?" Davey murmured, slowly peeling off his mask.

Deeks said nothing, he couldn't he was in shock.

Blood started to dribble down his nostrils and mix with his saliva, even more disturbingly blood started to trickle out from his ears.

"Momma!" Davey yelled, the sickening sound was bloodcurdling, it was the reason Deeks didn't sleep for several weeks after, the sound haunted him. Deeks stood rooted by that perverse cocktail of fear and shock as Davey ran towards the house, which appeared through Deek's eyes to be in slow motion. Davey's eyes dripped with tears as the burning sensation of vomit scorched his throat.

Davey's mask sat in the grass next to Paul's quivering body, the creases in it gave the sadistic illusion that it was actually smiling.

CHAPTER 20

Room 287

The Slammer's fermenting mask rested on the desk of a luxury room at The Billington in New York City, that overlooked the Mecca that is, Madison Square Garden.

The room was lit by early afternoon sunshine as it surged in through the gigantic window that separated the room from a small balcony area. Warm vapour from the bathroom seeped into the room, which was surprisingly high end to what some wrestlers were used to, but when staying in The Big Apple, they did like to indulge a little.

The radio played the days headlines through crackles and breaks, the newsreader's tone remaining drone and lifeless through each story no matter whether it was a tale of positivity or not.

"...Professional Wrestling to blame..." The words slapping Joe in the face as he exited the bathroom, one towel wrapped around his waist, another frantically rubbing against his mop of hair, trying to help quicken up the drying process.

The words halted him and he glared at the radio, listening intently.

Professional Wrestling was never mentioned on the radio or in the tabloids, or even on mainstream television unless something unpleasant had happened, then the vultures were out.

"...Eight year old, Paul Norris of Morgantown, Vest Virginia is currently in critical condition at a local hospital. Specialists have said that the child may never walk again"

"Fuck!" Joe said shaking his head "Poor kid."
He continued to dry his hair and sat on the edge of the bed.

"...Was hit on the head with a chair by his brother, Ten year old David Norris who was quoted as saying, 'I saw 'em do it on TV.'"

"Here we go!" Sighed Joe "Grab your torches and pitchforks, because all of a sudden what we do is real and not phoney."

"...Trauma suffered has severely damaged his spinal cord which may see him live out the rest of his life as a paraplegic."
Joe rose from the bed and discarded the towel behind him, running his hands through his damp hair.

"...His mother, Juanita Norris was irate...'These goddamn wrestlers are to blame for this! They should all be burnt alive for what they've done to my baby boy!'"

"Betcha you told him hundreds of times how fake we all were too, didn't you Mrs Norris?" Joe seethed.

"...Spokesperson, Wally Dominguez for Wrestling..."

"Fuck, Wally, you're famous!" Joe scoffed as he walked across the room towards the desk where the radio sat.

"We are deeply saddened by such a tragedy. But, I cannot reiterate this following statement enough, that all our wrestling superstars are highly trained professional athletes and children should not imitate or copy their performances or actions. Our events are solely intended for the fans viewing pleasure."

Joe switched off the radio and sighed. He felt all manner of emotions from that particular radio transmission and he could feel his blood start to boil up inside of him. Once again filling him up with that uncontrollable hate.

"No!" He growled, trying in vain to fight against the inevitable as his eyes met that taunting sneer from his mask once again. Mocking him and almost controlling him "Fuck!" He roared as veins popped out of his temples, pulsing like worms squirming under his skin.

He grabbed at his head and with an ear splitting wail he emptied the desk of its contents before collapsing in a damp mess on the floor of the hotel room.

Room 194

The shades are partially drawn in Room 194, with shards of sunlight cutting through the vertical blinds, striping the dingy room in bands of light.

Ace Armstrong lies like a starfish on the bed, completely naked. His body writhing as he groans in discomfort or pleasure, or maybe his groans come from somewhere in between.

The exquisite frame of a woman stands next to him, clad in a black PVC military style dress, a zip running through the centre of it but stopping south of her chest, allowing her huge cleavage to remain visible. She slowly strides around the bed in thigh high black leather boots, stabbing at the carpet with sharp six inch heels. Slowly she brushes a cat of nine tails style whip over his torso, red marks and welts can be seen on his now goose bumped flesh. He nibbled his bottom lip with excitement.

"More!" He murmured, he was almost begging her for more of what he'd just received.

"Fuck you!" The woman growls and stops the caressing with the whip just as it was reaching his genitals, his penis twitches with anticipation.

She walks away from him and around the room, the PVC clinging to her hourglass figure like a second skin. All that can be heard is the quiet squeaking of the PVC.

He closes his eyes and awaits something, anything. She keeps him waiting on purpose.

"Oh, Please, Mistress Hellanor!" he whispers.

"I'll tell you when it's time, you little shit! Stop your begging! You're fucking pathetic!" She seethes, spitting her insults from bulging cherry lips. Her face is slender and attractive, a scar or burn mark peeps out from under a mass of vibrant red hair that cascades down and covers most of her face. All of this under a black military style peaked cap.

"Dirty little worm!" She growls "I'm in charge! You got that?"

Armstrong smiles, his penis starting to come to life with the mere thought of what she can (and will eventually) do to him.

"Yes!" He rasped.

"Yes, what?" She shouts storming over toward the bed and lashing his torso with the whip. It flicks across his skin and he bites down on his lip again, almost drawing blood. His penis rises and he groans for more "Yes, Mistress!"

Room 109

The contents of Sunset Glen's large intestine hits the porcelain bowl of his ivory white streamlined toilet. He always struggled with his nerves before shows and always had to have a 'PMS' (Pre Match Shit) before go time. The fear of losing control of his bodily functions and soiling himself in the middle of a match haunted him. Hell, he'd seen it happen, and that poor guy never lived it down. The guy was wearing white tights too.

Room 256

A large black man, standing at almost 7 feet tall, and seemingly as wide across, struts around the room with his cell phone clutched to his ear, long flowing dreadlocks covering the majority of his face.

"Yeah, I'm here for a few shots for Raggu. I'll be back in Studd on Friday and I'll get you your stuff then."

He struts over to the bed where a holdall sits patiently waiting for him.

"Of course I've got it, girl!" he scoffs "You know me!" he adds laughing, flashing a line of golden teeth "I've got you covered, you know that."

He opens up the bag and all manner of illegal substances stare back at him.

"Take it easy! Chill out, yeah?" He growls, his face and demeanour changing like the wind and now he looks irritated. His lived in face contorting into a frown, the laughter lines manifesting themselves in abundance, but there is no humour in these lines.

"Look! Mandrillus is a man of his word, you'll get your fuckin' stuff, okay?"

He rolls his eyes at something the person on the other end of the cellphone says and sighed.

"That's just paranoia from the withdrawal, There ain't nobody watching your sorry ass, believe me!"

He pushes his dreadlocked hair out of his face and rubs at his throbbing temples "I know...I understand that, but there ain't a lot I can do about that at the moment."

He strolls towards the window and pulls open the glass door that leads onto the balcony, the sun shines in his eyes and he squints, his ears are bombarded by the sound of traffic from far below.

"What was that?" He asks not hearing "Oh, yeah!" he says walking back into the room and sliding the door back in place behind him.

"I'll be there, just hang tight a couple of days."

Room 226

The silence is eerie as the World Tag Team Champions, Devastation are sat either end of a small table enthralled in their daily game of chess. Veteran Frank Crane (Famine) and his son Damian Crane (Plague), the only Father and son team in professional wrestling history. Together they have dominated the Tag Team division for years, holding on to a record breaking six reigns as champions. But, at this moment in time they don't care about any of that, this is Father and Son time.

Damian's bishop takes Frank's knight. He smirks and looks up at his Father, he loves these moments with him, even though he never beats him, he enjoys it nonetheless.

Sunlight streams through and illuminates Frank's hagged face, his wrinkling bald head reflecting the light into his sons eyes, it makes Damian snigger.

His Father looks up from the board and gives him a perplexed stare while stroking his fingers over his thick greying moustache and then smiles.

"You think you've got me don't ya, kid?" Frank asks.
Damian shrugs his shoulders, but smirks with confidence.

Frank thinks about his move for another few minutes, lulling his son into a false sense of security and with the swift flick of the wrist, his rook glided through Damian's queen leaving his king exposed and unprotected.

"Check!" says Frank, his moustache rising on either side of his face, as he watches his son's face fall.

"Damn it, Dad!" Damian groans.

The two sit and laugh, and Damian takes time to take a mental photograph of this moment because he knows that his old man is ready to call it quits.

Room 116

"...You always say that." Snivels Sebastian as he sits naked on the edge of the large double bed, his rotund stomach hanging down between his legs, trying to conceal his private parts that very rarely see action these days.

"It's not you, Darling, really!" Crystal says trying to console him, by rubbing her hand on his back. "It's me!" She sighs and sits next to him, wrapping herself up in her silk dressing gown.

"You always say that too." He weeps "It's because I'm fat isn't it? That's why you don't want to make love to me anymore."

"No! Of course not!" She growls, hurt by his comment "You think I'm that shallow?"

"I don't know what to think anymore!" he says turning to her with tears rolling down his oval shaped face.

"I..." for a moment she looks into his sweet blue eyes, her husband's eyes, the eyes of a man that loves her with every inch of his heart. She almost spills the beans. The words dance around on the tip of her tongue, the truth is tantalising and yearns to escape. But her eyes look away and down at the carpet that is so soft between her toes. She knew that if she told him, it would all end and it would break him.

"Is there something you want to tell me?" He asks, she remains silent, her gaze still drawn to her feet in the shameful way a child would if they had done wrong.

"Is there?" He asks again, starting to feel like there is something.

"No!"

He looks away, at anything apart from her as he plucks up the courage to say the next words that could mean everything.

"Do you still love me?"

"Yes!" she answers immediately, there were no lies in her answer, she did love him.

Their drifting gaze met again and now she too had tears welling up in her beautiful grey eyes, the shroud of moisture appearing to make them sparkle, almost hypnotising.

"I love you so much, Crystal. Just tell me what I need to do and I'll do it!"

"I don't know, Seb. It's my head... I'm just so messed up right now, I don't know why." She started to cry, tears of guilt. He cradles her in his arms and kisses her on the head.

Room 231

Rambunctious laughter fills the air, as Emily Kincaid and Megan Powers lie on the large double bed watching a Bret Lennox movie on the wide flat screen television fitted to the wall, a large bowl of popcorn resting in-between them.

"Oh my god, Meg!" Laughs Emily as she doubles over in hysterics.

"I'm being serious!" Megan giggles.

"And he hit on you, while he was taking a piss?"

"Damn right he did! Dirty little shit!"

They both laugh together again, and Megan launches a handful of popcorn into her mouth and crunches down on them.

Emily grabs a handful of the popcorn and puts a few pieces in her mouth, chewing delicately and changing positions to lying on her stomach. She looks up at the screen as Bret Lennox creeps through the dingy cabin in the wintery horror classic, Maple Falls Massacre, obviously topless and showing off his slender physique.

"Oh, but just look at him Meg!" Emily swoons "Isn't he magical? You should have so gone with him! Whether he was pissing at the time or not!"

"You are out of control girl! We've got to get you laid." Megan says playfully shoving her.

"Please do!" Emily sighs.

"You know if you pause this film at the correct time you can see his dick, right?" Megan announces matter-of-factly, like the statement she just made was common knowledge. Emily suddenly gets on all fours on the bed and begins frantically rummaging through the crumpled bedsheet.

"Em? What's wrong?" Megan asks a little taken a back.

"I'm looking for the remote!" She cries.

"You slut!" Megan laughs and pushes her off the bed. Emily hits the ground with a thump and they both roll around in fits of laughter.

"Megan?" Emily says pulling herself back up the bed so her head is peering over the side at her and says with all seriousness "I really need you to find the remote, like yesterday!" She is showered by popcorn and she falls back to the floor laughing.

Room 201

The tranquil music of panpipes and running water softly flows around the room surrounding the meditating Jungle Jim, who is sat in his underwear crosslegged on the carpet in total relaxation. His diaphragm pulls itself in slowly, filling his lungs with air before letting out any negative vibes that have found a place to stay, it will only be a short stay as Jungle Jim does not do negativity.

The sound of the running water ascends into the air and out of the open window where it is immediately swallowed up by the traffic far below on the bustling streets of New York City.

Room 103

The room is dark, the blinds drawn, all manner of clothes lie in disarray on the floor, along with champagne bottles and pizza boxes. On the desk, rolled up bills sit caked in the residue of a fashionable cocaine known as Stardust, and the mirror above the desk boasts the words 'Johnny is God' scribbled on it with red lipstick. On the large double bed 'Magnificent' Johnny Midnight sleeps soundly in a mass of female bodies, it's impossible to tell just how many, some of them under the blankets, some of them are sprawled naked over him or hanging off the bed. Legs and arms twitch in their dreamy states, like the tentacles of some alluring octopus. Johnny begins to snore loudly.

Room 224

"I love you too, pop!" Cries a mask-less Mr Canada as he sits on the floor of his hotel room cradling his United States title in his arms, while his Father talks to him on the other end of the phone, his voice rising out from the loudspeaker.

"What you've got to remember is that this was your dream, and you're living it, Keith!"

"I know, Pop, I know." He sniffs.

"And, yes you're gonna miss home now and again, but that's all part of the game isn't it?"

"Yeah, I miss you and Ma, so much!"

"And we miss you too, Son. But you have to look at what you're doing. You're living your dream! There aren't many folk on this planet can say that. Do you think it was my dream to work down at the mill for forty years?"

"No, Pop."

"Hell, I wanted to play for The Blackfoot Ridge Barbarians! I was gonna be the next Wayne Gretzky!"
Mr Canada chuckles and wipes his nose with the back of his hand.

"Take the ball and run with it, kid. And just enjoy this time, it isn't gonna last forever is it?"

"No! And I know you're right... Just sometimes my anxiety gets the best of me and I'm just not very confident in myself."

"It's a tough life on the road... Just remember we're only a phone call away or you can 'Skip' us, if your Mother can figure out how the damn thing works!"

"Skype, Pop." Mr Canada laughs.

"Whatever! Just know this!" his Father paused as if filling up with emotion himself "We both love you very much and I am so very proud of you and what you have accomplished. So very proud!"
The words resinated with him and he burst into tears again, those words that he had longed to hear from the person that mattered the most.

Room 195

Billy Bronx had taken his book out onto the balcony for some peace and quiet. Well, it wasn't peace or quiet but it was still quieter than the sordid cacophony that was seeping through the wall from next door in room 194. Something flickered and shone in his eyes distracting him from his reading and he looked up at the gargantuan structure of mirrored glass adjacent to The Billington. He squinted to see if he could see what was shining in his eyes. It was coming from one of the windows of that neighbouring building and after a few seconds it stopped. He shrugged and went back to his book, asking himself the question that the said book had proposed to him, If you held a dinner party with famous people that are no longer with us, who would you invite?

CHAPTER 22

Randy Rogan leans back in his recliner, breathing a sigh of relief. There was nothing like being back at home and in his comfy spot. The fact that he could only hear the loud clicking of the clock on the mantlepiece indicated that the house was indeed empty. He looked around at his fabulous house that his chosen profession had built for him and he closed his eyes.

Just forty winks while Martha's gone to collect Jimmy from his friends house.

He drifted away and thought about a lot of things. The past, from starting his adventure off in a piece of shit ramshackle building, the persona's he went through until he found one that worked, the people he'd met along the way, the revolving door of acquaintances that had been made and lost. The first match he had, the first time at MSG, and all the matches in-between and those that followed. Some matches he can't even remember anymore, some blurred together to create a work of fiction that never actually took place and some lost and forgotten altogether. He thought about what his aim was when he originally started and how it changed when his little family came along. He smiled to himself, content with his career and understanding that his personal goals that he had set had been achieved. He thought about the other wrestlers and what they'd be doing today, show day before a huge event at Madison Square Garden. The anticipation and excitement they'd be feeling, what would they be doing to prepare? The gym, the tanning salon (for some), eating a nice lunch in a nice restaurant and then hanging around in the dressing rooms for the rest of the night until their matches. Randy realised that he would now sooner be here, sat in his comfy spot with his family, and that the excitement that he would have once had burning inside him was rapidly fizzling out. But, that feeling in front of that crowd, that feeling was very difficult to recreate doing something else, near on impossible. It's that feeling which is the reason that most of the wrestlers do what they do, for the adulation and the acceptance, maybe never having that in their real lives. This gave them their moment to shine and be who they were truly meant to be, the person that their society, or family or circle of friends wouldn't allow them to be.

Rogan thought for a moment, thought about the present, thought about how lucky he was to walk away from the business unscathed, apart from a few knocks here and there, he'll still be able to play ball with Jimmy and run around and have fun with him, watching him grow. It was then that he realised that this life now, being a Father and a husband were the important things, he no longer needed acceptance from strangers but from his own unit and that's what he had. In fairness he had that all along, but sometimes one must cross that bridge to realise that the grass is no more greener than the plot he left behind.

He smiled and thought of how lucky he has been to live the life that he has lived, to see the things he has seen and he was so thankful that it helped build their nest egg. He was even more thankful that he could now finally take the time to enjoy what he had built. In a way he was starting a new chapter of his life and he couldn't wait.

"Daddy!" Jimmy wailed as he exploded through the front door and shot straight down the hall and into the lounge where his Father was relaxing.

"You're home!" Jimmy yelled again and launched himself on top of his Father.

"Ooh! Watch it there, Champ!" Randy scoffed with a smile caressing his lips.

Martha appeared in the doorway and smiled "I think he's missed you."

"You think?" Randy laughed "How's it going, Champ?"

"Great!" Jimmy cried and then wrapped himself around his thick neck and squeezed with everything he had "I've missed you so much!" he sobbed tears bleeding from his little eyes.

"It's okay, I'm here now. Don't be sad." Randy said squeezing him back.

"I'm not sad, Daddy. I'm so happy!" Jimmy cried.

Martha stood at the doorway with tears rolling down her cheeks, mirroring her son's sentiment.

Randy looked up at her with his eyes glazing too and he squeezed Jimmy tightly and kissed him gently on the head.

"A couple more trips and I'm all yours, for as long as you want me, Champ."

"I love you, Daddy. You're my hero!"

The tears came now for Randy, there was no way of stopping them, but to be honest he didn't want them to.

Martha joined them on the recliner sitting on Randy's knee, they kissed and they cried together.

"I love you guys so much, The Three Amigos."

CHAPTER 23

The clangorous sound of weight plates colliding with each other fills the air and bizarre grunts and groans gush from the overexerting specimens at Strongbow's Gym.

An unmasked Slammer gets in his daily workout, leg day and he's squatting heavy. The excessive amount of plates rattle on the cold steel barbel as it rests across his broad shoulders, he controls his breathing as he slowly squats down and then rises again constantly repeating the almost regimental pace and pattern. He watches himself closely in the mirrored wall and is completely zoned out from all those around him going about their routines. His face flushed with colour and the veins raising on his neck indicate that his set is coming to an end. He's feeling it now and knows that these will indeed be the last few repetitions.

Satisfied with what he'd accomplished, he waddled forward, still carrying a burden of colossal weight on his shoulders and slotted the barbel safely back into the brackets of the squat rack. The sound of metal on metal sings again and this seems to bring him out of the zone, like someone ringing a dinner gong. He leans on the now secured barbel and looks into the mirror, watching each bead of sweat fall from his mop of hair. His breathing pattern is now a little heavy and he can feel the rapid beating of his heart that is working overtime to pump blood around this mammoth individual. He gives himself time for it to return to normal and in the meantime his gaze wanders, looking at the life that goes on around him through the reflection of the mirror. He can see all and watches unnoticed by anyone else.

Naturally his eyes focus on familiar faces, Jungle Jim sinks into a cobra position as he continues on his yoga program that has been working wonders for him. He has said that he feels ten years younger and has already noticed the difference it has made to his once weary joints. He has talked about one day creating his own program.

Kami Kajeu saunters along on the exercise bike, as if having a quaint little ride down some country lane, not expending too much energy. Slammer sees a few young wannabes laughing at Kami as they walk passed and Slammer scowls.

Little fuckers! He may not look like an adonis, hell, a lot of these punks in here probably think he doesn't belong here, but I tell ya, that fucker can go in the ring. He does what he needs to do here and nothing more. The guy's got an engine I tell ya, never seen him gassed or blown in my life.

Stomp and Tusk are lifting heavy on the bench press, eagerly cheering each other on in a friendly competitive way. Both of them clad in the standard uniform of brightly coloured Zubaz pants, vests and fanny packs.

Yellow Feather works with kettle bells.

Bella Marie lifting heavy being spotted by Mistress Evil.

Pedro Passion is at the water cooler taking time out from his workout to chat to a few fans.

His testosterone levels move up a notch and his eyes linger longer than they probably should as he focusses his attentions on René who is putting her inner thighs through a burn. Her body hugged tightly by a second skin of cerise spandex, and Slammer is boorishly and perversely staring as her legs open and close.

Damn! I wouldn't mind a ride on that myself.

He wipes the sweat from his brow with a towel and starts to wipe down the equipment he has used.

It's not until he finds himself staring at Emily Kincaid and Megan Powers on the treadmills, their breasts crammed into tight fitting sports bras and rising and falling in unison, does he realise he has to stop staring at people.

I'm either gonna get slapped or get thrown out for having a rod in my Zubaz! I really need to get laid.

He is about to leave, throws his towel over his shoulder, retrieves his drinks bottle and takes a swig when he notices Johnny Midnight. His grip automatically squeezes his bottle, already he can feel that redness flashing in his head, just the sight of him triggers his rage.

He scowls as Johnny leans on a piece of equipment letting the smoothness of his tongue dazzle some beautiful looking gym bunny. Johnny laughs and she flutters her eyelashes at him and whips back her long brown ponytail. It isn't until Johnny lifts up his vest showing off his incredible abdominal area to her and then taking her hand to stroke them with, does Slammer growl with annoyance. He squeezes the life out of the bottle and water squirts and dribbles onto the floor as he bounds over to where they are.

"Excuse me, Miss!" Slammer says politely, managing to keep his face from contorting through the anger that was welling up inside of him, also glancing at Johnny's face that was now sneering at him for interrupting "Is this guy bothering you?"
She looked up at Slammer a little shocked and taken aback "I...Oh, erm..."

"The lady is fine jackass! Now move on!" Johnny seethes.
Slammer turns his attentions to him and his face glows with anger, again inside his brain being cooked in a bubbling pot of fury.

"You want to make something of it, little man?" Slammer growls.

"I'm fine!" The gym bunny says, but her words falls on deaf ears.

"The lady said she's fine, retard!" Johnny growls and the two move in face to face, well, face to chest, but their eyes are fixated on each others.

"Oh! You want some do you?" Slammer barks gripping the water bottle tighter and tighter.

"You just take your fucking best shot you dumb son of a bitch!"

"Look, I said I'm fine! You don't need to..." She tries to say but Slammer interrupts.

"It's about time someone put you in your place!" Slammer growled again, his fist tightening and clenching, veins standing to attention once again.

"You're one stupid fucker! You're next in line to be the top dog and you're willing to throw all that away because you're fucking jealous of me getting my dick wet!"

"What?" shouts the gym bunny and slaps him across the face before storming away.

Johnny just laughs it off "Oh well, you win some you lose some. Guess you lose more than you win though right big guy?"

"I'm gonna..."

"You're gonna what? Hit me? Do it! Go on! Fucking do it! But, I guarantee I'll kick up such a stink that Raggu will send you packing and then who'll be next in line?"

Slammer simmered down, Johnny's words dancing in his head and ringing true. He knows that's exactly what would happen and then he'd be in the same position as Nemesis. The boot would well and truly be on the other foot then.

Jungle Jim and the Rhino Brothers had seen what was about to take place and had come over to calm the situation down. Jim had seen what Slammer could do first hand when he was provoked and although he thought Johnny could be a dick too, he didn't want to see the same thing happen to him that happened to Nemesis.

"C'mon guys, let's calm down." Jim said.

"Hey, Jimbo, I haven't got a problem!" Johnny before pointing in Slammer's face and adding "Tell this guy!"

"Leave it, Joe. C'mon now!" Jim pleads.

"Watch it!" Slammer seethes pointing back at Johnny, blood boiling again, trying desperately to control it.

"Or fucking what?" Johnny yelled, causing everyone in the gym to stop what they were doing and stare at them.

Slammer looked around and he sees everyone looking at him, judging him, mocking him, laughing at him, angering him.

There is silence, apart from in Slammer's head there are howling shrieks of pain.

"Fuck it!" Slammer growls and launches the crushed up water bottle across the gym before marching towards the locker room.

"What a fucking freak!" said Johnny shaking his head.

"Give it a rest, Johnny!" Jim says as he goes after Slammer, concerned that he may hurt somebody or even himself.

Johnny talks to The Rhino Brothers filling them in on what happened, meanwhile over at the treadmills Emily turns to Megan mid stride through pants of exasperation "What do you think Johnny's favourite sexual position is?" Megan nearly falls off the treadmill.

In the locker room, The Slammer clears it from anybody getting changed when he charged in and started violently head butting the metal doors of the lockers again and again, relentlessly bombarding it with dents.

"Joe, Is everything okay?" Came Jim's voice and a caring hand on his shoulder.

"Fuck!" Screamed Slammer, spinning around and grabbing Jim by the throat and actually lifting him off the ground and ramming him into the lockers.

Jim spat out some incoherent nonsense and started to turn a shade of beetroot. Slammer looked into his eyes, he knew by the way they were almost bulging from their sockets that he could kill him now if he wished.

Do it!

He shook his head trying to remove the thought from existence. If it could be thought, it could be said, if it was said it could be done.

Do it! Do it! Do it!

"No!" He screamed and let go of Jim, turning around disgusted at himself, as Jim slowly slunk down to the floor holding his throat and gasping for air.

"I didn't mean to do that, Jim. I'm sorry if I hurt you."

"That's it, Joe!" gasped Jim, struggling to fill his lungs again "I'm through trying to help you, you're on your own!" And with that, Jim leaves the locker room.

The Slammer sat down on the bench and stared into a mirror adjacent to him, he wore the mask in the reflection and it seemed to grin wildly back at him, the distorted reality created by his mind, he felt like he was being taken over and had no control of it.

But Jim was wrong, he wasn't on his own.

He was never alone.

The rage was always with him.

CHAPTER 24

Glen shuffled out of Louis Raggu's office, an actual meeting room this time not a janitors closet. Better arena, better facilities, but the same scrap piece of paper with Raggu's name scribbled on it just to show his importance. He closed the door behind him and a huge sigh of rejection left him. He held in his hands a musty old black mask, a large white X stitched on the forehead of it.

The mask of the infamous, Dr. X!

Glen felt like crying, what was he supposed to do now? He felt like a complete failure, and somewhere down the corridor he heard laughter. He felt like it was aimed towards him and his whole wrestling career. The laughter was indeed hysterical and it reverberated off the corridor walls like a pinball trapped in a never-ending game of ricochet. Glen felt like it was Madison Square Garden itself mocking him.

He was staring hard at the mask, wandering where he could go from here and he didn't see Randy Rogan approaching.

"You okay, Glen?" Rogan asked.

"Huh?" Glen said looking up a little perplexed.

"You look a bit upset. Are you okay?" Rogan asked again and then saw what he was holding in his hands. "Ah! Good old Dr X, huh!" Rogan chuckled.

Glen took Rogan's chuckling the wrong way and lowered

his head again, his body language causing him to hunch over and slouch as if his body were hanging from a noose.

"I don't know what to do with this shit!" Glen sighed.

"Glen, I'm going to tell you something right now that my mentor, 'Uncle' Sam Reagan once said to me."
Glen's ears pricked up by the mention of such a legend's name and he was a little startled that someone was actually taking the time to converse with him.

"He told me that there's no such thing as a bad gimmick."

"Really?" Glen asked.

"Really!" Rogan nodded "It's all about what you do with it. They fail when the performer doesn't believe in what he or she is doing. The fans can sense that, they pick up on that when wrestler's aren't one hundred percent committed. That's why they fail."

"Yeah… I guess that makes sense." Glen smiled, looking at the mask a little differently now.

"The people haven't taken to Sunset Glen, have they?"

"No" He sighed shaking his head.

"Think of this as a do-over. You get another shot here. Granted the gimmick is as old as the hills, but it's already established, it has history to it and some value. You can take that and use it to build something for yourself. Put your own stamp on it and make it yours!"
Glen's body language began to change and he seemed to rise up and stand tall from the pep talk that a veteran was giving him.

"It'll work, Glen." Rogan placed a hand on his shoulder "But, only if you give it everything!"

"I'm gonna do it!" He beamed.

"That's the spirit!"

"What should I do out there though? They'll know it's me out there!" He sighed, deflating again with negativity.

"They won't, Glen." Randy shook his head "Become the Dr X character. Yeah, that's exactly what it is! It's a character. So play it like one. Up to now you've only worked babyface, yeah?"

"Yeah."

"Well, like I said, it's a do-over. It's a fresh start! Play the character like all those nasty villains you used to watch in movies when you were a kid. Be dastardly! Be conniving! And cheat! You'll get the heat and it will be so far from what you've been doing, they won't know it's you."

"Yeah! You're right!" Glen said again upbeat and stuck out his hand for Rogan to shake it. Rogan smiled at him and shook it.

Laughter bounced down the corridor again and found them, Glen's face dropped.

"Probably laughing at me again!" He moped.

"Glen!" Rogan sighed "You need to stop being paranoid. They're not laughing at you!"

"They're not?"

"No! Look around, there's nobody here!"

They looked up and down and sure enough there was not a soul in sight.

"Look, even if they do laugh at you sometimes, it's just schoolboy stuff, ribbing and such. Laugh with them instead of taking it to heart and they'll come round to ya."

"Thanks so much, Randy!"

Glen scuttled off down the corridor looking at the mask.

"Oh and Glen?" Rogan called, stopping Glen in his tracks and causing him to swivel on the spot to face him.

"Yeah?"

"Have you got some black trunks?"

"Yeah, why?"

"Make sure you wear those with the mask." He smiled and gave him a wink.

Glen looked at the mask again and gave him a huge toothy grin and nodded before scampering away.

Rogan watched him disappear and it made him smile.

Sometimes it's not about you, it's about building others and giving back.

Rogan knocked the door and he heard the croaky reply from the other side of Louis Raggu for him to enter.

The cigar smoke was thick and almost shrouded Raggu and Wally. With a half chewed cigar protruding out of his greasy maw, Raggu sat at the head of a long table, with several unused chairs surrounding it. Wally sat next to Raggu and papers were strewn across the tabletop, all manner of shows and storylines scribbled down on them. They looked up and smiled at Rogan as he entered, closing the door behind him.

"Randy!" Raggu beamed "What can I do for you, Champ?"

He carried on sifting through papers while Wally jotted down the card for the evening.

"Louis!" Rogan said and then paused, not for dramatic effect, but for doubt. For a split second he was apprehensive about finishing the sentence because that would mean it's all over.

Louis and Wally looked up at him a little concerned.

"Is everything okay, Randy?" Louis probed.

"I'm done!" Rogan announced, it felt like a weight had been lifted from around his neck, he felt free. Well, almost free.

"Randy, come and sit down. Wally! Go and take five."

Wally stood up to leave.

"It's okay. Wally can stay." Rogan smiled.

"No, it'll give us time to talk things over. Besides, he's got errands to run." Raggu said waving a hand at Wally to leave.

"I do?" Wally stood looking puzzled about what errand he had to run.

"Yeah, you do!" Snapped Raggu "Coffee, black, pronto!"

Wally nodded and smiled at Rogan before leaving the room.

Rogan sat down next to Raggu and, Raggu adjusted his rotund frame on the chair to face him. He smiled around his cigar and Rogan thought that the speech was coming to try and change his mind, that the company needed him and they couldn't do without him. That speech never came. He snubbed out his cigar in a glass ashtray that sat next to him on the table.

"Okay, Randy!" he smiled at him, it was a gentle smile. A look that he had never seen on his face before. For the first time in twenty years, Rogan felt like the real Louis Raggu was sitting in front of him. Not the conman promoter everyone perceived him to be or the persona of a hard ass that he allowed people to see.

"So, what would you like to do? How do you want to go out?" He asked softly.

Rogan was taken aback and didn't quite know how to process this kind and caring, Louis Raggu. This was obviously why he wanted Wally to leave the room, not even he had seen this side of him.

"You're asking me?" Rogan finally said.

"Of course!" Raggu laughed "It's your career after all."

"Well, I..." Rogan laughed "I hadn't thought of it! I thought you were going to try and talk me out of it!"

"Don't get me wrong, I'm devastated! I'd love you to stay." He scoffed holding his hands in the air. "You're the biggest draw I've ever known in this business! I'd be a fool to want you to go anywhere!"

"Then why let me?"

"I'm not a complete bastard, Randy." He chuckled "Although some might believe that. It's your life and I get that you've had enough and want to go and spend the rest of your life with your family and watch that little scamp of yours grow up. You've worked damn hard over the years to not only reach the top, but to stay there for so long. It's unheard of really. And to go out while you're still on top? Well, that's what dreams are made of!"

"Wow! I assumed this conversation was going to be totally different." Rogan laughed.

"Never assume anything in this business, Champ!" Raggu winked and smiled again.

"Ain't that the truth!"

"You're welcome to talk yourself into staying if you wish!" Raggu laughed again "But, going out while you've still got all your faculties and the fact that you're still the champion means that's how you'll always be remembered by the fans. Not one of those poor bastards that keep going and going until people see them as washed up has-beens! It tarnishes their legacy. This way you'll always be the champion in people's eyes." Rogan smiled at him, he felt every word Raggu had said.

"But how do you want to go out?"

"I don't know. Obviously drop the title..."

"Yes, A true champion going out on your back." Raggu laughed and again which this time turned into a coughing fit.

"Fucking cigars!" He moaned before getting back on track with the conversation "I want to give back to you for everything you've given me, Randy."

"Well, thank you!"

"You're gonna work tonight against The Masked Mandrill..." Raggu stopped himself mid sentence when he saw the look on Rogan's face "Something wrong? Have you got heat with Mandrillus?"

"Oh, no! No, not at all! I just thought that tonight I could try something a little different?"

"Okay!" nodded Raggu leaning back in his chair "Shoot!"

"I want to work Dr X!"

"Glen?" Raggu yelled almost toppling from his chair.

"Yeah!"

"Why on earth would you..."

"I want to give back. I think the reason he has never gotten anywhere is that nobody has ever taken the time help him."

"I guess you're right." Raggu nodded "Okay, you've got Dr X in the main and God help you!"

"I'm certain I can help him be something."

"Hey, you go for it! Knock yourself out!If you can get a match out of him, that may go down as your greatest accomplishment in professional wrestling."

They both laughed.

"I'll take that challenge!" Rogan grinned smugly.

"Okay so Dr X tonight, and that's it?"

"What do you mean that's it?"

"You can finish up Friday in Studd City."

"What about the rest of the days? I thought it was New Jersey, Memphis, then a double header in Studd?"

"It is."

"I don't understand?"

"I'm giving you these few extra days to spend with your family. It's Spring Break! Go away for a few days or something."

"Are you sure about that?"

"Yes, of course I am. It'll give me a few shows to put an angle together so that we can take the strap off you in Studd on Friday."

Rogan leant back in his chair shaking his head in disbelief, he actually felt a little emotional that he had made such an impact on somebody that they would want to treat him so well and show him so much respect.

"That means a lot to me, Louis. That you've been so gracious about this. I hope me being the champion doesn't cause you too much of a headache about who to put it on and such." Rogan said as he stood up and held out his hand for Raggu to shake.

"Sit back down." He said still smiling "Wanna help me out with it?"

"Me? But, I've never booked anything in my life!" Rogan replied slowly lowering himself back down into his seat.

"You're too modest, Randy. Almost 40 years in this business and you've been at the top for the majority of it. You know a thing or two, believe me!"

"Okay." Rogan nodded. "What do you wanna do?"

"I think we both know by now that The Slammer is the next guy."

"Yeah!" Rogan agreed, with a gentle nod of his head.

"I know he can be a bit of a live wire!" Raggu announced holding his hands up like he's taking the blame for it "But, I'm confident I can mould him into the face of the company."

"Okay." Rogan nods again "So, me versus Slammer in Studd? Passing the torch?"

"No! Not so fast! You know the deal. The money is in the chase. I need it on a heel."

"Right, okay. How about Kami?"

"No disrespect meant, but, I don't want to flog a dead horse."

"Ouch!" Rogan laughed.

"You guys have had your feud for the past twenty years! It's time for some fresh blood."

"So who do you have in mind?"

"Johnny."

Rogan thought about it for a moment. It did make sense as the people would pay good money to see a despicable heel lose the title, especially if it's The Slammer chasing him for it.

"Okay. No problem!" Rogan nods.

"Great! I've got three shows to get Johnny in place to be number one contender. Any thoughts?"

"I'd have him go over tonight and tomorrow."

"Agreed."

"Who is he working?"

"Tonight it is Yellow Feather, and tomorrow it was supposed to be Ace, but he's erm... missing in action. And to be honest I don't think we'll see him again."

"Why? What's happened?" Rogan asked.

"Have you not seen the internet?"

"No, I have it on my cell phone, but to be honest I don't know what I'm doing with the blasted thing!" he laughs, slightly embarrassed that modern technology is whizzing passed him so fast.

"Here, let me show you." Raggu sniggers, and slides his touch screen cell phone off the table and taps away at it with his stubby index finger. "These photographs have been leaked online and now they're all over the place!"

Raggu turns the phone around and Rogan leans in to let his weary squinted eyes focus and there, is an image of Ace Armstrong completely naked on all fours, with a gigantic dildo hanging out of his ass, while a red headed mistress whips him.

"Shit!" Rogan gasped, his eyes like saucers.

"Yeah!" Raggu shook his head, a mixture of annoyance and hilarity about the whole situation duking it out on his face, the one minute he's grimacing, the next he's holding back sniggers. "So, yeah, safe to say, we won't be seeing him again."
There is an awkward silence for a moment, none of them wanting to talk about what they'd just seen.

"Right, so I was thinking, I've got Clayton Tex coming in and they could work tomorrow night."

"Sure! Tonight I'd have Mr Canada distract Yellow Feather and Johnny can roll him up. He gets the win and Yellow Feather isn't effected by the loss too much, because it was shenanigans."

"Plus, it helps build the Canada/Feather feud over the United States title." Nods Raggu in agreement "I like it!"

"Then have him beat Tex…"

"Clean?"

"Yeah, I think so. Clean win will give him that bit of credibility and they'll take him seriously."

"I was thinking about a Battle Royal? Have the winner become the number one contender?"

"Good idea!" Rogan agrees.

"Then give him another high profile win before he faces you?"

"Sounds good to me." Rogan nods.

The pair smile at each other, respect for each other etched on their faces.

"Thank you for everything, Randy. It's been a pleasure working with you." Raggu says sincerely while placing a hand on his shoulder.

"They didn't have any coffee, so I got you tea!" Wally announced bursting into the room.

"Fuck and damn it, Wally!" Growled Raggu "Don't you ever fucking knock!" And with that, the Raggu that everyone knew and nobody loved was back. As Wally waddled back to his seat with hot cups of tea, Raggu slyly winked at Rogan. Rogan smiled shaking his head.

He's the biggest work in the business. The son of a bitch is working everybody!

CHAPTER 25

"...Epic battle in this contest between two big fan favourites!" Comes the over enthusiastic and dramatic tones of Milton McQueen.

"You can say that again, McQueen! It's an irresistible force meeting an immovable object!" Yells Bunk 'The Hunk' emphasising to the people watching at home what a clash of titans this match is.

Billy Bronx lays in on The Slammer with several clubbing forearms to his broad trapezius area, the sound of muscular flesh meeting like a piece of rump steak hitting a butchers chopping block.

"I'll give you a few more then start your comeback." Bronx murmurs.

The Slammer pulls himself back onto all fours and nods.

The crowd roar for The Slammer, his name chanted over and over again in unison. Any calls for Billy Bronx are consumed and muted. Billy takes the time to look around at the crowd, playing up to it like it's getting to him that they're not chanting for him.

"Damn, Joe! You're fucking over like rover!" Bronx says, subtly shaking his head in disbelief, he had never witnessed the crowd get behind anyone like this before. With Billy's attention not fully focused on the matter in hand he clubs the rising Slammer again, but the timing was off and as Slammer turned his head to see where Bronx was he is met in the face by a flailing elbow.

"Whoa!" Bronx cries "Sorry man!" he follows up with a whisper as he goes to grab Slammer's head.

Blood drips from The Slammer's nostrils and splatters the canvas below him, he stares at the mat that soaks up the blood as it rains down recklessly.

"Are you okay, Joe?" Referee Kenny asks in a concerned manner, but The Slammer doesn't answer, he's now transfixed by the blood. It seems to drip in slow motion now, every drop sounds like a gunshot as it hits the mat and merges with the rest of it to create an ever changing Rorschach test before his eyes.

Then the redness consumed him.

He rises snarling like some deranged creature from the bowels of hell, blood mixed with saliva flicking out from the gaps in his gritting teeth.

He stares at Bronx, who looks frozen and static.

"Joe? Are you okay, man?" Bronx asks and throws some meaty forearms into Slammer's massive chest, but he doesn't register Bronx's question or his blows and skulks towards him almost stalking him.

Bronx tries to talk to him, he can see that he has a faraway look in his eye and it scares him, but Slammer can no longer hear his voice, nor the thousands in attendance cheering his name. All he hears is the blood falling from him and pounding on the canvas.

"Best just go home, boys!" Says Kenny trying to get in-between them but is just brushed aside by the massive bulk of The Slammer.

"Yeah, let's take it home, Joe!" Bronx murmurs as he approaches him and is met by a legit kick in the gut, the force causes Bronx to immediately double over in pain.

"What the...Joe? What're you..." Kenny says trying to grab at The Slammer's bulging bicep in an attempt to pull him back. The Slammer swiftly turns and looks at Kenny. There must have been something that terrified Kenny because he immediately let go and backed off slowly. He watched on powerless as The Slammer thrust Bronx's head between his thighs hooking him around the waist, amazingly hoisting the hefty frame of Billy Bronx with sheer animalistic strength, Bronx was not ready for the manoeuvre (which happened to be a devastating Power Bomb) and was not positioned correctly to safely take the move. The Slammer held him up in the air before driving him down to the canvas, the aim normally to bring the opponent down on their backs and safely bump the move. But, this was neither thought out nor safe, and Bronx was driven down to the mat unceremoniously onto his neck. There was a sickening crunching and cracking sound as Bronx was folded up, all his weight coming down on his neck.

"Oh shit, Joe! What the fuck have you done!" Yelled Kenny as he slid down to the side of Bronx who lay motionless on the canvas.

The Slammer stood over him, breathing heavily as the crowd shouted 'Slammer Time' (The name that had been given to his finishing manoeuvre), for they did not know that this wasn't all just part of the show.

The Slammer started to shake off whatever it was that had burrowed into his brain and made him do these things, and looked down at the prone body of Billy Bronx who had tears in his eyes, unable to move. Everything was moving in slow motion again, Kenny's arms were flung up into an 'X' to indicate to the backstage area that there was indeed a legitimate injury and straight away the medical team came rushing down towards the ring with Wally in hot pursuit.

"What have you done?" Wally screamed at The Slammer as he knelt by Billy's side and held his hand.

The Slammer had no answer, as he had no memory of what had taken place. He turned on the spot and looked at the crowd, the majority of them still cheering his name, except for the fans that were smartened up, they knew something was wrong and focused concern towards poor Billy Bronx.

"Kenny! Get him the hell out of here, before they turn on him!" Wally said and Kenny herded the zombified Slammer out of the ring.

As The Slammer staggered back towards the curtain, a stretcher was wheeled passed him. He turned to follow the stretcher and looked at Bronx still motionless in the ring, a brace being wrapped carefully around his neck.

"What have you done?" He murmured before he felt the nudge in the back from Kenny to move along. He looked down at his white boots, the toe ends stained with a dusting of his own blood, he felt like throwing up.

Five minutes later that's exactly what he did.

CHAPTER 26

From the Diary of Randall Rogan

Tuesday, April 23nd.
Home. Long Island, New York.

I had to feel for Glen tonight, stood there behind the curtain, shaking like a shitting dog. But, I tell you something, the bastard nailed it! He was obviously nervous and you could see he wasn't comfortable in the mask, but I gave him another few words of encouragement before he left for the ring. I basically took full responsibility for the match, to lift off any pressure that was resting on his shoulders. Hell, I am the veteran here, I should be able to take guys like this and have a great match.

I know Raggu wasn't convinced and this was probably Glen's last chance, if this didn't get over then he'd probably be getting the future endeavours speech. Raggu was that dubious of Glen in the Dr X gimmick that he'd actually set up some plants at ringside to lead the booing, but you know what? That little bastard never needed them. As soon as the fans saw that Dr X mask they erupted with a mass of heckles and jeers. It worked, I knew it would, but there was the matter of the in ring work.

I did have to lead him around the ring a few times, but he got it, he followed instructions. I was really pleased to see him take on the character and make it his own. He skulked around the ring and everything was slow and methodical, just what the character needed to be. I basically moved myself into positions like a true professional most of the time to see what he did, he got it. The old tricks like choking on the ropes and such, really gets the heat from the crowd. But, yeah he did good and I think it saved him his job. I just hope for his sake that he can take the little nuggets I've given him and learn to use them in other matches with other workers who may not be as accommodating as me.

It's too bad about Billy. A really great guy and doesn't deserve that to happen to him, nobody really deserves that. His career is over. A broken neck.
It would really make me think twice about putting The Slammer in that top spot if I was in Raggu's shoes.

It's good to be home and in my own bed tonight... Couple of days with the family now before I head to Studd City for my last match... Those words 'Last match' send shivers down my spine... wow!

Forgive me for I'm leaving you here while I go and make love to my wife.

CHAPTER 27

Mark Schroeder anxiously hurried through the crowded streets of New York City. He ignored the pungent smell of sewage that rose up out of the drains. He ignored the mass of people standing in his way by barging past them, almost knocking several pedestrians over with his round frame and his oversized rucksack that was stuck to his back, making him resemble a giant tortoise. He ignored their yelling and curse words. He ignored the loud droning sound of car engines that rolled along slowly, almost fender to fender. He ignored the obnoxious horn blowing from the impatient drivers and amazingly he managed to ignore the tempting smells wafting from the chilli dog cart on the corner of 8th Avenue and West 33rd Street.

He ignored everything around him because he was excited to get his greasy digits on the latest issue of pro wrestling magazine, Pro Wrestling FIRE.

Mark knew that there was only one particular newsstand that sold it in New York. Many wrestling magazines had now gone out of circulation with the rise in popularity of the internet and the majority of fans went there for their wrestling news. Mark was old school and preferred to feel the pages between his fingertips, the smell of the ink. It was the nostalgia more than anything and this was a way of keeping that nostalgia and those memories of his childhood alive. He can still remember going into the store when he was a child with his mother and buying his first wrestling magazine, in 1990. He remembers fondly the article about Curt Hennig's feud with Kerry Von Erich. He'd collected them ever since.

Finally after an exhausting thirty minute walk he finally laid eyes on the newsstand sitting just outside Central Park on West 59th Street. He smiled and waddled quickly towards it.

It took him a few seconds to catch his breath, he was very obese and that jaunt had really taken it out of him.

The old man behind the newsstand stared at him waiting for him to speak. Mark's face shone from the sweat that dripped down his face and matted his hair.

"Can I get ya something?" The man finally said, out of curiosity more than anything.

"A copy of FIRE!" Mark panted and he held out a crumpled and now slightly damp five dollar bill.

"The what now?" The man replied, looking bewildered at Mark's request, his wispy grey eyebrows rising up his wrinkling bald head.

Mark sighed "The wrestling mag?" He said scoffing immaturely, almost arrogantly like the man should know what it is.

"Oh!" The man chuckled.

He took the money and handed over the magazine, the cover of it presenting Megan Powers, with the headline 'Powers leads the revolution'.

"Ain't you bit old for that now?" The man asked and was met by burning eyes through his chubby and greasy face.

"You know it's all fake don't you?" The man added and Mark could feel his blood boiling. He was about to erupt when something caught his eye. It was Randy Rogan's face on the front cover of The Times. A passport sized photo of Rogan in the top corner, it's amazing that he saw it at all. The words 'Thank You Randy' in blocked font underneath it.

"What?" Mark said to himself, the old man held out Mark's change in his hand and looked bemused again at him.

"You okay?"

"Yeah!" Mark finally said, his boiling blood simmering now and his brain twitched with intrigue "Keep the change. I'll take a copy of The Times too."

The man passed over a copy of the newspaper and laughed "To be honest, there's probably more real news in your wrestling magazine!"

Mark ignored him and walked away with the magazine rolled under his arm, hastily trying to open the newspaper up to see why his wrestling hero was on the front page.

"Page twenty, page twenty..." He chanted as his fat fingers struggled to sweep through the pages. Finally he arrived at the double page spread that had a huge picture of Randy Rogan draped in the American flag. Pictures of lots of other wrestlers giving a tribute and a few words about him and his career and then he saw the words, 'Randy Rogan Retires' in massive bold letters.

"No!" Mark murmured, his bottom lip quivering and his eyes glazing with inevitable tears. He read the words again in his head, each word felt like it was being stamped out before him.

"No, no, no, no!" He growled and scrunched up the newspaper in his angry grip. He stood in the middle of New York City and scrunched up the paper in his hands and screamed at the top of his lungs. Tears cascaded down his round face as onlookers glanced at him like he was crazy, and then went about their daily routines without another thought about it, this was New York City after all.

He must have zoned out because he came to on his knees on the sidewalk with a police officer standing over him.

"Hey! I said are you okay? Because if you're a loon, I'm gonna have to take you in." The officer said.

"Huh?" Mark said looking up at the officer and then down at the newspaper.

"No, I'm fine, just had some bad news that's all."

"Then move it along. This ain't no place to be having no breakdown."

"Yes, Sir!" Mark said and gathered up the scrunched up newspaper and pulled himself up to his feet before scuttling off down the sidewalk and through the West Drive entrance to Central Park. As he entered the park he glanced over his shoulder to make sure the cop had moved on, he had indeed, he had bigger fish to fry.

Mark found a bench and dropped on it unceremoniously.

He was immediately surrounded by pigeons who obviously thought that maybe some brunch was in their   future, they thought wrong. He placed the newspaper and magazine on the bench next to him and struggled to take off his bulging rucksack.

"I can't believe this, I can't believe this!" He said over and over again, flustered as he finally successfully removed the rucksack and then dropped it to the floor. The pigeons dispersed, frightened by the discarded bag and flew away leaving Mark in peace.

"I won't believe this. It must be a mistake! It has to be!" he snivelled, opening the newspaper once again out in front of him. His eyes flitted everywhere at once and then settled on the small photograph of 'The Korean Kraken' Kami Kajeu and through glazed eyes he read on.

RANDY ROGAN RETIRES!

FELLOW WRESTLERS SHARE THEIR THOUGHTS ON A 35 YEAR CAREER

ARTICLE BY SAL EVERS

Kami Kajeu.

"I have been one of the most successful villains in professional wrestling history. But, my legacy in the history books should have an asterisk by my name, because I would never have reached the heights I did without having Randy there to play the fly in my ointment."

Rhino Brother, Stomp.

"I came into this business idolising Randy Rogan, to me he was everything pro wrestling was supposed to be. I had the chance to work with him once, a small show out in the sticks in

Hope Springs. I'd been wrestling a few years, thought I knew the lay of the land, you know? Well, in one match with Rogan it opened my eyes even further. He taught me more in that one match than I had learnt in three years prior!"

The Slammer.

"Randy is the greatest wrestler to ever step foot in the squared circle and anybody that says different can meet me outside!"

El Corazon De Plata.

"I first met Randy on the loop in Mexico, such a true gentleman and a professional. He will be sorely missed by the wrestling industry."

'Magnificent' Johnny Midnight.

"Let's face it, he's the reason we're all here."

Megan Powers.

"I had the pleasure of tagging with him numerous times. A true great and his presence and leadership will be missed."

Sebastian Churchill.

"A lifelong friend, and you can't say that about many in this business. In the wrestling business everybody wants to take, all he wanted to do was give. There is a reason he has had such a long distinguished career because his passion for what he did set him apart from everyone else. I'm going to miss him on the road, he is like the brother I never had."

'Big' Bella Marie.

"Goddamn! What a legend!"

Jungle Jim.

"I've never met anyone in this business like Randy, and I don't think I ever will meet anyone like him again. A true general, a true professional!"

Devastation Member, Famine.

"Hell, will anyone ever reach the heights he has? Highly unlikely! To be on top for that long... Nobody is ever gonna top that."

Clayton Tex.

"The guy is an icon. He has surpassed all his predecessors achievements and will leave behind an illustrious legacy."

Puma Kid.

"I'm so choked up right now. He was my hero and I'm not afraid to say that. To see him walk away is gut wrenching. I think it will leave a void in wrestling itself that will be very difficult to fill. I'm just sad that I never got to share the ring with him."

Pedro Passion.

"It's come as a shock to us all I think. I just can't remember a time when he wasn't here!"

Sunset Glen.

"Thank you, Randy. For everything!"

Tears spilt from Mark's eyes and speckled the paper in his lap, causing the ink to become wet and smudged.

"I don't believe this is happening!" he sobbed "What about me, Randy? What about your fans? The people that depend on you?"

He took out his cellphone from his pocket, and ancient looking touch button device with a tiny screen. He held the star key and it unlocked. The screen indicated to him that he'd had 86 missed calls from his Mother. He wanted to call her back and tell her how he felt, maybe he should call her back and tell her that he is actually still alive, it had been three months after all. But their last meeting didn't end well, how dare she tell him that watching all this wrestling bullshit was gonna cook his brain and he'd never get a wife or a job living in the basement with his face glued to the television day and night. He decided not to call her and slotted the cell back into his coat pocket.

"Fucking Bitch! What does she know anyway?" He seethed.

When she called them all a bunch of fakers was the last straw, and Mark left to follow the circus that is Professional Wrestling around the United States. Sleeping in street corners, benches and burnt out cars, just so he could follow his heroes, well, his hero, Randy Rogan.

"What will I do now?" He cried openly, unconcerned about the odd looks he was receiving by passersby. He looked down at the newspaper article again and at the end of the article it read 'Randy Rogan's last match will be in Studd City at the Patera Sports Arena this Friday, where he will defend his World Heavyweight Championship against the number one contender that has yet to be named. To witness Randy Rogan's last match contact...'

Mark looked up and wiped the tears from his doughy face "I've got to get to Studd City!" he sniffed.

CHAPTER 28

"...A special Tag Team attraction match tonight here in New Jersey and the crowd are loving every minute of it!" Milton McQueen yells into the microphone of his headset, trying to make himself heard over the roar of the crowd.

"These people are going bananas!" Bunk 'The Hunk' adds.

"Yellow Feather nailed Mr Canada with that Enzuigiri to the back of his head and they're both down! The referee starts the count, he's up to 5..."

"They're starting to stir, McQueen!"

"Yellow Feather is crawling towards his corner, looking to tag his partner The Slammer."

"But, don't count out Mr Canada, he's almost within reaching distance of Johnny Midnight!"

"The race is on!" McQueen shouts enthusiastically, building the drama for the inevitable hot tag.

"Look at Slammer! He's like a caged animal on that apron! He's chomping at the bit to get in there!" Bunk screams.

"And there's the tag!" Milton McQueen emphasises the importance of it by going up an octave "And here comes The Slammer!"

"But here comes Midnight too!"

"The crowd have erupted here! As The Slammer bounds into the ring, he ploughs down Midnight with a shoulder tackle!"

"But Midnight is straight back up and..." Bunk says before he is cut off by McQueen.

"Oh! He is met by a hefty lariat from The Slammer!"

"But Midnight is up again..."

"But, he's staggering all over the place, Bunk. That big clothesline rang his bell!"

"I'm glad I retired!" Chuckled Bunk.

"Look at this!" McQueen gasped in awe "The Slammer is hoisting Midnight up over his head and military pressing him!"

"Holy Cow!"

"Oh, but here comes Mr Canada again to break it up!" McQueen's tone lowers and sounds as disappointed as the crowd, they show their displeasure with a chorus of boos and McQueen continues again "The people of New Jersey did not like that, one iota! Now both of them are going to work on The Slammer."

"Wait a minute Yellow Feather is climbing up to the top rope!" Bunk yells again as if to turn the attention away from the beat down "Midnight has spotted him." Bunk laughs, rooting as always for the bad guys.

"But it's too late!" Screams McQueen "And Yellow Feather nails him with a big Missile Dropkick and Midnight hits the mat!"

"Mr Canada sees Yellow Feather though and charges him..."

"Oh! But Yellow Feather saw him coming and a big body Backdrop over the top rope and to the outside!"

"Looks like the United States champ took a nasty bump."

"Yellow Feather is saying something to The Slammer."

"Maybe he's asking if he's okay. You know how they say that don't you?" Bunk pauses for dramatic effect "Hey how are ya, hey how are ya!" He chants.

"Would you please stop!" McQueen spits.

"The Slammer is smiling and nodding at something here...What's happening... Wait, he's hoisting up Yellow Feather over his head!" McQueen gasps.

"He's gonna launch him onto Mr Canada!"

"Oh my God!" McQueen screams matching the crowd as The Slammer launches his own partner over the top rope and out on top of Mr Canada. "What a great show of teamwork and creativity there..."

"Look out, McQueen!" Bunk sneers "Slammer is too busy showboating and doesn't see Midnight."

"Midnight sneaks up as his back is turned and... no!"

"Rolls him up!"

"One, Two... He's got a handful of tights!" Growls McQueen seemingly not impressed with the rule breaking.

"Three, Yes!" Bunk screams "He did it! Midnight pinned The Slammer!"

"Midnight just got in Slammer's face and said something to him." McQueen states "And whatever he said has not gone down well with the big man. He's being restrained by the referee and his own partner!"

"Mr Canada and Johnny Midnight are all smiles as they make their way back down the aisle."

"The Slammer is not happy."

"Can you blame him?" McQueen yells.

"You're spitting on me, man! Sheesh!"

Backstage behind the curtain Mr Canada and Johnny Midnight shake hands and catch their breath.

Raggu arrives all smiles chewing on yet another cheap cigar, closely followed by Wally, drawing a line through something on his clipboard.

"Great Match, Boys! Really good stuff!" Raggu scoffs patting them both on the backs before recoiling from the sweat that was now on his palms "Yeah, just what I wanted!" he added wiping his moist hands on Wally's shirt.

"Glad you liked it, Mr Raggu." Johnny said wiping hair away from his face.

"Please! It's Louis! Call me Louis!" Raggu slithers like a snake and coils an arm around his shoulders leading him away from Mr Canada, who looked on a little dejected like he'd had nothing to do with the match.

"Yeah, Louis, sure!" Johnny shrugged nonchalantly.

"You wanna know something, kid?" Raggu whispers.

"What's that?"

"You're gonna take..."

"What the fuck is your problem, faggot!" Screamed Slammer bursting through the curtain, Yellow Feather in hot pursuit and trying to pull the gargantuan back, but soon losing interest when he was pushed aside.

"What is your problem?" He asked Johnny again, walking up to him and ripping his mask off.

"Let's calm the fuck down!" Raggu yelled standing between them "What is this all about?"

"That little shit, keeps fucking with me! Saying shit to me in the ring..."

"Oh, quit your whining! You Momma's boy!" Johnny laughed.

"You little Fuck!" Growled The Slammer and lunged for him, arms stretching out as if he was going to ring his neck. Everyone who was backstage at the time steps in between him and Yellow Feather, Mr Canada and Wally hold The Slammer back.

"You're a dumb fuck!" Johnny shouts smiling at him, antagonising him more and more.

"Right, enough!" Raggu shouts and there is finally silence and The Slammer stops struggling "I'm sick of all this bullshit! What is this, high school?" He asks, there is no reply.

"Look, if you guys don't realise that you two together are money then you're bigger idiots than you look!"

"Hey, it's not me, it's..." Johnny tries to speak but is cut off by Raggu again.

"Shut up! You're just as bad for poking the fire!"
He turns his attentions to The Slammer "You have the world at your feet, Joe! You're a fool if you throw it away now! You're skating on thin ice as it is with what you've been pulling lately!"

The Slammer attempted to speak and then realises there is no point, he knows he is damn lucky to still have a job.

"You guys don't realise that I can make and break any of you! I could pick two new guys right now and make them instead if that's what you want! Is that what you want? Or do you want to make some money? Some real fucking money?"
He is met by nods from the two, both of them now annoyed at themselves for having to agree with the other.

"Right! Good!" Raggu says calming himself and sucks on the cigar for a few seconds.

"Right, this Friday in Studd! Against Rogan for the strap..." He suddenly announces.
There is a pause while everyone sucks in air and seems like they are all holding it in, scared to breathe out incase they miss something.

"Johnny! You're going over!" Raggu declared before walking away leaving everyone looking around at each other gobsmacked.
Johnny smiles a wry smile and winks at The Slammer.

CHAPTER 29

From The Diary of Randall Rogan

Wednesday, April 24th
Home. Long Island, New York.

It felt great to be woken up by my little champ today. Although his methods leave a lot to be desired. Jumping up and down on my head shouting 'Wake up, Daddy, wake up!' isn't the most subtle of alarm clocks. But, I wouldn't change it for the world.

Martha and I made love last night, it was like we were teenagers again, there has only ever been one woman for me, she's everything I need and want. I love her so much. Maybe when I'm all done and settled I'll take her away to Hawaii, we never really had a honeymoon as I was always on the road. Come to think of it I can't remember the last time she had a vacation and she deserves one. I can organise it all and drop it on her, she'll like that. I may even organise renewing our wedding vows on the beach... Yeah that would be really nice, I think she would appreciate that. In some ways it will be very fitting as it's like I'm starting my life again, so why not!
They say that news travels fast, well, that saying is definitely true in pro wrestling. I've already been bombarded with phone

calls, text messages and emails from people either sending me their best wishes or trying to book me for interviews or appearances. By the look of the article in the New York Times it would appear that Raggu let the cat out of the bag. I get it he's a business man, cashing in on my story, It just would have been nice to be the one that dropped the news.

I watched the show last night. All the guys and girls pulled it out of the bag, proof that we are just cogs and they no longer need me. Time to spend some time with the family now for a few days while the gang hits Memphis and then Studd for back to back shows on the Thursday and Friday. I'll meet up with them on the Friday, for the last time.

Life is changing, changing for the better.

CHAPTER 30

The sound system of the Porteau Palace in Memphis echoed through the old building, indicating that the evenings show had indeed started. The broom closet muted the blaring sound of eighties rock music, as Miss Crystal sat on an upturned mop bucket staring longingly at the illuminated screen of her cell phone.

The smell of cleaning products frustrated her nostrils, causing them to twitch rapidly. She didn't dislike the aroma, she was used to it now as a janitors closet or broom closet was a regular meeting place for her and Johnny's shenanigans. The smells conjured pleasant memories of orgasmic pleasure.

"Where the hell is he?" She sulked as she tapped out a text message with her heavily manicured nails attacking the screen like a flurry of pecking beaks.

The reply comes quickly, short and sweet reading 'I'm not coming' the name above the message, Johnny.

"Fuck!" she growls, her normally beautiful face contorting unattractively.

"You're not messing me around, Mr Midnight!"

She rings his number, her face glowing with annoyance waiting as the phone rings out.

"What's up?" Comes the nonchalant answer from Johnny Midnight.

"'What's up!' What do you thinks fucking up?" She shouts down the phone "I've been waiting for you for the last hour!"

"Yeah, I can't make it, Im busy."

"Busy? I'm sitting on a fucking bucket in a dirty old broom closet waiting for you! So get your ass here now!"

There was a pause for a moment and he didn't answer.

"Hello?"

Nothing.

"Johnny! Don't ignore me!" She sighed "Please talk to me. Why are you being so distant?"

Johnny sighed and then said, "Look, it's been fun but it's over now. I'm moving up in the world and I don't need the excess baggage."

Crystal sat shocked, tears welling up and then falling down her cheeks, mascara merging with the tears and slicing her face with two lines of black.

"But..." She tried to speak, but she choked on something rising up into her throat, it felt like her heart.

"I've made up my mind. We're done." He said finally and hung up the phone. She dropped her cell phone to the floor below, the hard floor chipping away at a corner of it, she didn't care.

The three year affair flashed before her eyes, mental images from their time together filled her minds eye, two perfect forms writhing together in a contorted dance of passion and sin. She already felt guilt because of the whole sordid ordeal, but Johnny had become like a drug to her, she couldn't do without him.

Now, he was gone and she was left with sadness, anger and self pity to join her overwhelming burden of guilt. The light from the phone's screen died, shrouding her in total darkness as she sobbed her heart out.

CHAPTER 31

"Ladies and Gentlemen! It is now time for the main event of the evening!" Crowed Waylon 'The Voice' Voight as he stood in the glowing spotlight with microphone in hand, his unmistakable succulent voice rippling in waves. There was a flurry of cheers throughout the crowd at the announcement and anticipation grew, all of them wondering what will be announced.

"The next match will be a twenty man over the top rope Battle Royale!" Voight growled emphatically. His enthusiasm was met with a lukewarm reaction, many younger people in the audience cheered, they knew that this meant that they would get to see twenty wrestlers all battling it out in the ring at the same time, which was obviously an impressive sight to behold, especially for the eyes of youth. For those who groaned at the announcement it meant the mundane paint by numbers style attraction that they had become so accustomed too, and most of them only felt that it was exciting when it got down to the final four.

"Twenty men will start in the ring." Voight continued "When a wrestler is thrown over the top rope and both feet touch the floor, he is eliminated!"

The crowd caboshed this announcement with no real reaction at all, some had already left at the announcement of a Battle Royale to examine what drag ends remained at the concession stand.

Voight's next announcement stopped many of the naysayers in mid gripe.

"The winner of the match will become, The Number One Contender to The World Heavyweight Championship!" He bellowed and that was met by a cheer from the crowd.

Many hurried back to their seats, they now realised that this match had meaning and wasn't just a throw away match.

"And!" Voight said loudly, interrupting the stirring crowd as they hurried to put their point across to their friends who they thought could be the winner. "The winner will take on World Heavyweight Champion, Randy Rogan, this Friday in Studd City!"

The crowd erupted. Now they were truly invested and potentially about to see the next champion begin his journey to greatness. The news had obviously been out now that Rogan was indeed retiring and that the show in Studd City would be his farewell match. The majority who were smart to the wrestling business knew he would be dropping the belt to whoever won this match. The age-old tradition being upheld by Rogan and going out on his back when his time had come. It made sense that the retiring or leaving wrestler was no longer going to be there and didn't need the win. But the challenger would still be there and a win could help build that particular character.

There are exceptions to the rule, but nine times out of ten this is the way it ends. The promotion will still try to push and tell you that the champion will want to go out on top and with the title, allowing them to forfeit it later on, but the majority will indeed believe that the challenger will take the title.

"Here are the competitors!" Voight purred again as generic eighties rock music came blurting out of the speakers and the curtain began to twitch.

Behind the curtain twenty eager wrestlers stretched and waited for their names to be announced. Raggu stood underneath a piece of paper tacked to the wall, which contained the relevant information that the wrestler needed to know.

BATTLE ROYAL

~~BILLY BRONX~~ CLAYTON TEX
ROXY HORROR
PUMA KID
KRONG
YELLOW FEATHER
SEBASTIAN CHURCHILL
EL CORAZON DE PLATA
THE MASKED MANDRILL
FIRECRACKERS
BELFAST BRAWLER
~~ACE ARMSTRONG~~ DR X
ACE IS A BUMMER!
RHINO BROS.
KAMI KAJEU
MR CANADA

FINAL FOUR: SLAMMER, MIDNIGHT, PASSION, JIM

SLAMMER & MIDNIGHT DRAW. 20 MINS

"Right boys, don't fuck this one up. Joe and Johnny, you are the last two. Do not go over the side that faces the hard cam. Do you understand?"

Johnny nods as he slots a piece of gum into his mouth and starts to chew on it, The Slammer answers "Yeah, sure" shrugging as he slides his bulbous cranium into a new silver mask, dotted with blue and red stars, his old one still covered in blood from his last match.

"I mean it boys, you can't fuck this up. You're going over the top simultaneously, it's gotta look like you're both hitting the floor at the same time. We have free roaming cameras round there so we can choose which angles to show, but the hard cam side will expose it if it doesn't go to plan."

They nod again at Raggu to indicate they do indeed understand.

"Good! The rest of you, do what the hell you like!" Raggu says walking away.

"Guys! We're stealing Ace's finish tonight!" Yells Stomp with a playful snigger. Everyone turns their attentions to Stomp who has his partner Tusk bent over in front of him simulating that he is penetrating him from behind. A large rubber ball clasped in Tusk's mouth and a crosseyed expression on his face, as Stomp vigorously thrusts his pelvis into his rear.

Everyone erupted into hysterics as the introductions start.

"Introducing first!" Voight announces, and the human adonis that is Jungle Jim leaps through the curtain and lands in a crouching position, clad only in his loin cloth and animal tooth necklace while looking around, almost surveying the crowd.

"From the deepest darkest jungles of Buenos Aires... Jungle Jim!"

The crowd fondly cheer for Jim and he makes his way down the aisle to the ring.

"Next up we have hailing from Paradise City, Las Vegas, Nevada!"

Pedro Passion arrogantly sashays through the curtain blowing kisses to nobody in particular. His purple trunks plastered with templates of red lips and his sleek physique slathered in a layer of baby oil.

"Pedro..." with massive emphasis on the o "Passion!"

The crowd serenade him with boos, some cheers from Smarks leak through, longing to see Pedro turn Babyface.

"From Austin, Texas... Clayton Tex!"

Clayton Tex jogs out from behind the curtain, clad in tight denims and slick tan cowboy boots, waving his cowboy hat in the air with a rambunctious cry of 'YEE HA!' The crowd responding with a minor cheer, having not really seen too much of him in their territory before.

"From Tran..." Voight purrs in a more lower sultry tone "...Sylvania! 'The Time Warped Treasure' Roxy Horror!"

Roxy Horror provocatively struts down the aisle, a strange sight of a man with a chiselled physique, shaved head and hairy torso clad in fishnet stockings, suspenders, corset and long velvet evening gloves. His face heavily made up, lips pouting surrounded by a heavy five o'clock shadow.

The crowd attack him with a showering of abuse and jeers. Some Southern states still not ready for such a character or lifestyle.

"From Parts Unknown, Puma Kid!"

He launches himself out from the curtain to rising cheers, his small frame springing up and down like he was a living breathing pogo stick. His turquoise and silver sequinned mask resembled that of a jungle cats in it design, pointed teeth hanging over the cut out mouth section, two ears sprouted from the top of his head and it was finished off with white fur trim.

"COME ON PEOPLE!" He screamed, his hands balled into fists as he nodded in acknowledgement of the crowd.

The crowd cheered again and with a slap of his spandex covered thighs (that matched the colours and design of his mask) he jogged down towards the ring.

"From The Wilderness of Blackfoot Ridge" Voight lowered his tone to build the drama "Seven Feet of Animal Man Beast..."

A huge bear of a man standing at almost seven feet tall, and looking as though he had been sleeping rough for a month, growled through broken, misshapen teeth, the fans were delighted in returning their jeers and curse words in his direction.

"KRONG!" Voight growled.

His blotted barrelled torso was squeezed untidily into a one strapped brown singlet and standard worn black wrestling boots. He had gone bare feet in his early stages of the gimmick but numerous broken toes made him rethink that part.

"And now the former two time United States Champion... Yellow Feather!" Voight exploded with enthusiasm which was mirrored by the fans as they saw him trot out from behind the curtain, his hand raised in the air, his palm positioned like the blade of a tomahawk.

"Being accompanied by..." Voight began and then stopped himself mid sentence when a robe clad Sebastian Churchill stepped out and realised that he was without his beautiful valet, Miss Crystal. But ever the professional Voight thought on the spot "...Ladies and Gentlemen, due to the dangerousness of such a match, Miss Crystal will not be allowed at ringside for her own safety." A groan rippled over the crowd who always look forward to seeing such a beauty.

Sebastian Churchill turned his warty nose up to the ceiling and ignored the crowd as his name was announced by Voight.

"From Durango, Mexico!"

El Corazón de Plata burst from the curtain, silver mask and tights emblazoned with a heart design on them, and came out to cheers.

"El..." Voight put extra emphasis on the word rolling it around expertly with his tongue "...Corazón de Plata!"

He ran to the ring, a matching silver cape fluttered behind him like some metallic super hero, all the while his ageing physique wiggled uncontrollably with each bounding stride.

Another masked man sauntered through the curtain before his announcement had even started. A tower of a man dressed in suit trousers and a smart white shirt, black suspenders cutting through the shirt and holding his trousers on. The shirt rolled up to his elbows showing off his massive dark forearms as he gestured to the crowd with his middle finger.

"The Masked Mandrill!" Voigt said quickly.

His mask displayed the colours and pattern of an alpha male mandrill, as his long dreadlocks cascaded down his back.

The crowd wained wearily but not for long as 'The Voice' erupted with "Lenny and Duke... The Fire Crackers!"

The crowd were back up again at the sight of the two young good-looking guys in flamed emblazoned tights leaping through the curtain. Females in the crowd screamed as if The Beatles had just took centre stage, the duo bounced around excitedly, their thick mops of blonde and brown hair whipped around like rockstars from the eighties.

"From Los Angeles, California!"

The crowd already knew who it was and spat a barrage of curse words and ridicule.

"'Magnificent' Johnny Midnight!"

At the announcement of his name they booed again, it seemed to rise into the ceiling of the hall and do a circuit before attacking him again like hungry buzzards as he strutted arrogantly through the curtain.

"You're looking at the next champion!" He yelled and grinned obnoxiously, with aviator sunglasses balancing on the end of his nose and a bright cerise leather jacket hanging off his shoulders nonchalantly.

"From Belfast, Ireland!" Comes the next announcement "The Belfast Brawler!"

Groans from the crowd as a red headed lout, clad in ripped jeans and t-shirt strolled down the aisle, not acknowledging the crowd at all, but cracking his knuckles in preparation for throwing a few potatoes.

The ring had started to fill up now and with fourteen wrestlers in there, ring announcer Waylon 'The Voice' Voight had manoeuvred himself onto the outside of the ring. He stood adjacent to the timekeeper's table where an old man sat, hammer in hand eager to sound the bell and start the match.

"From parts unknown... Doctor! X!" Voight hissed the letter X like it had left the mouth of a snake.

The crowd were silent and Glen felt like a rock was lodged in his throat, making it difficult for him to even swallow.

Oh, no, not again! He thought, his black mask concealing a face of disappointment.

But as Glen walks out he was taken aback when he was hit by an onslaught of boos from the crowd.

He immediately hunched himself over as if he were a mad scientist's slave and lurked down the aisle, stalking all who waited in the ring. His mask hid his face and he was thankful because he was smiling.

"Stomp and Tusk!" Voight growled "The Rhino Brothers!"

The two gargantuan beasts traipsed down to the ring, as always Stomp was overly vocal towards the fans "You're looking at the only endangered species in professional wrestling! Ain't nobody like us!"

Tusk strode up the steps to the ring apron and gestured he was going to break someone, maybe everyone who stood before him.

Stomp bounded up onto the apron and pointed at the wrestlers in the ring gathered around staring at him and yelled at the top of his voice "You know what time it is boys?" before sticking his thumb up in the air "It's 'Wus tha yo fumb?' time, baby!"

The wrestlers in the ring immediately started laughing and had to turn away from him to stop themselves from becoming hysterical. It was a difficult feat for the ring full of wrestlers to conceal their laughter and shoulders rose and fell rapidly as faces were hidden from the crowd.

"Four time Heavyweight Champion of the World!" Voight announced with all the pomp and circumstance that it deserved "From Pyongyang, North Korea!"

Hatred oozed from the crowd like a toxic gas as the large waddling bulk of Kami Kajeu made his way slowly to the ring.

"'The Korean Kraken' Kami Kajeu!"

The hatred was so much, not just because he was the heel and that's the way it was, nor was it the unrest with North Korea itself but because they knew he was a major player in the match and could very easily come away the victor. As the fans were thinking this, he was thinking how cold the wooden flooring of the aisle was on the souls of his bare feet.

"The United States Champion..." Voight paused to let the crowd finish their verbal massacre of Kami Kajeu and when they realised who was next, the same abuse was aimed at the curtain as Mr Canada strode out proudly. Wearing his United States title around his waist he waved a large Canadian flag over his head.

"It's the 'Canadian Hero' Mr Canada!" Voight growled, voice finally croaking slightly, he had definitely earned his money tonight.

"And, Finally!" He announced, again giving the people enough time to realise what was happening "'The American Hero'!" The crowd erupted into a frenzy while The Slammer's huge frame strode out from behind the curtain with his hands on his hips, head nodding toward the crowd.

Voight announced his name, but it was already drowned out by the roaring of their crowd shouting 'SLAMMER! SLAMMER! SLAMMER!' Over and over again they chanted in a relentless hypnotic rhythm.

The Slammer dived into the ring and everyone backed off to allow him the spotlight. The eyes of the wrestlers danced around at each other waiting for someone to make the first move.

With all the pieces in place, the bell rang and the carnage ensued as twenty gladiators clashed in what could be seen as a modern day coliseum.

CHAPTER 32

The roaring of an excited crowd rebounded down a long narrow corridor of The Porteau Palace. The old pictures of people that have performed there in the past tremble against the harsh concrete wall that had been caressed fairly recently, with a paintbrush of a non offensive neutral colour. The cheap plastic frames that are constructed around the said pictures and show posters, rattle with the energy emanating from the building's main hall.

Miss Crystal staggers down the corridor, one high heeled stiletto on, the others whereabouts unknown. The missing shoe causing her to limp unevenly, the one heel clicking on the polished wooden floor, sounding like the soothing ticking of a clock. Her long slender evening gown of black sequins shimmered under the strip lights overhead dazzling like a nights sky. She staggered and fell into the wall, which luckily for her held her upright. She staggered on sliding against the wall, stirring the hung pictures and leaving them crooked as she continued on her way. Sliding against it like a slug, leaving a trail of picture frames in disarray in her wake. Her mass of platinum blonde hair had been swept up on top of her head and originally been held there by a clip, the clip was gone and her hair sprouted out in all directions like the leaves of a jungle plant.

She sobbed with each flustered step and for the first time in her life, she looked hagged almost unattractive. Her wine coloured lipstick unceremoniously smudged across her face and a tirade of salty tears had smeared her mascara into a chaotic frenzy, but most disturbingly of all were her wide dilated pupils that stared into the abyss, seemingly detached from the vessel that was staggering down the corridor. She saw the figure of someone appear at the end of the corridor but through her drug fuelled haze, she could not identify the owner of this blurred apparition that stood before her.

A voice called out to her, it sounded like her name, but what was her name? It sounded like a question, but who was asking her questions? Her guilty conscience asked, and what did they ask she thought, her head racing but irresponsive.

"Crystal?" Came the voice again, this time loud. She heard her name and the distorted vision approached her, closer until he was on her.

She fell into the man's arms and he caught her, staggering back under her deadweight.

"Crystal?" He heard again "What's wrong? Are you okay?"

The answer to both questions was the same.

No.

He lowered her down to the floor and cradled her in his arms, she looked up at him and saw many faces, all of them dancing in front of her eyes like a kaleidoscope of masks, rotating fiery like the objects in the window of a slot machine, spinning rapidly until her disillusioned mind could piece the correct features together.

"Johnny..." She slurred.

"No, it's..."

"Sebby? It's Sebby, I'm so sorry my love." She said her head beginning to clear now and tears streaming again from her eyes.

"No, Crystal, It's Wally."

Her eyes opened and the face now matched the voice, Wally knelt looking down at her with concern "Are you okay?" He asked.

Crystal laughed hysterically almost as though she was possessed by some demon "No!" And then continued laughing while pulling herself up to a seated position.

"Have you taken something?" He asked in a concerned tone.

There was no reply as she tried to shake the cobwebs.

"Crystal! Have you taken something?" Wally asked, this time more firmly.

She nodded and she wore an expression of embarrassment on her face.

"Jesus!" Wally sighed "Cocaine?"

She nodded and the waterworks started again.

"Why..." Wally began to ask and stopped himself, he knew the answer "Is this because of Johnny?"

"Yeah!" She sobbed.

He held her closely and she let him.

"We need to get you to the hospital. Let me get word to Seb and..."

"No!" She shrieked "No hospital, don't tell Seb, he can't know about this!" She said frantically trying to get to her feet, she did and staggered, her footing still uneven and she leant up against the wall again.

"Then what? I can't leave you like this?" Wally pleaded.

"I'll just sleep it off, I'll be fine." She said scooping makeup out of her moist eyes.

"What's going on?" Came a call from down the corridor. Wally turned to see Mistress Evil hurrying towards them.

"Is she okay?" Mistress Evil asked warmly, a look that you would never see from her when she was out under the spotlight.

"She's..." Wally started, but was interrupted by Crystal "I'm fucked up, Suzanne. I am fucked right up!"

"Shit!" Mistress Evil said and came to her aid to steady her, gripping her firmly by her arm.

"Suzanne, can you get her to her hotel?"

"Yeah, sure!"

"Thank you. But, Seb mustn't know about this, okay?"

"Yeah, I understand. He won't hear anything from me." She nodded and cradled Crystal's petit body in her masculine frame.

"C'mon, let's get your bag and we'll get you to bed." Mistress Evil said tenderly and with that she helped her down the corridor.

Wally watched on and sighed, he slipped a hand inside his polo shirt and rubbed his Saint Christopher that hung around his neck, he didn't even realise he was doing it. It was a trait of his that he did when he was worried about something or someone and in this profession he had seen many people lose their lives because of such recreational habits. People he'd loved or been in love with, friends that he enjoyed conversing with or people he just enjoyed being around. His eyes had seen so much death, there had been too much of it in professional wrestling for his liking.

As he watched them walking away down the corridor and disappearing around the corner he hoped, (and tonight he would pray) that he wasn't witnessing the collapse of yet another life.

CHAPTER 33

"...Crowd is electric here at The Porteau Palace in Memphis! We're down to the final five in the..." Milton McQueen announces to all watching in TV land.

"Make that four, McQueen!" Bunk interrupts "There goes Kami Kajeu!"

"Oh, I stand corrected! A double clothesline from The Slammer and Yellow Feather, teaming up to eliminate the former four time champion, Kami Kajeu!"

"And one of the odds on favourites to win this thing!"

"Wait a minute, Yellow Feather and The Slammer just made eye contact."

"It's a stare down, McQueen!"

"These people are going nuts here! Two of their fan favourites could be looking to do battle here. They're circling each other and it looks like it's going to happen!"

"This reminds me of the time Mr Spock and Captain Kirk fought each other with those weird axe things!"

"Will you be serious!" McQueen snaps at him.

"Well, it's up there!" Bunk scoffs but is ignored by McQueen.

"Now, if Midnight and Passion were smart they'd stay out of sight and let these two eliminate each other."

"They know what they're doing, McQueen! They don't need advice from you! You see they're staying in the..."

"Midnight and Passion attack Yellow Feather and The Slammer from behind, just before they are able to make contact with each other." McQueen turns to Bunk "Guess they're not so smart after all, Bunk!"

Bunk grumbles under his breath.

"But, they're mounting a comeback here, with each of them nailing some solid right hands, wait! What a despicable act by Midnight, he went downstairs and nailed Yellow Feather between the legs!"

"Nothing despicable about that in this type of a match, McQueen. Anything goes!"

"Yellow Feather drops down to the mat in agony and now the two of them are going to work on the big man."

"As big as The Slammer is, even he can't take on two guys, McQueen."

"The Slammer is up and grabs both of them around their throats!"

"Looks like it could be a double chokeslam coming up!"

"It would appear that way...No! Passion and Midnight cut him off with kicks to the midsection and The Slammer doubles over in pain."

"It looks like Pedro Passion and Johnny Midnight might have made a deal here. Maybe they're looking to share the prize money?"

"Well, they can't both share a title shot! I wouldn't trust either of them as far as I could throw them, Bunk!"

"You're so untrusting, McQueen. You always think the worst of people." Bunk sniggers and is yet again ignored by the professional Milton McQueen.

"The Slammer stands upright but staggers back towards the ropes, Midnight and Passion hit a double dropkick and The Slammer goes over the top rope and he's out!... No! No! No, he hung on and landed on the apron."

"I thought he was a goner, McQueen!"

"Me to!"

"Oh God! Wait? Did we just agree on something?"

"Well, we can agree that those dropkicks were a thing of beauty."

"They sure were, McQueen."

"Let's get another look at those on the replay." Bunk groans in appreciation of such a sight "In total unison. What a team these two would make!"

"I can see it now! 'Passion and Midnight'"

"That sounds like a bad detective series!"

"I'd watch it!" Bunk shrugs.

"Back to the action and the duo stalk Yellow Feather who is starting to rise and... He attacks them both with chops"

"Oh my God! Did you hear those chops?"

"The crowd showing their appreciation for those reverse knife edge chops."

"Yellow Feather does throw those with some flair!"

"And a big tomahawk chop to the head of Midnight and he goes down! Now he is unleashing an assault on Pedro Passion forcing him back to the ropes. Passion manages to push him off, but there's that ear splitting war cry from Yellow Feather and he charges Passion!"

"Passion sees him coming…"

"He drops his shoulder and backdrops Yellow Feather over the top rope! Oh, he's outta there!"

"Smart move by Pedro Passion, using Yellow Feather's momentum against him."

"Pedro is mocking the grounded Yellow Feather, thrusting his…"

"Oh he's giving it to him alright!"

"What's this? From behind…"

"No!" Bunk cries.

"Midnight with a sneak attack just came up from behind while Pedro was distracted and dumped him over the top rope!"

"Pedro is furious!"

"I can't say I blame him! No honour amongst thieves, Bunk."

"Damn it!"

"Looks like 'Passion and Midnight' has been cancelled after just one season, Bunk!" McQueen laughs to himself, very proud of his quip.

"I'll do the funnies if you don't mind, McQueen!"

"Well, there's nothing funny about this for Midnight, because he has dropped to his knees in the centre of the ring. He thinks he has won! He seems to have forgotten all about The Slammer, who is rising up on the apron behind him!"

"Holy cow! He rose up like some gigantic sea creature and look at that…"

"Yes, that huge grin from ear to ear like a Cheshire Cat as he steps over the top rope and slowly walks up behind the unsuspecting Johnny Midnight."

"Oh, this is not good!" Bunk sighs before shouting "Look out, Johnny!"

"What the hell are you doing?"

"Well, if all these pencil neck geeks can cheer Slammer on, then I can cheer Johnny on!" Bunk smirks matter of factly.

"You're supposed to be an impartial broadcast journalist!"
Bunk just grins at him and McQueen shakes his head at him "Never mind."

"Oh, Johnny's seen him!"

"Midnight turns around ever so slowly and now he's face to face with a monster!"

"Run, Johnny! Run like the wind!"

"Theres no place to run and he throws a couple of shots, but they have no effect on The Slammer! He hits back with a flurry of blows of his own that hit the mark and leaves Midnight reeling."

"He whips Midnight into the rope and Oh! What a big boot to the kisser!"

"Midnight is down and looking for a way out, but there isn't one and The Slammer hoists him into the air for a big body slam!"

"Even I felt that one, McQueen!"

"Slammer with a handful of hair as he peals the motionless, beaten carcass of Johnny Midnight up from the canvas."

"His luscious hair!" Bunk groans in shock "He'll pull it out! He can't pull hair surely?"

"Anything goes in this one, remember Bunk?" Scoffed McQueen and is immediately back to calling the action "The Slammer picks Midnight up like he is weightless and parades around the ring with him draped over his shoulder."

"Looking for a running powerslam maybe?"

"No, he's charging the ropes he's going to put him straight over the top!"

"No!"

"If he does, this one is over and we have a new number one..."

"Thumb in the eye by the Magnificent One!"

"What a shortcut!"

"But it worked."

"It did indeed and it stopped the big man in his tracks. Midnight slips off his back and grabs the large cranium of the masked man, as if he's looking for a suplex?"

"Maybe looking for that, 'Magnifi-Plex!'"

"But what good would that do him here?"

"Well, it may wear him down."

"You're right, Bunk!"

"Don't sound so surprised! Sheesh!"

"He's hooked up that leg and is looking to interlock those fingers and deliver a modified Fisherman Suplex."

"Here we go!"

"No! The Slammer blocks it and breaks Midnight's grip and he grabs him around the head now for a...No! Wait a minute!"

"Oh wow!"

"Suplex by The Slammer! They've..."

"Both of them suplexed over the top rope and out to the floor!"

"The crowd is stunned into silence at the Porteau palace here in Memphis!"

"I'm in shock!"

"Both men going over the top rope, in a dangerous suplex manoeuvre, the momentum forcing them both over the top and out. Wow!"

"What happens now?"

"The referee's look confused."

"Those idiots! But what happens now, McQueen?"

"I don't know, Bunk! I have never seen anything like this before!" McQueen shakes his head "This is unprecedented."

"Damn it! McQueen! I need to know these things! I've got money... I mean I'm a broadcast journalist and the people need to know the outcome!"

"The Referees are discussing it now."

"The Slammer is back in the ring and holds a clenched fist in the air, he thinks he's won it."

"Now, Johnny's joined him, and he's prancing around with both fists in the air. I think he's won, McQueen."

"We don't know for sure. Wait a minute... I'm getting some information through that we are going to have a look at the instant replay. So we should be able to tell you in a few moments folks. So please stay with us."

"How come you get the information? Nobody ever gives me any information!"

"Here we go and here is the replay."
There is silence as the replay is played and examined closely by the announcers.

"Well, I'm afraid we can't tell from that manage point."

"No, on my monitor it looks like Midnight won!"

"What?"

"It looks like The Slammer touched down first."

"You're out of your mind!" McQueen   "It's clearly indecisive!"

"Don't yell at me!" Bunk moans defensively "I'm entitled to my opinion."

"Sorry folks, but we don't have... Oh! Midnight and The Slammer are having an altercation in the ring."

"It's just handbags, McQueen."

"The Referees are in the ring and separating them."

"Both these guys think they've won this!"

"There's our head official, referee Bernie Barnes discussing something with the ring announcer. It would appear that they have made a decision."

"Those idiots couldn't make a decision about what they were going to have for lunch, let alone something as important as this!"

"I'm hearing again from the back that they have checked multiple camera angles and they are still stumped! But, they're now going to play another angle for us so hopefully..."

"Here it comes, McQueen!"

"No, It's still inconclusive."

"But, what does all this mean, McQueen?" Bunk groans grabbing a handful of McQueen's tuxedo and shaking him.

"We're about to find out! Let's go to 'The Voice' Waylon Voight for the result."

"Ladies and Gentlemen..." He pauses until he has everyones attention, a nervous calm shrouds the crowd "Here is your winner..." again he pauses and looks at head official Bernie Barnes for confirmation again, he gets it from a nod of his head.

"And the winners of the match, 'Magnificent' Johnny Midnight AND The Slammer!"

The crowd jeer loudly not happy at the outcome. The pushing and shoving starts in the ring again, yet again the referees have to play peacekeepers as they separate them.

"Ladies and Gentlemen, ladies and gentlemen, please!" Voight says excitedly "I have just been informed..." Again he has hush and the people's attention fixated on his every word "...Due to the controversial nature to the end of this match, tomorrow night in Studd City, The Slammer and 'Magnificent' Johnny Midnight will go one on one and the winner will be named the number one contender to Randy Rogan's World Heavyweight Championship!"

There is a roar from the crowd, very happy at the announcement.

"The Magnificent one doesn't look very happy with that announcement!"

"And why should he! He just won that match and now they're pulling the rug out from underneath him!"

"Oh, it would appear that Voight is not yet finished."
Voight holds the microphone in the air and the crowd simmers down again.

"And the match will be..." a pause again and it's as if the air was sucked out of the building as everyone held their breath "A Steel Cage Match!"
The crowd erupted like a Vesuvius of euphoric emotion as the colour drains from Johnny Midnight's face.

CHAPTER 34

There was a buzz of anticipation and excitement around the Richland Coliseum in Studd City. The whole roster was eager to see how Randy Rogan's retirement and the imminent number one contender's match between Johnny Midnight and The Slammer would affect the landscape of professional wrestling. It was in many ways a passing of the torch to the next generation. Some were all for this change, the younger workers with the all or nothing styles could see that the change in direction was imminent and they were watering at the mouth with the possibilities. They believed it was now their time to shine, their stars obscured by larger than life planets that forbid them the space to fully shine.

Others believed that this could well be the beginning of the end and the business would suffer without a true draw at the helm. The old school mentality rearing its wrinkled neck and casting a finger of negativity in the direction of the young upstarts that look to take what was built by them. Each of them fearing that the storytelling would become a thing of the past and that the exhibition style bouts that had become commonplace on the independent scene. The constant use of unnecessary sequences and dangerous stunts would soon muscle out the history and true art form of what they did all their life. Feeling that their life's work was being made a mockery of.

Realistically, neither side was right or wrong, both sides arguments had some merit to them, evolution is always inevitable and cannot be fought against and then there is an old saying, 'If it ain't broke, don't fix it'.

What really was needed was something in the middle that would cater for and attract both ends of the spectrum. Only time will tell whether this gargantuan task can be undertaken.

As workers went around their last minute routines before bell time, Johnny Midnight casually walked through the arena. He felt in a daze and it was as if he could hear every thump of his heart echoing in his eardrums. He knew that he was on the verge of getting to where he always wanted to be and where the arrogant side of his personality believed he deserved to be.

On top. His persona that came across to others wasn't to far away from the real man that hid behind the bravado, maybe that is why he had been so successful in his role as 'Magnificent' Johnny Midnight because the character and the man were so similar that it felt natural to him. But even still, behind the prima donna attitude there was still that small part of him that had once been a child dreaming of becoming a World Champion.

A roguish, almost childlike grin quivered across his lips as he thought about the days gone past as a child looking up at the ring watching his heroes do battle. Randy Rogan versus El Talón being the first match he saw live with wonderment in his eyes, his hero was indeed the man that he would face tomorrow for the most prestigious prize in the game. Not that he would tell Rogan that, nor anyone else for that matter, his arrogance and personal insecurities would not allow it. Plus he didn't want to be referred to as a 'Mark' by taunting peers. His hair was slicked back and moist, getting longer, it now fell between his shoulder blades and it slapped against his wellformed muscular back as his gleaming black leather boots squeaked on the linoleum flooring of the corridor. He had chosen to wear his new pair of black trunks that had been painstaking hand made by a very talented seamstress he knew in Europe, her work second to none in quality. The design simple but effective, all black with subtle diamanté stones sewn in to give the illusion of shining stars on a void background, the rear emblazoned flamboyantly with the word 'Magnificent' in silver and dotted randomly with the same shimmering diamanté stones. His spandex covers that fit snugly over his kneepads also mirrored the same design. Tonight he wanted to be dressed all in black, to tie the visual that he was indeed the villain, it made him feel like the dastardly outlaw from an old western. He smiled again, continuing on his journey towards the locker room, maybe playing out some other childhood fantasy of cowboys and Indians in his head. For the first time in a long time he felt like himself. Not the Lothario that most took him for, yes, he did frequently enjoy the company of women and recreational habits that some found unsavoury, but he was a young man enjoying his freedom and sowing his wild oats. He wasn't hurting anybody, well, apart from the occasional broken heart here and there, but he just wasn't ready to be tied down.

This business only works if you're single he thought. So many times had he seen marriages of other wrestlers end because of their shenanigans on the road, or even couples who start of thinking it's great sharing the same experience and dream, only for one to become bitter at the others success and then breaking up and then still having to see them everyday.

No, he believed where he was and what he was doing was right for him and if occasionally he had to deal with a case of herpes then so be it. He heard the tail ends of peoples conversations as they stood around talking about their matches.

"I'll work the leg tonight." Pedro Passion said to Puma Kid, who answered in an eager and youthful reply "That's cool. I can hit an Enziguri for the double down then."

Johnny making a mental note not to work The Slammer's leg in their match. He was a stickler for wrestling psychology and he believed that every match should be different. The crowd would soon get bored if in every match they witnessed a wrestler attacking the opponents leg. He believed that wrestlers should ask each other what manoeuvres, sequences, spots and finishes they were doing on a show then there was less chance of seeing things repeated, which can really grate on the average wrestling fan.

Plus, if the finish to his match was for instance a piledriver, if they used that move in the opening match then the move would lack its appeal by the time the main event rolled around. Even more so if the said manoeuvre was kicked out of or not used for the finish, it could bury the main event match and maybe the whole show depending on the story being woven in.

Megan Powers, Emily Kincaid, René and Mistress Evil stand around talking about their upcoming tag team match. Johnny noticed them standing in their revealing outfits, cut low around their breasts exposing their rouge contoured cleavages. Their tight shorts that almost sliced their buttocks in half, this was just how his mind worked, he was a male chauvinistic pig and leered at women like pieces of meat. Yet the women still came to him so he had no need to change his way of thinking.

To look at them all standing there was an odd sight, Megan Powers was tall and strong, clad in the brightest of yellows and reds, her hair rising out from her head like moulded candy floss. She towered over the dainty, delicate flower that was Emily Kincaid, who was dressed like the stereotypical farmer's daughter in a checkered blouse tied provocatively enough so her chest could be seen, worn denim Daisy Duke style shorts with her feet tucked snuggly in to brown leather cowboy boots. The ensemble was topped with a cowboy hat sitting back on a head of dutch braid.

Then next to them was the muscular pale physique of Mistress Evil. A black PVC swimsuit with a zip passing from navel to neck, gave her the look of some sensual vampire from some gothic horror film. Red contact lenses were shocking and off putting, and the extraordinary red flash of hair that was swept back like a huge comb that you would find on the head of a rooster.

Then René the French Canadian, former glamour model turned wrestler, naturally beautiful but over elaborate plastic surgery to her breasts, cheeks and lips made her look cheap and false. The facade finished with an abundance of make up and a mass of platinum hair.

The sight of them made Johnny smile again, this time with lust, various scenes flitting rapidly across his minds eye as he focused on the cheeks of Megan's rear trying to escape her outfit. To him they looked like a box of opened chocolates, all the different flavours and textures enticing him.

"So when Emily goes up top..." Said Megan, who was the senior in this matter and leading the conversation with that layout of the match. "René, this is where you come in."

"Okay!" she agreed through her pouting fishlike lips.

"Good! Just make sure you push her off the top." Megan added.

Emily and René watched on with saucer like eyes in awe and clung to every word, not wanting to miss anything and be blamed for any mistakes out there, both of them so wanted her approval.

Mistress Evil lights a cigarette and slides it between her crimson lips, and nodded at everything Megan said.

"So, while I'm distracted Suzanne you roll me up?"

"Got it, Meg!" Mistress Evil scoffed, cigarette wiggling up and down in the corner of her pursed lips.

Johnny walked past, his eyes tracing over them with a sickening debauched gaze. He quickly steered his gaze away from them and pretended to concentrate on the corridor up ahead. He could feel their eyes burning into him, this excited him, his dick twitching with arousal in his tight trunks. It did his libido the world of good to feel desired, maybe he was wrong and not all of them yearned for him, but they were still looking, he could feel it. Besides, he knew that Emily definitely would not turn away his advances. Her tongue was constantly hanging from her gaping jaws whenever he was near, her cowboy boots splashing around in a puddle of drool. He wanted to keep her like that, it meant he had a back up if ever the water hole was running dry.

He had already tasted what René had to offer, she was easy, too easy really. Mistress Evil well, he wasn't brave enough to take on such a challenge just yet, although he did have the distinct feeling that his advances would fail on her because, I have a dick he thought.

Megan was a prize he thought, a little bit older than him and still very attractive, it was the experience he was after, her experience. Yes, after Crystal, Megan was next on his Hitlist.

"Hi, Johnny!" swooned Emily as the other girls rolled their eyes.

Johnny just nodded.

His face soon fell when he saw Sebastian Churchill approaching. Clad in his wrestling gear which was a regal maroon shade tonight, a matching robe tied around his waist with expertly crafted sequins sewn into a floral arrangement. He wore a look of a man with the weight of the world on his shoulders, he looked straight on not even seeing Johnny, his mind a million miles away.

Johnny saw something completely different, and with that, created his own painting from his own mix of watercolours. To him he looked like a husband on the warpath, a husband that had just found out the sordid secret of his wife's love affair with one of his peers. Sebastian neared and Johnny actually balled a fist up in preparation that he would have to defend himself, he was adamant in his assessment of the situation. Sebastian was almost right on top of him now and surely were about to clash.

"Oh! Hello, Johnny!" Sebastian smiled in his corse cockney accent "Didn't see ya there, mate."
Johnny nodded, unclenched his fist and carried on. He stopped when he heard the girls ask how Crystal was feeling, she had been conspicuous by her absence Johnny thought and wanting to know the gossip he halted. He looked around and noticed that there was a piece of paper with the evenings card scribbled on it.

TAG TEAM CHAMPIONSHIP
DEVASTATION (C) v FIRECRACKERS (15 MINS)
(COUNT OUT)

PUMA KID v PEDRO PASSION (12 MINS)

PROMO WITH THE SLAMMER (MANDRILL CHALLENGE)
SLAMMER OVER (5 MINS)

POWERS & KINCAID v EVIL & RENE
(20 MINS)

INTERVAL
SEBASTIAN CHURCHILL v YELLOW FEATHER (12 MINS)
MR CANADA DISTRACTION.

RHINO BROS. v LOS COLIBRIES (10 MINS)

DR X v JUNGLE JIM (6-8 MINS)

CAGE MATCH
JOHNNY MIDNIGHT v THE SLAMMER (30-40 MINS)

He started to pretend to look at it so he could eavesdrop on the conversation. It gave him a sweet sense of satisfaction to see his name underlined and going over in such a huge match. He skimmed over the other matches and listened as Sebastian told them that she was still sick and back at the hotel tucked up in bed.

The girls fussed over him with sympathy and Johnny moved on. Moving on like he was in life and his relationships.

CHAPTER 35

An intimidating shadow caressed the worn ring canvas, that was heavily stained with the sweat of the nights earlier contests. Already drying and seeping into the fabric from the heat of the powerful spotlights that hung above the ring like orbiting planets.

The Slammer stood in the ring, hands gripping his hips and chest expanded like the pose of some gloating super hero, but to a lot of people that is exactly what he was.

Milton McQueen stood next to him dwarfed by his colossal size and almost consumed by his daunting shadow. The crowd that are already riled up into a frenzy in Studd City, start to simmer down to hear their hero speak.

McQueen stares up at the monster of a man, straining as his outstretched arm hoisted the microphone up to the jaws of the masked gargantuan.

"Good people of..." The Slammer speaks into the microphone, his voice low but welcoming, it reverberates through hidden speakers in the large domed building of The Richland Coliseum "...Studd City!" The crowd cheered in unison at the mention of their hometown.

The Slammer nods in response to the crowd and speaks again.

"Everything I've ever done in this business has led up to this night! All the sacrifices I've made, the training, the travelling, as all led me to this point! To finally be within arms length of a shot for the World Heavyweight Championship!" He pauses as the crowd show their appreciation with a rising cheer of 'You deserve it!' that floods the arena.

"I know that I will have to take on my good friend Randy Rogan! He's been a mentor to me and a good friend. But, I know that deep down in my heart I can beat you Randy." He points into the camera for all the viewers watching around the world. There is no malice in his tone nor arrogance, just confidence. "I believe that it is my time! It's Slammer Time!" The crowd roar again and rhythmic chants of 'Slammer Time, Slammer Time!' fill the air.

"But, there is one person that stands in my way as I teeter on the verge of greatness. That person is none other than, 'Magnificent' Johnny Midnight!"

The crowd boo loudly at the mere mention of his upcoming opponent's name.

"Hell yeah! Boo that punk!" The Slammer's voice rises, spitting with passion and anger, the crowd are with him hanging on every single word. He has them, like wriggling fish on the end of a line.

"He doesn't deserve to be in the position he's in! He's lied and cheated to get to where he is, using short cut after short cut to get this opportunity! Is this who you want as your next champion?"

"No, no, no!" Comes the response, each word spat out like bullets pouring out of the hot muzzle of a machine gun.

The Slammer looks around at the crowd and nods again with agreement, the spotlight reflecting off the golden trim of his stars and stripes design on his mask.

He is just about to speak again when he is interrupted by another booming voice.

"I don't know who you think you are kid!" Comes the laid back growl of The Masked Mandrill who glides down the aisle with a microphone gripped in his hand.

"But, there is a pecking order around here!" He seethes and is met by a bombardment of abuse from the crowd, some of it even becoming personal and racial. He ignores it all, he's heard it all before.

"It goes like this!" He snarls as he sluggishly stomps up the steel steps and onto the apron. He pauses and takes in the hate from the crowd, golden teeth flicker in the lights as he smiles sadistically, a dark face hidden under the red and blue pattern of a Mandrill's war paint. He turns his attentions back to The Slammer who waits patiently.

"First come, first served!" Growls the Masked Mandrill stepping over the top rope and walking up to meet him in the centre of the ring. A stare down ensues and the two lock eyes and push out their large muscular chests. The two of them evenly matched in size and stature, neither of them backing down from the other.

"I've been here way longer than you! I've dominated everyone in this company! If anybody deserves a shot at that title, it's me!" He growls his head stretching forward to meet The Slammer, his dreadlocks whipping out behind him like the tail of an angry scorpion. The Slammer obliges and the two butt heads and snarl at each other like duelling stags. Milton McQueen remains sandwiched between the two angry giants and tries to keep order.

"Now, just wait a minute you two! Settle down!" McQueen cries as the two push into each other with their masked foreheads.

"Gentlemen! Gentlemen please!" He screams and finally manages to leaver the two apart. The crowd loving every moment of this and chant for The Slammer.

"You can't just come down here and..." McQueen sounds off at The Masked Mandrill and is immediately interrupted.

"Little man! I can do anything I damn well please! That's why I'm issuing a challenge to this piece of trash! I want you, right here, right now!"

"Now wait just a minute, Masked Mandrill, The Slammer has already been contractually obligated to wrestle against Johnny Midnight tonight in a steel cage match! He can't just..."

"I accept!" Snarls The Slammer much to the pleasure of the crowd.

The Masked Mandrill smiles knowing that he has just weaved his way into the title picture that he technically has no right to be in.

A referee jogs down to the ring and slides in getting between them both telling them to back up into neutral corners before he can start the impromptu match.

"Ladies and Gentlemen it would appear we have a match!" McQueen announces as he scrambles to get out of the ring before the carnage ensues. As the referee bends through the ropes to talk to the ring announcer, The Masked Mandrill attacks The Slammer. He sends him hurtling out of the ring and on to the thin matted area that protects the wrestlers body from the cold unforgiving concrete that lies hidden beneath.

The bell rings signalling that the match is indeed underway and the crowd already get on The Masked Mandrill for a despicable act of unsportsmanlike conduct. He hits back with the uncouth gesture known as the forearm jerk, which only acts to stir the pot of emotion that is bubbling in the stands.

The Masked Mandrill is quickly out after The Slammer and lays in some stomps to the thick trapezius area of 'The American Hero'. He then makes the mistake to get tangled up in a war of words with a group of rowdy fans, spitting expletives at each other, but in doing so he had taken his eye off The Slammer, who has risen from the ground like some angry demon, his fists clenched and muscles taut as he turns to the unsuspecting Masked Mandrill and grabs a handful of his cascading dreadlocked hair and yanked him around. He began unloading with meaty right hands to the forehead of The Masked Mandrill who teetered on the spot like a spinning dreidel, threatening to topple with each connected blow.

Grabbing the back of The Masked Mandrill's head, he slammed him down towards the apron of the ring. The Masked Mandrill striking the mat with the clammy palms of his hands to create the echoing thud, then snapping his head back from the impact to give the illusion to all that his bell had just been well and truly rung. The Masked Mandrill staggers backwards, his tacky dark flesh suddenly covered with goosebumps from the cold steel ring post at his back. He leant up against it, eyes rolling in his head as he waited. The Slammer was amped up and so were his fans all cheering him on as he unleashed a roaring war cry and charged at the unsuspecting Masked Mandrill. He moved and The Slammer connected with the solid steel ring post like a runaway locomotive ploughing into an unyielding buffer stop.

The Slammer takes the impact on his wide chest and then collapses to the floor again. The Masked Mandrill shakes away the cobwebs from his head and then again upsets the crowd with taunts over the carcass of their fallen hero. He yanks him up by the back of his mask and starts to try and untie the laces that secure it onto his head and conceal his mysterious identity. There is a gasp from the crowd, of astonishment and intrigue, some in the crowd longing to see who is under the mask.

"The world's finally going to see what an ugly bastard you are!" Yells The Masked Mandrill as his sweaty fingers struggle to untie the tight laces.

The Slammer rises again and knocks Mandrill's hands away, his mask now hanging loose at the rear, his sweat matted brown hair spilling out as he adjusted the eye holes so he could see his opponent. The Masked Mandrill charged him and The Slammer drops a shoulder and back body drops him onto the floor, his back arching up from the thin protective mat in pain.

The Slammer adjusts the loose mask again and sees The Masked Mandrill crawling around the ring on all fours in an attempt to escape. The referee joins them on the floor now to get the action into the ring but The Slammer ignores him, brushing him aside as he gives chase. The Masked Mandrill sees the fuming tyrant picking up speed behind him and makes it to his feet and now a game of cat and mouse ensues. They manage half a lap of the ring at full speed before their huge frames start to tire. The Masked Mandrill makes a swift detour and slides in under the bottom rope, the exit was so sharp that The Slammer tries to do the same, but his rubber soled boots slip on the mat as he tries to change direction and nosedives dangerously towards the steel steps situated around the ring post. The crowd gasps as he hurtles towards the steps and his head strikes the corner, shredding the rugged material of his mask and carving out a shockingly deep wound into his cranium. The Slammer collapses into the steps and then to the floor, blood spewing from the wound. There is an eery hush that falls over the crowd as well as The Masked Mandrill who watches on in shock. The referee is soon at the side of The Slammer, his head writhing around in a groggy rotation. The referee speaks but he does not hear him. There is blood, so much blood that is mopped up by his mask like a hungry vampire. The wound can be seen, pumping out blood with reckless abandon and finally The Slammer can focus and sees the referee's terrified face shouting at him. He still cannot hear his words, all he sees is blood, all he sees is red.
Red.

The blood bubbles and boils and The Slammer is up to his feet once again, blood vomiting uncontrollable from the wound and down his face and torso, dripping onto the floor. The crowd look on nauseated and the referee makes an 'X' shape with his arms over his head to indicate to the backstage area that he is hurt and hurt bad.

"No!" The Slammer growls, blood filling his mouth, the metallic taste causing him to cringe and spit it out onto the floor. He grabs the rope and pulls himself up into the ring. He can hear The Masked Mandrill ask him if he is okay but he ignores him and drives towards him. The Masked Mandrill knows that they've got to go home and go home now. He makes as though he is going to nail him with a double axe handle blow, holding his arms up over his head and leaving himself open for The Slammer to make his move.

The Masked Mandrill looked into The Slammer's eyes, and they scared him. A man that does not scare easy saw nothing in those eyes but hate. Luckily for him something must have clicked in The Slammer's head, maybe the severity of the problem snapped him back to reality and he lashed out with a worked boot into The Masked Mandrill's gut. As he doubled over, The Slammer trapped his head between his thighs all the while blood dripped down rapidly staining his opponent's shirt. He locked his hands around the waist and in one huge hoisted movement, brought him up for a devastating power bomb back down hard to the mat, but safely. He collapsed on top of him and the referee slid into the ring and slapped out a rapid three count.

The Slammer fell back onto the mat and looked up at the lights, they appeared pink to him through blood smeared eyeballs. He saw people surrounding him but heard nothing, all he heard was the throbbing of his head as blood spurted out of the three inch gash that had now scythed out a dwelling place across his head.

CHAPTER 36

Randy Rogan reclined back in his favourite armchair with an ice cold Bobby's Light gripped in his hand, the smell of sizzling steak floating out from the kitchen. He sighed a contently "I could get used to this." As he smiled to himself, taking a swig from his bottle.

"Don't get too used to it!" Martha called from the kitchen "You're gonna be cooking for me when you get back!"
He laughed and then smiled to himself.

"Anything you want, honey."
He stared at the large flatscreen television that was fixed on the wall, just thirty minutes ago it had been showing Jimmy's favourite cartoon, Monster Meals and now had The Slammer making his way down to the ring for an interview with Milton McQueen.
He watched on and his mind wandered. It then did the darnest of things, it told him he was making a mistake.
How can you leave this all behind? Look at the ovation he is getting! That could be you! Why are you leaving anyway, you love it there! No, I really don't, I hate it! I despise the world, it's like an unrelenting cancer that sucks the life out of people then spits them out to fester... But, I love it. No! You miss it! I do! I don't I...

The house phone rings and tugs him out from his musing battle with his conscience, a bittersweet fight that had no conclusion.

He heard Martha's slippers attacking the hard wooden flooring of the hallway and stopped the constant ringing with a cheery greeting. Her voice moved up an octave when she realised she new the caller and obviously someone she liked. After a few seconds of chewing the fat, her voice got louder as she entered the lounge. Randy turned around to look at her, she stood smiling, holding the phone to her ear. He smiled at her, he loved her so much, her hair swept up in a casual bunch on the top of her head, her apron that read 'Don't Piss Off The Cook' emblazoned on it. The apron hugged her beautiful pear shaped figure and he loved her as much as they day they met. He smiled goofily at her and she glanced at him and shot him a confused look as if to say, 'Why are you being weird?'

Then said her goodbyes and held out the phone for Randy.

"It's for me?" Randy asked.

"Yeah, it's Bob."

"Bob?"

"Yeah, Bob! Bob Belaire!"

"Oh! Bobcat!"

Martha rolls her eyes, always finding it quite childish that the men in her husband's profession refer to each other as their working names.

Randy takes the phone and settles back into his recliner.

"Bobcat, my old Buddy! How's it going?" He asks.

The Masked Mandrill strides down the ring and Randy swigs his beer.

"How are doing you old goat?" Bobcat chuckles down the phone.

"Nearly over that finish line my friend." Randy laughs.

"Yeah, I'd heard."

"News travels fast!" Randy scoffs swigging the beer again.

The Masked Mandrill hands out some verbal to The Slammer on the massive screen.

"Now, why I'm calling you is because I have a proposition for you."

"Now, wait a minute, Bobcat. I'm not ready for no comeback yet! After tomorrow, I am done!"

"That's what they all say!"

They both laugh.

"It's nothing like that." Bobcat says.

"Okay, shoot!"

An impromptu match starts on the screen which raises Randy's eyebrows, surprised that they have thrown this spot in before The Slammer has a big match later on that night.

"I have a Wrestling Convention coming up in Ontario on Saturday. I know it's late notice but I'd love it if you could be there."

Randy's face contorted as he mulled over the offer, one eye watching the screen as The Masked Mandrill bulldozes The Slammer out of the ring.

"I don't know, Bobcat..."

"It's nothing major. It's just signing autographs, plus a meet and greet with the fans. Maybe a few photographs."

"I don't know, Bob." Groaned Randy "I was hoping to be finished up and back home by then."

Martha appeared next to him wiping her hands on a towel. She had obviously been listening to the conversation and mouthed the words 'do it' to him. Randy mimes back 'Are you sure?' And she smiled and nodded before kissing him on the head and returning to the kitchen.

"C'mon Randy, it would be a nice send off for you and you'd get to see some of the old boys and girls too!"

Randy loses himself in thought.

Maybe this is the best way to move forward. There is always going to be that little demon inside that pokes you with his flaming pitchfork, with each annoying prick he would whisper 'Comeback, comeback, comeback' And you know you don't want that. But yet you will still miss aspects of the business. Maybe this is a way to stay involved without actually being involved.

The Slammer hits a backdrop on The Masked Mandrill on the screen and the sound of Milton McQueen's over enthusiastic yelp snapped him from his thoughts. He'd almost forgot he was on the phone to Bobcat until he spoke.

"Are you there, Randy?"

"Yeah, sorry, Bobcat!"

"I know you're in Studd tomorrow night, and they are willing to fly you out the next morning. They really want you there, Champ. What do you say?"

"Okay. I'll do it!"

"Great! Can't wait to see you again."

"You too, buddy!"

"I'll get the information emailed over to you now and I'll see you Saturday?"

"Okay. See you then!"

The phone is hung up and The Slammer's head explodes against the steel steps as blood erupts from his head like a volcano.

"Oh, Shit!" Randy gasps rising out of his seat.

CHAPTER 37

The Slammer sat back in a foldout chair in the pristinely decorated locker room. A silhouette of red against surroundings of white was a sight to behold, almost artistic in someways, in other ways enough to give you nightmares for the rest of your life.

A flustered gaggle of people (that included Louis Raggu and Wally Dominguez) flitted around anxiously like bees, buzzing with questions, shouting and shrieking incoherent nonsense. This is how it all appeared to The Slammer, who watched through a cataract of flowing crimson.

"We've gotta get that mask off and see what we are dealing with" He heard someone say, he thought it could be the medical officer, but he couldn't be sure as the voice came from behind him. He looked down to the floor and watched as the drips of blood rapidly peppered the gleaming tiles below. Each droplet that collided with the tiles changed the picture that The Slammer was looking at, like a disturbing macabre kaleidoscope.

"Somebody cut that damn mask off!" Shouted Raggu, he'd suddenly appeared in front of him. The Slammer recognised his hideous choice of footwear, tired and worn leather sandals, with his fat toes bulging out of the end of them, swelling like a line of cooked sausages. Blood dripped onto his sandals and trotters, Raggu recoiled, quickly moving his feet out of the way of the splash zone. This made The Slammer smile.

"Are you okay, Joe?" Raggu asked warningly.

"What the fuck do you think!" The Slammer barked as he sat up right in the chair. Blood now trickling down the curvatures of his muscular physique, framing each abdominal muscle in bright red plasma.

"I'm just concerned about you, Joe. We all are!"

"We need to get that mask off!" Shrieked the medical officer again, he could see him now through the blood soaked shroud standing talking to Raggu. "But, we need to do it slowly and carefully..."

"Oh, for fucks sake!" The Slammer bellowed and with that grabbed the shredded mask and ripped it off his head. Hair and flesh that had become attached to the inside of it, quickly left with a disturbing sickening tearing sound as the mask flew through the air and blood was flicked all over the room, raining down on everyone in the vicinity. They all stopped for a moment, frozen in animation like they were ivory statues in a garden somewhere in ancient Greece. It was not the flicking of blood that disturbed them, but the wound that glared at them, like the angry slanting eye of something possessed, crying constant tears of blood. But the most sickening thing of all was the glistening of something whitish from inside. It was his skull. The bone peaking through the oozing of blood, catching the light from the strip lights that sliced the ceiling above, causing it to dance on the solid surface, appearing to wink at the onlookers.

"What the fuck are you all waiting for?" The Slammer growled "Stitch me up, for christ sake!"

Everyone suddenly started flitting around again as though they had been left on pause and waiting for someone to press the play button again. The medic dabbed at the wound with some gauze, immediately a red mass of blood soaked gauze was dropped unceremoniously on the floor with a splat. The Slammer looked down at it and then another mass of blood-soaked gauze joined it. It looked like the contents of someones stomach had just emptied out in front of him.

"Fuck" The Slammer murmured, realising just how serious this could be.

"I'm not going to lie to you, Joe, this doesn't look good at all!" Raggu says through a contorted brow of concern.

"Is that supposed to make me feel better?" laughed The Slammer.

More gauze fell but with less blood on it.

"Well, At least the bleeding has stopped." Said the medical officer.

"Is that good, Doc?" The Slammer asked.

"Of course!" He chuckled trying to make light of the situation, but soon stopped smiling when The Slammer turned his head to make eye contact with him. The face of a man that looked like he'd survived a massacre, his face streaked with red war paint. "Yes, It is good. We don't want to lose anymore."

The medical officer prodded his finger around in the wound, the excess flesh flapped around like curtains near an open window and with each prod, The Slammer winced. It was if his finger was actually pressing into his brain.

"Take it easy, Doc!"

"My apologies" He said "I'm going to clean this up as best I can, but you're going to need to get to a hospital and get it stitched up and maybe a head scan"

"Fuck that!" The Slammer growls.

"Sorry?" The medical officer gasps almost taken aback.

"Can you stitch me up?"

"Well, yes" He stuttered "But, you should really get checked out by..."

"No!" He growled again. "You stitch me up now. I've got another match to prepare for"

"Whoa! Time out!" Raggu intervenes holding up his plump little hands in the shape of a T "What the hell are you saying, Joe? You can't go back out there now! Not after this!"

"I fucking can and I will!" He could feel that red mist descending again but he fought it, he knew he needed to try and stay level headed here or they will probably have him condemned.

"Joe, there's a gaping fucking hole in your head!" Raggu shouts pointing at his wound. With that comment Wally, who had been standing in disgusted awe swallowed hard, turned a strange colour and left the room.

"You don't think I don't know that, Louis!"

"Look, I can't let you go out there like this, Joe. Surely you understand it's too dangerous?"

There is a pause and nothing is said between anyone, finally there is a huge sigh from The Slammer and he wipes the dried blood out of his eyes. Everyone believing now that he has come to his sense with such a sigh.

"It's for the best, Joe" Raggu said placing a hand on his huge boulder like shoulder "You're health is way more important and I don't expect you to step back out there and jeopardise..."

"Look! It's like this!" The Slammer announced calmly "The doc is gonna stitch me up, nice and tight! And then I'm gonna go an change my gear and be ready for that cage match"

"I can't let you do that, Joe"

"Oh yes you can! For years I've been told I've got to do this and got to do that to reach that brass ring. Well, now my fingertips are within touching distance of it and I'm not giving up that shot now."

"There will be other times Joe. You go away sort yourself out and it'll all still be here waiting for you."

"Bullshit. I've seen it happen to too many guys. They go away when they're white hot and then come back and people don't care. They had their moment, their chance and then it's gone. So stitch me up and get me back out there!"

Raggu sighs and looks at the medical officer.

"Doc, do you think it's safe for him to go back out there and wrestle tonight?"

"No."

"Bullshit!" The Slammer growls.

"He could have a concussion or worse, a fracture to the skull." The medical officer added.

Raggu looked into the eyes of The Slammer and for the first time ever, he could see Joseph Fox. Jr looking back at him. The kid that got into the business to prove to his step father that he could be something. He could have sworn he almost saw tears welling up and he sighed again.

"Can you stitch him up?" Raggu asked the medical officer.

"Yeah, sure. But, he'll have to sign a Waiver"

"Joe, will you sign a wavier to let him stitch you up?"

"Yeah, now get on with it!"

"Will you also sign a wavier for the company too. Freeing us from any liability if something happens to you out there tonight?"

"Yeah. Now just do it already."

Raggu nodded to the medical officer and turned to leave the room leaving the following words to float around the blood stained locker room.

"I hope you know what you're doing."

CHAPTER 38

Randy sits in his recliner, an empty plate on top of a lap tray, the knife and fork left discarded together in a transparent shallow plash of blood from the evening's steak. His eyes remain glued to the screen as Milton McQueen announces that the Cage Match main event will amazingly, still be going ahead.

"That crazy bastard!" He said to himself, shaking his head in disbelief "I can't believe that Raggu would even entertain the idea"

"Daddy!" Came a bellowing interruption from Jimmy, launching himself at his father and grabbing him in a loving headlock.

"Whoa, Champ!" He holla's, the tray and contents almost sent flying from his lap.

"Mommy, said it's time for bed now" He grins a loving smile of innocence. He stood in front of him, his gangly limbs and protruding pot belly hugged tightly by his pyjamas that depicted the fan favourite tag team, The Firecrackers on them. The legs and sleeves rising up his arms and legs as though they had shrunk in the wash. Randy could do nothing but smile back with pure love.

"Watch this." Jimmy says and then begins to wobble one of his front teeth back and forth with his tongue, his eyes almost going crosseyed as he tried to concentrate on what he was doing.

Randy laughed.

"Isn't that something." Randy chuckled and reached out with the tip of his finger and wiggled.

"Mommy said it will fall out soon, then I'll get a dollar from the Tooth Fairy!"

"You sure will!" Randy smiled, putting the tray down on the coffee table "Hey, it's one of the front ones isn't it?"Randy enquired playfully as he stood up to fall height.

"Yeah?" Jimmy said gaping with confusion.

"Well, that means you get five whole dollars for one of those!" Randy said enthusiastically.

"Five dollars!" Jimmy whispered slowly, his eyes growing wide as though he'd just discovered a treasure map "Oh, wow!"

"Anyway, time for bed. Hop on." Randy says bending over, his spine shrieking as he did, he sold no effect of this to his son as he shouted 'Yippee' and mounted his back.

"You ready?" Randy said standing up straight.

"Yep."

"Hold on tight, Champski."

Jimmy flung his arms around his neck and gripped his hands together tightly as Randy wore him on his back like a novelty backpack.

They passed Martha who was standing in the doorway and had watched the whole affair take place, a loving smile etched into her homely face.

"Night Mommy!" Jimmy shouted as they passed her and Randy winked at her.

"Goodnight Boo." She said and watched as they climbed the stairs.

"Up the stairs..." Randy said as they creeped up slowly "Went the bears..." he added and then paused to let Jimmy fill the gap with "Up, up, up!"

They both laughed.

Randy thought that the stairs would become his new nemesis in his coming years. His knee joints creaking as much as the old wooden steps, it was if they were having a competition to see who was the loudest, who had the best squeak.

"Quicker Daddy, quicker!" Jimmy yelled digging his bare heels into his side like a jockey would a racehorse.

"Hey, take it easy there, Champ." He moaned "I can't go any faster. You're getting as heavy Kami Kajeu!"

They arrived at the top and Randy groaned in relief, then shuffled along the corridor to Jimmy's room.

Inside Jimmy's room was like an Aladdins cave of wonders. He wasn't spoilt as such, but he had everything he wanted or what he and Martha thought he wanted. In truth he had too much and rarely played with the majority of it. The posters of himself and his peers filled the walls. Randy wondered whether he would actually grow out of wrestling as he grew older. Was he only interested in it because he did it for a living? Again the conscience battled each other in Randy's head, duelled over what was right for his son's future. What if he wanted to become a wrestler? Would he let him follow in his footsteps? Would he want him to? A side of him thought it would be nice to share the experience with him and then get to live through it all again, watching on and being proud of his son's achievements in what had been for him a way of life. Then the other side to the coin, being in that world that can be so toxic and offer all manner of tempting delights that can lead to wreck and ruin.

No, he had decided long ago that it will be his choices of what he wants to do in life and he will respect that and accept it, offering support to whatever he chooses to be. Better to chase his own dreams, not someone else's.

"Are you ready?" Randy asked him as he pulled him over his shoulder and held him in his arms.

Jimmy smiled that excited smile again and nodded frantically.

"Okay... You asked for it!" Randy said and with that held him up above his head in and military pressed him before letting him fall onto the safe soft landing of his bed.

"Nice bumping, kid!" Randy smiled as his son bounced back up and then began jumping around the bed excitedly.

"I'm going to be World Champion like you when I'm older Daddy."

"I'm sure you will be!" He said grabbing him in a bear hug, more to stop him bouncing around than anything, but looked into his eyes lovingly "You can be anything you want to be."

Jimmy stopped bouncing around and stood in the grip of his Father's loving bear hug, thinking. The cogs of a seven year old's think tank working.

"Can I be an aeroplane?"

"Well... No, Champ."

"Oh!" Jimmy dropped his head looking sad.

"But, you can be a pilot! And pilot's fly aeroplanes."

"Oh yeah! And helicopters!"

"And helicopters." Randy nodded in agreement.

"Oh, wow! I could really be a pilot?"

"Of course you can."

"Wow!"

Randy pulls back the duvet and places Jimmy inside and pulls the duvet up under Jimmy's armpits. Jimmy again looked deep in thought.

"Why are you stopping wrestling?" He asked almost with sadness in his voice as if he was sad for his father having to stop doing something that he loves.

The fact is he didn't love it, not anymore. But, yet he did love it. It was almost like a smoker going cold turkey and giving up smoking. You know it's no good for you but you always crave having one more drag.

"Well..." Randy sighed sitting next to him on the bed and running his fingers through his son's mop of hazel hair, thinking how did I ever make another life as lovely as this little boy. "When you do something for a very long time it can sometimes get you down and when that happens, it's no longer fun anymore"

"So when something is not fun you can stop?"

"Yeah, kind of, in some things."

"I'm gonna tell Mommy that I'm gonna stop eating peas then. That isn't fun at all!"

Randy laughed.

"Yes, but that's different, peas are good for you, they give you muscles like your old man."

"I guess. But they sure taste gross."

"How about you choose a different vegetable? Which ones do you like?"

"I don't know... Carrots and broccoli are okay I guess."

"Okay, then, we'll compromise."

"What's that? Is that a vegetable too?"

"No." chuckled Randy "It means you never have to eat peas ever again."

"Never again! Never ever!" He gasped.

"Never ever!"

"It's a deal!"

"Hold on there a minute, Tex! But you have to pick a vegetable in its place. You understand?"

"I think so." He mulled over the question "No more peas. But, I have to have broccoli or carrots?"

"Yes."

"Okay." He shrugged, and the fist pumped the air "No more peas!"

The two laughed and Randy kissed him on top of his head and started to leave.

"So, do you not like wrestling anymore then?" Jimmy said, his question made Randy sit back down.

"Sometimes we have to make choices in life and sometimes those choices are very hard to make. I was just getting very tired and I missed home, I missed you and your Mommy."

"So, it was like you had to pick between wrestling or us?"

"Yeah."

"That's a tough choice."

"Not really." Randy chuckled "I'm always going to pick you and Mommy over anything else."

"Okay." Jimmy shrugged and turned over to go to sleep. Randy looked at him as he sank down into the bed and became one with the duvet, hugging his favourite stuffed toy close to his face, close enough to smell all this familiar smells that make him feel safe and secure.

"Goodnight Champ." He said as he walked towards the door and flicked off the light switch.

"Night night Daddy." Comes the sleepy reply that ended in a full on yawn.

"Love you." Randy added with a smile again, staring at the curled up lump in the bed and wondering how he ever made something so perfect and how quickly he had grown. He would leave early in the morning and probably not see him, but he felt content that he could spend the rest of his days seeing him and watch him grow into whatever he wants to be.

"Daddy?" Came a weary croak as Randy had turned to leave.

"Yeah, Champ?"

"I'm glad you chose us over wrestling."

"Yeah, me too." He smiled and closed the door.

CHAPTER 39

The Slammer and 'Magnificent' Johnny Midnight sit perched high above the ring on a fifteen feet high steel construction. A structure of unforgiving girders, joints and brackets, all fused together to create the menacing cage that surrounds the ring.

Cameras flash, the light colliding with the steel and giving it the illusion that it has been forged from the stars themselves. The eager fans trying to capture a rare moment and keep it with them forever, something to tell the grandchildren about.

Where were you when The Slammer battled Johnny Midnight in a steel cage they will ask. This question will be asked many times, but not for the reasons that you perceive.

"The Slammer and Johnny Midnight are duking it out at the very top of the cage!" Milton Mcqueen gasps in amazement.

'These people are loving every minute of it, McQueen!" Bunk 'The Hunk' adds.

"They sure are, and for good reason. What a battle!"

"These people are sadistic! Finding entertainment in such a barbaric contest!"

The Slammer and Johnny Midnight teeter back and forth as each throws their weary blows at each other as they straddle the very top of the cage. Every time they move the whole structure sways with them, the sound of steel crunching and clanging together is terrifying, looking as though any moment the whole erection could come crashing down.

"The Slammer looks like he's gaining the advantage here with several right hands to Midnight's forehead that have gone unanswered" McQueen reacts to the one ended battle that is taking place high above them.

"Johnny is on woozy street!" Bunk adds.

Midnight leans back, baking under the heat of the spotlight that is in closer vicinity than normal. Sweat cascades down the ripples of his physique and his eyes roll back in his head.

"You ready?" Midnight murmurs, heard only by The Slammer's ears.

"Yeah!" The Slammer answers and starts to manoeuvre himself round at the top of the cage, placing his feet on the rungs of two of the separate panels that make up the corner of the cage. He grabs Midnight's sweat doused jet black hair in his giant mitt and moves him into position carefully at the top of the cage. The two have never seen eye to eye, especially in recent months with the two of them vowing for the same position within the industry and neither ones ego willing to take a backseat. Tonight they are working in tandem and the results have been very positive, putting on a great match thus far which has had the fans on the edge of their seats. It truly is amazing what can be accomplished by people, even those of who we don't always agree with if we just let go of the ego and work together. The Slammer readies himself and is about to latch onto his opponent and deliver a devastating move from the top of the cage. He grabs onto Midnight's head wrapping a gigantic arm around it as Midnight sits on top of the cage waiting patiently. The Slammer takes the moment to look out at the frenzied crowd, through the gloom and bright flashes of cameras, he tries to come to terms with where he is and how he got here, trying to take in the moment. He looks majestic in his new gear, all in red, peppered with golden trimmed white stars throughout the tights and a red mask emblazoned with one star on his forehead.

Red.

His current outfit red for much different reasons than the ones he has had to throw into the trash prior to this match.

Red.

The adrenaline shuddered through his body with urgency as if it had someplace to be, and the fine hairs that sprouted from his tanned, muscular frame and stood to attention. A moment, that was truly one to saviour.

Red.

His head exploded with pain, he immediately grasped his head in his hand, as if it would help to sooth it, it didn't.

"Joe? What the fuck's going on, man?" Midnight whispered, sensing that something was wrong, it was taking too long and he turned his head slightly to see what he was up to.

"Are you okay?"

Underneath the mask, where the twelve stitches sit tort through The Slammer's flesh, screamed with pain, as if some creature wished to be let out. The redness fell again, but he fought it, for this time the whole affair was so painful. He grabbed at the mask with both hands, his tearing talons trying to pry the pain from his face. In doing so he became unbalanced and looked   as though he would topple backwards into the ring. Midnight thought fast and grabbed a handful of The Slammer's waistband and held it tightly, and with the other hand gripped the top of the cage he was sitting on. He held on for dear life.

"Jesus, Joe! What's going on?" He winched through gritted teeth, concealing the fact he is holding him up from onlookers.

"Are you okay, man? Speak to me!"
As The Slammer's head rotated slowly in a circle on the support of the large bulging trapezius muscles, Midnight bravely (or insanely) released the cage and started peppering The Slammer in the torso with very light looking left hands.

"Come on, Big guy! We can't fuck this up. Not now!" Trying with all the control in his hands to save the match, make it look as though he is indeed putting up a fight and it is this that is the cause for The Slammer's pain.

"The Slammer looks like he's in trouble up there, McQueen." Bunk states with real fear in his voice.

"I think you could be right, Bunk." McQueen acknowledges and thinks quickly "He may be reeling from the effects of earlier on in the evening."
Finally The Slammer started to come round. What lasted a few minutes, felt like a lifetime to both The Slammer and Johnny Midnight, who was still holding on to a handful of The Slammer's tights. So tightly gripped in fact that his hand had turned disturbingly pale.

"I'm... okay now." He grounded and moved closer to the cage positioning himself back where he needed to be.

Johnny Midnight loosened his grip on the tights and let out a breath of relief.

"We doing this now? We good to go?" Midnight asked The Slammer who still looked groggy.

"I..." was all he spluttered as though he was disorientated.

"Suplex!" Called Midnight and synched his own head into the arm of The Slammer and then flung his other arm around the neck of the big guy. Instinct must have taken over as Midnight basically set himself up for the move and The Slammer held him tightly before hoisting him up vertically into the air and then dropped backwards. This was a risky move at the of best of times, but made even more dangerous when the driver of the train is out of it. They fell through the air and it was if time stood still, it seemed to take forever for them to come down. Gasps and shouts sounded muted and eery. Finally they both hit the ground safely and lay motionless.

"Suplex from the top of the cage!" Screamed McQueen, emphasising just how much of a huge move it was.

"They fell eighteen feet!" Embellished Bunk, with equal enthusiasm.

"They're both still down! Doesn't look like...No, wait... The Slammer is twitching and so is Midnight..."
The pair lay in the middle of the ring, the silhouette of the cage bars dominated them, as if they had been dismembered by these thick black swipes of sharp shadow.

"Everything okay?" Called referee Bernie Barnes through the cage. He'd been joined by the medical officer and a brood of other referees and officials all concerned at what they had seen.

"Joe?" Asked Midnight turning to face him.

"Huh?" He replied.

"Are you okay?" Midnight asked, with worry in his voice, he knew that The Slammer was struggling. He didn't like the guy, he never would, but he's not the complete bastard that everyone thinks he is. There was a pause and he saw The Slammer's eyes finally focus as if life had been breathed back into him.

"Yeah...I'm okay now."

"You remember where we're going next?"

"No!" The Slammer groaned and held his throbbing head again "I can't remember."

"Okay." Said Midnight "We are gonna milk this double down okay?"

"Yeah."

"Take all the time you need. I'm gonna wait for you to start coming up before I make my move."

"Yeah, sure... okay."

"Good! You're gonna head for the cage, I'm gonna head for the door. I'm gonna crawl real slow like, okay?"

"Yeah, I'm with ya."

"When you're at the top I'm gonna see ya and shake the cage, that's when you hook your foot up and hang upside down."

"Yeah, I remember now."

"Then I just kind of fall out of the door for the win."

"Yeah, I'm ready!" The Slammer says and starts to rise from the puddle of sweat that has manifested underneath his gargantuan bulk.

The crowd go insane when they see The Slammer rising to his feet.

"The Slammer is up! The Slammer is up on his feet!" Cries McQueen.

"I didn't think either of them would get back up from that!" Bunk said in awe.

"The Slammer is swaying back and forth but he's made it to the cage and he's looking up at it again. Holding his head again, obviously the effects from earlier this evening have indeed taken their toll."

"If he'd got any sense, he'd go through the door!"

"You're right, Bunk. In his condition the easier and safer option would be to go through the door. But, these guys are warriors and sometimes the biggest battle they face is against themselves, to see if they really can achieve."

"Yeah? I call that being stupid! If there's an easy way out. You take it!"

"That says a lot about you, Bunk!"

"What is that supposed to mean?"

The Slammer's clammy hands grab onto the bars of the cage and he slowly starts to climb it. Behind him Midnight slides across the moist canvas towards the door in the corner, dragging his prone body with his forearms, he looked like an exhausted skink trying to find cover from the hot desert sun.

"We've got a race on now as The Slammer is nearing the top of the cage and Midnight is slowly dragging himself towards the door!"

"It's like the hare and the tortoise!" Bunk yells.

"The Slammer has reached the top!" Milton yells.

The Slammer once again straddles the top of the cage and wearily looks out at the mass of moving shapes and flashes of light that surrounds him. He looks down and he can see that Midnight has pulled himself to his feet and is loitering with intent around the cage door. He makes eye contact with Midnight and without saying a word or gesturing he knew it was time, it was just one of those senses that you get when you get the business and how it works, timing, timing is everything. The Slammer attempts to climb over, the uncertain teetering cage frame wobbling which each movement. He starts to scale down the other side, Midnight waits for The Slammer to slip and slot his foot in-between the bars, that will be his cue to shake the big mass of metal. The pain drills into The Slammer's head again, this time the pain is relentless and it screams in his head like harpies from hell. His hands instinctively go up to his head again and he loses his grip on the cage and he falls.

There was an enormous gasp in unison, that seemed to suck all the air out of the arena, leaving behind a deathly void of silence.

The fall was later described as a swan dive, but it looked more like a gannet swooping down and cutting through the water in search of sardines, unfortunately for The Slammer there was no ocean to break the fall or revive him on his landing. He collided with the floor headfirst and lay motionless, blood again flowing through the eye holes of his mask as old and new wounds leak tears of crimson.

Midnight stood like a statue his hands still out in front of him ready to shake the cage wall.

Shock had taken him and this showed by the stupid grimace that was moulded into his face. The look was mirrored by every single person in the building as an eerie hush fell over the arena.

The medical officer and officials rallied around his gargantuan adonis, it was like a God had fallen to earth and no-one really knew what to do.

The medical officer was afraid that he might have broken his neck and refused to move him. He checked for a pulse and was at least relieved to find a pulse, but was still not convinced that a fall like that would not have done any damage to his neck and spinal cord.

A gurney came hurtling down the aisle and fellow wrestlers along with it to see if he was okay and if they could be of any help. All the Baby-Faces of course, Jungle Jim, The Firecrackers, Yellow Feather.

All the fans were now standing, their heads bobbing back and forth as they stretched up onto tiptoes trying to get a better look. Some were even crying at such a travesty, but there were some of course who jeered through the masses, believing it to be part of the show, an act, predetermined. Fake.

Slowly the medical officer used scissors in his gloved hands to carefully cut through the blood soaked mask of The Slammer. Slowly the mask was removed and placed next to him. The Slammer's hand instinctively grabbed it and held it tight, ringing out the blood that had been soaked up by it. It seeped through creases of his hand, he was unconscious but would not let go of the mask.

Raggu and Wally stood and watched, horrified and distracted, selfishly Raggu was already thinking of where they were going to go next as The Slammer had technically (unintentionally) become the winner of the match because he escaped its restraints first.

With the mask now taken away and his face again caked in crimson mask, disgustingly cell phone cameras snapped away as a minority of disrespectful fans took photographs of The Slammer's face. What kind of a world do we live in when a person's initial reaction is to take out their phones and capture other peoples misfortunes?

The old wound had reopened and a larger divot had appeared in the top of his head. It resembled a crater like geyser, any minute now a blast of heated water would surely burst from it.

The medical officer noticed something that confirmed something to him and he turned to Raggu standing behind him and shook his head. A pinkish fluid had started to trickle from his ears and nose. The look told everything Raggu needed to know.

Suddenly, The Slammer's body started to convulse as a seizure took hold of him, something he had suffered through many times before, but always by himself, not shared with thousands of people.

The Slammer was in urgent need of hospital treatment.

The Slammer needed immediate surgery.

The Slammer was done

CHAPTER 40

Louis Raggu swiftly tore through the small packet of sugar and sprinkled it into his black coffee, that sat before him on a small glass coffee table in the lobby of Buchanan Suites in the north of Studd City.

As he swirled the sugar around the coffee with a spoon, he sighed a heavy sigh, the kind that a man sighs when he seemingly has all the worries of the world upon his shoulders. He taps the spoon on the lip of the coffee cup half a dozen times, relieving it from excess moister and placed it down on a napkin that lay on the table, it acted quickly to absorb the coffee.

Raggu sighed again and stared into the thick dark liquid that danced around before his eyes. The darkness of the hot beverage mirrored the burdensome bags that hung from his eyelids. Another night of no sleep had taken effect and strong black coffee seemed to be the only thing that kept him going.

He sat alone in the lobby, no Wally at his side this morning for it was too early and Raggu needed to get his game face on to tackle today, especially with what had transpired the night before.

He couldn't face Wally without a plan. He dared not have a plan of action to tackle such a dilemma. As far as Wally was concerned, his boss always had a plan and knew exactly what to do in any situation. What Wally didn't know was that Raggu was usually up two or three hours before, wracking his brain to come up with solutions.

Last night, well, last night took the biscuit.

"What a fucking night!" he groaned to himself, taking a small cautious sip from the smouldering coffee. As he swallowed he replayed the events of last night in his head and what he was going to do next. As the captain he needed to steer the ship and he needed to steer it in a totally different direction.

He shook his head seemingly at a loss and picked up his cell phone, activated it, used his fatty stubby thumbprint to open the lock and listened again to the voicemail that he received from the SCPD in the early hours.

The following report was made by Detective Clyde Stevens of the Studd City Police Department at 00:02 on Friday 26th April.

Joseph Fox Jr. AKA 'The Slammer' was taken to St. Vincent's Hospital around 22:13 on Thursday 25th April, where he was immediately admitted to theatre where he was set to undergo emergency craniotomy surgery, under the supervision of Doctor Simon Calloway. Unfortunately...

The Slammer lay on the operating table of the theatre. The blinding light that hung over the table illuminated his motionless body but that was all, anything not touched by the light was in total darkness. Anything out of that circle of light seemed lifeless and void of emotion. His clammy bulk of flesh shone under the illumination, flesh that was pasted with dried blood. His rugged face was patched with cleansed areas and blood stained areas, like the paint of a native American. His head had been heavily bandaged which had seemed to stop the bleeding, with just a patch of drying blood seeping through the final layer of gauze.

His breathing appeared normal as he lay unconscious. The shredded and stained mask still gripped tightly in his hand.

"Okay Nurse. We're going to need those bandages off to see what we are dealing with here." Came a voice through the blinding light.

"Yes, Doctor!" Came the muffled reply.

A figure clad in teal from head to foot stepped into the light, it was obvious from the stature and build that it was a female, the head and face covered with surgical cap and face mask, leaving only her eyes visible. She began unravelling the bandages, unveiling the wound.

Another nurse came into the light and took the blood drenched bandages from her and disappeared.

"Ooh very nasty." Said Dr Calloway, leaning over the prone body of the Slammer poking softly at his wound with a gloved finger "Definite TBI, several fractures in the skull..." He then ran his finger over the large divot in his head "Damn, what hit him a bulldozer? I'd say a haematoma too. That takes priority. Thats what we will deal with first."

The lights gleamed off his circular spectacles giving him the illusion that he didn't have any eyes at all, but two bright white lights gleaming in the hollowed out sockets of his dark face.

"Do we have an IV ready to go?" Asks Dr Calloway turning away from the patient to look into the darkness.

"Just about ready to go, Doctor." Came the muffled response of a man. Another teal figure comes into view. This time the tall and skeletal physique of a male nurse.

"Good! Let's go Nurse!" Calloway said sternly.

"Yes Doctor." The nurse responded and nodded, then attempted to inject the general anaesthetic through an already inserted cannula. "Readying it now!"

"Can I get a countdown after the injection please?" Calloway adds.

"Signs are good." Comes the voice from the nurse "Starting the countdown now."

10.

The Slammer's eyes start to flicker as if he were deep in sleep.

9.

The sound of the cranial drill being tested shudders through the theatre like the contents of a busy bee hive.

8.

The heart rate monitor beeps, a little faster than Dr Calloway would like.

"How's that heart rate Nurse?"

"Levelling off now Doctor."

7.

The metallic rattle joins the cacophony as tools are placed in arms reach.

6.

Dr. Calloway turns away to organise his tools and makes sure he has everything he needs.

5.

The Slammer's eyes twitch again, rapidly.

"Erm, Doctor?"

4.

The Slammer's body starts to twitch and the heart rate rises again.

3.

Dr. Calloway turns rapidly.

"What the hell is going on?"

2.

"He's coming out of it!" Shrieks the nurse.

1.

The Slammer's fingers clench around the mask in his hand and he sits up bellowing a war cry that could have woken the dead. He is immediately blinded by the light and turns away almost growling like a grumpy bear witnessing that first bright sun of spring after a long winters nap.

"We need to sedate him!" Yells Dr. Calloway, but his words fall on deaf ears as The Slammer jumps from the operating table, swatting the spotlight away with a gigantic arm. As the nurses move in on him to try and tackle him, he punches the slender male nurse in his face. The sound of his nose breaking against his fist is gut wrenching and blood immediately seeps through his face mask, as he falls onto the table unconscious.

"Get the fuck away from me!" He roars and grabs a small female nurse by her head and squeezes it tightly like he was juicing a lime. Her screams echoed around the theatre and must have effected The Slammer's ears because he let go of her and she fell to the floor, lacerations dug deep into her temples.

He wobbled and then staggered knocking over all manner of equipment and medical instruments as he clawed at his throbbing head.

"We need help here!" Dr. Calloway screamed heading for the door, but he was grabbed by the scruff of his neck and flung over the table into a mass of scalpels and various tools that once lay on trays. The metallic shriek of raining tools pierced through The Slammer's sensitive brain again and caused him to wince with discomfort.

Finally he looked at his clenched hand that homed his mask and smiled a sadistic grin that could have been from Satan himself. He placed the tattered mask over his head once again and felt okay, his unsightly wound still showing and the skin with a patch of hair still flapping around every time he moved.

Dr. Calloway tried to pull himself off the ground and tipped over a metal dish that would have held part of his cranium no doubt. The metal ringing as it hit the hard tiled flooring caused The Slammer to howl and he grabbed at his head again. Then he stopped suddenly, all he could hear was the clanging of a ring bell and the spotlight shone down on a frail female nurse cowering defencelessly in the corner of the theatre. To The Slammer this looked like his next opponent, bathed in the spotlight of the dark and dingy arena. There were ropes behind her and people cheered him on 'Slammer, Slammer, Slammer' he heard the ghosts of the past call in unison and he moved in on her, his menacing gargantuan shroud of shadow smothering her.

...Dr Calloway received only minor injuries, the worst being two broken ribs, Nurse Timothy Dunn suffered a broken nose and concussion, Nurse Debra Miller and Doctor Gail Constanino escaped without injury. Trainee Nurse, Miss Rena Huffman is currently in critical condition after suffering a intracranial aneurysm. Unfortunately Nurse Rose Whistler lost her life at the hands of Fox, suffering a broken neck. Fox fled the scene and has not been seen since. He is now wanted for three cases of assault and murder.

It will have to be seen whether Fox is mentally fit to stand trial for these crimes.

Detective Clyde Stevens

The coffee mug made an ugly scraping sound as it met the glass surface of the table, Raggu rubbed a hand over his damp receding hairline. He pulled out a small notepad from the chest pocket of yet another grotesque looking shirt and started to jot down some notes. Still he struggled with what to do next given that The Slammer ordeal wasn't the only thing that happened last night that forced him to alter his plans.

Mandrillus Kalu AKA 'The Masked Mandrill' emigrated from the Democratic Republic of Congo in Africa when he was just aged twelve. Emigrating may be the wrong word, escaping may be more fitting. He escaped the war torn town he lived in, stowing away on a cargo plane until he reached South America, finally settling in Venezuela where he lived on the dirt streets of a small town on the outskirts of Caracas. It was there that he was discovered by the local drug baron, Eduardo Colón who happened to be driving through the flea bitten town in his immaculate white Rolls Royce, that was as out of place in such a rat invested dump as a full belly of food was. Colón took young Mandrillus in and taught him the trade. Soon Mandrillus was hopping over the border to deliver all Colón's magical South American sugar to the connections over in the United States. One of his best customers happened to be Vinnie Valentine of Studd City. It was through this connection that Mandrillus moved to the United States and settled in Forge City where he set up his own operation and struck up connections with 'The Coyote' Eduardo Gonzalez. He found himself in the bizarre world of wrestling and realised that he could make more money selling to the professional wrestlers. The athletes that needed unattainable items to help them perform or survive the rigours on the road. Cocaine, uppers, downers, marijuana, pain pills, viagra, the most popular being anabolic steroids.

Mandrillus stood in his hotel room at the Buchanan Suites in a tight pair of boxer shorts, that looked the brightest of whites against his dark skin, he cared nothing about what drama had taken place that evening at the Richland Coliseum. He smiled that sparkling golden smile of his as he opened up the suitcase that sat on the bed.

"The candyman is in town and look at all those sweets, girl!" he chortled, turning his attentions to his guest "Didn't I tell you I'd look after you?"

Swaying back and forth on a chair, looking very skittish sat a dirty looking girl, dressed in a short denim skirt and laddered black stockings, while a large jacket shrouded her small frame. Several holes peeked out from the material and some had even been repaired with black electrical tape.

She nodded at Mandrillus vigorously, her greasy dark hair dripping down in front of her face, hiding the pretty features of what appeared to be a once attractive girl, now replaced by the ghostly gaze of a heroine addict.

"Yeah, yeah, I know, I know! Just give me the stuff, man!" she spits rapidly, before sniffing and wiping the contents of her streaming nostrils on her coat sleeve.

"Patience, Princess! Patience!" Mandrillus scowls not liking to be rushed or told what to do, ever.

He sieved through the mass of baggies, boxes and bottles made of glass and plastic, prescription stickers half scratched away on the majority of them.

"Now, how much you want? A baggie?"

"Half!" She hacked.

"Half!" He boomed, followed by an irritated sucking of his glistening nuggets that were merged into his teeth "Fucking Half, girl!" He shouted again picking up the bag of powder and waving it at her "You call me up noon and night whining about you need this shit! I listen to all your shit and all you want is half a baggie?"

"I've only got a twenty." She says quietly.

He clenches his large hand around the baggie and squeezes it. He takes a deep breathe and leans down to her level, staring her right in the eyes. His dreadlocks dropping over his face, giving him the appearance of a caged animal trapped behind long slender bars.

"Now you listen to me!" He said quietly and calmly but his face meant business "You wanna fuck me around, turning up with twenty bucks? Damn girl! I don't deal my shit with no hopers, this stuff is the real deal and you have to pay real deal prices!"

He smiled at her, it was a menacing golden grin.

"You think I'm a street corner hustler, just out to try and get what he can? Then think again, bitch!"

The girl swallows, her wide eyes peaking out from behind her curtain of hair.

"I'm the top fucking dog!"

He stands back up to his full height, almost seven feet of it and holds the baggie out in the palm of his hand, his wrist and fingers dripping with gold.

"So, how much do you want?"

"Oh, I think I have got a hundred after all." She said pulling out a crumpled up bill from her deep pocket.

"Yeah, I thought you might!" He laughed, snatching up the grimy bill with the scrunched up picture of Benjamin Franklin looking up at him.

"Girl? Don't you ever go trying to fuck me!" he said matter of factly as he threw the bag into her lap "Because your ass will lose!"

There is a loud resounding crash and the door to the hotel room swung open violently. The loosened hinges groaned in pain and shards of splintering wood burst from the area where the lock was once nestled safely in place. As the door swung open it revealed two police detectives, who quickly moved inside with guns clenched tightly and aimed directly at Mandrillus.

"Freeze, you fucker!" Came the growl from Detective Freeman.

"SCPD!" Called his partner Detective Graham.

"What the fuck?" Mandrillus shouted and rummaged around in his suitcase grabbing a large Magnum Research Desert Eagle "Fuck you pigs!" He growled ready to take aim with his oversized handgun.

"Get your fucking hands up, Manny!" Came the purr of the girl behind him, he felt the cold nose of her police issue Glock tickle his flesh as she pressed it up against his kidney area.

"You little bitch!" He whined and dropped the gun to the floor with a thud.

"Turn around slowly big man!" She added.

He turned around placing his hands on his head and stared angrily at the petite frame of Officer Valerie Nash aiming her handgun back at him with intense delight on her face.

"Great job, Nash! Well done!" Graham said smiling, a gleaming grin that was more than just a proud superior.

Other uniformed officers enter the room with guns fixed on the huge man, just incase he tried something.

"Cuff him, Richard!" Said Graham.

Detective Freeman moved in cautiously and took his wrist and latched on the first bracelet "Don't you go doing anything stupid now, Big man!" Freeman said taking hold of his other wrist.

"Hey, my brutha! Help me out here?" Mandrillus groaned.

"I'm not your 'brutha'! You fucking jackass!" Freeman seethed cinching in the second bracelet real tight.

Mandrillus grimaced as his hands were now locked tightly behind his back.

"The hell you are! You're that white man's brutha! Need to break those shackles my brutha! Step out of the white man's rule!" nodding his head towards Detective Graham who was now putting his gun back into his shoulder holster.

"Get the fuck out of here!" Freeman growled and pushes him towards the door, the uniformed officers stepped out cautiously with guns still locked on him as they lead the way for Detective Freeman.

Mandrillus eyeballed Nash on the way out and then growled a metallic snarl in Graham's direction. Graham smiled back smugly "You know what's a real shame?" he said, his words causing Mandrillus to stop and look at him bemused.

"What's that?" He asked.

"I was looking forward to watching you get your ass kicked by some other fucker in spandex tonight."

"Oh yeah?"

"Yeah! I've had tickets for a while. Would have been nice for my kids to see a real life loser up close and personal."

"Fuck you man, and your fucking ugly kids!"

"You're the one that's fucked, buddy." Smiled Graham "I hear they like 'em big up at Skelter!"

Freeman pushed Mandrillus on his way and began reading him his rights as they disappeared down the corridor of the hotel.

"Well done, Officer Nash." Graham said, smile shining through the shrubbery of his auburn beard.

"Do I get a promotion now?" She grinned dropping her dirty coat to the floor and revealing a netted shirt that hardly covered her bra underneath.

"We shall have to see!" Detective Graham smirked and slowly closed the door behind him.

Raggu was still busy writing when Wally appeared in the chair opposite, he hadn't noticed him at all, but he heard another mug of coffee slide over to his line of vision and looked up to see him sitting there.

"Good morning Wally! Didn't see you there."

"Are you okay? Please tell me you've had some sleep?" Wally asked.

"Yeah, yeah, slept like a dog."

This was obviously a lie, three hours at the most would have been the correct answer.

"So!" sighed Wally "What are we going to do now?"

Raggu closed up his private notepad and slid it back into his chest pocket, clippings the pen in next to it. He picked up the coffee, sipped it and sank back into the chair.

"I know exactly what we are going to do."

"Really?"

"We build someone else!"

"But who? They're dropping like flies!"

"The title is going to be on Midnight, yes?"

"Yeah, but what about..."

"Give me chance, Wally!" Raggu snapped wearily and then sighed "Sorry about that" He sighed and took a sip of coffee as if that may help his mood. "We are going to bring Nemesis back and we'll have him chase Midnight. We should be able to gain sympathy for him with what happened to him at the hands of The Slammer and then he can chase for the title."

"Great!" He shrieked enthusiastically, he'd always had a soft spot for Nemesis, knowing that he was one of the good guys and easy to do business with.

"I've got my eyes on a young kid, goes by the name of S.D Douglas. Thought we may be able to sprinkle some magic dust on him."

"Sounds good to me!"

"I also want to introduce a Women's title and have Megan take that."

"Great!"

"Well, needs must. You have to keep the machine moving, Wally."

Raggu sinks back into the chair and finally feels like he can rest before another big night in the wrestling industry.

CHAPTER 41

From The Diary of Randall Rogan

Friday, April 26th
Flight L3 1616, From New York to Studd City.

Firstly, I'd like to take back my initial feelings on flying to shows. I had complained about how the majority of the industry's top stars fly now more than road tripping. Flying is great! Maybe it's because I have been travelling alone these last few years, distancing myself from the others that my mindset has changed. But, maybe it's my age and I just want less hassle. Either way I think I will continue to fly instead of face the riggers of the road...What am I saying? After this weekend I won't be on the road and my next trip will probably be to Hawaii to renew my wedding vows. Yes, I have booked it, and no I haven't told Martha yet.

To say that today was a little bit surreal would be an understatement. As I sit on another plane writing this, the realisation had finally hit me, well, it smashed me in the face like a Giant Nagata stiff right hand. I'm not embarrassed to say that I just excused myself to go to the bathroom cubicle, where I spent fifteen minutes crying.

It's such a huge event, something that I have done for my entire life is coming to an end.

Are the tears through sadness or through happiness?

If I'm completely honest they're a little bit of both. You could call it an amalgamation of grief and relief. It's the end for 'The American Man' Randy Rogan and the beginning for 'Father and Husband' Randall Rogan.

Life starts now!

I would like to say that all the anguish and trepidation that I have felt this morning and through last night's broken sleep was due solely to my retirement. But, I think a lot of it stems from last nights events.

Seeing Joe fall from that cage (after already suffering that appalling injury early on) sickened me, it actually scared me. I mean, that could have been me! That was my initial and selfish thought, really I think that is human nature. We are first hit with shock and then I think our brains compute it as 'Phew, at least that wasn't me!' I don't think we can change that, that's just how we think. I really feel for Joe, he's had a rough time of it of late, I know he has had some personal demons to battle, I don't really know what they are, whenever I tried to talk to him about things he would get defensive and close up.

So, I thought I wouldn't pry it wasn't my place to, he'd tell me when he was ready.

Maybe I should have carried on prying, I guess that's my guilt to live with if he doesn't come out of this.

I do believe that a lot of it has to do with the pressures of the business though, especially as he was set to be the next guy, it's not for everyone, you have to be made of different stuff. I'm not saying stronger, but different.

You have to have the right mentality and I think if you're already a bit of a loose cannon and dealing with the inner turmoil of holding back the reaper, then you're doomed from the get go.
I hope he is okay though, but it didn't look good.

Raggu sent me an email last night (as I wanted the card) and also he filled me in with what had transpired incase I didn't know. I did know I watched it live in a puddle of my beer that I had dropped as I shot up from my recliner, gaping in shock. After a while I thought I probably looked like that famous painting by Edvard Munch, 'The Scream'.

Raggu told me that he had been taken to the nearest hospital (St. Vincent's I believe) and would undergo surgery for what is believed to be a fractured skull and a possible subdural haematoma.

I still haven't heard anything of how it went, whether it was a success or not. Or whether he even survived such an ordeal! I'm no brain surgeon but it sounded fucking serious to me. I just hope he's okay.

I like to document all my matches, have done since my very first match, so I will scribble down tonight's show and add the match, venue, date and result to my records when I get home...

It will be the last thing I add to those records...

Crazy!

Joe falling from that cage just keeps replaying in my minds eye over and over again... Still selfishly thinking...

'That could have been me.'

FALKINBURG ARENA,
GRENOBLE, STUDD CITY

Sebastian Churchill vs Clayton Tex (12-15 mins)

6 Man Tag
Puma Kid, El Corazón de Plata & El Flamingero vs El Talón, Mr
Canada & Dr X (12-15 mins)

René vs Emily Kincaid (10 mins)

Pedro Passion vs Jungle Jim (15 mins)

World Tag Team Championship (3 way)
Devastation (c) vs Rhino Bros vs Firecrackers (20-25 mins)

Yellow Feather vs The Masked Mandrill (15 mins)

Megan Powers vs Mistress Evil (10 mins)

World Heavyweight Championship
Randy Rogan (c) vs Johnny Midnight
(30 mins)

CHAPTER 42

Megan is swamped by her fellow female wrestlers, Big Bella Marie, Emily Kincaid, Mistress Evil, Vicious Veronica and the masked Grass Snake, all congratulating her in the locker room.

"I'm so pleased for you, Meg!" Emily squeals grabbing her tightly round her neck and nearly causing her to fall over.

"Take it easy, Em!" Megan laughed.

"Yeah, congratulations, girl! If anyone deserves it it's you." Bella Marie brims.

Rene leans on the wall next to them, a sour look on her face like she'd been sucking on a lemon "Yeah, I guess!" She scoffed under her breath.

The comment was only heard by Mistress Evil and she moved up real close to her and whispered in her ear "You'd better watch that forked tongue of yours, René. It may get your scrawny ass in trouble!"

"Screw you, dyke!" René growled.

Mistress Evil immediately grabbed her by her throat and swung her around until her back connected with the wall of lockers. The clamour halted the girls merriment and they all looked to see what was going on.

"Whoa! What's going on?" Megan asked.

Mistress Evil ignored her and squeezed René's throat until she started to turn an unpleasant colour.

"Now you listen here you little tramp! Don't you dare come in here with your green scrawny ass thinking that you have a right to fucking be here! You've gotta earn your right, you hear me?" She screamed at her, René struggled to breathe but nodded frantically.

"All these girls have earned that right! Nobody here has got where they are through sucking dick apart from you!" And with that she let go of her and backed off towards the others who stood there still unaware of what was said to cause such a ruckus.

René slid down the lockers holding her throat and gasping for air.

"Mr Raggu is going to hear about this!" She said through heavy breaths.

"Go on! Tell the fat cunt! I'd do the same to him too!"

René climbed to her feet and ran out of the locker room.

"What was all that about?" Big Bella asked.

"She was disrespecting us." Mistress Evil shrugged.

"Girl! Your ass is crazy!" Chuckled Bella Marie.

"Anyway!" Mistress Evil said planting a kiss on Megan's cheek, painting it with a large red lipstick mark "Congratulations. It's great to finally see that we're going to have a Women's Championship after all this time!"

"Love you girls!" Megan said beaming from ear to ear as they all huddled together in a large affectionate clinch of comradeship.

The door opened and in shuffled Miss Crystal, dressed in casual sweats her hair tied back in a scruffy ponytail, her face looked grey and frail.

"Crystal!" Emily cried and they all approached her and hugged her. She looked tired and weak, but her face brightened when she saw them.

"How have you been, Crystal?" Grass Snake asked

"So, so!" She shrugged, even that gesture seemed to make her body ache.

"Are you working tonight?" Emily asked in surprise.

"No, I've got to take some time off." Crystal said meekly almost embarrassed by the sentence "Looks like I've gotta go into rehab." Her face glowed with discomfort.

"Hey, I've been there!" Mistress Evil said, "It ain't no picnic believe me. But it will be worth it in the end." She said with a caring smile and hand on her shoulder.

"I'm gonna try my best." Crystal said smiling back at them, gazing at all their faces and seeing pity in their eyes, but also love. She didn't want their pity but she did need the love.

"Are you going to watch the show?" Megan asked.

"Yeah, It's a big night for the business. I have to be here."

"Get in here, girl!" Bella Marie yelled and grabbed her, pulling her into her bulging bosom and squeezing her tightly "I ain't never letting go!" She yelled and the others huddled around again in cackles of laughter.

CHAPTER 43

Randy Rogan sat all alone in the locker room as he taped up his wrists. The sound of tape being ripped was all that could be heard apart from the very distant reactions of the crowd out in the main hall.

He wound the tape around his left wrist, several times and then pressed it down into place rubbing his fingertips over his wrist, taking longer than he ever had before, to feel the rough texture of the tape. He couldn't believe that this would be the final time that he did it, something that seemed so insignificant the other thousands of times that he had done it. But now it seemed like the most important thing in the world. He stood up and waited for the inevitable weeping of his ageing joints. He found himself laughing as he stretched and all 33 vertebrae in his spine chimed like someone dragging a percussion stick over all the bars of a xylophone. That would always be with him he thought, a souvenir from this adventure.

He walked through the locker room, the familiar smells of stale sweat and muscle balm fluttered around his nostrils. He looked around and surveyed the room, glancing at everyone's bags and cases that homed their personal effects, treasures that kept them safe. The familiar smells that their items must have to them, smells of home and of loved ones, charms if you will to keep away the demons of the road and remind them what is waiting for them back at home.

Randy knew that soon he could have those scents under his nose forever, and not have to ever be without them again. The regular clothes of his peers hung up on the pegs provided or left thrown unceremoniously on their bags or the benches. To Randy these discarded items of clothing were like the skins of the wrestlers, the outside world membranes that they wear everyday in the real world but take off when they need to perform, when they need to become someone else. Which is the false skin?

He arrives at the full length mirror and stares at his reflection, for a moment he sees that wiry teenager that started sweeping the ring and fetching and carrying for the wrestlers, back in Long Island. Then before his very eyes he saw himself manifest into that bleached blonde clean shaven blue chipper that he was when he started off, a turquoise singlet cutting into his ripped physique. As age took hold and his row upon row of shredded abdominal muscles gave way to one rotund mound and a more natural hair colour with a thick moustache balancing across his top lip, the singlet gone and replaced by lime green trunks. The reflection changed again, and the trademark stars and stripes that he inherited from his mentor, 'Uncle' Sam Reagan. Then numerous titles appeared and disappeared around his waist or draped over his shoulder, showing all his illustrious accolades within the blink of an eye. Then his current reflection pulsates into view and he stares at what he is now, what he has become. Red trunks and red knee pads, flashed with stripes of white and blue and silver sequinned stars dotted throughout, flickered in the light and made him feel like he was somebody. He smiled, years of mental and physical abuse and he was still happy with how he looked, he wasn't sure how long he would look this way though, not with Martha's wonderful homely cooking every night. But to say he can walk away from it with only minor aches and pains was victory within itself.

"Good Job, Old Man!" He chuckled to himself and found that he was doing various poses in front of the mirror, his face contorting with each pose, something he hadn't done since he was a freshly picked strawberry and believed his own hype. He looked over to where his items were and there was old faithful, lying on the bench winking at him so seductively, like a secret mistress that you've had to call time on because your wife was becoming suspicious.

Please don't leave me. I love you, I'm forever yours.

These are the whispers that tempt him to go back on his word and carry on this adventure. He strides over to it quickly and grabs it as if to shake that other woman and tell her 'no' and to 'leave me alone, it's over now'.

He stares at it for the longest time, it's heavy, but to him it's weightless, it's a part of him.

"Randy?" Came a voice from behind, he span around on the spot, a little embarrassed that he hadn't heard anyone come in and couldn't remember how long he'd actually been standing there.

"Huh?" Randy said goofily and as he turned he saw his opponent for the evening and the man he would be passing the torch onto, 'Magnificent' Johnny Midnight.

"Can I talk to you?" He said.

This was a line that Rogan had heard dozens of times during his career, it was usually followed up with 'I heard you've been saying this!' or 'So and so said you'd said this!'

Nine times out of ten that is how these conversations end up going, the majority of the time was just bullshit or things had been taken out of context and there had been a mountain made out of a molehill.

"Yeah, sure!" Rogan sighed.

Here we go. What have I said now and who to?

He searched his mind for any conversation that he had had where he had made any derogative remarks about Johnny. He could think of none.

I'm too old for this schoolyard political bullshit! Fuck it! Why should I care either way? After tonight I'm done anyway.

But he did care, he was passionate and protective about his reputation, he hated seeing it tarnished by others and their misrepresenting of the facts.

All I've ever tried to be is a good guy and help people where I can. Yeah I've made mistakes and misjudged situations myself, but none of the mistakes I ever made were done in malice. I really shouldn't let this bother me so much but...

"I wanted to say thank you." Johnny said interrupting Randy's argument with himself.

"What?"

"I wanted to say thank you!" Johnny repeated.

"For what?" Rogan snapped and then immediately wondered why he did.

"For being my inspiration and the reason I got into the business in the first place."

"Oh!" Rogan said rather sheepishly.

"Obviously, I would also like to say how grateful I am that you're putting me over tonight." Johnny was so solemn it was a side that Rogan had never witnessed from him before. In fairness he hadn't really got to know him and maybe that's his fault, maybe he should have got to know him a bit better instead of listening to everyone else's opinion on him. Listening to the bullshit of others, exactly what he'd just been arguing about with his own conscience.

"Well, thanks! Look I'm sorry I snapped at you just now."

"Hey, it's cool I get it."

"You do?"

"Yeah! It's Pro Wrestling! Everybody's shields are up. There are so many poisoned tipped darts flying around in this business, you have to keep your defences up!"

"Too true." Rogan laughed and a gong was struck in his head, the realisation that everybody feels the way he does, everybody is in the same boat and all suffer with the same anxieties and inadequacies. Some just hide it better, some of them just want control of the oars instead of all rowing together.

"Sit down, kid." Rogan said openly with a friendly smile and sat down on the bench.

"Thanks!" Johnny said and sat next to him.

Rogan looked him up and down, he was a good-looking guy, good physique and he knew there was nothing wrong with this in ring work. In fact he looked like a million bucks in his special gold trunks that he'd had made especially for this evening. Gold attire was surefire advertisement that the said wrestler was going to win a title. "So what shit do you want to get in tonight?" Rogan asked, assuming that was where the conversation was going to next.

"Oh, we can talk about that later. I'm happy to go along with whatever you want to do out there."

"Oh? Okay!" Rogan nodded, very surprised and totally thrown off by him. He made the mistake of judging him like a lot of the younger generation and was expecting him to list of an array of moves that Rogan would enviably shoot down because there was no need for them.

He was pleasantly surprised.

"I'm trying to make amends." Johnny started and looked down at the floor as if he were embarrassed to say the words "I've been a complete dick and I know everybody hates me."

Rogan wanted to intervene and tell him that he was wrong, but he couldn't say that, that was peoples verdict on him. Dick.

"I know I came in here hot off the Indies and it was daunting you know? To come in here and everywhere I look I could see the guys I grew up idolising when I was a kid!"

"Yeah, I get that. I've been there myself." Laughed Rogan.

"Well, I just wanted to come in and do my best, but then that turned into wanting to have the best match every night and not care whether I was stepping on other peoples toes. I know it pissed a lot of people off when I'd go out there and do spots that they had planned or I'd do too much."

Rogan was surprised that he realised that he was doing too much.

"I guess I just wanted to be noticed, so I went all out every match."

"That's understandable, everybody wants to be noticed. It's like we're fish in an aquarium. People only want the pretty, colourful flashy ones."

Johnny nodded in agreement.

"But, all those fish make that tank work. Yeah, it's nice to have the clown fish and the angel fish to look at, but the tank needs the likes of Amano Shrimp and Ramshorn Snails to remove the algae. They're not attractive in the slightest but they get the job done."

"Yeah!" Johnny laughs appreciating the metaphor "I've let my ego get out of control and have developed a huge chip on my shoulder. I want to change that and I hope to have similar conversations with the other guys after tonight."

"That's very professional of you, kid. I for one appreciate that. I'm sure some of the old guard will too."

Rogan holds out his hand and Johnny's shakes it.

"I will say one thing though, Johnny."

"Yeah, what's that?"

"I know that you've got a weakness for the ladies."

"Hey, I'm not going celibate for you, Man!" He laughed.

"I'm not going to ask you to! There's worst demons to have in this game." He chuckled "But, just be careful who you are jumping in and out of bed with. I mean rats are well and good but when you start shitting on your own doorstep, that's when it can get unpleasant."

"Yeah, I hear ya. I'll try. Really I will." He laughed not sounding very convincing, Rogan shook his head and laughed with him.

"Oh, Raggu said that he wanted me to get some colour tonight. I haven't got a clue how to do it? Could you show me?" Randy smiled and all of a sudden he felt like he was back in 1986 again.

CHAPTER 44

CHAMPION VS CHALLENGER

'Magnificent' Johnny Midnight had already made his way down the aisle, as it is customary in the industry the challenger enters the ring first. Randy stood behind the curtain ready to go, for the last time. The curtain fluttered slightly due to a breeze that worked its way around the arena causing it to gape slightly, giving him a glimpse of what awaited him, standing room only in a jam-packed arena. Thousands had crammed themselves into Falkinburg Arena to witness Rogan's last hurrah.

He felt slaps of support on his back and backside, his tight buttocks hardly moving in his tight fitting spandex trunks. There were muffled 'go get ems' and 'good lucks' but he couldn't really hear them, he was in the zone. Already his mind was visualising the match that he'd put together with Johnny earlier, he was a very visual person and saw everything play out in his head like a movie before hand, it was just how it was with him. He often thought that in another life he may have been a film director. It was just clear to him, in his minds eye he'd already had the match.

He cracked his neck viciously from one side to the other and the sound of his leather jacket creaked with each nervous movement of anticipation. The long tassels that hung from the sleeves tickled his exposed thighs as he straightened his jacket into place, hoping that everyone could see the stars and stripes logo that he'd had airbrushed on the back of it for this special occasion. The words 'One last time' emblazoned across his shoulders in a graffiti style font, in the colours of the national flag.

The butterflies bumped into each other in his gut, why did he feel so nervous? He had not felt this nervous since his debut where he threw up in a trashcan before going out. In truth he hadn't felt those butterflies for a long time, and it's been said many times that when the butterflies stop fluttering it's time to call it a day. But they were back in full force tonight, he smiled to himself, he had missed them.

His music kicked in, it was show time, he nodded his head to the tune and then started stamping his foot, waiting for that moment, that very moment in the song where he would burst through the curtain like he had thousands of times before.

"One more time." He said and stepped through onto the aisle.

The crowd exploded when they saw him and he stood for a moment longer than he ever normally would, just to take it all in. He looked around and felt proud to see so many people with beaming smiles on their faces calling his name. The t-shirts that had his likeness or logo embellished on them, the foam fingers that waved in the air and most touching of all was seeing the arena filled with flags of his country that he held so dear. He started to move on when he felt the urge to cry, but as those boots started slapping against the aisle he was back in the zone.

He slapped hands that stretched out over the guardrails to touch him, grasping fingers tugged at his jacket. It was almost like Beatlemania as he struggled to make his way to the ring, past the masses of flailing arms lurching towards him, like the tentacles of some sea creature or reaching hands of the living dead in some zombie movie. Finally he made it and skipped up the steps onto the apron, opening up his jacket to show off his World Heavyweight Championship, another cheer from the crowd that was somehow even louder. It was a rarity indeed to receive the pop on top of the pop.

Rogan wipes his feet on the apron, like a polite visitor that has been invited into someones home for the first time. He stepped through the ropes and walked into the centre of the ring, to soak up the incredible atmosphere.

He nodded in approval and acknowledgement of his adoring fans, tonight they were giving him everything, so that's exactly what he would give them, everything.

The music died and a constant chant of 'Thank you Randy!' rose up from the crowd and seemed to spiral around the arena as if it were caught on the ever so popular Mexican wave. The reason it seemed to come from everywhere at once was simple, everyone in the arena was chanting it. This brought tears to Randy's eyes again and he tried to take his mind off by settling into his corner and slipping off his leather jacket. He managed to force back the tears and stepped forward again to the centre of the ring where a nervous looking Johnny Midnight was waiting to meet him. Veteran referee Bernie Barnes smiled at him as he pretended to read them the rules of the match, he'd known Randy since he was a small kid sweeping arena's and fetching and carrying. Bernie had personally asked Louis Raggu to be assigned to this match, he had so much respect for Randy.

"You ready, Champ?" Bernie asked.

"I think so." Chuckled Randy and unbuckled the belt that was synched around his waist so tightly. He stared at the championship, it had never looked so beautiful with the spotlight reflecting on its golden plates, the tiny rubies that had been painstakingly secured in place, at the hands of a very talented craftsmen all those years ago. He rubbed his fingers over that eagle that he'd come to know so well and lifted it up to his face kissing it one last time and savouring that familiar cold metallic taste in his mouth. He lowered it and handed it to Bernie who smiled again "It's been a pleasure, Randy." he said

"Yeah, one hell of a ride!" Randy said as he witnessed the championship being held aloft in the air by Bernie for all to see.

Randy was pleased to hear the reaction of the crowd for the title, it was nice to know that it still meant something to the people and that holding it meant something too. He was proud as punch to be able to say that he helped make it as prestigious as it had become.

"Thirty years of my blood, sweat and tears have been spilt over that thing, kid. Now it's your turn." He said to Johnny as the two of them stood face to face in the centre of the ring "I hope you're ready for it?"

"I hope so too!" Johnny said breathing long and deep as his glance shifted for a moment to the title, probably pinching himself that he had even made it this far.

"Well, you made it to the dance. Are you ready?" Asked Randy as they stood face to face "Shall we dance?"

"As long as you don't tread on my toes, old man!"

"Old man is it? Oh! We are on!"

Narrow smiles caressed the lips of the two readying titans, not enough for any of the crowd to notice.

The bell rang to indicate the match had officially started and the smiles disappeared immediately. Kayfabe was in full effect and it was game time.

The pair circled each other, you could say it resembled a tiger circling its prey, looking for that opening, for that advantage, but these were both tigers, both of them alphas, fighting for territory and survival and in the end there can be only one winner.

They lock up using the oldest wrestling hold in history, the hold that has become synonymous as the starting stance for wrestling since grappling had become a thing thousands of years ago, and now all those years later in modern day it still lives on. An arena swelling to the brim with people to watch two men sweating under the harsh spotlights pay tribute to that specific hold, the collar-and-elbow.

Their tort biceps and brachioradialis muscles collide with a solid thud gripping each other firmly like birds of prey latching onto their unsuspecting victims with tapered talons. They jostle for position for a moment, their faces contort, grimaces painted on for effect but there is no pain or struggle.

"Ready?" Rogan murmurs.

Midnight grunts back a response that he is. On hearing that Midnight is indeed ready, Rogan pushes him off with all his might sending Midnight down to the canvas with so much velocity that the momentum propels him out through the ropes and onto the floor. An impressive looking feat, Rogan who was the bigger of the two now looked stronger and more dominant as he flexed his muscles in the direction of his opponent, who had popped up immediately onto his feet, his face slathered with humiliation.

The crowd ate it up, cheers for Rogan and an earful of jibes and obscenities for Midnight.

Midnight slides back into the ring under the bottom rope and charges Rogan out of sheer embarrassment, as he attempted to put Rogan in his place. Rogan is ready for him and a carefully placed hand behind Midnight's head as he passes, sends him over the top rope, back to the outside of the ring.

The crowd again roar in a frenzy of adulation for the champion and ridicule for the challenger who is once again left dumbstruck at ringside.

Rogan laps up the enthusiastic praise from the crowd and showboats for them with a muscular montage of varying poses.

Midnight is soon back in the ring, his cheeks puffing like a pissed off adder ready to spit venom. He takes exception to Rogan's gloating and grabs him mid pose spinning him around to face him. Midnight berates him with a mouthful of abuse that ends with a schoolyard push to the chest.

"Slap me!" Midnight says under a gritted teethed mask of annoyance. Rogan immediately obliges and whips the palm of his right hand across the cheek of Johnny Midnight's pretty face. The sound was like a gunshot going off and Midnight was sent crashing down to the mat again as quick as a snapping mouse trap, he rolled out the ring gently rubbing his sore cheek that was already glowing and throbbing like the pulsing of a police car's cherry.

Midnight walked around the ring, shaking his head in disbelief, trying to figure out how to play the game against the champion. He wore a look of a man that was doubting himself, a look that had very rarely (if ever) been seen etched on the face of 'The Magnificent One' before. He stood out at ringside for a while (maybe too long) and the crowd were getting restless.

"He's milking it too long, Bernie." Rogan said to the referee "Get him back in here."

"C'mon, Johnny get back in here!" Bernie shouted at him and started to count him out, a raised hand indicating to all what number he was currently up too.

Midnight pulled himself back onto the apron and grasped the top rope, glancing at Rogan, the eye contact was there and Rogan knew exactly what to do. As Midnight returned the fast ball of abuse he was receiving from some loudmouth in the crowd like a professional tennis player, Rogan grabbed the top rope and yanked it towards him bringing Midnight in the hard way over the top rope with a front flip landing unceremoniously on his backside. Midnight hurried back to his feet. Now he's hot and vexed to the point that he will try anything to get his hands on Rogan. He makes the mistake of charging towards him again and Rogan adjusts his body and hooks his arm under Midnight's armpit. He used his own momentum against him to flip him over in a hip toss manoeuvre sending him back down to the canvas.

"Arm drag!" Muttered Rogan.

Midnight hears and lunges at him, allowing Rogan to take his left arm and force him down to the mat with a twist of his body. Normally he would hold onto the arm and work over it to weaken it or maybe to give himself and his opponent a breather, but not tonight. He lets go of the arm on impact and Midnight is soon back to his feet and coming again.

"Gorilla press!" Rogan croaks and Midnight positions himself as he moves forward at speed to take the said move. Rogan places a hand just underneath his throat, positioned comfortably on his collar bone while his other hand grabs his thigh, high up near his groin and hoists him up straight into the air. Midnight pushes himself upwards with hands placed on Rogan's thick trapezius muscle, the sight is really quite magnificent, as Rogan walks around the ring with him held up in the air for all to see.

The crowd cheer wildly, some of them pleading with him to throw him out of the ring or even into the pig pen with the rapid boars to let them have their way with him.

Rogan declines and drops Midnight crotch first onto the top rope. Midnight's eyes bulge as the tort top rope connects with his testicles and his mouth gapes in a comical manner as the crowd feel his pain with a mimicking 'Oohing' sound in unison, as he sits uncomfortably perched on the top rope.

"Hold on to your nuts!" Rogan says as he approaches him and grasps the top rope tightly, then he begins shaking it up and down, uncomfortably the rope rubs against his inner thighs and collides with his private parts until he is flung back into the ring, where he cups his baby maker in his hands, hoping that they have remained intact.

Midnight scowls and stands up to full height and again foolishly races towards Rogan who drops his shoulder and sends Midnight spilling over the top rope with a back drop, Midnight finds himself once again on the outside of the ring.

Rogan takes the time to strut around the ring again, grinning like the cat that got the cream and if Midnight continued to use his frustrations to spur him on, then he will not be receiving even the smallest taste of cream tonight.

The announcers argue over the headsets as they talk about the match to the people watching at home. McQueen believing that Rogan is just too experienced for Midnight and that he will successfully go on to retire as champion of the world. As usual Bunk 'The Hunk' disagrees and insists that Midnight is just feeling out Rogan, and it's only a matter of time before he makes a mistake and then Midnight will make his move.

Rogan feels short-winded and pants like a dog, his pulse rate rising. He takes a minute while Midnight is again playing the crowd outside and retrieving that much needed heat from them.

Blown up? Already? Can't be!

He takes a deep breath in and his whole ribcage shudders, it was a nervous shake that reverberated all over his body.

Nerves? Really?

He smiled and took the moment to take stock, he wasn't blown up it was just nerves, it felt extraordinary to him that he could still be nervous after thirty plus years of doing something.

I know why you're nervous, Old Man! Because you don't won't to fuck this up. You won't! Now, get your shit together.

Midnight cautiously slunk through the ropes and back into the ring, this time it would appear that Midnight was indeed trying another tactic. Done with the hotheadedness approach that had failed him numerous times, he stalked Rogan slowly and appeared to want to try his luck at locking up again.

"You ready to go again?" Midnight asked.

"You know it, kid." Rogan answered and the two lunged at each other to lock up once again.

This time Midnight used his speed (which was his asset against this particular opponent) and slipped out of the collar-and-elbow tie up and took Rogan's head in a headlock. He hooked his hands together in that favoured butcher's grip and began to squeeze. In reality, the muscles in his arms were flexed and the face was grimacing but the hold was a loose as a politicians morals.

"Are you okay, old man?" Midnight grimaced.

"I'm good. Just keep it goosey loosey, kid, gooesey loosey."

"Okay, where'd you wanna go from here?"

"I'll attempt to grab the rope. You switch up into a wrist lock."

"Gotcha!"

Rogan shuffles slowly across the ring, twisting his body and trying to reach for the rope, if he reached it then Midnight would have to release the hold. Midnight needing to keep control of his stronger opponent, grabs at Rogan's arm that is within touching distance of the top rope. Holding Rogan's arm by the wrist he twists around causing his arm to go tort and he drops to his knees, discomfort shown on his ageing face. Midnight positions his fingers in place so he has a good grip and forces his thumbs into the base of the palm, applying pressure on the ulna and radius where his forearm meets his wrist and forces his hand backwards.

"Ease up!" Rogan grimaces and Midnight loosens his grip slightly but still his face remains the same, as though he were applying an immense amount of pressure.

Rogan rises up from his knees, a layer of grime already staining his once pristine knee pads, he may have been annoyed at this after the match, but he knew that these particular knee pads were to be auctioned off for a local charity and they seemed to pay more handsomely for items that were spoilt in someway or another. He swivelled his body, took hold of Midnight's wrist and with a quick spin he reversed the hold and now Midnight was on the receiving end. The two exchanged reversals, each of them getting the upper hand on each other if only for a few moments before being outsmarted. They were locked in a circle of oneupmanship that neither looked like winning, technically they were matched in every way. Then the crowd watched on in appreciation for both wrestlers and the art form of professional wrestling that was on display, their motion was so fluid that they looked like two dancers gracing the canvas in coordinated choreography.

Finally reaching a stalemate, Rogan uses his larger frame to force Midnight back to a corner, the referee is immediately there calling for a break, they both submit to the referee's wishes and release each other. While Bernie eases Rogan back to the middle of the ring to give his opponent space, Midnight hatches a despicable plan. He turns around and fumbles around trying to untie the rope that keeps the turnbuckle pads in place. The crowd exploded ferociously at Midnight, calling to the referee to turn around and witness this treacherous unsportsmanlike behaviour.

The referee turns around but, Midnight is conniving and hides what he was trying to do, but the referee's interruption was enough to foil his plans of removing the pad and exposing the steel turnbuckle that lay underneath.

"Hey! What're you doing, Johnny?" Bernie enquires with air of suspicion.

"Whoa, Man! Nothing!" Midnight gripes, holding his hands up in the air showing the official that he has nothing concealed in his hands and a false face like butter wouldn't melt.

The competitors look as though they are going to lock up once again when Midnight takes a short cut by driving a knee into Rogan's solar plexus, causing him to double over with the sudden impact. Midnight sees his chance and takes it by grabbing Rogan's head in another Headlock. Rogan soon over powers him again and pushes him back into the corner once again. As the referee retreads his steps by breaking them up and moving Rogan back to the centre, Midnight continues with his loathsome deed and quickly unties the rope from the turnbuckle pad until it comes off in his hand. He then disposes of it over the top rope and with a wink to the crowd that infuriates them, he saunters back to tackle the awaiting Rogan.

Now, Midnight had an ace up his sleeve, with the turnbuckle pad removed he was obviously scheming of a way to plough the champion's face into the exposed steel bolt, that was supposed to be used to adjust the tension of the ring ropes, not reconstruct Rogan's facial features. It was a hand he could play later on for neither Randy Rogan nor the referee had noticed that it had been removed.

Midnight rushes towards Rogan, trying old tactics and possibly hoping that he wouldn't be expecting it, but Rogan is too slick again and sidesteps the incoming magnificent missile and Midnight hits the corner at full speed, his sternum compressing as they hit the firm pads. Luckily for him it was the opposite corner to where he'd been laying his trap. Rogan grabs a handful of Midnight's thick greasy hair and lifts him up into position. The referee gets on his case for the hair grabbing and Rogan apologises like the role model he is. Midnight sinks into the corner holding his chest.

"Okay, you ready now?" Rogan asks as he looks out at the people with the open palm of his hand in the air, almost asking for their approval.

"Yeah, beat down?"

"Yeah!" Rogan grunts, before asking the crowd "Shall I?" The crowd call back with an immediate response that he should indeed.

Rogan takes the palm of his hand and spanks it across Midnight's chest. The sound of chopping flesh on flesh carries around the arena and rides a wave of 'Woo' that blares from the crowd.

He strikes again with the reverse knife edge chop and the crowd respond again.

"Okay, let's go!" Rogan says just before hitting a final strike that left the indentation of his hand on Midnight's blemished chest.

Rogan grabs him by the arm and tugs him out of the corner with the intent to send him into the opposite corner, but Midnight holds on. With a quick dos-à-dos he manages to reverse the Irish Whip manoeuvre and send Rogan hurtling towards that corner with the exposed steel turnbuckle. Rogan hits the corner back first and goes down instantly favouring his back.

The crowd are hot now and extremely unhappy with Midnight for his deception to gain the upper hand and also the referee, for not seeing such shenanigans going on right under his nose.

Midnight is quickly on the downed champion like a shark that smells blood in the water and unleashes a tirade of viscous looking stomps and kicks to the wounded area.

Rogan tries on several occasions to make it to his feet but every time he rises up onto his hands and knees, Midnight lashes out again. The rubber sole of his boot pounding down on his injured back.

"Get some heat." Rogan murmurs through the gritted teeth, of what appears to be excruciating pain.

Midnight stops with his attack and turns his attentions to the crowd, with arms stretched out either side he spins around on the spot showing how superior he is to them all and to his downed opponent. They fire back with a rising chorus of boo's. It would seem that they all know this song and are in good voice this evening.

Rogan crawled towards the ropes, hoping that he could pull himself up with their help, but when he gets there Midnight is on him again and drapes his throat across the middle rope and leans on him, causing him to choke and splutter, spittle spraying from his mouth and settling in his beard. The referee immediately intervenes laying on the count to break the hold or he will be disqualified and blow his chance of becoming the Heavyweight Champion of the world. But Midnight knows that he has a five count and bends the rules enough to break the hold on four. Midnight is backed off by Bernie who gives him a tongue-lashing for cheating so blatantly.

Midnight takes no notice and attacks the ropes behind him using the momentum to send him striding towards Rogan who still remains draped over the middle rope, gasping for air. Midnight launches himself and with open legs jumps and straddles the back and head of Rogan with a leapfrog body guillotine. He stays in the position for a while gloating to the crowd, sitting on the back of his neck and adding insult to injury. Another rapid count from the referee is enough for him to dismount quickly and back away again as Rogan's limp carcass falls to the floor. Not knowing whether to hold his back or his throat.

"Is this all he's got?" Midnight yells pointing at the crowds fallen hero, they show their disdain and Midnight laughs it off. Seeing Rogan starting to rise again he approaches him, to stay on top and hopefully do more damage to his already injured back, with the main objective being to soften up that area for his finishing manoeuvre, 'The Midnight Feast'.

Midnight yanks Rogan up by his head and lifts him up as if to possibly perform a bodyslam, but instead holds him there for a moment for all to see before bringing Rogan's back down onto his knee for a devastating backbreaker. He lets Rogan fall to the mat with agony dripping from his middle aged face, with his face contorted it made him appear older than his years and sympathy oozed out from the crowd.

Rogan clutches at his back and his body arches, almost convulsing through the damage caused by Midnight's excellently executed backbreaker. Midnight takes the time to gloat again, once again adding fuel to the fire of animosity that bubbles away under the crowd.

Rogan rises again and murmurs to Midnight to stay on him. Midnight obliges and delivers an elbow drop to the small of his back, causing Rogan to become grounded again. Midnight rolls him over and attempts a cover, it's a nonchalant effort not even hooking the leg to stop Rogan from kicking out and even with the injured back, Rogan is out on the count of one.

Midnight's arrogance may well be his downfall.

There is a subdued cheer from the crowd, more through relief that their hero is still not out of this match yet, down but not out. Midnight moans at the referee that he should be counting faster and while doing so, Rogan has managed to get to his feet, still favouring his back. Midnight gives him a swift kick to the stomach and then as Rogan doubles over, he hooks up his head with his arm before wrapping Rogan's hanging left arm around his own neck. He hoists him into the air before falling backwards with a snapping suplex. The ring quakes under the impact, the sound of Rogan's body being dumped to the canvas in such a fashion carries around the seething sea of humanity all calling for Midnight's head. Rogan's body again arches off the mat, contorting with pain.

"Clutch." Rogan winces through a sad face of torment, rolling over onto his front to help set up the move for Midnight. Rogan never once remained motionless while down, he had to appear to the crowd that he still had some fight in him. Many made the mistake of lying dead when they have taken big moves. He continued to crawl towards the ropes.

Midnight stomps on his lower back and that halts the crawling for a moment while he positions himself for one of the most devastating submission holds in Professional Wrestling. He grabs Rogan's arms and places them on his thighs. He interlocks his fingers and muzzles his mouth while cradling his chin, then he sits down on Rogan's lower back, causing his whole upper body to become curved in an unnatural position. With the camel clutch locked in place, only time will tell whether Rogan has enough to escape as many have fallen to this hold. The hold itself looks agonising, in truth it's not too far away, it can be very uncomfortable if left in the hold for a while. Rogan and Midnight take the time to have a breather and talk about where they are going to go next, with Rogan's mouth covered by Midnight's hands, he can talk quite freely without anyone seeing him communicating.

"You okay, Kid?"

"Yeah!" Midnight murmurs through gritted teeth, his arms tort as if the hold will end in Rogan actually being split in half. They both remain quite comfortable for the time being, albeit hot and clad in a thick layer of sweat caused by the humidity, the spotlights and the exertion of doing such things under these conditions.

"Good, good!" Says Rogan "So far so good, Kid."

"How long you wanna keep it like this?"

"There's no rush. We're gonna wait for them to decide. Don't make the mistake of going too early, they want it, but the timing has to be right."

"Right, gotcha."

"But, we've gotta dick tease these bastards, Kid. We're not going to break when they come up and fire up straight away."

"We're not?" Midnight says looking shocked and stares at Bernie who is smirking back at him, pretending to check on whether Rogan is going to give up or not.

"That's what they'll expect. I gotta sell this back too. So we come up once and boom, back to my back and back to the hold."

A lightbulb goes off in Johnny's head somewhere, that moment when people get it has just hit Johnny Midnight.

"We will milk it again and then wait for them to come up again."

"Will they come again?"

"They'd better!" laughs Rogan "Then we break the hold and I'll hit some fire."

"Got it!"

Rogan stares out into the crowd and latches onto a small boy in the first row, wearing a Randy Rogan shirt and a gigantic foam finger protruding from his right hand. It looked ridiculous like in a cartoon when someone would accidentally hammer their thumb and it would throb and quadruple in size comically.

"Right, here we go!" Rogan says.

He makes eye contact with the boy in the crowd, the moment is electric, the boy's eyes widen and you can see him glance around to see if his hero is looking at someone else. Rogan manages to loosen an arm from around the confines of Midnight's knees and reaches out towards the child as if pleading him to come and help him. The child turned to his father and his brother he mouthed something to them and his father patted him on the back, probably not believing him. But the boy was not deterred and he started screaming and chanting for Rogan.

Rogan communicated back rapidly opening and closing his hand towards the boy as if trying to grab the invisible words leaking from his mouth ,and using them to prop himself back up.

"Here we go!"

The boys chanting was soon picked up by several others in the crowd and Rogan slipped another arm free and now both hands open and closed rapidly in the direction of the chants. Soon it snowballed and more and more chants rose in the arena. Rogan started to nod his head and then the whole arena was calling in unison 'Let's go Randy, let's go!' And that's just what Randy did. He managed to get to his knees, still with Midnight straddling his back and with his hands clenched tightly around his greasy beard. Rogan got to one foot and then the other, still with Midnight on his back. Rogan cradled his legs in his arms as Midnight shook his head in shock and confusion and then backed him off into one of the corners. Midnight released the hold and Rogan staggered forward holding his back, much to the delight of the crowd. But as Randy bent forward trying to get his breath, Midnight is quick to shake off the effects of Rogan's escape and climb up to the middle rope where he jumped off, and with clenched hands delivered an axe handle smash to the wounded area. Rogan fell to the ground once more in agony and Midnight was again back on him without a moments thought, again applying the dreaded camel clutch.

The crowd boo loudly and then settle down again, they needed a rest just as much as the wrestlers after that one, but they would soon return in full force.

"That was incredible!" Johnny gasped.

"Told ya. Next time they'll really explode!"

It didn't take long, they did explode and all it took was that one reaching hand again, they immediately went with him, so the escape this time was much quicker, they were ready for it. That was the art, making them feel part of the show, making them believe that their actions had a significant effect on the match. Acknowledge the support and they will be there for you, ignore them and they'll leave you to rot in the camel clutch.

Rogan rose again, almost identical to the last time only a little quicker, but as Midnight hung on to him like a bull rider at a Rodeo, expecting the same backing into the corner sequence, Rogan through a spanner in the works by throwing himself backwards, so Midnight took the impact and Rogan landed on top of him. The crowd erupted again as both men struggle to get to their feet now, Rogan still jabbing at his injured back with a balled up fist as if to try and kickstart it again.

Midnight throws a wild right hand but it is blocked by Rogan's meaty forearm and he fires back with a right hand of his own that causes Midnight's head to snap back on his neck. It was a very nice sell and it made Rogan's shots look devastating. Again and again Rogan uses the handsome face as his own private punchbag as he gets into a rhythm. But, just as it looks as though Rogan is back in this match, Midnight jabs a thumb in the eye of the champion interrupting his attack. Midnight tries to shake off the dizzying effects of Rogan's hefty rights and can be seen rubbing at his jaw, Rogan staggers off holding his eye. The referee and the crowd team up to berate Midnight again for dubious tactics, but he ignores them. Instead he swings a whirlwind righthand towards Rogan, but the wily old veteran had his number and quickly ducked the swing.

Hey batter, batter, batter swing, batter batter! Rogan thought and laughed to himself.

The momentum of missing the right hand causes Midnight to spin on the spot and with his back to Rogan, he takes full advantage lifting him up by his hips and driving the base of his spine down onto Rogan's bended knee with authority, in a reverse atomic drop. As Midnight sells the effects to his derrière he turns slowly to be met by a slab of Rogan's arm that collides with his chest knocking him down to the canvas. Rogan holds his aching back again but drops to the canvas and covers Midnight, making sure to hook a leg to make it difficult for Midnight to escape.

"One...Two, Two count!" Indicates Bernie who holds two fingers up.

The crowd thought it was enough and a gasp of 'almost got him' hissed from them like the sound of leaking gas.

They rise again, but this time it is Rogan that has the advantage and he grabs Midnight and hooks him up for a suplex, maybe looking for some payback from earlier on in the match.

He attempts the manoeuvre once more but is halted by the pain in his lower back. However with the people cheering his name he gives it all he's got and hoists Midnight up in the air, but Midnight manages to kick his legs and unbalance Rogan causing him to slip down behind the champion and jab him twice in that injured kidney area. Then Midnight clasps his hands tightly around Rogan's waist and falls back taking Rogan with him in a German suplex. Rogan's shoulders hit the mat and Midnight expertly bridges on the top of his head and toes as to keep his own shoulders from being counted down.

The referee is down quickly and counts "One...Two..Thr...No!"

Rogan just about comes out the back door and for the moment manages to hold onto his title.

Midnight cannot believe it's not a three count and sits in shock next to Rogan who still keeps coming, trying to rise up again.

"Referee!" Midnight yells at the top of his lungs and holds out three fingers to him, but the referee shakes his head and holds up two in response. Midnight grabs at his sodden hair and screams in annoyance.

"Time to shine, Kid." Rogan says pulling himself to his feet "Get your shit in now."

Midnight grabs Rogan and manages to lift the large opponent up into a body slam, not going for a cover as he was placing him into position for a following up move. He exits the ring and settles on the apron. He looks out at the crowd, all of them booing him apart from a gaggle of females blowing him kisses, but this was too important for him to get side-tracked now. He climbs to the top rope and some of the crowd hold their breath. Since making it to the big time he hadn't pulled this move out yet. On the Indies he would do it every match, the majority of that crowd are numb to it now, but this crowd had never seen him perform it before and watched on in anticipation of what he was about to do. He looked down at Rogan as he stood on the top rope and thought about what he said earlier, this was a special match and called for a special move.

"Always keep something in reserve." He whispered to himself and with a deep breath and with a bend of the knees, he threw his body into the air feet first. His body whipped around and came hurtling down to splash the prone Rogan in a perfectly executed a shooting star press.

The crowd gasped, some even applauded him for such an amazing piece of athleticism. He lay on top of Rogan who actually gasped for air himself, the landing being so on target that it knocked the wind out of him.

"You okay?" Midnight enquired.

"Yeah!" Rogan groaned "Think I've shit my trunks!"

They both chuckled for a moment, then Midnight lay on him and the referee counted.

"One...Two...Three!" Calls Bernie and Midnight rolls off him with hands raised in the air, but Bernie interrupts the premature celebrations immediately when he sees Rogan's foot draped over the bottom rope.

"No, no, no!" Bernies yells.

"What?" Midnight screams.

"Foot on the rope!" And with that points to show Midnight that it is not over yet.

Midnight looks like he's out of ideas and foolishly attempts to ascend the ropes again. Is he looking for the same manoeuvre again or something even more stupendous?

It does not matter because Rogan is up on his feet and hits Midnight with a few shots to the gut before climbing up to join him. With Rogan on the middle rope on the inside and Midnight on the outside with one foot up on the top, Rogan grabs his head and positions him for a superplex which could well finish the job. Midnight taking advantage of that injured back of his, sinks his knuckles into the fleshy area around his kidneys causing

Rogan to let go of the hold and with it, any intentions of going through with what he had planned. With Rogan doubled over and Midnight perched above him, he saw his opportunity to try another high spot and leapt off the top rope flipping over Rogan, but grabbing his thighs on the way down bringing him down to the mat with an impressive looking sunset bomb.

Midnight holds on to the downed Rogan and the ref counts again "One, Two, Th..." Kick out! Rogan survives again and Midnight collapses backwards to the mat shaking his head in disbelief. Searching the corners of his brain for the answer to the question he's been asking for the past twenty minutes, 'What is it going to take?'

As Midnight is lost for a moment of self denial in his own ability, he doesn't notice that Rogan has pulled himself back to his feet by holding onto the rope. The crowd definitely noticed and they start clapping in unison. Rogan grips the top rope tightly and begins to stamp his feet in harmony with their rhythmic applause, nodding his head as the claps get faster and faster.

Midnight is there again trying to play party pooper to the Rogan farewell celebration and lays in some clubbing forearms to the top of his back, but Rogan doesn't feel them. He's in a whole other zone now and the adrenaline has started to kick in. He turns to face Midnight who looks gobsmacked and whips him with a slicing Mongolian chop, flooring the challenger. Midnight rises quickly enraged and again making the mistake of letting his emotions cloud his judgement. He attacks Rogan with his arm outstretched to deliver a clothesline, but Rogan has his number, he ducks the oncoming outstretched slab of meat and spins rapidly on the spot, delivering a stiff spinning lariat that floors Midnight again. He bumps hard but is back up again and seemingly hungry for yet more punishment, as Rogan meets him with a bionic elbow which Midnight bumps and bounces right back up from. His ego even getting in the way of his pain threshold now, unfortunately for him he runs straight into a big boot to the face that knocks him staggering back into the corner. Rogan moves in now, feeling he is in a rhythm with the increasing pump of the adrenaline flowing through his body which momentarily masks the pain in his lower back. He grabs Midnight's arm and yanks him toward the opposite corner (with the exposed turnbuckle bolt protruding from it) with an Irish whip. Midnight is quick like a cat and jumps up onto the second rope to stop himself eating the steel and jumps backwards, turning himself around in midair to crossbody block the oncoming Rogan. Amazingly, Rogan seizes him out of the air and turns him around driving him into the mat with a crisp scooping powerslam.

Rogan covers him, hooking the leg as standard for the veteran, but Midnight is out of the pinning attempt with half a second to spare.

The crowd are riled up into an absolute frenzy now, all of them 100% behind their hero, chanting nonstop now for their champion.

Rogan rises up and looks out at the crowd. If it is possible, it seems to get louder. He nods in appreciation of them and holds a thumb up to the sky, they scream as they know what's coming next. He turns that thumb around so it's facing downwards, as if he were some Roman Emperor calling for his gladiator champion to finish off his latest opponent. With the thumb swiftly whipped down, Rogan roars "For Old Glory!" and picks Midnight's lifeless body up and places him on his shoulder in a reverse fireman's carry. Everyone knows that he is going for his finishing move that was known as 'Old Glory Driver' (In some circles the move was known as the tombstone piledriver).

This is exactly what the people want, they want to see him defeat Midnight in the centre of the ring with his finishing move and then retire as champion.

Rogan positions him into place but Midnight's greasy flesh helps him slide off his shoulder end ing up behind him. Midnight getting desperate now, grabs a handful of Rogan's hair and attempts to ram his face into that dangerous hunk of metal again. Rogan places his boot on the middle rope and blocks his attempt and then drives Midnight's head into it instead. Midnight falls to the canvas clutching his forehead. With Rogan's kidney starting to burn again, Rogan collapses too.

They lay next to each other, the spotlights cooking their flesh from above. Steam rising off their exhausted bodies and drifting through the crisscross of vanilla lights.

    "You okay, Kid?" Rogan asks turning his head slightly to see if Midnight was okay with the blading process.

    "Yeah, I think so." Midnight answered, a little trepidation warbling in his throat as he answered.

Rogan looked on and could see Midnight's right hand quivering.

Bernie knelt between them as if to check that both competitors were indeed okay and able to continue. "Think he may need a bit of reassurance Randy." He whispered and Rogan nodded.

Bernie rose to his feet and started to put a count on both of the fallen combatants, they would have ten to answer the call if they failed to do so, the match would end in a draw.

"He's counting already!" Midnight squealed in panic "I haven't done it yet, I'm not going to have time!"

"Take it easy, Johnny. You've got plenty of time. Bernie knows what he's doing. We got a nice slow count going on here. We've got all the time in the world."

"I don't know whether I can..."

"Just breathe, kid. Take the gig and dig it in at your hair line."

"Okay!" Midnight says his voice quivering.

The sharp shard digs into his flesh, pecking at him like the beak of a buzzard it goes just deep enough as it needs to be and blood already starts to make an appearance.

"Okay, now twist that little son of a bitch."

Midnight twisted it slightly, but nothing else happened.

"Twist it again. A little sharper this time."

He did as he was told and now the flow came, it was warm as it dribbled down his hands. The sensation was strange but it was also exhilarating Johnny thought as he slide the small blade into the waist band of his trunks.

"Okay, Bernies on seven, let's go." Rogan advised and they both started to rise again.

Rogan held his back again, selling the effects with a furrowed receding hairline and puppy dog eyes. Midnight's face was drenched in a constant flowing of crimson, the crowd gasped at the sight of it. Seeing the females in the crowd recoil at his face was a rarity for Johnny, but it also meant that he had gotten the desired effect, and the blade job was a success.

They both staggered around the ring and then came fill circle, facing each other once again like the very beginning of the match. Rogan moves into action quickly as he picks up Midnight for the Old Glory Driver. This time there is no escape for the befuddled Midnight as he hangs lifeless in Rogan's tight secure grip, his head smearing blood onto Rogan's large thighs as he readied the move. Rogan growled in pain for his back as he jumped up into the air and came crashing down to the mat on his knees. The point of the move to drive Midnight's head straight into the canvas. Rogan let go of Midnight and let him dissolve into the canvas along with the sweat and blood seeping from his body. Rogan slowly   drapes his tired body on top of Midnight's and the referee counts again.

"One... Two... Thr...! Two!" Shouted Bernie long and loud, much to the surprise of the gasping crowd.

Amazingly Midnight managed to escape the pin with a twitch of his shoulder that could have been down to a knee jerk reaction more than anything, but whatever it was, Midnight was still in this match and it was time for the shocked champion to ask himself what more does he have to do.

Now Rogan is the one who is trying to pull out all the stops and climbs up to the top rope. With a wave of his hand, gesturing for the people to stay with him, they comply and chant his name again long and loud as he stands on the top rope for possibly the last time in his career. He looks around taking it all in then with a leap of faith, delivers a picture perfect top rope elbow drop on the bloody mass of flesh that is 'Magnificent' Johnny Midnight. He covers him again with a draping arm for Midnight to again find something from somewhere and kick out at two and a half again.

The arena is filled with gasps.

In their eyes, Midnight wasn't even in the same league as Rogan before this match but now with how it has been worked out, it has also made Midnight look like a main event player to them.

Rogan looks out to the crowd astonished, the same gaping faces stare back at him.

"Welcome to prime time, kid." Rogan pants. He knows that Midnight has just made the step up, and they will accept him as a top guy now. They may not like him, but they will at least acknowledge that he deserves to be there.

Rogan stands up again, this time he grimaces with the pain of his back and looks out at the crowd for an answer to defeat Midnight, they don't have one but they continue to holla in support. Rogan is taking an awfully long time to make his next move and alarmingly starts to climb the ropes again, but this time his positioning is very different as he looks out to the crowd with his back to his downed opponent. The crowd immediately rise to their feet as they look on in awe of what this man, at the end of his career is doing. With no fucks given he throws himself backwards and for the first time in his career attempts a moonsault. As he soars through the air, everything appears as if in slow motion. But when he nears the canvas, Midnight is no longer there, having taken the precaution to roll out of the way and Rogan hits the ring with an horrendous thudding sound.

As the crowd groan for their fallen hero, the bloodied mess of Johnny Midnight staggers to his feet. He grabs Rogan's arm quickly spins him around, rolls over him, rolling him up in a magistral cradle to try and score a surprise win.

"One, Two, Thr…"

Rogan kicks out.

Both men rise again, but Midnight grabs Rogan by his trapezius muscles jumping up high into the air pulling Rogan's body down onto his waiting knees. Rogan calls out in pain as he feels the impact of Midnight's knees crushing into his spine with a nasty 'Back Stabber'.

Johnny Midnight has finished messing around now and grabs the legs of the downed champion. He intertwines his legs around his own turning him over while cradling his legs under his arm, before sitting down abruptly on the lower back of Randy Rogan.

Rogan's arms flail around and clutch at his sweaty hair from the pain shooting into his lower back as Midnight tries to synch down with the submission hold that he calls 'The Midnight Feast'.

How long can Rogan hold on in this torturing hold? The crowd are soon by his side again calling his name. They spur him on once more and he pushes himself up onto his hands. He starts to pull himself towards the ropes, the crowd scream and Midnight shakes his head. Rogan groans in agony but finally manages to grab the bottom rope.

The Referee taps Midnight on the shoulder to release the hold but Midnight thinks he has won the match, he thinks that Rogan has tapped out and conceded. While Midnight is arguing with the referee, Rogan somehow again uses that intestinal fortitude to drag himself back up the ropes and moves back to the centre of the ring, refusing to lay down and die. Midnight is given the signal by Bernie that he is back on his feet and a red faced Midnight leaps into the air athletically kicking Rogan in the back of his head, flooring him again. With Rogan again down on the canvas, Midnight tries to lock in his devastating finishing hold. This time Rogan uses all his might to push Midnight off, the two rise up again facing each other. Wounded and battered like two templar knights on the bloodstained battlefield of The Holy Land. Blood still oozes from Midnight's handmade wound and drips from his nose and chin onto the canvas staining it with dark red droplets. He hits the ropes and dives at Rogan, who catches him and drives him down to the mat for a ribcage shaking spinebuster. But, Rogan's back is too injured for him to attempt a cover and slowly they rise to their feet again.

"Shall we go home, Kid?" Rogan asks under his breath.

"I thought you'd never ask!" he scoffed under heavy breathes.

Rogan turns around and is almost taken by surprise as Midnight launches a crescent kick towards him. Rogan manages to catch his foot and spins him around to disorientate him, then goes for the Old Glory Driver once more. Surely hitting this now with everyone so tired, would be the end of it? But Midnight manages to wiggle free and scoop Rogan up in his own finishing manoeuvre. What insult to injury it would be if "Magnificent" Johnny Midnight defeated Randy Rogan with his own move! Luckily for Rogan, he is too heavy and his deadweight at this late stage of the match has worked in his favour. Midnight drops him back down to his feet, looking incredibly exhausted.

Midnight sways in the middle of the ring on the verge of passing out it would appear. Rogan has a little left in the tank and hits the ropes for momentum and charges towards him, but as he nears him, Midnight drops down as if to attempt a back drop to the onrushing Rogan. He manages to see this, and flips over him for a sunset flip. Unfortunately for Rogan, Midnight reads this and sits down right on top of him. He hooks up his legs and with no way to kick out, the referee counts "One...Two...Three!"

The bell rings to indicate the match is over and there is a new World Champion.

The people are stunned and then boos haunt the arena like a hunting owls predatory cry.

The two of them lie again on the canvas looking up at the lights, their chests rising and falling rapidly.

"Randy?"

"Yeah, Kid?"

"Thank you." He chokes, trying to hold back his emotions.

"It's been a pleasure Kid. Don't fuck it up!" he laughed and continued to lie their looking up at the lights and remembering the hundreds of other times he lay there in the same predicament. There were tears in his eyes when he heard the unmistakable enthusiastic cry of Waylon 'The Voice' Voight announce...

"And New! World Heavyweight Champion... 'Magnificent' Johnny Midnight!"

Rogan looked to where Johnny once lay, but now there was nothing but a blood stained canvas.

He had already left to embrace his new championship, which he cradled in his arms like it was a newborn, then kissed it lovingly, not the way he would kiss one of his many ring rats, it was almost a caring kiss. He held the title high in the air as it was custom for people to take photographs and such. The news was probably already being circulated around the world on the internet that there was indeed a new champion of the world. Strangely Midnight left the ring early, under a chorus of jeers from disgruntled fans in the crowd. Some of them even going as far as launching soda cups at him as he fought his way back up the aisle. Rogan caught a glimpse of one hitting him on the top of the head and it made him chuckle, as ice cubes burst out of a cola drink and dripped down his back. "Count yourself lucky Kid. When I was your age it would have been filled with piss."

He started to hear a gentle clap caress over the crowd and then it grew in volume as he sat up with moist eyes.

Bernie knelt in front of him and thanked him for everything that he had done for the wrestling business. He even had tears in his eyes too as he told him that if it wasn't for him keeping the business afloat through the dark times, then his children may not have eaten some weeks. Rogan appreciated that immensely and Bernie left the ring and joined the announcers and officials outside at ringside applauding him.

Rogan finally rose to his feet and cried without feeling stupid because the people in the crowd were crying too. There wasn't a dry eye in the house as they said goodbye to one of the greatest in the business the only way they knew how with a roaring chant of "Thank You, Randy! Thank You, Randy!"

He waved to them all as he stood in the middle of the ring his face damp with tears and perspiration, and did what only true legends would, he continued to sell the back.

CHAPTER 45

When Randy shuffled through the curtain for the final time in his career, he was suddenly confronted by a blockade of people waiting for him, everyone was there from his current wrestling fraternity, smiles on some faces, tears in the eyes of others. They instantly burst into a ruckus of applause and hollering that took him by surprise.

He was so taken aback by the whole affair that he seemed to drift back in time, once again riding the nostalgia train with the next stop being Memory Lane Station.

He heard muted congratulatory bleating and felt the caress of warming hugs, handshakes and kisses on his cheeks, but again he wasn't there. He was suddenly transported on the other side of such farewells all those years ago. Goodbyes that he himself had said to old legends of the game and old friends long gone from the business, sadly some long gone from this world.

He felt the warmth, love and support and he appreciated it, but at that moment he was trapped in a daze, a daze that was showing him flashes of all those he'd said farewell to over the years. They appeared before him in the places of the well-wishers as if like spirits, pleasant shadows from his past. The sight of them made him smile, seeing them applaud him too.

The likes of Colt Hansen, 'The Samoan Warriors' Sina and Fiti, The High Chief, Jack Dynamo, Magnus Meadowlark, Captain

Yankee, Golden Velvet, 'Beautiful' Bob E. Dassler, Professor Sakata and of course 'Uncle' Sam Reagan.

Gazing at the transparent slender face of his mentor Sam Reagan again made his eyes well up to the brim, and when he smiled at him and lifted up a thumb of acceptance, he melted.

This was purely all his own imagination but to him he had accomplished everything he had set out to do and deep down he knew that his hero, mentor, teacher and friend was proud of him and that was all he needed.

The flood gates opened and the eery holograms of yesterday dissolved.

Randy fell into the arms of Sebastian Churchill and the two of them cried together as rising applause and cheers surrounded the pair. Randy had survived thirty plus years in the wrestling industry at the very top of the mountain and came out unscathed on the other side.

CHAPTER 46

Room 191

Mark Schroeder had booked into the Buchanan Suites late afternoon that day, knowing that all the wrestlers stayed here when in Studd City. In fact he had a whole notebook filled with all the hotels and inns that the wrestlers stayed at in almost every state. He'd even kept a tally of how many times a said wrestler had stayed in each hotel and even kept a log of the room numbers.

He was always a little bemused that Ace Armstrong would book into one hotel with the other wrestlers and then usually hightail it to the cheaper parts of town where he would then check into a really cheap room for a few hours before returning back to join the others. To say that Mark was a little naive to the things that go on in the real world was an understatement to say the least and it was also an understatement to say that he took his Pro Wrestling very seriously. It had become an obsession to him, so much so that he left home months ago and has had no contact with his Mother or any other members of his family since.

He sat on the edge of the bed and gazed into the mirror on the dressing table of the small hotel room. His sockets were deep from lack of sleep and puffy and moist from fresh tears. He returned to the hotel a few hours ago, straight after the last match of the night, for once he didn't wait with the others for autographs and photographs, he had too much on his mind. His eyes seemed to leak uncontrollably like a sink pipe that was in need of a plumbers wrench.

He didn't like the reflection he saw. The sad round greasy face, with a sprouting of facial hair in random places, keeping the greasy raised heads of his acne company. He had thought that this patchy monstrosity of bristles would make him look more like his hero, Randy Rogan. He had wanted to grow a beard like his for the longest time but his heavily acne scarred skin wouldn't allow it. He scowled at the failed attempt now, he no longer wanted the beard.

"I'll shave it off!" He spat and stood up, tearing away at the American flag bandana that was tied ever so tightly around his dirty greasy receding hair. The bandana had left a red line across his forehead as though he'd been scalped by some native that had yet to take the trophy.

As he stood up dressed in dirty sweat pants and an over sized t-shirt that clung to his rippling torso, he looked at the design on the t-shirt and he made eye contact in the mirror with Randy Rogan that was growling back at him.

"Fuck you, Randy!" He blubbered, his bottom lip wobbling like Jello "You're no hero of mine!" And with that defiant act of betrayal he tore the shirt off, leaving him disgusted at his obese physique that was peppered with bed sores underneath the folds of his unwashed flesh. He grabbed his bag and stormed off to the bathroom, again he found himself looking in the mirror, hating what he saw, trying to shut the doors on reality and the life he left behind. That is why he had escaped that world and stepped into the strange world of Professional Wrestling, it was escapism yes, but he had taken it that step too far and to him this was the real world and everything outside it may as well just have been a soap opera playing out around him.

He abandoned his travel bag on the closed seat of the toilet and rummaged around inside it until he found a plastic carrier bag that contained his wash things, they weren't used very often. He removed a razor from it and dropped the carrier back into his travel bag. The razor had no protective sheath on its business end of things and rust had started to appear on the jagged blade, revoltingly old scraps of hair from shaves of the past had clung to the razor blade and refused to leave. Mark didn't care about such things and ran the hot tap until steam started to rise from the basin. He had no shaving foam or cream, such things were luxury to him so he picked up the small block of hotel soap and rubbed it together under the hot water until there was some sort of lather forming in his chubby fingers. He smeared it unceremoniously on his cheeks, dabbing in random areas. Even though he was in his thirties he had lived a very sheltered life back in Illinois with his Mother and Father. With his Father bedridden for years and almost in a tranced state due to the medication he was on, he'd never had anyone to show him how to shave. Unless the heroes of Pro Wrestling started putting out pampering vignettes, then he would never know.

"Shaving sucks!" He moaned as he attacked his face with the razor, it tore at his flesh like a vulture hacking through the carcass of a wild boar.

Those shaving lessons would never take place, especially when his Father passed away around a year ago. That was the main reason for him leaving, he did not see eye to eye with his Mother and they fought like cat and dog. Neither of them ever letting up or willing to give an inch.

He swilled the razor in the water and then turned off the tap as he discarded the wet soapy razor back into the carrier bag.

"I just wanted to be like my hero." He sighed, feeling the tears coming again "And now he's gone! Fucking gone and left me all alone!" He cried again and then wiped away the condensation from the mirror hung above the basin. What stared back at him was the worst possible hack job of a shave ever witnessed. Hair still remained in places, soap clung to some of it in clumps and blood oozed out of small lacerations all over his face, as though his flesh was suffering from some kind of pox. He stared deep into his reflection and started to cry heavily now. He may have told himself that it was due to his hero retiring, that Rogan has left him alone in the word with no direction, but the truth of the matter was that he was grieving and was suffering from guilt. Grieving for the loss of his Father sure, but the guilt is not for leaving his Mother without a word, but guilt because before he left he emptied the Schroeder family life savings that was hidden in a shoe box under his Mother's bed. Leaving poor Mrs Schroeder to pay for her husband's ludicrous medical bills that had mounted up due to his illness.

"What have I done?" He bawled and collapsed to the floor of the bathroom sobbing, the real world burrowing into the forefront of his mind now, and with the retirement of Randy Rogan and no longer being able to focus on him and what he was doing, he had left himself open for a dose of reality.

"Damn it Randy, it's your fault!" He screamed and lashed out at his travel bag that sat on the toilet, the bag hit the tiled floor and the contents spilled out in front of him as he sobbed into his hands.

What was most disturbing about the contents that'd been poured out onto the floor was that it contained a small Ruger Blackhawk revolver.

His hands parted from his face like theatre curtains as he gazed at the revolver. He didn't like to think about the past again, he preferred to submerge himself in the life of wrestling, but suicidal thoughts had always been with him. In a way, wrestling had been good therapy to keep those intentions at bay.

But with all that had happened tonight and his mental state causing him to be at an all time low, Mister Ruger Blackhawk looked awfully inviting.

He shot up immediately and rushed to the sink and ran the cold tap, splashing at his face.

"His first world title reign was in 1994, he defeated 'The Reflection' Rex Regal in long Island, New York. Second reign 1996, defeated Kami Kajeu at Madison Square Garden, New York City. Third reign 1998, defeated Kami Kajeu in Portland, Oregon..." He chanted to himself, using his knowledge of wrestling and his hero's achievements always seemed to calm him down, nothing could happen to him when he did this. He splashed his face and looked into the mirror this time he was flabbergasted to see Randy Rogan looking back at him.

Just one pull of that trigger and it will all be over, Mark.

"No!" He squealed the tears starting to fall again.

You'll do as I say, kid! I'm the main man and you'll do whatever I tell you to do! If I tell you to train hard, eat right, talk right, fuck right, shit right, you will!

"No, no, no!" He sniffed "Fourth reign 2005, defeated El Talón in Mexico City, Mexico. Fifth reign..." He continued his mantra to no avail.

Don't tell me what I've done you fat fucking fag! Those were my damn achievements not yours! What achievements do you have to your name? None!

"Please stop!" he whimpered and fell to the floor cowering up against the toilet, trying his upmost not to look at the revolver.

Oh, I'm sorry, I beg your pardon. That isn't fair, you've done some shit, right? Like hiding from your poor sick old Daddy when he needed you! Or how about not being bothered about getting off your fat ass and getting a job!

"I can't work I have a condition!" He grizzled.

Or worrying your poor Mom sick, leaving her to pay all those bills and of course, there is your masterpiece! The theft of all your family's money, so you can follow wrestlers around like some slut of a ring rat! Take a fucking bow you sad fucking piece of shit!

Rogan had stopped speaking and Mark reached for the revolver, he stuffed the barrel into his mouth and his finger quivered over the trigger. He gagged on the barrel and vomited.

"I can't do it. I should, but I can't." He cried and dropped the revolver down to the tiles once again.

You can't even kill yourself. What a fucking loser!

CHAPTER 47

Room 225

There was a nasally grumble that escaped from Randy Rogan as he lay on his bed in his hotel room. He was still fully clothed and his diary sat open on the bed, almost mimicking the gaping maw that projected the animalistic calls from his throat. It was obvious that he had been putting the finishing touches to his wrestling chronicle, filling in the last page on his wrestling adventure when the Sandman came calling. There had never been a more content sound than the sound of Randy Rogan's snoring that night. All the stress, anxiety and the riggers of thirty plus years had drifted away, seemingly leaving his body with each boorish exhale. It was as if he had been cleansed mentally and physically, the proverbial weight well and truly lifted.

Without a care in the world now, he slept like a baby. Rogan was finally at peace.

Room 220

Emily Kincaid sat up in one of the two single beds that sat in room 220. The lights were off and she was bathed in a bright flickering beam from the television. They were showing one of her all time favourites, Some Like it Hot. So part of her didn't care that she couldn't switch off and sleep. The adrenaline that still pulsated through her body would not allow sleep anytime soon anyway. She was content, but every so often her gaze would drift away from the comical antics of Jack Lemmon and Tony Curtis and stare at the empty single bed that sat next to her. The bed that belonged to her best friend and travelling partner, Megan Powers. It sat lifeless and untouched, caressed with grey and white toned light, giving it the appearance of some cold slab in a morgue.

"Where the hell is she?" Emily sighed.

She never felt complete unless she had Megan with her to protect her, she was the big sister that she never had. She felt so alone when she wasn't there, and homesick, the distance from home never seemed so bad when there was somebody there to talk to.

On this particular night Megan had said she was going to stop in the bar for a while and have a few drinks before retiring. It was in fact a huge night in the history books for Professional Wrestling. The torch had been passed and the new champion Johnny Midnight wanted to celebrate. That night the drinks were on the champ!

"I might have well stayed down there! It's not like I'm getting any sleep." Sighed Emily.

She looked at the clock that flashed back at her in red neon indicating 1:34am, sighed again wondering if Megan would ever return.

"Maybe she got lucky?" Emily asked herself "Fair play if she has! She could do with a good seeing to!"

She stares back at the screen watching Tony Curtis and Marilyn Monroe embracing in a toe curling kiss and she sighed again, sinking under the blanket and grabbing a pillow to her chest tightly.

"So could I."

As she settled down for the long haul hoping that she would drift away into the land of nod, hopefully in the arms of Johnny Midnight who was waiting for her on the other side of dreamland.

Her eyelids flickered as if being attacked by the strobing light of the television, almost hypnotising her into slumber and just as her eyes closed there was a loud bang and a boisterous ruckus from the room next door.

"What the?" She sat up startled only being asleep for a matter of seconds and then was traumatised for a moment not knowing where she was.

The ruckus was louder, as if something were being thrown aggressively against the furniture.

She sat up in the bed, adjusting her nightgown and put her ear up against the wall. She knew that Johnny had the room next door and she listened intently to see what was going on.

She was taken aback when she heard a female squealing groans of ecstasy, she slid down the wall in a sulk.

"Well, whoever you are, you're a lucky bitch!" She scowled.

Room 221

Johnny Midnight's aggressive groans matched that of his female companion's jubilant yelps of pleasure.

The headboard for Room 221 had never been rattled in such away, as it clashed violently with the vanilla decor, no doubt loosening some plaster in its wake.

Beautiful ripe tanned buttocks had emerged in front of him as the female positioned herself on all fours on the bed. Johnny grabbed at her cheeks as she buried her head into the dishevelled duvet, with playful giggles.

"You like that!" He growled grabbing at her bubble like rear and then slapped at it, leaving a blushing handprint on the tender flesh. She groaned again as a mass of brown hair cascaded down over her head. She giggled, and a muffled voice asking "Give it to me!"

"With pleasure!" He smirked and positioning himself on one kneeling leg he inserted his pulsating manhood into her moist gape and thrusted emphatically. The vigorous slaps of his groin on her backside echoed through the room, and with each groan of pleasure he was spurred on to go quicker, using yet another exuberant burst of energy.

Now the sight of a man and a woman enthralled in a sweat clad battle of who finishes first, may not phase some people. Most will enjoy the twitch of arousal in their loins as two beautiful athletic bodies writhed into each passionately.

That is understandable. But this night of passion was shrouded by a cloud of humour, for any lucky onlookers who managed to witness the events would notice that, 'Magnificent' Johnny Midnight was indeed wearing his newly won World Heavyweight Championship belt around his waist as he ploughed into the superb peach that arched up to meet his amorous advances.

"Who's the champ? Who's the champ, baby?" He moaned through gritted teeth of concentration.

"I soon will be!" Came the reply as she rose up onto all fours and whipped her hair back revealing, Megan Powers enthralled in a moment of orgasmic pleasure.

CHAPTER 48

It was the early hours of Saturday morning and the Buchanan Suites was now as quiet as a morgue. The partying down in the bar that will no doubt go down as another legendary tale. Rhino Brother Stomp had organised a huge game of spin the bottle which saw some audacious and peculiar matchups and those that failed to comply with the rules of the kiss had to pay the price, and a dare was imminent. All was going swimmingly in a drunken haze until Pedro Passion refused to kiss Sunset Glen so Stomp hit him with a dare that couldn't be comprehended by the sober minority in the bar. On seeing the dare played out, some of them made a sharp exit, others watched on in awe, the rest just wanted to have another story to tell. Pedro had boasted before that he could do such things that no other man can and was always mocked for such a proclamation. Tonight he was challenged and with a cloud of Tequila blinding his better judgement, and a roomful of his peers, he accepted. Pedro Passion would indeed attempt auto fellatio.

Although details of this tale may change throughout the years, one thing will remain the same, and that is that he was indeed successful.

Mark Schroeder crept up the two flights of stairs in the dead of the night, his destination, Room 225. His reason for visiting his wrestling hero at such an unsocial hour was unexplained. Perhaps he could no longer hold in what his career had meant to him personally. It was focussing on Randy Rogan and his struggles over the World Heavyweight Championship that helped him to deal with his Father's illness. Was he merely stopping by to say thank you? The reasons unclear but he moved with hesitation and some reluctance as if battling against his own conscience. The short trip up the two flights seemed to take several minutes, in fact, it was almost 25 minutes. His moral compass flickering from shall I or shan't I in rapid succession.

Finally he reached the floor, several doors on either side lay before him in the gloomy corridor where his hero lay asleep behind one of the doors. He took a deep breath and shuffled his rotund frame down the corridor. He had an awful suffocating feeling like claustrophobia setting in, caused by the doors that sandwiched him in and a layer of perspiration seeped out of his pores.

Why had he made this journey at such an unholy hour? Surely Randy Rogan wouldn't take kindly to be woken in the early hours, would he? Surely anything he has to say to him can wait to the convention tomorrow?

These and a dozen other things were things that he asked himself as he arrived at Rogan's door.

He pulled out a sweat clad trotter from the confines of his overcoat pocket and then attempted to knock the door. He raised it and then stopped himself, shaking his head and stuffing his hand back into the deep pocket. He could hear the loud snoring of someone content and deep in dreamland, he'd lost the battle now, the time had passed. He could not with good conscience knock that door now and wake his hero from his slumber.

"I'll tell him tomorrow." He whispered, his hand jiggling around in his pocket and tears forming in his eyes again. To him this was like losing his Father all over again and he just couldn't deal with that. Rogan had been his surrogate Father for years, Rogan just didn't know it. Passing on little tidbits of information, encouragement and support to Mark through the television   and computer screen or through the pages of magazines. His hand again escaped the confines of his pocket and suddenly wiped at his eyes and his dribbling nose with the back of it, smearing a tacky layer of mucus over it and then his demeanour changed to that of anger.

"No!" He seethed "You'll tell him now! You'll get it all off your chest! He can't do this to you." He started to snivel again and his head dropped, the courage had once again left him "He can't leave me!"

He hung there in front of the door, swaying slightly back and forth, like washing on a clothesline, drenched in sweat and tears, quivering in an imaginary breeze.

His hand delved back into the pocket and again nervously rummaging around.

"I have to give this to him now!" He cried.

The gift that he wished to give Randy was a mystery because as he raised his hand once again to knock the door he was disturbed. A few rooms down he heard a door open slowly. This was enough to send the skittish Mark Schroeder into retreat, and he waddled quickly away towards the stairwell again. He knew it was probably best to leave now anyway as he was due to catch the early train, an incredibly tedious train journey from Studd City to Seattle and then onto Calgary, Canada. He needed a head start if he were to be on time for the convention. Besides it would give him a chance to read the entire Top 500 Pro Wrestlers for that year in the latest special edition magazine that he had just purchased.

CHAPTER 49

Megan Powers slithered out of Johnny's room, slowly closing the door behind her, the latch clicking quietly back into place to secure it. The noise still sounded loud to her ears and she winced standing motionless in the corridor for a second or two. Her hair was in disarray and her skin flushed from the evening of pleasure with the new champion of the world. She crept barefooted across the worn unattractive carpet that was in desperate need of modernisation, her clothes and heels gripped tightly to her ample bosom as she moved surreptitiously towards the next room. She dug out her keycard and held it for a moment, gently pressing her ear up against the door. She heard nothing and hoping that Emily was asleep, she let herself into the room as quietly as she could. Megan froze on the spot as Emily stirred, the mass of duvet squirming like some gigantic grub as she turned over and spilled out from its confines. She was still fast asleep and Megan breathed a sigh of relief. She stared at Emily, she was so sweet and innocent, lost in her own world of dreams, oblivious to what her friend had been up to this evening. Megan felt low, real low.

"Meg, you're the worst friend ever!" She murmured dropping her garments on the floor and sliding into her bed as quiet as a church mouse.

"What an utter bitch you are." She told herself as she fell fast asleep.

A few minutes later in the room that Megan had just escaped from, Johnny Midnight waltzed out of the bathroom, a towel wrapped around his waist and body sodden. He whistled a little tune and felt on top of the world. He grabbed his newly won World Heavyweight Championship belt that lay strewn on the unmade bed and smiled.

He rubbed his moist fingertips over it like 34 other men had done in the past and shook his head. A part of him could not believe that he had actually achieved the goal, that he was now seen as the greatest Professional Wrestler in the world. He felt content and smug as he draped it over his shoulder and looked into a full length mirror that was fixed to the wall. He posed with it, remembering when he was a child and along with his friends would make their own championship belts from cupboard boxes and parade around as if they truly were at the top of the mountain, now he actually was.

There was a soft tapping at the door.

"She can't get enough of me!" He smirked. He placed the belt back down on the bed and strutted over towards the door, readying himself for another matchup with the stupendous Megan Powers.

"You want another shot at the champ!" He scoffed arrogantly as he opened the door, but what he saw chilled him to the bone. A sight so terrifying that it was if his blood congealed within his veins.

All 6 feet 10 inches of The Slammer stood before him, filling the doorway with his enormous frame. It looked like The Slammer to him, but there was something slightly off about him, as if his mind wasn't fully there. He was still wearing his wrestling garbs that were coated with dried on blood that appeared almost brown in the gloom of the corridor lights. His shredded, blood soaked mask covered most of his face, like The Phantom of the Opera, doing a terrible job of covering up the horrors that lay beneath.

"Joe?" Johnny said his Adam's apple wobbling in his throat.

The Slammer scowled, and those eyes showed nothing but hate, whatever had laid dormant behind those eyes for so long was finally free. He lunged at Johnny, grabbing his throat with a huge pair of mitts that clamped around his neck like two monkey wrenches.

Johnny tried to fight but to no avail, as he was easily forced back by this human wrecking machine that had already claimed the lives of several innocent people over the last couple of days. The door was slammed shut by a flailing leg of The Slammer like the whipping tail of an angry Iguana, and clenching his grip around Johnny's neck, he hoisted him off the floor.

Johnny gagged and struggled for breath as the colours in his face moved through a gradient of reds and purples. Just when Johnny's eyes were about to roll back in his head and call it a day The Slammer let go.

It was not through compassion or a change of heart, but to launch him across the room, where he collided with the wall and then fell unceremoniously onto the bed next to his beloved new championship belt.

Johnny gasped for air and clutched at his throat that had already been tattooed by The Slammer's thick fingerprints.

The Slammer stalked him like some jungle predator, almost toying with him.

"Please... Joe... you don't... have to do... this." Johnny struggled to say, fighting to get each word out.

The Slammer just looked at him like some zombie, remorseless and robotic.

To Johnny he didn't look alive, it was as if he were walking on a different plane.

The Slammer's dead eyes just stared through him, and flaps of tarnished flesh hung from his broken cranium. The dishevelled mask unable to conceal the matted blood and flesh that clung to his face. Then to make matters worse, The Slammer smiled and suddenly the life was back in his eyes again. This scared Johnny more than the stalking animal that he first appeared to be, because he was indeed in control and hadn't lost himself to madness after all. This made him even more dangerous.

"I've come for what was promised to me!" The Slammer growled, the sound of dried blood in his throat gave it a sadistic edge.

Johnny looked over at the belt sitting on the bed.

"Take it! It's yours!" He coughed and spluttered "You can have the fucking thing!"

The Slammer laughed and it was sickening.

"Oh I will take it." He cackled "The old fashioned way." And with that he grabbed him by the scruff of the neck and lifted him into the air in what resembled his finishing manoeuvre and whispered "It's Slammer Time!" Before bringing him forcefully down on the back of his neck. There was a gut wrenching crack as several bones in his neck snapped, and his prone body folded into himself like a human accordion.

The Slammer smiled and reached out to take the Championship from the bed when he was halted by the groaning and blubbering of Johnny, who was still very much alive and in considerable amount of pain.

"Still some fight left in ya I see?" The Slammer grumbled and grabbed a handful of Johnny's thick black hair and pulled him up from the carpet. His towel fell and he was left to dangle lifelessly in The Slammer's grip, as tears started to roll down his face, the tears shed with the realisation that he was indeed paralysed.

"Joe..." He muttered through a quivering bottom lip.

"Shhh!" The Slammer whispered softly and placed a finger on his moist trembling lips. "Remember Kayfabe! Don't use my real name you Mark!" And with that, grabbed him with both hands and twisted his head violently until there was another sickening crack and when Johnny's head drooped forward against his chest, his eyes were glazed and soulless. The Slammer let go of him and his naked carcass seemed to seep to the floor like melting clay, forming a puddle of dead flesh for the maid to discover in a few hours time.

The Slammer took the World Heavyweight Championship title and gazed at it, the mistress sang back to him in that succulent voice of hers, she had found her latest chaperone.

The Slammer smiled and uttered only one word, the one word on every wrestler's lips from the moment they first dreamt about being part of this business until the moment they left. The one thing that matters to all, to be a "Champion."

CHAPTER 50

Randy Rogan watched on in awe as thousands of people, some of them dressed up as their favourite characters from film, TV and comic books sauntered around losing themselves in a fantasy world for the day. He'd never been in this environment before and felt a little out of place, not to mention a little awkward when scantily clad females (almost) dressed as their favourite   comic or Manga characters embraced him for photographs. He had no idea who they were supposed to be and felt like a dirty old man next to these young exposed bodies.

He was however pleased to see so many familiar faces that he'd known throwout the wrestling industry, who were also there in the Wrestling section of the convention, all of them siting at one long narrow table with their likeness emblazoned on promotional posters hung behind each of them. Rogan had to laugh at some of them though, who had wrestled in the earlier 70's or 80's and now look nothing like the picture that hung behind them.

But I guess that's just how people remember them. That will be me one day no doubt!

He was happy to be sitting with Nemesis, who he hadn't seen since he was let go due to his altercation with The Slammer. He was in high spirits and was very smug when talking about what had happened to The Slammer over the last couple of days, his face actually beamed stating "It couldn't have happened to a nicer guy." They also chewed the fat about life in general and Randy was pleased to hear that Raggu had contacted Nemesis and offered him a spot back on the roster. They laughed and chatted about times spent together on the road and in the ring, both of them completely unaware of the news that was currently breaking on the internet. The deaths of two wrestling personalities were currently snatching the headlines on all the major news sites. 'Magnificent' Johnny Midnight was found tragically murdered in his hotel room, and then the news filtered through that Crystal Churchill had been discovered in the restroom of The Falkinburg Arena, dead by an apparent overdose.

Randy felt a little nervous by the whole affair and even expressed such apprehension to his old friend and organiser of the event, Bobcat Belaire, who reassured him that everything will be fine.

He stared at the tower of 8 x 10's with an older picture of himself on it and wondered if he'd even make a dent in them. He passed the marker pen around in his fingers nervously.

My obvious concern is that nobody will come. I've never ever felt like a celebrity and still feel awkward in these meet and greet type situations. The scale of this thing is just ridiculous! The amount of people here, just to meet people is astonishing, I just can't get my head around it.

Bobcat Belaire stood at the entrance to the wrestling section and watched as herds of people clambered towards the tables forming lines at the table in front of the wresters. Randy's mouth gaped when he realised that his was by far the longest of all the lines. He looked over at Bobcat who smiled back at him and held up a thumb, he knew all along how marketable and how much in demand Rogan was.

"Looks like someone's over!" Laughed Nemesis with a nudge to his arm.

"Yeah, I guess I am." Laughed Randy, who had been so genuinely taken aback by it all. He'd been working so hard for so long that he had never stopped to smell the roses, that he was in fact a big deal.

Maybe I will do more of these conventions.

People of all ages came and went and he signed whatever they wanted signing, posed for photographs and selfies with everyone and even chatted a while with some that wanted to tell him how much they respected him and how they loved him.

It was a huge ego stroke for him and even one day into his retirement the inevitable question came, and it came way to frequently "When are you coming back?"

Never.

After hundreds of autographs had been signed, Randy flexed his fingers trying to shake off that numb feeling from the repetition and getting some blood back to them. He stood up and cracked his back like he had done a thousand times before his matches, it was stiff but he could certainly get used to making a living this way, it was a lot easier than getting thrown around the ring every night.

As he stood he noticed his number one fan, Mark Schroeder in the line and was actually pleased to see him and threw his hand up in a friendly gesture.

Must not have seen me.

Mark looked blank as if he were in a world of his own, but Randy sat back down and went back to signing.

"You know that guy?" Nemesis asked.

"Oh, yeah! It's Mark Schroeder of Chicago, Illinois." Randy was actually amazed that he remembered where he came from in all honesty, but he had decided that these hardcore fans were the key to keeping his name alive in this industry, so he was going to do his upmost to stay in contact with them. He was even toying with asking Mark bout starting up a fan club for him and pay him for running a website. He thought this would be a nice gesture on his part to say thank you for all the support over the years.

"Looks, like one too!" Chuckled Nemesis.

"What?"

"A Mark!" He laughed again.

"Yeah, I guess. But they're the reason we are here, Paul. Don't forget that."

"Yeah! I guess you're right" Nemesis agreed, never ever looking at the fans as the reason he gets to actually do this for a living and without them he wouldn't be here now. Randy could almost see Nemesis thinking his last statement over and he was much nicer to the next person that wanted an autograph. With one sentence he had changed the way that Nemesis looked at the fans.

Mark appeared looking tired and clammy, trotters still sunk in the pockets of his dirty overcoat, with his rucksack stuck to his back like the shell of a dung beetle

"Oh, Hi Mark!" Randy said pleasantly and smiled a genuine smile.

Mark said nothing and blankly looked at Randy.

"It's good to see you." Randy said and his face contorted a little bemused by Mark's perplexed look.

"I'm your number one fan." He murmured under his breath and a tear started to roll down his cratered cheeks.

"Hey, it's okay, Mark." Randy said standing up a little concerned "There's no need to get upset."

"Everyone I love leaves me." He sniffed.

"Sorry?" Randy said not quite hearing him under the snivelling.

A revolver left the confines of Mark's right pocket, gripped in his fat sweaty hand.

To Randy it all happened as if in slow motion, he saw the gun appear but it did not register. He saw the tears streaming from Marks eyes, Nemesis rose next to him and lunged forward towards Mark, Bobcat's face at the entrance terrified Randy, his eyes like glazed saucers staring back at him. He didn't even hear the gunshot and he felt nothing as he looked down to see blood seeping through a torn hole in his white t-shirt. He fell backwards, but he felt no impact from hitting the floor as he lay looking up at the lights of the convention hall. There was no sound. He heard only the slow beating of his own heart, a sound that grew quieter and slower with each beat. He saw his Wife and Son flash before him, everyone he ever knew in or out of the business hurtled past in rapid succession as though he were watching his life back on an old VHS and someone just hit the fast forward button.

The bright lights above blinded him and he blinked rapidly, when he looked again everywhere was dark and he lay in the middle of a ring, the heat of the spotlights failing to warm his cold flesh, and the sound of the crowd cheering was distant, but it was there as he closed his eyes and lay on the blood stained canvas.

THE END

From The Diary of Randall Rogan

Saturday, April 27th
Buchanan Suites, Studd City.

Well, It's done.

I have so many emotions rolling around my head right now, but I feel so relieved! Relieved that it is all over and now I can spend my time with the two people I love the most.

It's a strange feeling, really... It's hard for me to write anything, I just want to sleep. I feel like I've got thirty years of sleep to catch up on. It's as though I left everything in the ring tonight and walked out as me, the true me. I shed the skin of 'The American Man' and left it on the canvas.

Now, I'd just like to disappear up into the mountains somewhere and live out a life of solitude with just a few special people. What I wouldn't give to gaze on mother nature in all her glory! Waking every morning to mountains, trees, lakes and snow! Watching the wildlife and how they live their lives without such distractions and share in that peaceful life with no politics and bullshit. I guess I'd just like to escape now and to be left to my own devices.

The best way I can put it is... it's like a book that has come to its end. I've closed it up and now I've placed it on the shelf. It's there if I'm feeling nostalgic and want to have a look through it and reminisce, but I'll probably never read it again.

Now, I start a new book and a new chapter.

WRESTLING TERMINOLOGY

(For the readers unfamiliar with Pro Wrestling)

Kayfabe: A term used by people within the business as a code when discussing wrestling matters in public without revealing the scripted nature.

Ring Rat (or Rat): A promiscuous person, often a young female, who attends professional wrestling events primarily to seek sexual liaisons with wrestlers.

Mark: A fan who believes that the characters and events of some or all of professional wrestling are real. The term can also be applied to a fan who idolizes a particular wrestler, promotion, or style of wrestling to a point some might consider excessive.

Booker: Constructs the matches and storylines for wrestling shows.

Greenhorn/Green: A wrestler who is in the early stages of their career and may be prone to make mistakes because of their inexperience.

Babyface/Face: A good guy or fan favourite.
A Gig: A small blade is used for cutting oneself to add drama to a match. Term is also referred to as 'Blading', 'Bladejob', 'Gigging', 'Juicing' and 'Getting Colour'.

Heel: A bad guy or villain.

Pop: This refers to a positive reaction from the crowd.

Heat: The crowd reacting to the Heel, usually with jeers and booing for not appreciating what antics the Heel is doing. Also can refer to real-life animosity between those involved in a professional wrestling angle, or match.

Over: Wrestlers can be over as either faces or heels. The term suggests that the fans are buying into what the wrestler is selling, meaning his character. Also, 'Going over' means winning a match.

Jobbing: When a wrestler is booked to lose a match it is described as 'A job' or 'Doing the job'. Wrestlers who routinely (or exclusively) lose matches are known as jobbers.

A Shoot: When a match, angle or promo becomes real.

A Work: Anything that is planned to happen.

Angle: A fictional storyline. It is not uncommon to see an angle scrapped due to it not getting over with the fans.

Blow Off: A final match to end a feud or storyline.

Botch: A mistake made during a match or promo.

Broadway: A match that goes to a time limit draw.

Bump: The term for falling when taking a move.

Calling it in the ring: To make up moves and storytelling in a match on the fly, rather than rehearse them in advance.

The Card: The lineup of matches that will make up the show.

Tag Team: A wrestling duo that take part in matches that pit two wrestlers versus two wrestlers.

Drop: Losing the title.

A Stable: A group of three or four (on some occasions more) wrestlers joining forces.

False Finish: A pinfall attempt which is kicked out of, usually after a finisher or series of high impact moves, and usually kicked out of just before the referee counts to three. This builds crowd anticipation towards the actual finish.

The Finish: Planned end to a match.

Foreign Object: A weapon that is not allowed to be used in the match.

Strap: Championship title (or belt).

Gassed/Blown Up: Out of breath or exhausted during a match.

Fire/Fire Up: When a wrestler shows a considerable amount of enthusiasm when mounting a comeback.

Go Home: To finish a match. One wrestler would tell the other to 'go home' when it is time for them to execute the planned ending for their match. Referees may also tell the wrestlers to go home if they are running short on time or about to run over.

Hot Tag: In a Tag Team match, the face's tag to a fresh partner after several minutes of being dominated by the heel team, usually immediately followed by the freshly tagged partner getting in a quick burst of offence.

A Draw: A wrestler who fans are paying to come and see. Some may only be attending the show because of the specific wrestler.

No Sell: To show no reaction to an opponent's offensive moves.

Potato: A strike to the head which makes real contact.

Ring General: An experienced wrestler who knows how to work a match to its full potential.

Rub: Helping a less popular wrestler get over by associating them with a more prominent or popular wrestler.

Push: The promotion getting behind a fan favourite by giving the said wrestler opportunities, involving them in major storylines and usually making the wrestler a champion.

Turn: A switch in alignment of a wrestler's character.

Ring Psychology: The process of wrestling a match in such a way that the crowd becomes emotionally involved. Performing an engaging match requires acting skills and a good grasp of dramatic timing.

Sell: To react to something in a way which makes it appear believable and legitimate to the audience.

Smark/Smart Mark: Someone who has inside knowledge of the wrestling business, but is not speaking from their own personal experience with the business, getting their information from dirt sheets and websites.

Smart/Smarten Up: Knowing The inner workings of the wrestling industry.

Spots: Any planned action or series of moves.

High Spots: Big moves or sequences, which could include top rope manoeuvres or dives to the outside.

Squash: A one sided match when one wrestler is booked to dominate the other.

Spotfest: A match that mainly contains spots after spots with no real story to the match.

Rest Hold: A loose hold applied during a match, during which wrestlers catch their breath or plan the next series of spots together.

Stiff: Using excessive force when executing a move, deliberately or accidentally.

TITLE HISTORY

WORLD HEAVYWEIGHT CHAMPIONSHIP

KRISTOFF VON HACKENSCHMIDT	17/5/1938	MUNICH, GERMANY
BILLY LINCOLN JR.	1/1/1942	NEW YORK CITY, NY
CAPTAIN PROPAGANDA	3/4/1947	NEW YORK CITY, NY
BILLY LINCOLN JR. [2]	26/12/1947	BOSTON, MA
GRIPPER BURKE	19/04/1950	FORGE CITY, FG
MAN MOUNTAIN DAWSON	20/2/1952	CHICAGO, IL
GRIPPER BURKE [2]	17/6/1952	PITTSBURGH, PA
BILLY LINCOLN JR. [3]	7/3/1953	NEW YORK CITY, NY
BUTCHER BROWSKI	8/9/1954	CHEYENNE, WY
CHIEF CROWFOOT	10/12/1955	BOSTON, MA
THE WIZARD	2/2/1960	STUDD CITY, ST
VACATED DUE TO FORCED RETIREMENT	10/1/1963	
DAN DYNAMO	17/5/1963	NEW YORK CITY, NY
THE MARAUDER	8/11/1965	BALTIMORE, MD
DAN DYNAMO [2]	6/6/1966	MIAMI, FL
DINO DEKKER	13/11/1968	TORONTO, CANADA
'UNCLE' SAM REAGAN	18/1/1969	WASHINGTON, DC
MAXIMILLAN LUFTWAFFE	2/8/1971	NEW YORK CITY, NY

UNCLE' SAM REAGAN [2]	1/1/1972	ATLANTA, GA
'MAGNIFICENT' MAGNUS MEADOWLARK	12/7/1974	PHILADELPHIA, PA
DAN DYNAMO [3]	10/3/1975	SANCTUARY CITY, AK
ABEL CAIN	11/9/1975	NEW YORK CITY, NY
THE HIGH CHIEF	22/4/1978	NEW YORK CITY, NY
EL CORAZÓN PURO	10/10/1980	CANCUN, MEXICO
THE RUSSIAN BEAR	21/2/1981	MOSCOW, RUSSIA
'UNCLE' SAM REAGAN [3]	16/7/1981	WASHINGTON, DC
VACATED DUE TO INJURY	14/12/1983	
ABDULLAH 'THE SCREAMING SHIEK'	15/12/1983	PORTLAND, OR
CAPTAIN YANKEE	3/3/1984	NEW YORK CITY, NY
'THE SAMOAN WARRIOR' SINA	2/5/1988	CHARLOTTE, NC
CARLOS MORALES	27/8/1988	SAN DIEGO, CA
GIANT NAGATA	4/4/1989	TOKYO, JAPAN
NAGATA REFUSES TO DEFEND TITLE OUTSIDE JAPAN		
CAPTAIN YANKEE [2]	4/7/1989	OSAKA, JAPAN
VACATED: INJURED BY MASKED MACHINE	1/6/1991	
THE MASKED MACHINE	7/6/1991	ALBANY, NY
CAPTAIN YANKEE [3]	12/12/1991	DAYTON, OH

'THE REFLECTION' REX REGAL	24/7/1992	LOS ANGELES, CA
ARN ARMSTRONG	27/2/1993	SAN ANTONIO, TX
JAMES VAN COLT	19/1/1994	BOSTON, MA
'THE REFLECTION' REX REGAL [2]	8/9/1994	CLEVELAND, OH
'THE AMERICAN MAN' RANDY ROGAN	22/12/1994	LONG ISLAND, NY
'THE KOREAN KRAKEN' KAMI KAJEU	8/11/1995	SHANGHAI, CHINA
'THE AMERICAN MAN' RANDY ROGAN [2]	6/11/1996	NEW YORK CITY, NY
'THE KOREAN KRAKEN' KAMI KAJEU [2]	20/3/1998	HOUSTON, TX
'THE AMERICAN MAN' RANDY ROGAN [3]	9/9/1998	PORTLAND, OR
VACATED DUE TO INJURY	23/12/1999	
VINNIE VALOR	1/1/2000	KANSAS CITY, MO
'THE KOREAN KRAKEN' KAMI KAJEU [3]	20/3/2001	SAN FRANCISCO, CA
AXEL JACKSON	7/8/2001	STUDD CITY, ST
STRIPPED: NOT IN A POSITION TO PERFORM	6/6/2002	
HIRO SHINZAKI	21/6/2002	TOKYO, JAPAN
EL CORAZÓN DE PLATA	4/3/2003	NEW ORLEANS, LA
EL TALÓN	1/2/2004	MEXICO CITY, MEXICO
'THE AMERICAN MAN' RANDY ROGAN [4]	10/6/2005	LONDON, ENGLAND
THE MASKED MACHINE [KAMI KAJEU] [4]	4/7/2008	NORFOLK, VA

'THE AMERICAN MAN' RANDY ROGAN [5]	13/9/2009	SANCTUARY CITY, AK
EL TALÓN [2]	5/10/2014	SASKATOON, CANADA
'THE AMERICAN MAN' RANDY ROGAN [6]	2/11/2015	NEW YORK CITY, NY
MAGNIFICENT' JOHNNY MIDNIGHT	26/4/2019	STUDD CITY, ST
VACATED DUE TO TRAGIC DEATH OF MIDNIGHT	27/4/2019	
OLYMPUS	1/7/2019	DETROIT, MI

UNITED STATES CHAMPIONSHIP

DAN DYNAMO	20/4/1960	CHICAGO, IL
COLT HANSEN	12/3/1965	CAMDEN, NJ
THE MARAUDER	7/12/1967	HOUSTON, TX
'THE GREASER' BRAD DIMUCCI	20/1/1967	STUDD CITY, ST
SHALLOW GRAVES	3/7/1968	CALHOUN, ST
COLT HANSEN [2]	10/2/1969	AUSTIN, TX
'SHRIEKING' ARAD	16/12/1970	NEW YORK CITY, NY
JACK DYNAMO	14/2/1972	DENVER, CO
'SHRIEKING' ARAD [2]	16/3/1975	NEW YORK CITY, NY
CAPTAIN YANKEE	3/7/1975	MINNEAPOLIS, MN
SHALLOW GRAVES [2]	1/2/1976	GREENSBORO, NC
FLYING EAGLE	13/5/1976	RALEIGH, NC
'THE SAMOAN WARRIOR' SINA	7/12/1976	CHARLESTON, SC
CAPTAIN YANKEE [2]	21/10/1977	FORGE CITY, FG
VACATED DUE TO INJURY	11/6/1978	
ABDULLAH 'THE SCREAMING SHIEK'	8/12/1978	NEW ORLEANS, LA
EL CORAZÓN PURO	4/4/1979	PHOENIX, NV
'BEAUTIFUL' BOB E. DASSLER	9/11/1979	RICHMOND, VA
EL FUEGO DE LOS OCHENTA	23/7/1980	STUDD CITY, ST

GEORGE W. SAINT	20/8/1980	VANCOUVER, CANADA
'BEAUTIFUL' BOB E. DASSLER [2]	24/12/1980	NEW YORK CITY, NY
CAPTAIN YANKEE [3]	6/6/1981	PORTLAND, OR
THE RUSSIAN BEAR	17/9/1981	NASHVILLE, TN
'UNCLE' SAM REAGAN	1/5/1982	CEDAR RAPIDS, IA
DR X	27/8/1984	CANTON, OH
FLYING EAGLE [2]	11/10/1985	CHARLOTTE, NC
'DELICIOUS' DANNY	3/4/1986	ATLANTA, GA
OUTBACK ZACK	10/11/1986	BOSTON, MA
DR X [2]	3/2/1987	COLORADO SPRINGS, CO
'THE AMERICAN MAN' RANDY ROGAN	26/11/1987	CHICAGO, IL
VACATED DUE TO INJURY	15/4/1988	
STARBURNER	13/5/1988	HOUSTON, TX
PROFESSOR SAKATA	20/2/1989	BLUEFIELD, WV
BOBCAT BELAIRE	27/10/1989	ST. LOUIS, MO
THE KOREAN KRAKEN' KAMI KAJEU	16/12/1990	SAVANNAH, GA
UNCLE' SAM REAGAN [2]	25/8/1991	NEW YORK CITY, NY
EL TALÓN	19/11/1991	ROANOKE, VA
NEMESIS	18/1/1993	DAYTONA BEACH, FL
SEBASTIAN CHURCHILL	6/7/1994	PITTSBURGH, PA
NEMESIS [2]	8/9/1995	KANSAS CITY, MO

STRIPPED DUE TO MISSING DATES	1/6/1996	
SEBASTIAN CHURCHILL [2]	1/6/1996	JACKSONVILLE, FL
NEMESIS [3]	22/3/1998	FORGE CITY, FG
PEDRO PASSION	7/8/1999	LOUISVILLE, KY
JUNGLE JIM	16/9/2001	ASTORIA, OR
SEBASTIAN CHURCHILL [3]	3/3/2002	JACKSON, MI
ACE ARMSTRONG	14/7/2004	LAS VEGAS, NV
DR X [3]	19/12/2004	MAPLE FALLS, CANADA
DR X UNMASKED AS SEBASTIAN CHURCHILL		
SEBASTIAN CHURCHILL [4]	19/12/2004	MAPLE FALLS, CANADA
ACE ARMSTRONG [2]	13/8/2005	LOS ANGELES, CA
THE MASKED MANDRILL	14/1/2006	WASHINGTON, DC
PUMA KID	22/4/2007	NEW YORK CITY, NY
PEDRO PASSION [2]	11/5/2008	SAN DIEGO, CA
THE SLAMMER	30/12/2009	CHICAGO, IL
VACATED DUE TO INJURY	10/5/2012	
SEBASTIAN CHURCHILL [5]	11/5/2012	ALBANY, NY
BILLY BRONX	3/4/2013	DALLAS, TX
PEDRO PASSION [3]	7/6/2013	MINNEAPOLIS, MN
NEMESIS [4]	29/5/2014	BANGOR, ME

'MAGNIFICENT' JOHNNY MIDNIGHT	16/3/2015	SANCTUARY CITY, AK
YELLOW FEATHER	23/6/2017	CHATTANOOGA, TN
'MAGNIFICENT' JOHNNY MIDNIGHT [2]	11/1/2018	RIVERTON, WY
YELLOW FEATHER [2]	13/8/2018	ALBUQUERQUE, NM
MR CANADA	20/4/2019	SANCTUARY CITY, AK

WORLD TAG TEAM CHAMPIONSHIP

THE DYNAMOS [DAN & JACK DYNAMO]	1/10/1963	RIO DE JANEIRO, BRAZIL
THE SAMOAN WARRIORS [SINA & FITI]	3/4/1968	CLEVELAND, OH
THE DYNAMOS [2]	13/7/1971	NEW ORLEANS, LA
THE SAMOAN WARRIORS [2]	6/12/1971	NEW YORK CITY, NY
THE NATIVE AMERICANS [HIGH CHIEF & FLYING EAGLE]	1/2/1972	NEW YORK CITY, NY
THE SAMOAN WARRIORS [3]	27/6/1972	PHILADELPHIA, PA
THE AMERICAN CONNECTION [SAM REAGAN & CAPTAIN YANKEE]	30/5/1973	HAMBURG, PA
THE MONSTERS FROM THE MIDDLE EAST [ABDULLAH & ARAD]	9/11/1973	NEW YORK CITY, NY
THE AMERICAN CONNECTION [2]	8/5/1974	PITTSBURGH, PA
THE MONSTERS FROM THE MIDDLE EAST [2]	13/5/1975	LONG ISLAND, NY
THE NATIVE AMERICANS [2]	27/9/1977	ALLENTOWN, PA
THE DOCTORS OF X [DR X & DR X]	3/11/1978	NEW YORK CITY, NY
THE AMERICAN CONNECTION [3]	12/12/1978	NEW YORK CITY, NY
VACATED DUE TO INJURY TO REAGAN	1/3/1979	
HAMMER & SICKLE	4/3/1979	NEW YORK CITY, NY
THE AMERICAN CONNECTION [4]	11/12/1979	WASHINGTON, DC
THE TOKYO GIANTS [GIANT NAGATA & GIANT ROBOTO]	3/3/1980	BOSTON, MA
EL REY DE LOS REYES & EL GRAN POLUELO	4/8/1983	CANCUN, MEXICO

THE FLATLINER BROTHERS [A-TAK & SUICIDAL SID]	17/2/1986	HARLEM, NY
THE TOKYO GIANTS [2]	6/5/1987	TOKYO, JAPAN
TEAM U.S OF A [SAM REAGAN [5] & RANDY ROGAN]	14/3/1988	NEW YORK CITY, NY
THE DEVIL'S REJECTS [DR X [2] & THE MASKED MACHINE]	10/10/1988	CHICAGO, IL
THE NEW AGE AZTECS [CUTTHROAT & DELMONTÉ]	16/7/1989	MAPLE FALLS, CANADA
THE TERRIFICS [TERRIFIC TIMMY & DELICIOUS DANNY]	23/7/1989	JACKSONVILLE, FL
THE NEW NATIVES [FLYING EAGLE [3] & YELLOW FEATHER]	19/11/1989	NEW YORK CITY, NY
THE TERRIFICS [2]	23/2/1990	LAS VEGAS, NV
RANDY ROGAN [2] & NEMESIS	30/7/1990	STUDD CITY, ST
THE DEVIL'S REJECTS [2] [DR X [3] & THE MASKED MACHINE [2]	17/10/1990	HARTFORD, CT
STRIPPED WHEN REJECTS ATTACK OFFICIALS	31/1/1991	
THE SPACE MOUNTAINEERS [BUNK THE HUNK & DIRTY MARTIN]	1/2/1991	GRAND RAPIDS, MI
THE NEW NATIVES [2] [FLYING EAGLE [4] & YELLOW FEATHER [2]	11/8/1991	NEW YORK CITY, NY
THE SPACE MOUNTAINEERS [2]	3/12/1991	DETROIT, MI
NEMESIS [2] & RANDY ROGAN [3] [2]	6/4/1993	FORGE CITY, FG
TOKYO ARSENAL [GIANT NAGATA [3] & KAMI KAJEU]	9/8/1993	LOS ANGELES, CA
STRIPPED WHEN NAGATA IS FIRED	2/1/1994	

THE DELIGHTS [DELICIOUS DANNY [3] & PEDRO PASSION]	3/3/1994	ASTORIA, OR
THE RIOT BROTHERS [MATT RIOT & PAT RIOT]	13/6/1995	SANCTUARY CITY, AK
THE GRINDHOUSE SLAUGHTERHOUSE [THE SWINE & THE MASKED MACHINE [3]	7/9/1995	NEW YORK CITY, NY
NEMESIS [3] & ACE ARMSTRONG	10/4/1996	EL PASO, TX
THE GRINDHOUSE SLAUGHTERHOUSE [2] [THE SWINE [2] & THE MASKED MACHINE [4]	3/9/1996	CALHOUN, ST
THE NEW NATIVES [3] [FLYING EAGLE [5] & YELLOW FEATHER [3]	11/2/1997	BIRMINGHAM, AL
THE SAVAGE MANIACS [JUNGLE JIM & KRONG]	5/4/1997	OKLAHOMA CITY, OK
VACATED WHEN KRONG ATTACKS JUNGLE JIM	6/6/1997	
DEVASTATION [FAMINE & PLAGUE]	10/6/1997	BOSTON, MA
LOS COLBRÍES [COLIBRÍ UNO & COLIBRÍ DOS]	22/8/1999	GREENSBORO, NC
DEVASTATION [2]	10/9/1999	ANAHEIM, CA
THE CANADIANS [BOBCAT BELAIRE & THE CANADIAN KID]	3/8/2001	MONTREAL, QUEBEC, CANADA
THE MERCENARIES [KAMI KAJEU [2] & EL TALÓN]	10/11/2001	SAN FRANCISCO, CA
THE AMERICAN ALLIANCE [RANDY ROGAN [4] & THE SLAMMER]	4/7/2003	WASHINGTON, DC
VACATED WHEN ROGAN IS INJURED	7/9/2003	
DEVASTATION [3]	8/9/2003	NEW YORK CITY, NY

THE RAINFOREST ELITE [JUNGLE JIM [2] & ACE ARMSTRONG [2]	2/11/2005	CHICAGO, IL
DEVASTATION [4]	18/6/2006	NEW YORK CITY, NY
THE PUMAS [PUMA KID & PUMA DARK]	7/4/2008	RICHMOND, VA
THE MERCENARIES [2] [KAMI KAJEU [3] & EL TALÓN [2]	1/11/2009	LOS ANGELES, CA
THE AMERICAN ALLIANCE [2] [RANDY ROGAN [5] & THE SLAMMER [2]	9/8/2010	LONG ISLAND, NY
THE GRINDHOUSE SLAUGHTERHOUSE [3] [THE SWINE [3] & THE MASKED MACHINE [5]	13/12/2010	HOPE SPRINGS, OR
NEMESIS [4] BILLY BRONX	12/3/2011	TUSCAN, AZ
THE LOVE RANCH [LANNY LOVE & C.H LANDEL]	7/6/2011	CHICAGO, IL
THE AMERICAN AVENGERS [ALAN BAMMER & KEN TUCKIE]	8/10/2011	MANCHESTER, ENGLAND
DEVASTATION [5]	16/7/2012	ORLANDO, FL
THE DIAMOND DOGS [ZIGGY & IGGY]	12/3/2014	SEATTLE, WA
PEDRO PASSION [2] & JOHNNY MIDNIGHT	6/8/2015	NEW YORK CITY, NY
THE PUMAS [2]	7/11/2016	STUDD CITY, ST
DEVASTATION [6]	16/2/2017	MIAMI, FL

A Special Thanks

I owe a debt of gratitude to everyone that I stepped foot in the ring with, whether I was against them, as a tag team, in battle royal type shenanigans, or just had the pleasure to share a locker room with. Also a huge thank you to all the promoters that booked me and saw potential in my work, as well as the referees, managers, photographers, announcers and supporters.

I have indeed learnt from them all and I thank them all.

Lance Storm, "Hooligan" Marcus Kool, Dan Ryder, Becky Ryder, Nemesis, Sal Americana, The Hunter Brothers, Mark Clarke, Matt Clarke, Jesse Jones, Joey Ozbourne, "Golden Boy" Cameron Knite, Steve Valentino, The Bouncer, British Born Steele, Jasabel, The Judge, Lord Graham Thomas, Bobby Riedel, Johnny Ova, Kekoa Mana, Chris Brookes, Daniel Moloney, Damian Dunne, Pete Dunne, Spud, Jonny Storm, Dave Mastiff, El Ligero, Millie Mckenzie, D'Lo Brown, Chris Hero, Super Dragon, Low Ki, Abyss, Jerry Lynn, AJ Styles, Blue Meanie, Tracey Smothers, Al Snow, Steve Corino, Joel Pettyfer, Raven, The Sandman, Jody Fleisch, Colt Cabana, Chad Collyer, David Starr, Harlem Bravado, Scotty 2 Hotty, Doug Basham, Bram, Marty Scurll, Nick Aldis, The Blossom Twins, Robbie Brookside, Eugene, SoCal Val, Danny Hope, Jemma Palmer, Faye Palmer, Liam Perrin, LJ, Kieran Young, "The Boss" Neil Edmunds, Christopher Drew, Charles Kesley, Ryan Parrott, Saul Adams, Dave Sharpe, Carson Bailey, RC Chaos, Puma Kid, Harry Cruise,

Brandon Thomas, Carlo Cannon, Falcon, Ace Anderson, The Elliot Jordan Experience, Maddog Maxx, Carl Mizzery, Luke "Dragon" Phoenix, Corey Americana/Pain, Bert Fabulous, John Harding, Kris Navarro, Joey Syxx, Jack Gallagher, Romeo Vain, Damo Scorpio, Kit Knox, Tommy Gunn, Adam Maxted, Nathan Jones, Zack Gibson, Kim Roxx, Joey Sanchez, Joe Black, Jayme Future, CJ Connors, "The Don" GBH, Francesco Messina, Miguel Tabone, The Iron Serb, "Heavy Metal Maniac" Marc Hogan, Athena Furie, Shauna Shay, Barbie Rogue, Nightshade, Shax, Evelyn, Luke Basham, Jimmy Vice, Eddie Cobain, Shane Hardy, Drake Wynter, RJ Mann, Daniel Valentine, Killian Jacobs, Christopher Royals, Shorey, Ajax, Regan, Gianni Valletta,Jack Quinn, Vardas, "Glamorous" Roddy, Ron Corvus, Red Scorpion, Kat Von Kaige, Xia Brookside, TJ Sky, Joey Scott, Stixx, Doug Williams, Sebastian Knight, 2K, Spindoctor, Nik Dutt, Frank Wesker, Kieran McQueen, Big Richard Action, The Beast, Weasel, Big Rich, "Tomcat" Kev O'Neil, Scott Mack, Terry Thatcher, Lacey Owens, Al Crowley, "21st Century Hero" Luke Douglas, Dan Tucker, Jem MTX Brown, Jack Storm, A Star Athlete, Innocence, Alex Gracie, Bobby Barratt, Alex Shane, Bill Duffy, Lacey James, Kade Callous, King Khan, Skull, Rob Hunter, The Disciple, Laken Xander, Bubblegum, Andy Boy Simmonz, Caiman, Cyanide, Ricky Knight, Sweet Saraya, Stephen Perrin, Luscious Latasha, Gabby Gilbert, Alpha Brothers, Chris Petherwick, Kenny Killbaine, Dominita, John Copping, Stephen Keane, Edwards, Ricky Rowley, Hari Singh, White Tiger, Wolf, Gremlin, Jimmy Casino, Angel Gonzales, CJ Rawlings, "Spiritwalker" Luke Douton, Keith Myatt, Rigour

Mortis, Damian Grant, Heratio, Lucien L. Jones, Carnage, Derice Coffee, RJ Singh, Joey Hayes, JJ Jenkins, Great Tsunami, "Gentleman" Gilligan Gordon, Jack Banting, "Playboy" Phil Bedwell, Geraden, Staxx, Mega Pegasus, G The Ghetto Superstar, Sy King, Magik, Jack London, Mooga, Ice XVII, Kristen Lees, Matt Mensa, The Chemical Brothers, Shawn Scott, Romeo, Hex, D-Mac, The Babyfaced Pitbull, Shawn Hughes, Psycho, Tom Patrick, Adam Pendry, Rob Blayze, Kai Saxon, "Renegade" Ian Rogers, Platinum Page, Daniel Standring, Chandler Scott Lee, Violet Vendetta, Youths Gone Wild, Beer Fuelled Violence, Mike Wyld, Gangster, Templeton Cruise, Brett Banner, Alex Graves, B52, Marcel Gibbons, Paul Malen, Jules Lambrini/Ash Steele, Nick Knight, Jay Icon, Sam Green,Kelly Louise Foxall, Anna Summers, "Gentleman" Christopher Locke, Ric Violent, Ryan Smile, Ronin, Jonny The Body, Abbas Rezazadeh, Corey Johnson, Chris Stone, Aaron Lee Dovey, Scott Dovey, Aphrodite, Viktor, MK McKinnon, Nate Lewis, Shabazz, Bacardi, Tommy White, Dave Pearson, Dave Williams, Chris Dutton, Julian Perkins, Red Tiger, Ryan Myatt, T-Bone, "Dirty Dancin" Danny McGuff, KC Sunshine, Gabriel Kidd, Dave Preston, Sean Midnight, AJ Hughes, Aiden Potter, LMR, Drill, Max Inferno, Phil Woodvine, Kris Godsize, Colin Russell-Ames, Daniel Delgado, Matt Burns, Seb Stead, Tom Lancaster, Gordon Harris, Amanda Littlewood, Mark Shelton, Marc Lungley, Andy Johnson, Gareth Holloway, Liam Pinches, Jacob Caslin, Derek Caslin, Pete Stevens, Joel Allen, Chris Roberts, Ben Roberts, Ben Hubbard, Dan Cottingham, Damian Hill, Oliver Newman, Stuart Smith, Keith Massey, Darren "Jig" Withers, Tracy Jenks, Paul

Sinclair, Kylee Russon, Sue Hannah, Simon Brown, Peter Staniforth, Kriss Sprules, Melicious, Kevin O'Neil, Steve Sykes, Steve Saxon, Vicky Grindley, James Worthing, Tom Baker, Matt Reid, Bobby Barratt, Steve "The Barman", Chris Hubble, Matthew Brown, The Stoke Crew (Sarah, Charlie, Charles, Skye, Jim), The Worton Family, The Probert Family, The Brookes Family, Helen & Dave, The Harris & Dawes Family, The Rowley Family, The Cottingham Family & the best gear maker in the business, Sarinah Penders at Airhead Diva Design.

Thanks to Seb Stead for the use of the photograph.

A WORD FROM OUR SPONSORS...

OTHER WORK AVAILABLE

Monster Home

Vatican: Angel of Justice

Vatican: Retribution

Blood Stained Canvas

Maple Falls Massacre

Fear Trigger

Welcome to Crimson

Monster Meals

COMING SOON

Vatican: Unholy Alliance

Visit the website www.djbwriter.co.uk

Follow author Daniel J.Barnes on social media
@DJBWriter on Facebook, Instagram & Twitter.

Proud to be part of the Eighty3 Design family. For all your website and graphic design needs.

www.eighty3.co.uk

Printed in Great Britain
by Amazon